KARABIAN RED

Ashley N. Silver

KARABIAN RED

First Edition: November 2022

Library of Congress Control Number (LLCN): 2022915232
ISBN: 978-1-7370642-0-6 (hardcover)
ISBN: 978-1-7370642-1-3 (paperback)
ISBN: 978-1-7370642-2-0 (ebook)

Edited by Stacy Dymalski
Cover design by Michelle Rayner of Cosmic Design

www.ashleynsilver.com

KARABIAN
RED

Ashley N. Silver

For the little girl who thought she didn't like to read.

A NEW MONSTER

She wore the red dress, because she had her heart set on being as formidable as possible.

Sure enough, the king's cabinet of advisors, commanders, and councilmen were all staying near the outer edges of the viewing platform and keeping their eyes trained on the test field in the distance. Anything but meeting her eyes.

Good. She smiled, and straightened her papers at the table. Her hands were stained crimson from working with the explosive powder she'd designed, nearly up to her elbow, like two long gloves permanently fused into her skin. They looked like blood, and Jemisha Kazem wouldn't have it any other way.

Unlike the three chemists who had failed before her, she was the only one who'd earned a name that wasn't her own, something they called her behind her back in the hallways, meeting rooms, and even on the city streets.

The lady with the red hands.

And if the test today went as planned, she'd be more than that.

She tucked wisps of her black hair behind her ears as the breeze picked up, and stepped around the table to the very front of the platform, beside the king.

Shallow, grassy hills stretched all around the platform, and in the distance, a tiny brown spec signified the singular barrel of her explosive. A thirty-yard fuse stretched through the grass, and some unfortunate soul who'd lost the coin toss was walking toward the end of it with a torch in hand. Thirty yards, and yet she'd still insisted that the man with the lighter run after the flame took.

"The formula seemed promising this time, much more potent than the previous batch," said the king of Brighton, by way of greeting.

A hillside was still dented and charred black, visible east of the platform, from that supposedly *weak* batch that had been tested six days prior.

King Hector's gray and black hair matched his charcoal-colored jacket, and he stood with his arms crossed as he squinted across the test field. On his opposite side, his son, Kassian, was mirroring his father's stance.

The prince turned to her. "Have you decided what to call it yet?"

"Nightfire," she announced. She'd decided on the name last night, as she stared into a spoonful of the bloodred powder. Not just because the cloud it produced was as black as night, or because it blossomed like a bouquet of flames, but because of the night Brighton's original royal family had been assassinated twenty-two years ago. The king now only made it onto the throne because he was the closest in relation after the graves were dug.

She was only ten at the time. She recalled how the next morning, two men in official red uniforms had knocked on the door, lowered their hats over their hearts, and announced to her mother that her father would not be returning from his post. A wing of the palace had been set aflame by bloodthirsty radicals, and her father was not the only guard who'd been trapped inside.

Even now, with a new palace constructed closer to the middle of the city of Northgate, the tragedy of the old palace lingered. Repaired, but permanently scarred by the fire, it served as inspiration for ghost stories, storage, and now the location of her lab.

But as of today, revenge for all of that needless death—her father's death—was closer than ever. A report from the singular spy Brighton sent to Dale, the island nation in the west, had arrived that morning before dawn. It confirmed everything she'd hoped.

The rumors were true. The whispers were more than they seemed. The man responsible for the deaths of the original royal family was hiding in Dale and being sheltered by their strength. After all this time, finally, they had a lead.

And now it was time for blood.

The king gestured to the man on the outside edge of the platform with the flag, a workman who was lucky enough not to be lighting the fuse today, who dutifully waved it, signaling for the man in the distance with the torch to light the oil-soaked rope.

A distant, golden line of fire snaked through the grass, and the lighter was already running in the other direction.

She listed through her calculations in her head as the flame sped toward the barrel. Of all the formulas she had assembled for Brighton's king, something about this one felt different. The numbers and compounds balanced each other perfectly, like they were meant to fit together, pre-ordained by some omnipotent angel of death. Maybe it was, but Jemisha preferred to think that she alone was the only monster capable of bringing this new weapon to life.

All chatter behind her fell silent as the last few yards of the fuse burned away.

Light stung her vision, and an ungodly boom hit her ears and reverberated through the cavity of her chest. A shock sent everyone on the platform lurching back, some falling over completely. The smell of smoke, ash, and the bitter concoction of chemicals singed her nostrils as she gripped the edge of the table, righting her stance.

Shielding her eyes from a searing gust of air with her hand, she watched as a plume of black smoke, as black as onyx, climbed into the morning sky. Bursts of fire rippled and sparked within the cloud. It expanded outward with a vengeance, like a massive skirt, and she heard the man with the torch scream as the hem ate him alive.

God, it's horrific, hideous—those were her first thoughts, for a split second. She didn't need to look around at the men on the observation platform to know they were still cowering as the shadow stretched over all of them. But then Jemisha couldn't help it. She laughed. She felt like she'd tamed a wild horse, finally gotten it to yield to her will. *My monster. She's absolutely stunning.*

The test field was seven miles west of Northgate. It was secluded, far from the main roads and hidden among grassy hills. Evidence of the explosions had never been big enough to reach beyond it. The common folk weren't meant to know about the crown's secret tests or her explosive. But this was something different altogether. The plume was still growing taller; by now, the city might already be able to see it rising above the horizon—and it was far from done.

Jemisha snatched up the paper with the formula on it, and clutched it over her heart.

What they saw today was produced by only a single barrel. *One.* Which meant the hard work was over; now it was just a matter of making much, much more.

It's more powerful than I thought. And now everyone is going to see.

CHAPTER ONE

The bitter tang of metal wafted through the air like smoke. An entire wall of the forge opened to the grassy hillside, but the smell of coal and iron always lingered.

I walked along the back wall, past the storage bins and tools all hanging from their designated nails. The tongs in my hand had grown heavy over the hours, weighed down even more by the carefully sculpted chunk of metal between the pinchers. It was far from done, but it had the basic shape of a knife—there would always be time to grind it down later. I remembered the first time I had actually made anything without help. It seemed so complicated then. The end result was a hideous section of metal with a warp so bad it could have been part of a child's slingshot; I hadn't hardened it at the proper temperature—which was precisely how I learned to go to the barrel of oil with a sense of urgency.

I marched up to the oil drum that was just outside and plunged the glowing yellow piece of iron into it, turning my face away from the scorching plume of smoke and flames that came up. Stirring the unfinished blade around, I prayed that it wouldn't emerge warped and bent out of shape, as it often did near the end of the day, when I had the least amount of time to fix it.

I dragged the back of my gloved hand across my forehead as I waited, certainly leaving streaks of coal. I squinted at the dark smears going up my arm, layered over skin turned bronze after so many hours in the sun. Strands of my ebony hair crossed in and out of my vision as a gust of wind rolled over the hill.

I withdrew the unfinished knife from the oil, no longer glowing, glancing over it as I made my way back to my anvil.

Good. No obvious bends.

I hung up the tongs on my way, able to tolerate the heat that the blade still carried through the leather of my gloves. I held it up to one eye, looking down from the end of the tang to the point. Beside me, Harris was wiping his hands clean with a rag, having already finished putting everything at his station in order.

"Got a warp?"

"No, thank god," I set the blade down on the anvil. The fact that it didn't wobble back and forth like a seesaw was even better. I took off my gloves and tossed them onto the table between us, "I think it's the first cooperative blade that I've made in days."

He smirked at me, holding out the rag with one long, darkly-colored arm. The patterns of scars where he had accidentally burnt himself stood out much lighter, almost shining. "Don't stay late again—you know you don't get paid after hours. Just finish it tomorrow morning."

I took the cloth to work on the smudges around my hands. I didn't have as many burns as he did. I hadn't been here as long as he had. Still, I could point out the few whitened lines where I had mistakenly bumped a piece of glowing hot metal. "Yeah, yeah, I know. I just never seem to finish evenly; the last blade is always the one I leave as a work in progress until the next day."

"I can't imagine the anxiety that must cause," he joked, heading toward the main building that sat behind the forge. I followed, leaving the cloth and the knife by my anvil as some of the other blacksmiths pulled the heavy doors on the western wall closed.

"It's terrible; I can hardly sleep, and the thought eats away at me all night." I grinned at how well I had added the theatrics to my voice.

Harris looked over his shoulder to scoff, nearly laughing, "Oh please, Ignatius, you never sleep."

We joined the nine other smiths in a line outside the main building, passing the sign that read, "Salona Forging Co." in white painted lettering.

"But," I added, "I get some of my best ideas when I should be sleeping."

"And some of your worst, too." He gave me a pointed look.

"That's fair."

The line moved quickly. In the doorway was the forge owner's wife, Margaret, with a joyful round face and unruly curls of brown hair. She counted out small silver coins, using the top of the railing by the steps like a table. She placed the neatly organized stacks of money into the calloused palms of each worker until it was only Harris and me left.

She handed Harris his week's pay with a smile, and he waited off to the side as I put out my hand.

Still smiling, she picked up the coins, but held them inches from my palm and raised one eyebrow. "Are you going to be wise with your money this time?" she asked.

I grinned, "Hey, I only gambled that *one* time—and trust me, I've learned my lesson."

"I should hope so," she laughed, placing the money in my palm. The weight of it always seemed strange, like I was a child and it was something fragile that I had been told not to touch.

"I just know," she continued, "that you also have a habit of giving it away."

I stuffed my money into my pocket, knowing that most of it wouldn't be there for long. "Ma'am, you worry too much. Am I not the perfect example of a responsible young man?"

I saw Harris roll his eyes on the edge of my vision, and Margaret chuckled, waving us off, "Quit flashing that charming smile and just try to make good decisions. I expect both of you back on time tomorrow."

"We'll do our best," Harris joked, as we made our way along the footpath that led down the slope and connected to the nearest street. He flipped one of his coins into the air with his thumb, catching it again easily.

"You going to take your usual route?" he asked.

"Yeah, but I'll catch up with you and Everett later, same place as always."

He flipped his coin again, and the light from the red sunset behind us winked off one of its sides. The sky itself had been as gray as dishwater for days, turning sunrise and sunset dull and crimson, but the smoke still showed no signs of retreat. People had been blaming a wildfire up north, but there were also rumors of some kind of mishap.

"You know you don't have to help them," Harris reminded me, with a twinkle of understanding in his dark eyes. "Not when it becomes an obstacle, and not when they're such conniving little shits."

"I was a conniving little shit," I said, "and it's not really that bad financially. You remember what those places are like—"

"A damn chicken coop."

"Yeah, and the weakest ones are pecked nearly to death over simple things like food. Wouldn't you have appreciated the extra help?"

Harris made quick work of avoiding the question, answering instead, "It's just a waiting game, when it comes down to it." He brushed a hand over his short, black curls. "We all had to get through it, same as them." Only he had it worse. All the kids with darker skin did. I didn't understand when I was little; he was just my friend with the bright, wide smile and the patience of a saint. But even back then, I knew the way he was treated wasn't fair. Wasn't right.

"It's a long waiting game." I remembered counting the days until I could leave for good, until I could turn a cold shoulder to that six-story brick building and the crowded, slanted street it resided on.

He shook his head as we came to the road, half smiling as he turned left, "Just be *careful*."

I turned right, following the rough, cobblestone road downhill into a line of shadow, "I'm always careful."

I didn't need to look back to know he made one of his precautionary faces; I'd seen that angled brow and dimpled cheek more times than I could count—it usually included the slow shake of his head, too. He was the responsible one, after all. He didn't dig himself into trouble, especially when it came to money.

The series of turns were an easy trip, one I suspected I could walk blindfolded. There was a bakery around the first turn, and the smell of fresh bread, pies, and cakes constantly drifted from its windows and doors. When I was six and Harris was seven, we'd stolen a pie along with two other boys our age. Harris nearly got caught and passed the warm dish full of apple pie into my hands, and I scurried out the window before anyone could stop me. The two other boys weren't far behind. Harris managed to wriggle free of the baker's grasp, and caught up with us a few blocks over. Naturally, we ate it all with our hands until the dish it came in shined as if it had been scrubbed clean.

We were in trouble up to our noses when mistress Helena found out. Her face had been a glorious shade of pink as she lectured us. I think Harris felt bad about it afterward. But if the thought crossed my mind at the right time, even today, I could still laugh about it.

A few streets down, I passed the school where I had attended a few of my weekly lessons—before I mastered the art of evading responsibility. The classrooms smelled of chalk, and the plain white walls were what I stared at while I considered ways to get out of them, as I forcefully ignored the cold ache in my guts every time I passed through the painted blue doors.

I crossed the road near the bar where I first learned what it meant to stumble into walls and laugh at things that weren't funny. Harris had practically dragged me out of there. He drank occasionally, but he never let himself anywhere near the threshold of losing control, or waking up with a light head and an endless need to throw up—a principle I quickly decided to adopt after that following morning.

When I recognized the short, lean woman walking up the street below me, I debated crossing to the other side of the road again, but opted for a tense smile instead. Better to stay on her good side; I'd owed her money since last year when the expert card-counter beat me at poker, and I had a feeling the grace period was near to running out. She smirked knowingly, her coffee eyes lined with kohl, and gave a nod as she passed. She raised one of her tattooed hands to grip the edge of her hood, keeping it secure as a breeze picked up. The first time I ever saw those black-inked snakes coiling up her forearms I was nine; she'd wrenched me out of the water near the end of a pier before shoving me into the capable hands of an elderly fisherman. By the time I'd stopped coughing up water, she was already gone. And I'd never quite been able to find the words to thank her.

At last, I reached the short, wide street that passed the front of a bank. The building had wooden doors with impressive carvings and white columns, and a small cluster of five orphan kids huddled by the farthest one.

I retrieved a portion of my money, not all of it, of course, but enough, and tossed it to the oldest boy. He was getting better at catching it…progressively.

"Don't waste it on stupid shit this time," I warned, as the other four huddled around him to count up the money.

"We won't," he said, sporting a mischievous grin and his chipped tooth.

"How's mistress Helena?"

"Mean."

"Loud."

"Looking more ancient by the day."

I couldn't resist a small laugh for the last one, "Be careful then, or she'll survive longer than all of you out of spite." As I turned to leave, I added, "I'll be back next week."

They nodded. The five of them, all thin, with messy hair and dirt scuffs, were like a mirror to my past. I had seen the reflection a million times, yet it always made me flinch.

THE TRIP across town was shorter than usual, and hints of smokey, bronze sunset were still trailing in the sky by the time I caught up with Harris and Everett.

Harris and I followed behind Everett as he complained about his day of work in the fields east of the hills—the job he'd taken after being fired from blacksmithing two months ago. The street ahead was dimly lit by a few hanging torches, casting an orange glow over the steeply angled road ahead of us. I could smell hints of cigar smoke drifting from some of the busier places a few blocks over, like an odd blend of freshly cut wood and hints of lilac. Then, of course, there was the tart fragrance of alcohol and poor decisions.

"Oh my god, you should have seen it! I was about ready to strangle the selfish bastard!" Everett went on, waving his hands, as he always did when he talked. "He comes at me with his shovel, after I've just given one of my *best* speeches on his lacking work ethic, and swings it at me," he flung his arm out wide for emphasis, the hazy torchlight shifting on his blonde hair. "I duck, and he starts swearing and going off, so I pick up the metal rake and bash him across the shin with it! Well that really pissed him off, let me tell you!"

As I chuckled at the colorful image in my head, I noticed a pair of men standing outside one of the buildings ahead of us on the left. I recognized the leaner one as Taz; we had been friends since he joined Harris and me on the pie-stealing expedition. But then the light from a nearby torch caught on the rich, auburn red hair of the second man, who was taller than Taz and built far stronger. My stomach sank.

"Shit," I muttered, tilting my face toward the cobblestones and allowing some of my hair to fall forward and hide my features.

Harris looked over at me with a scrunched brow, then glanced ahead at the small group. "Your bad decisions keep catching up with you. Do you have the money?"

"Of course, I don't have it," I whispered. "If I did, I would have taken care of it ages ago."

"Remind me again how giving away your money isn't a financial burden?"

"Shut it."

I can get away with walking right past him, can't I? It's dark enough, he probably won't see my face…

"Well, they're walking this way, so you better have a good speech prepared," he gave me a pat on the back.

Everett trailed off mid-sentence, stepping aside as the man with red hair, Malcolm, dropped a heavy arm across my shoulders, "Well, if it isn't my best friend in the whole world."

I glanced at Taz and he shrugged. His hazel, faintly slanted eyes were full of sympathy as he followed alongside us. His hair was a lighter brown than mine, and he smoothed it back as he ducked around a particularly strong cloud of smoke.

I heaved a sigh. "Before you ask, I still don't have it."

"Oh, you mean the forty pieces you've owed me for five months now? I'd nearly forgotten." Malcolm squinted his blue eyes, which were dark like the sea before a storm, and I shrugged his arm off as we all continued to walk.

"I'm working on it, alright?"

"Is your luck so bad that you keep gambling away everything you make?" asked Malcolm.

"No, I haven't touched a deck of cards in five months."

"After that bad of a loss, I'm not sure I would either."

I thought of arguing, but I couldn't. A collapsing building had more surety than my luck did that night—and that was being generous.

"Look, I can't conjure the money out of thin air. You're going to have to wait a little longer."

"I believe that less and less every time you say it," Malcolm shook his head, "and I've had to deal with people who owe me money plenty of times before. I know how this works."

I wrinkled my nose, "Maybe you've gotten too comfortable with winning games of chance then."

"I come up even without fail, and that's a lot better than most people. But you know that better than anybody."

"And you still play. You do realize luck can change?"

Malcolm pursed his lips. "We all have bad habits. At least mine isn't avoiding every issue that finds its way into my path."

"I'm a runner, what can I say?"

His brow wrinkled and he glanced at me sideways. I winked, pushed Everett aside, and tore away down the street.

I could hear Everett's laughter as he joined the storm of footfalls behind me.

I made it to the nearest intersection and turned right, then veered back up the busier street. I darted around a group of men and through a cloud of cigar smoke. About half way up, the road briefly leveled out in front of another bar, and the back of my throat burned by the time I made it there. I paused to decide on which way to turn, but I had underestimated my lead.

The world spun sideways as Malcolm crashed into me, and the faces outside the bar all turned our way. Harris skidded to a stop beside us. Taz and Everett were still running to catch up.

Having managed to stay on my feet, I shoved Malcolm back a step, but he was already laughing.

"You ass! You've probably had the money for weeks!"

"Trust me, if I did, I would have used it to get you off my back by now! Forty pieces isn't exactly spare change."

"Yeah, I know," he shoved me in return, "that's why I want it!"

Among the crowd, a woman was leaning on the railing outside the bar. Her blonde hair was braided from the top of her head and down past her shoulder; she wore all black, and the clean panels of her clothing fit together like armor.

"Mordecai, Eric," she called back through the hazy doorway, "come look at this."

Malcolm continued, "I'm not in the mood to wait another five months. If you have even a fraction of what you owe me, I want it now."

"Good luck with that."

Harris' eyes grew to the size of dinner plates. "Stop that, Ignatius. Don't turn this into a goddamn spectacle."

Taz joined him on his left, out of breath, and rested his hands on his knees. Everett wasn't too far behind.

"There are a thousand better ways to handle this," Harris added.

I considered how far another stretch of running could get me, if it was worth trying. At least then there wouldn't be half a bar watching the fight.

Apparently, Taz agreed. "Go find somewhere to talk about it, at least, before you start kicking each other."

"What if I'm in a kicking mood?" Malcolm remarked.

"I'm sure you can find something else to break a toe on."

Two men had joined the woman outside the bar; one had the precise demeanor of a bear, with wide sloping shoulders, black dreadlocks, and an arm coated by black tattoos that looked like writing. The other was taller, with dark blonde hair coiled into a knot on the back of his head. He had a belt with several knives strapped to it and a pearlescent scar running through his left brow onto his cheek. It gleamed in the low light and highlighted the angles of his face—which reminded me of a falcon, or something equally calculated and predatory. Both wore the same kind of black, uniform clothing as the woman.

At least everyone else outside the bar seemed to be losing interest, since no one had taken a punch yet.

Malcolm, Taz, Everett, and Harris followed my gaze.

"Money troubles?" the taller one asked. "I couldn't help but overhear."

Malcolm's expression was unmoved. "And who asked you?"

The scarred man took a sip from the amber colored drink in his hand, "At least tell me how much it is. I'm curious."

"Forty pieces," I muttered.

The corners of his eyes scrunched into a small wince, "That's unfortunate."

"That'll take a while to save, even with a decent income," the man with dreadlocks noted.

Yeah, good thing I've already handicapped that too.

The taller man and the woman glanced at each other. Her eyebrows lifted slightly, and he finished his drink. "You'd be interested in a way to earn a lot of extra money, I assume? All of you?"

Everett frowned.

Harris placed his hands on his hips. "This is the part where you give us a ridiculous sales pitch, isn't it?"

"A hundred pieces in six months," the woman parried, and she tossed a coin into Harris' hand, "give or take a couple of days."

Harris regarded the wide dot of metal with a curl in his lip, angling it up to the light. Taz's jaw fell open. "Oh my God," he walked over to get a better look, "that's a Queen Valinda."

Harris blinked, "So?"

Taz dropped his voice to a whisper, "They're solid gold."

Quickly, Harris lowered the coin and glanced around at the people nearby. "Shit, really?"

"Harris, put it away," I said.

"I could buy my own forge with a hundred pieces." He tucked the coin into his pocket and glanced carefully at the trio outside the bar. "You know how long I've been saving for that."

I nodded, "You set aside a third of what you had the day you aged out of the orphanage."

"What do you think, Taz?" Malcolm asked.

"I could afford the supplies I need to make art people would actually buy—it sounds great. I wouldn't have to dig charcoal out of the fire and scribble on used paper anymore. Hell, I could probably afford lessons too."

Harris nodded at me, "You could dig yourself out of financial ruin, with sixty pieces to spare."

"And turn Malcolm into a rich man in the process..."

"One-hundred-forty pieces," Malcolm contemplated. "I'll be honest, it's pretty tempting. I could do practically anything with that."

The man with the scar was drumming his fingers on the railing, his falcon eyes reading each of us. He had to be a military man, I supposed. All three of them did. But there was something about the way he stood, specifically. If the ground began to shake, and the streets cracked and buckled like dry clay, I had no doubt he'd be one of the few still standing.

"Then you're all willing to consider it?" he pressed.

"Tell us what the job is first," I said.

"You'd be part of a lower facet in the military, basically," explained the other man. "We can take you to talk it over with one of our superiors."

I looked to Harris. "Smells a bit like a scam?"

He shrugged, "They haven't tried to make us sign anything. We can go hear more and decide from there?"

We all looked at each other in silence.

What would I do with the sixty pieces I got to keep? I could use it to improve my career, I could travel, I could leave Salona for good if I wanted to —but where would I go? Maybe I'd use some of it to get the star tattoo professionally removed.

"Then I guess we want to learn more. Where do we have to go?"

CHAPTER TWO

The first giveaway should have been their clothes. The sleek black fabric didn't fit the mold of regular civilians; not only that, but I had noticed gold insignia embroidered onto their right shoulders a while ago. A thin ring enclosed a broadsword crossed by twin axes. The woman and the man with dreadlocks—who'd told us his name was Eric—bore two horizontal red stripes below it. Mordecai, the taller man with the scar, had four. But we followed them anyway because, supposedly, there was a military outpost where we could talk with *a superior.*

The second giveaway should have been how far we had gone in the armored carriage; I'd only seen a few of the trim yet sturdy transports before, because they usually resided in the larger cities. They were what people with influence used if they needed secure travel. The interior smelled of leather and polished wood, enough that I could nearly taste it. The cushioned seat below me was firm. New. We had made our way across to the northern side of Salona and crested the hill above the edge of town when Harris elbowed me. I followed his gaze to the door, and the polished smell turned sour when I noticed there were no handles on the inside.

Across from us, Eric was completely unbothered as he gazed out the carriage window.

Eventually, our transport cut off the main road and followed a narrower dirt road into the trees, up the hill, to what I assumed looked like a military outpost. A portion of the hillside and trees had been cleared away, revealing a flattened area of ground. On it sat high sections of wall that made a rectangle, probably crafted from the same trees that had been felled to make room for it; one tall tree trunk stood directly beside the others, sharpened into points at the top.

The third tell was when the heavy metal gate clanged shut behind us, but by then it was too late. The lock itself was a heap of metal more than twice the size of a fist, and the slats that secured it, I noticed, were each about the width and length of a billet of steel.

One by one, we exited the armored carriage behind Eric.

Wooden buildings stood in organized rows on either side of the rectangle, with a few smaller ones at the far end. The grass in the middle was flattened, almost to the dirt in some places. Other people wearing the same black uniforms, maybe twenty, were wandering about as well, and a few paused to look our way as Mordecai cleared his throat and tucked the massive gate key away.

Taz's mouth was pressed into a dash as he looked around. "I think I've seen enough. How about you?"

"Yeah," Harris nodded, "I think I'm good."

Mordecai shrugged, but the set to his shoulders was far too steady to be natural, like something rehearsed. "Don't be silly. You've been here for less than a minute."

"This isn't an Orvalian outpost, is it?" Malcolm asked, and at this point it wasn't a question.

"No," Mordecai conceded.

Now I realized why the scent of wood and leather had seemed so familiar; it was the same fragrance in the gambling hall with its round oak tables and leather-clad chairs. It was the smell of a bad idea.

Taz pointed toward the gate, nearly poking Everett in the face. "All the more reason I'd like to get going."

Creases formed at the corners of Mordecai's eyes as he said, "That's no longer an option, I'm afraid. You're all staying here."

"Like prisoners?" I asked.

He clicked his tongue, "I prefer to think of it as recruiting."

My stomach rose into my chest like I was falling, and I surveyed the iron gate and towering walls once again.

"So that whole speech about a job was a trick?" Harris retrieved the gold coin from his pocket, "Is this thing a knockoff too? I should have known a hundred pieces in six months was too good to be true."

The woman—Elysian—revealed, "Actually, that's the only part that wasn't a lie. If you survive, you get the money." She pointed her chin at the coin, "Feel free to bite it, if you want to be sure; real gold dents."

Harris arched one brow, but pressed the coin between his teeth anyway, and the rest of us huddled around. Sure enough, there were shallow indentations left behind.

"If I give it back, will you let us out?" He held the coin out, but she only shook her head.

"And you said *survive*?" Taz ran a hand through his light brown hair, "What are you expecting us to do?"

Mordecai began to slowly pace back and forth in front of us, and Eric waited on our right with Elysian. "In simple terms, you are being contracted by Brighton's government. Work is needed, and work is being found." He paused at the end of the line, in front of Taz, "Any previous occupations?"

When none of us spoke, Mordecai donned a serpentine smile and added, "We can do this the easy way, or the hard way. It's up to you."

My eyes snagged on the knives that lined his belt. There were likely more hidden in his clothes. And the other people circling like vultures—weapons indeed gleamed at their sides as well. The ones nearest the gate, who were doing a poor job acting as if they weren't eavesdropping on every word we exchanged, brazenly flaunted their crossbows.

Taz's eyes narrowed as he cautiously answered, "I work in a factory."

"What kind?"

"The building is shared by two companies; sometimes I work on the side that produces cloth, sometimes I work on the side that refines coal. I'm an artist on my free time."

Mordecai nodded indifferently and continued down the row. "And you?" he asked Malcolm.

"I'm a stonebreaker."

"That's grueling work," Mordecai nodded again, "I respect that."

He paused in front of me, raising his eyebrows rather than repeating the question. I felt the edge of my lip curl.

Impatiently, he remarked, "A professional beggar, perhaps?"

"Blacksmith," I spat.

He said nothing, continuing down the line.

"I'm also a blacksmith, but I dabble in engineering," explained Harris.

Everett folded his arms, "I work in a field."

"Not that much variety, but at least you all work in some kind of physical labor," Mordecai resumed his line of pacing. "That will help. You should all be strong enough to make it through."

I could smell the chopped wood it had taken to build the walls surrounding us and the structures within. The grass underfoot had been flattened from wear, reducing patches of it to packed dirt. Whatever this was, it had been here for a while.

The itch to run was strong, and blurred images of scrambling through the trees warped my thoughts. But the other black-uniformed men conveniently placing themselves in front of the gate kept my feet in place. For now.

Mordecai continued, "Brighton's military is in need of more people, but not for factory skills, stone breaking, blacksmithing, or farming. They are working to double the size of their army by the end of next month, give or take a week."

"What for?" I asked.

Harris was tense at my side, glancing at me out of the corner of his eye, and Malcolm crossed his arms.

"Well, why do you think they'd want a bigger army?"

"War?" Taz suggested.

"Exactly."

To my right, Malcolm wrinkled his nose. "Seems like a dangerous way to go about it."

"I don't dictate how things are done. My only concern is that I do my job and bring them the people they need; by law, six is the minimum number per rotation. An easy, even number for Brighton to divide up as it sees fit."

"There are only five of us here," I pointed out, with no small amount of satisfaction.

Mordecai's expression didn't falter one bit. "Oh, believe me, we're not finished. We'll have at least two more by the time this is all done."

Elysian—who I kept thinking looked like she was related to Mordecai in some way—and Eric nodded.

I bit my tongue to keep my temper at bay, thinking through all the ways I should have known better and all the red-flags I should have seen before we'd agreed to get into that armored carriage.

"Going to war is a taxing ordeal, and a substantial army is an important part of that," Mordecai added.

My face scrunched as I tried to form a question.

Harris beat me to it—using a much more tactful tone than I would have—asking, "But there hasn't been a war in decades, and the most recent one was in the south. Who does Brighton want to go to war with?"

"Dale, the island country in the west," Elysian answered plainly, like she was describing the weather or something else equally unimportant.

The image of the map crossed my mind, as I tried to recall where things were. I had never been to Dale, and I had never much cared to know more about it. But from what I understood, they mostly kept to themselves.

So then why are they Brighton's target?

Before anyone else could get a word out, Mordecai said, "You'll understand more clearly as time goes. But for now, your greatest concern should be that training begins first thing tomorrow."

Training? An invisible weight landed on my shoulders.

We need to think of a way to get out of here.

"It will be difficult because that's the way it was designed," Mordecai continued. "You have no choice, at this point, so I suggest you do your best to go along with it. If you choose to be resistant, uncooperative, lazy, or incapable, then you'll have to face the consequence for it."

Anger began to cloud my vision, and my hands curled into fists. "You think you can train us to be your pawns?"

This time, I ignored Harris's glance. My tone was sharp because I meant it to be, and there would be no calling it to heel.

Mordecai's face was stubbornly unchanged. "That's what they pay me for, so I do it. The same goes for everyone else here."

"What are you going to do when someone does eventually escape and tells the Orvalian military where this little setup is? I can't imagine they'd be too happy about it being so close to their border—we passed the marker on the way here."

"You aren't the first person to say that to me." He smirked tightly, stepping closer. "The second, actually."

I lifted my chin in defiance. Harris waited beside me like a statue, only his eyes moving as he watched our faces. On my opposite side, Malcolm and Taz carefully read every detail of the exchange. If they had a pen and paper they might have even jotted down notes. Everett was busy counting the men by the gate on his fingers.

"Sometimes examples have to be made, the least you could do for yourself is make sure you're not one of them."

So, this has been ongoing. I wonder how many people have already cycled through here?

Harris kicked the side of my ankle and shook his head.

"Does everybody understand?" Mordecai asked.

This time, I didn't say another word. If all five of us were going to find a way out, through the gate or over the wall, we needed time to come up with a plan.

Having been sufficiently threatened, we were herded into one of the barracks by the eastern wall. It was one room and not particularly large, but it was just big enough to hold the four of us and keep us from wandering around. Not only that, but it was sturdy; the floors didn't creak or shift, and there were no drafts coming through the walls.

A headache sprouted in my right temple as I scanned the space. The expanding pit in my stomach wasn't helpful either. I toed the back wall in frustration, and Harris watched me with his arms crossed and a wrinkled brow.

"Well, this is a disaster," Taz planted himself by the opposite wall and leaned against it.

"How could we be stupid enough to walk into this?" I wondered aloud.

Malcolm shrugged one shoulder, "It was a really good offer—we obviously aren't the first to fall for it either. Everybody needs money, so it makes sense for them to target that."

"At least they gave us water," Harris said, pouring himself a cup from the pitcher on the small table, "assuming it's not poison."

"No, there'd be no point in that."

I smirked, "But feel free to test it out and let the rest of us know if your throat starts closing on itself."

Harris, of course, did not hesitate to dump the full cup of water across my front.

"Are you bleeding?" Taz asked, and pointed, "What is that?"

I glanced down. The water had pasted my shirt to my chest, and red was visible over my heart through the fabric. "No, that's just my tattoo."

"It's as red as blood."

Malcolm's face fell slack, and a shade of color faded from his skin.

"I never knew you had one." Taz pressed, "What is it, if you don't mind?"

"It's a star—most of one anyway," I tugged the collar of my shirt down so that half of it could be seen. The star had eight points, and was about the size of a fist, but was not filled in entirely with red; the inside had been left hollow, so it was more like a thick, stark outline. "I actually have no idea what it means. I've had it since I was left at an orphanage as a baby."

Malcolm swallowed hard, "You don't know who gave it to you?"

"Not a clue."

He sat down in a chair and stared at the floor in front of his feet for a moment. I saw concern flash across Taz's face, and Everett ended his scrutiny of the door to listen in.

"I have it," Malcolm said weakly.

"What?" I asked, unsure if I had simply heard him wrong.

Malcolm added, "I mean I have one just like it. That tattoo. And I don't know how I got mine either."

Taking a seat immediately sounded like a good idea, but I braced my shoulder against the nearby wall instead. I tilted my head, suddenly dizzy. "You have the same tattoo and no idea where it came from? Same place and everything?"

"Different place," he corrected, "My left shoulder blade." He turned around, tugging the left side of his shirt off his shoulder so that everyone could see.

There would be no way *not* to see it. There it was. The same eight points, same blood red color, same size, same everything—just completely out of place. *Not on me.*

My mouth went dry, as if I'd eaten sand.

"Hm," Harris considered. "That's...odd."

Everett nodded, "They both look professionally done—if they're cheap they fade, especially if you've had them your whole life."

"Its color is identical," Taz noted, his eyes squinted at the marking, "That's impressive, considering how much variance there is between your skin tones."

Malcolm silently secured his shirt back into place. I crossed my arms.

No one said anything for a while.

It was like stinging nettle had left its mark in the shape of a star over the red ink, burning and refusing to let me forget that it was there. I had made myself used to it for so long, for my whole twenty-one years, as a matter of fact. I saw it every day. I always knew it was with me. Not worrying about why I had it to begin with had become like dealing with the weather when it turned sour; if it rains, it rains, and there's nothing anyone can do. But what about this?

"You know absolutely nothing about it?" I asked again.

Malcolm nodded, "Kids used to make fun of me for it. You know how they can be; they figured I was either cursed or a monster."

"Mistress Helena used to call me the star-spangled-shit," I added. "She was the woman in charge of the orphanage where I grew up."

"I grew up in an orphanage too, but I left the area. It was miles south of here."

Taz tapped a finger on his chin. "Is there any way it's a coincidence?"

"It's possible, I guess..." Malcolm said, and we looked at each other.

I finished the thought for both of us, "But unlikely."

Keys rattled on the other side of the door, and Eric stepped in. His chin was tensely set as he shoved forward another man: no, another prisoner.

He looked like he was in his early twenties, like the rest of us; in fact, he was probably Harris and Malcolm's age—a year older than Taz and me. He had black, disheveled curls of hair, and his skin was light, with scatterings of freckles. His eyes seemed unusual though, as he staggered to a stop near the middle of the room, turning to shoot Eric a fuming gaze. They were green. Like sage around the edges, and darkening to the color of pine in the center.

Without a word, and completely unfazed, Eric closed and locked the door as he left. I was beginning to think the swirling patterns of tattoos on his arm had been done in black specifically to match what appeared to be his consistent mood. Austere and unyielding.

The newest addition to our group looked around at the sturdy walls, hands in fists, with green eyes moving in slow sweeps. He was shorter than Malcolm and me, only by a little, but still more muscular and taller than Taz.

"Rough night?" I half-joked.

He glanced at me cautiously. "I've had better. Did they promise you money as well?"

"Unfortunately, yes," Taz sighed.

He walked toward the back wall, scrutinizing the rest of the room as he went. "Training to be soldiers in a pointless war," he scoffed, "So this is what life is going to be like until someone thinks of a way out of here."

As he passed me, I noticed an odd scar on his upper right forearm. It was circular, but with the kind of detail that a piece of lace might have. I squinted.

Is that a brand?

Before I could get a closer look, he tugged his sleeve down to cover it. He fixed me with a stern gaze as he paused, green eyes slightly narrowed in warning. I only blinked, packing the curiosity back into a jar.

He continued on, "This should be interesting. Does anyone have an idea yet?"

Harris shook his head, "Not yet. We were just about to start working on that."

The prospect of that was like a kick in the ribs. And that wasn't even accounting for the newly unearthed tattoo situation.

"At least they said we can get the money if we live," I offered. "But I guess we'll have to see about that too."

Green Eyes briefly examined the back wall. He kicked it lightly, like he expected it to topple over—and I wished it would—but it held strong nevertheless.

"Well, if we're going to be trapped, we should all at least know each other's names," he decided, and turned around. "I'm Evander."

I BARELY SLEPT. I wasn't sure what I was expecting; it certainly wasn't a full night of rest, but I had hoped for a little more than what I got.

We'd discussed ways to escape until my eyelids were heavier than rocks. Worse yet, we didn't make any progress toward a plan. Then, no matter how I tossed and turned, my thoughts continued to run around me like screaming children. The most obnoxious of them all was the one that kept reminding me what Mordecai had said: training starts tomorrow.

And now tomorrow was today.

Mordecai paced a line in front of us on the grass, like he had yesterday, only now he was carrying a crossbow. He wore the same black clothing from the night before, or maybe it was a clean set. I couldn't tell. The girl, Elysian, as well as Eric and a few other men were dressed to match.

"A soldier's job is not easy," Mordecai explained. "It is the farthest thing from it. But as long as you do what I tell you, you will have a chance. Got it?"

I took a deep breath to suppress a yawn. Silence answered his question, and apparently it was enough.

"Good." He clapped his hands together, jolting Taz, who had ever so gradually started to lean with exhaustion. "We have a lot of work to do. Or, I should probably say *you* do."

Work. I wondered what Margaret and everyone else at the forge had to be thinking. They would just be starting their shift, and despite all promises, Harris and I would not be on time. That damn knife I didn't finish would still be sitting at my station.

"Let's go." Mordecai led the way, toward the main gate, and we trudged after him, practically dragging our feet.

God, and it's only morning. How can I be this tired already?

Eric and Elysian were poised on either side of the main gate as Mordecai worked his key into the lock. The other reinforcements waited close by, each carrying a crossbow of their own and watching our every move.

Small creases formed at the corners of Harris's eyes as Mordecai pushed the main gate wide open. My feet became heavy, and seemed to stop on their own as I looked at the expanse of freedom ahead of us. After no one moved, Mordecai gestured out with his arm. "Go."

Just like that? You're handing us the chance to bolt on a silver platter?

A skeptical glance down the row, at all the tilted heads and fidgeting hands, would have been reassuring—until I saw Everett. His eyes moved between Mordecai and the open gate so fast that they blurred. By the time I opened my mouth to say something, it was already too late.

"Don't!"

He was running. Dirt flew into the air behind his heels as he swerved around part of the gate.

Mordecai crossed his arms and his lips disappeared into a line. But beside him, Eric had already taken aim. The mechanics of the crossbow clicked, and in that same instant, Everett fell forward like a tree. It wasn't until he'd skidded to a stop, no more than twenty feet away, that I could see the fletching on the bolt protruding from the back of his skull.

Harris clapped a hand across his forehead. Evander sucked air through his teeth. Malcolm wrinkled his nose, squeezed his eyes shut, and looked away. Taz turned around and threw up. When the fermented, acidic smell of vomit hit my nose, I thought I might just do the same.

Mordecai sighed, "Well, at least now I don't have to explain what happens if you try to run."

"You just *killed* him!" Harris pointed.

Taz was still bent over the glistening pile of vomit and clutching his stomach.

My stare kept wandering to the path Everett had taken, his steps still fresh in the dirt. Then the coppery smell of fresh blood, either real or a trick of my imagination, made my insides boil.

Mordecai squared his shoulders and strolled down the narrow dirt path ahead. "Come on. We don't have an entire day to waste standing around."

Eric nodded for the rest of us to follow him, and we did. Slowly. Watching every crossbow carefully.

The footpath snaked down the side of the mountain through the trees. I made myself concentrate on the sounds of boots crunching, birds, the smell of dirt and grass; not the fact that Taz was still donning an awful grayish hue, not that no one—not even Evander—was speaking, and not that there was a strange gap in our ranks like a missing tooth.

The hike finally ended near the bottom of the mountain where the trees thinned and a transport road sprawled from north to south.

A wagon was waiting on one side in the shade, with crates piled up on the back. The man in the driver's chair had a wide brimmed, straw hat that he had tilted down to cover his face; he glanced up from underneath the shadowed rim to nod as Mordecai passed him.

"There are three crates in this wagon," Mordecai reported as he cast a look over the side, "and there are now five of you. You would have been working in pairs to get them back up the mountain, but it'll still work with one less person."

I lifted my chin to get a better look at the crates. They were each about as long as a person, but wide all the way around.

Elysian retrieved several sections of rope from the back of the wagon, and with the help of the driver began fastening it to one of the crates.

"You want us to drag them?" Taz wrinkled his nose.

Mordecai pursed his lips. "I suppose you could always try and drive the wagon up a steep hill through the trees and *hope* that it doesn't get stuck. Of course, you're dragging them."

"What's in them?" asked Harris.

"Supplies for repairs, newer weapons, basic necessities that need to be replenished."

Both cringing, Elysian and the driver lowered the first crate to the ground, and Mordecai narrowed his steely-blue gaze at us.

"You two," he pointed to Taz and Evander, "work together."

He moved down the row as the two of them reluctantly picked up the ropes and started hauling the crate across the road.

"You two," he paired Harris with one of his henchmen. To his credit, the man didn't complain, and instead dutifully passed his crossbow to Eric.

"And I think you can figure out the rest," he waved a hand at Malcolm and me.

I re-traced the path we had taken in my mind, all of the twists and turns and steep rocky sections where tree roots poked out of the soil. Then I looked at the heavy crate as it waited on the ground, with ropes looped around and behind it and through the braided handle, with only the two ends left to hold onto.

"There are six other people here," I pointed out, eyeing the additional men with crossbows, "and you want us to deal with this all on our own?"

Mordecai shrugged, "They aren't here to make this easier for you. They're here to make sure that you can move a box up a hill without failing. And believe me—you don't want to fail on the first test."

"Is that a threat?"

"It's a warning." He pointed to the crate, "Now go."

I bit down on my tongue as I marched to my side of the crate, lifting the rope over my shoulder. Malcolm did the same beside me, keeping a peeved look directed at Mordecai the whole time.

"Well, this should be fun."

"Yeah, I can't imagine anything else I'd want to be doing right now," I grumbled.

The fibers of the rope bit into my shoulder as we followed the trail back up the hill, and the man in the straw hat drove the empty wagon away down the road. By the time we made it to the first switchback, my hands were burning from where I was holding the rope. Dryness closed around the back of my throat as I watched the ground, planting each step carefully for more leverage.

At least it kept me from re-imagining the way Everett fell, and the way the crossbow bolt poked out of his skull.

Keeping pace was key. As Mordecai led the way, setting a reasonable but speedy clip, it became clear that there would be no stopping until we made it back to the fort. Not unless we wanted to test the strength of his warning.

"I can't believe he has the nerve to call this a test," I grunted. "I could be getting paid right now, not giving a shit about their stupid war or this stupid crate."

"I wonder if he just wants to see one of us collapse," Malcolm offered, gritting his teeth to haul his corner of the crate over a protruding rock.

My side of the crate got caught on a tree root, but a harsh lean into the rope was enough to tear through it. "And now we need to re-think our escape; running for it at the right time isn't going to work the way we thought it would."

"Yeah, not unless we all learn how to dodge crossbow fire."

The steep, bumpy trail loomed ahead. The two other crates weren't that far in front of us, but it may as well have been miles. A droplet of sweat rolled off my forehead as I tried to readjust the rope for what had to be the twentieth time so far. The coarse fibers carved through the fabric of my shirt, sinking into my skin like claws.

"This thing is getting on my nerves," I complained, pausing in one of the few places where the trail went level. Eric and a few others waited impatiently behind us as I pulled my shirt off, wrapping it around part of the rope for additional padding.

Malcolm waited in silence, dragging his sleeve across his dampened brow, and said nothing as we started pulling the crate once more. We didn't speak again until the next switchback of the trail.

"Have you ever thought about what the tattoo might mean?" he finally asked, avoiding looking directly at me—at *it*.

If I could count up all the time I'd spent asking myself that question, it had to amount to days: sitting awake at night when I was younger, in nightmares, during the middle of the day if my mind had the chance to drift, and when I had to concentrate on pretending it didn't exist at all. It always found a way to sneak into my head. It was like a more frustrating version of dust; no matter how many times I tried to clear it away, no matter how many times I swept it out the door, it always found a way to come back.

"I have thought about it," I admitted. "I've tried to understand, and guess, and fill in the gaps. Each time I try, the more it feels like a waste of time. I'll probably never know the answer."

He tilted his chin down and frowned at the dirt. "You're positive? Were you left with a letter at the orphanage that could help?"

"By 'letter' do you mean a shred of paper with my name on it? Because that's all I got—and I burned that thing years ago. What about you?"

He shook his head, "Same thing."

I didn't regret watching that slip of paper burn, turning black, letting it curl and wither like a leaf. The smudged, hurried strokes of ink had always been more insulting than comforting; the least they could have done was write my name decently.

"Then I guess we're both useless," I said.

He winced. It could have been from the strain and the damn crate, but then again, that was the least of our problems.

The slope of the trail gradually steepened the farther up we climbed. We couldn't be much closer than halfway to the top, at best. My shoulder was bothering me less now that I had wrapped the rope with my shirt, yet the penetrating ache of a bruise was slowly spreading.

"You're probably used to working this hard, as a stonebreaker?"

He dimpled one corner of his mouth, "Swinging a sledgehammer all day has its perks, I guess."

After another switchback, I asked, "Aside from the fact that we have nothing to go off of, have you thought about what the star could mean?"

"No. I mean, I've thought about it, of course, but I have no idea," his brows pressed together as he looked at the ground. "Why is it a star at all? Why the color red? Why anything? I've tried..." his thoughts fell straight off the edge of a cliff.

"Tried what?"

He shook his head, "Nothing. It's all just a series of dead ends."

"What do you mean?"

"Everywhere I turn when it comes to that tattoo, all I find are brick walls."

I slowed my steps, which forced him to slow down as well, and I watched his face. He resisted my gaze, keeping his eyes forward. I could see the muscle in his jaw pulling tight. There was a faint flush of color going up the side of his neck. He glanced at me for barely a second as my pace slowed even more, noting the arch to my brow.

"No, that's not it." I considered. "Do you know something you're not telling me?"

His eyes narrowed, "And why would you think that?"

"I can see it in your face. You got tense when I asked you to clarify."

"I'm tense because I'm dragging a fucking crate."

We both ground to a slow stop, frowning across the trail at each other. His eyes were slits of blue as he examined my expression.

"How am I supposed to know that it isn't *you* who's lying, Ignatius? *You* could already know something and be hiding it from me."

"What would I gain from that?"

"I don't know, you tell me."

I let my end of rope fall to the dirt, pointing an accusatory finger at him. "You're dodging. You know you are."

"Hey!" Eric yelled from behind the crate. "We don't have all day! Get going!"

Malcolm didn't move.

I kicked the side of the crate, picked up my section of rope again, and leaned my shoulder into it. Plowing forward though the dirt, through twigs and over rocks, was much easier with fresh gusts of rage in my sails.

Through gritted teeth, I said, "You're a fucking liar and we both know it."

"Well, I think you're a liar, so I guess that makes us even," he huffed.

He could know anything—who gave it to me and why. He could know one or both of my parents' names, and even where they are.

I bit back another remark as the climb continued, my teeth locked together. There were no words between us for the rest of the trek. Just a steadily widening void.

CHAPTER THREE

"You seem agitated." Harris looked at me from under an arched brow as we worked to unload equipment from one of the crates.

"That's because I am." I shoved a cluster of spears into the storage shed, disregarding the loud clatter they made as they fell. "Did you hear any of our conversation on the way up?"

"You and Malcolm? No. I couldn't hear much of anything over the sound of crates grating over rocks."

"Well, then you were lucky." I tossed the one remaining spear through the door, watching as it flopped onto the pile with the rest.

"Was it about the money?"

"No. It was about the tattoos." I shot a look toward the middle of the camp, where Malcolm was helping Taz and Evander assemble wooden dummies with parts out of a different crate. Mordecai stood nearby to supervise. He would point and give out instructions whenever he saw fit, only glancing back at us whenever I threw something too loudly.

Harris sighed through his nose as I hurled a metal helmet at the back wall of the shed. "That bastard knows something about them that he isn't telling me. I can tell."

"*How* could you tell?"

"People act differently when they lie. He was saying something about the things he's done to try and figure out what it means, and he practically dropped dead mid-sentence. Then he tried to avoid it altogether."

Harris pursed his lips, "Are you certain you're not jumping to conclusions?"

"Please," I scoffed, "I'd fling myself off the top floor of a building knowing this shit was below me. Poker-faces don't fracture like that unless something's there."

"If you say so."

I had just begun stewing together a remark when the clang of the heavy lock on the main gate turned our heads.

Elysian and two of the other men walked though, their uniforms standing together like pieces of a black chess set. In her grasp was a child, probably no older than eleven or twelve, with lanky arms and legs that he hadn't yet grown into. He kept his head down like a kicked dog, his light brown hair falling forward to hide his face.

Elysian's shoulders were raised nearly to her ears as she dragged him toward Mordecai. I could see their mouths moving, but there was too much distance for me to hear a word between them.

"What's happening?" Harris asked.

I shook my head, "I don't know."

Malcolm, Taz, and Evander stopped their work with the dummies, and turned to watch as Eric joined the group that had walked in with Elysian. Harris and I silently crossed the grass to join them.

"What are they doing with a kid?" Evander's green eyes swept back and forth across the scene. I followed suit, trying to read expressions; Elysian, who had a watchful eye trained on all of us, was talking in a hushed voice with a crease in her brow; Eric was shaking his head, adding a few words from time to time as he gestured with an intricately tattooed arm; Mordecai was pinching the bridge of his nose like he had a headache, and his shoulders were drawn forward—the closest thing to a hunch that someone like him could possibly ever do. He spoke too, but only in short bursts.

Things began to fade into hideous clarity as the seconds drew on, our ears straining to hear.

"They can't honestly consider recruiting a child," Malcolm said, "Can they?"

"Is that what you think they're doing?" Harris asked.

"Why else would he be here?" I shook my head. "If they're this desperate to add to their army, at what point do they draw a line?"

"Just below age ten, apparently," observed Taz. "What do we do?"

"Fucking stop them, obviously," Malcolm asserted, and he walked toward them. Evander was quick to follow.

Taz, Harris, and I glanced around, and I quickly went to the open crate to retrieve one of the wooden staffs.

Harris's dark brows lowered. "A stick?"

"In case the carrot doesn't work."

Together, the three of us followed toward the larger group.

Mordecai's eyes rolled upward as soon as he caught sight of us, and he planted his hands on his hips.

"I didn't realize this place doubled as a daycare," Evander chided. The wide, easy smile it came with was nearly enough to mask his sarcasm completely. "Whose spawn is this? Not yours, I know that—" he swatted Mordecai's arm, "yours would look a lot more like a ferret."

Elysian heaved a sigh, still holding the boy like a wild animal. "He wandered too close."

"So, what are you going to do, send him into a battlefield?" Harris' eyes moved back and forth between them.

"It's none of your concern, actually," Mordecai bit out, staring at the main gate as it was locked shut, "and you all should be getting back to work. Equipment doesn't unload itself, and dummies don't stand up on their own." The corner of his eye twitched as he glanced our way, "The wooden ones don't, anyway."

Malcolm narrowed his eyes. "So, you're going to do what? *Get rid of him?* He's a kid!"

The boy still hadn't looked up, keeping his head bent toward his chest. His brown hair was a disheveled mess with a few twigs and blades of grass caught in it, and dirt scuffs covered one side of his body, probably from when he had been caught.

Mordecai pinched the bridge of his nose again, and by now he might have had a genuine headache. "Go back to work. Now. This has nothing to do with any of you, and it's my duty to keep this place under control. That, and I'm not exactly in the mood to ruin my career because one kid wandered down the wrong hillside."

Evander pursed his lips and trailed a critical glance from the toes of Mordecai's shoes up to the scar on his face.

"You can't kill a child for that," Taz argued.

Between Mordecai's sullen scowl and the kid, taut strands of anxiety began to lace up my spine and around my chest. "If you can't afford to let him go, then just train him like the rest of us."

He shook his head, and beckoned for Elysian to walk past us, "That's just as much of a death sentence." He withdrew one of the knives from his belt and it flashed in the light. "For the last time, go back to work."

Now the boy looked up with wide, round eyes, dragging his heels as Elysian reluctantly started to walk. She strained to avoid looking down at his face as Malcolm put out an arm to stop her, trying to reason with her.

I prodded Mordecai in the shoulder with the staff and sent him back a step. An unspoken threat rippled across his features like a heat wave.

"Don't you think the king of Brighton would be just as furious if he found out that you killed an innocent child?"

"Not if he's expanding his army by lying to people. He might be more aggravated by me bringing him a little kid, who will be mowed down like a blade of grass in a battle and add nothing to his forces. Do you think I want to do this?"

Behind me, Malcolm and Evander were arguing with Elysian and staying in her way. Taz and Harris waited beside me, each keeping an ear toward both conversations. Eric had taken a step back, waiting as some of his other uniformed counterparts watched from a distance.

Mordecai pointed at the end of the staff, which I had aimed

toward his face. The knife in his hand gleamed in the corner of my vision. "Put the stick down, boy. There's no need for it."

"Then you put your knife away."

His nostrils flared, and his knuckles whitened on the blade's handle. I raised the end of the staff higher, closer to his face, and secured it with my other hand.

"You don't want to test me," he maintained. "I'll agree not to hurt the boy. But if you strike me, it won't be him who should worry about his safety."

It was a conscious effort to keep from immediately swinging at him. Helping scam people into a system of involuntary labor was one thing, but it was another thing to drag a little kid into that same mess. One that sent my blood boiling. "If you agree, then put your knife away."

I looked over my shoulder as Elysian released the boy and he hid inside our ranks, wide brown eyes locked on Mordecai and his knife.

When I turned back around, Mordecai still had his blade out.

"Put the stick down," his tone sharpened like a piece of metal. "Now."

My jaw clamped as a spark of anger lit. I whirled the end of the stick down and it clacked against Mordecai's wrist; the knife landed on the grass by his feet.

He shook out his hand and his face reddened.

Somewhere behind me, Harris cursed under his breath.

"Oh, I see. You've officially decided that you're going to be a problem." Mordecai grabbed the end of the staff and pulled. I cringed as I fought his grip. Harris took hold of the back of my shirt, and I reluctantly let my weapon slide through my fingers.

Mordecai whipped the staff through the air expertly and tossed it well out of reach, near Eric. "There's always one that can't seem to learn how to bend. And the ones that don't bend, break."

Harris released me as I swallowed down the bitter taste of regret. The drumming of my heart landed in my stomach. A vein bulged from the side of Mordecai's neck that did not match his tone, which was well disciplined and steady, the mark of an expert. His four red stripes slinked across my thoughts.

With his uninjured hand, he grabbed a clump of my hair, and I winced as he led me away by it. His words came out evenly again, in stark contrast to the strength in his grip, as he said, "The only question that remains is whether you're a fast learner—in which case this will be over quickly—or a slow learner."

What?

He led me across the grass in the direction of the main gate. I thought nothing of our unwavering course toward the deep, wooden water troughs lined up to the right of it. Not until the last second, when a gasp caught in the back of my throat.

Oh shit!

Mordecai shoved my head and shoulders into the water, using his weight to keep me there. My breath knotted up in my chest as the cold water surrounded me. I tried to think reasonably, but the violent rush of panic blurred everything, and I clawed out at the edges of the trough. No matter how hard I pushed, no matter how much I tried to use my grip as leverage, Mordecai didn't budge.

I'd met the sensation of drowning once before, when I was nine.

Playing at the end of the dock and harassing seagulls was something I had done a thousand times. There were about ten of us that day, as gray clouds swam across the far edge of the sky and cold seawater lapped at the dock's sturdy posts.

Someone dropped their left shoe into the water and cried out after it as it sank. We all huddled on the edge, watching as its shape was swallowed up by the dark water and bubbles trailed behind it. A tendril of seaweed swirled with the waves.

"What do I do!" the boy cried. "That was one of my good shoes— the rest have holes!"

An older boy with freckles and large front teeth pointed, "Just dive in after it. Someone's gotta go get it before it sinks too far."

"Not me."

"Ew, no! There's seaweed!"

"Just leave it, there's a storm coming anyway."

The wind was sweeping in like cold beats of a giant bird's wing. I peered over the edge with everyone else at the deep blue and gray below us, as a few more tiny bubbles rose to the surface.

The boy stared down at his foot in its dirty sock and whined.

"You go get it!" The older boy said, and he pushed me.

I landed with a splash. The cold was everywhere and I held my breath. My eyes were squeezed shut as tight as they would go, and I could hear the gigantic purr of the water, could feel myself sinking.

My arms and legs flailed against the darkness but I still couldn't see, and I didn't want to open my eyes. Something brushed the side of my leg, and a slimy leaf slid past my hand. I recoiled from it, but then another flapped across my face. I reached to push it away, and all I felt were more lengths of seaweed.

Now my lungs burned, and the back of my throat was aching. I kicked and swatted and wanted to scream. My eyes flew open on their own and the water stung my eyes. Everything was dark and blurry, shadowy gray bleeding into deep brown and green, but at least I could tell light was filtering down from one direction. Up.

When I looked that way, I could see the rectangular shadow of the dock, the billowing ends of the seaweed, and the pale blue of the sky beyond, but it was far away, far enough for me to panic.

Air! It was all I could think. *Get to the air now!*

Instinct took over as I kicked against the water and pulled it past myself with my arms. I shoved sections of seaweed out of my way, cringing each time I had to touch the slimy, ropey vines. I didn't want to look down because I knew it was dark, and I had the unshakable sense that there was a monster waiting somewhere below me. It would certainly have hideous, beady eyes and long fangs, or arms with spindly, bony fingers at the ends and a tail like a snake. If I looked down, I might see it reaching after my feet.

It would never be happy with just a shoe.

The surface of the water broke past my face and I struggled for air against the pattern of waves, which would spill into my mouth at the worst times. I spat it out, coughed, and tried to take another frantic breath, still kicking and flapping.

A wave threw me into one of the dock's supports, and the barnacles on it scraped my arms and hands, but I held onto it regardless.

Finally, I had enough air to scream for help.

All of the other boys had fled from the end of the dock—to fetch help, they later told me—but it had been the woman with the snake tattoos, the card counter, who eventually pulled me up from the waves. She'd wiped my matted hair from where it was plastered to my face and set me on the wooden planks beside a gray-haired fisherman, leaving me in his care. With that, she vanished back down the other end of the dock and into the city streets. After I'd stopped coughing, and after I had vomited into the water, the fisherman walked me back to the door of the orphanage.

Harris was shocked when he saw me, and he sat down at my side after I'd been cocooned in blankets.

"What happened to you?" he asked.

Upstairs, we could both hear mistress Helena shouting at the other boys, and I couldn't resist a little bit of a smirk. "I went for a swim."

I never played at the end of the dock again.

Now the water was rushing in my ears once more, barely audible over my racing heartbeat.

I couldn't think. I needed air more than I needed to think.

Involuntarily, I gasped in water. My lungs had minds of their own now. I could feel the cold water accumulating in my chest, and there was nothing that I could do except for thrash helplessly. Blindly. Ringing filled my ears and my arms were sluggish and weak as I tried to pull myself above water. The panic and cold were blending with the sinking, dark sensation of losing consciousness.

At last, he let go.

I flopped onto the grass like a fish and started to heave up water and gasp for air.

Mordecai stood aside, with his arms crossed and tapping one foot as he waited for me to stop hacking up water. Once he decided that I had recovered sufficiently, he lugged me to my feet again and led me back to the rest of the group.

The mid-morning air was cold enough to sting my skin, as more water dripped from the ends of my hair, and my teeth chattered together.

He shoved me back into line beside Harris, who watched me like a concerned parent as I bent over to spit up more water. Nearby, the poor kid was practically hiding behind Taz, so pale he might have been on the verge of fainting.

"Anyone else care to test my patience today?" Mordecai asked, and the question was met with silence and wide-eyed looks. "Good." He leaned down toward me, as I carefully worked to stand up straight without sending my lungs into another fit. "And do *not* try to disarm me again."

I glared up from underneath my lashes, where droplets of water still clumped them together.

I didn't try, I succeeded! Did that bruise your pride?

He straightened, shaking out the arm that was drenched with water. "Now that that's settled, we have a lot of work to do." He pointed to Malcolm and Evander, "Finish assembling those dummies so we can stop wasting time."

"TODAY MIGHT JUST BE one of the longest days of your life. The first one always is, and it'll be one of several. However, I cannot emphasize the importance of these skills enough," Mordecai droned as he paced in front of us, Elysian waiting beside him. "They could save your life, when the time comes."

I had finally dried off from my near-drowning. Still, I paid less attention to what Mordecai was saying, and more on keeping the irritating rattle in my chest at bay, should I dare to breathe too deeply.

Harris stood to my right and had been kind enough to swat me on the back if another wave of coughs passed through. Malcolm was to my left. We had barely said a word to each other since this morning, a trend that appeared to be continuing. On his opposite side, the boy stood cowering, with his head down and his shoulders folded forward.

"As soldiers, your only task will be to kill effectively with weapons, but not be completely helpless without them," he dragged his stern eyes across each of our faces. "Understand?"

We all nodded stiffly.

He paused in front of the boy and nodded once, "What's your name?"

He flinched, slowly lifting his gaze to meet Mordecai's eyes. "My name is Nickolai."

Mordecai scrunched one corner of his mouth and sighed. Elysian, rather than enduring the fearful look on the child's face, opted to cross her arms and look at the grass in front of her shoes.

"Well, Nickolai, you should know that you're going to have to work harder than most if you want to make it out of this alive."

"The training?" he squeaked.

Mordecai nodded grimly as he clarified, "Yes, partly. Every one of you has to make it through training to be proficient." He looked around at the rest of us pointedly. "It is not my wish for it to be this way, but if you cannot complete the tasks you are given, then it becomes my job to get rid of you."

"You mean kill us," Evander sniped.

"Yes."

I toed at the grass, breathing shallowly to prevent a cough.

"We'll start with hand-to-hand combat, and then move to weapons from there," Mordecai resumed his line of pacing. "Since there are six of you, the pairings will work out evenly."

Oh no, not this again.

"How about," he squinted, "you two." He put Taz and Evander together. "And you two." He pointed to Harris and Nickolai.

Mordecai smirked faintly as he passed in front of Malcolm and me.

Please don't.

"Since you both seemed to be getting along so well earlier," he taunted, "you can work together for this too."

God dammit.

I bent my head to the side and coughed. Malcolm didn't say a word, clamping his jaw and looking at the ground as Mordecai continued past us.

"Alright. Now split off, and don't get too close to any of the other pairs."

Harris gave me a shrug as he and Nickolai passed. I bit down on my tongue as I returned to kicking the grass, and Malcolm was suddenly fascinated by everything that wasn't in my general direction. Neither one of us made the effort to move.

I guess we'll just stay here then.

Each group had loosely formed a circle, and Mordecai stood at the middle of it. "We'll start simple. I assume most of you already know how to throw a punch, but we'll go over it all the same." He raised his right hand to demonstrate, wrapping his fingers into a fist. "Keep your thumb bent around the front of the rest of your fingers so that it doesn't get jammed or broken, and do not hit with your knuckles, hit with the flat part between them and the first joint. Otherwise, you'll break your own hand. Make sense?"

Each of us held up a fist of our own, mimicking what he had done. Nickolai watched Harris's hand, and carefully folded each finger into the same place.

"Good. One of you, stand holding out your palms and the other will practice hitting. Then you'll switch."

Malcolm and I glanced at each other out of the corners of our eyes, and I held up a fist. He sighed, and reluctantly turned to face me with both palms up.

I slugged his right hand, not bothering to wait for Mordecai to give the command, and Malcolm's jaw clenched. I raised my eyebrows.

I know you know something.

The second time he was better prepared and didn't flinch. He molded his face into a blank mask, but I could still sense the tension underneath, coiling tighter like a spring after each hit.

"You know you don't *actually* have to hit me as hard as you can," he finally said.

"Why not? It's practice, isn't it?"

"Clearly, that's not all of it."

As I went to punch his right palm again, he moved it out of the way, "I'm not playing this game with you. I've told you everything I know about the tattoo."

"That's not true."

"Yes, it is."

"I don't believe you."

Mordecai shot a look over at both of us, and we returned to our fighting positions. Still, I couldn't help commenting, "It amazes me that you are so good at gambling, because your playing face is easier to see through than glass."

"Oh, so that's how you managed to lose so badly?"

"No," I disregarded his open palms, and sent a fist whirling toward his face but stopped it just before the end of his nose. He recoiled, then scowled. "That's how I'm going to figure out what you aren't telling me."

"Switch," Mordecai called from the middle of the circle.

Malcolm's hands were already in fists, and I squared my feet, putting up my hands.

I was ready for the first hit, and I didn't so much as allow myself to blink. He didn't say a word to me for the rest of the session.

Harris was especially kind to Nickolai, talking him through each rotation. He even made a joke about Mordecai, when his back was turned, of course, that got the kid to smile a little.

Taz and Evander talked through most of the rotations as well—mostly about fights, from what I heard. Taz had never tried to hit someone in his life; Evander, not surprisingly, had seen his fair share of what he called "brawls and other rigorous pastimes." During the fourth and final rotation, Evander not-so-subtly winked at Elysian, and Mordecai swiftly hit him on the back of the head.

"Quit making eyes at my sister or I'll gouge them out," he warned, but Evander only chuckled.

It was only about a half-hour before the moment I had been silently dreading arrived.

"You two," Mordecai pointed at Malcolm and me, "stand in the middle of the training area. The rest of you, form a line and stay out of the way."

I bit my tongue and stifled a sigh.

"Think of this as the first official test that you need to pass. It doesn't necessarily matter if you win the sparring match or not, just be careful not to lose more than once."

"So now it's a competition to weed out the weak?" Harris asked. "Isn't that a bit counterproductive, after going through all the effort of capturing each of us?"

"First of all, I never said that," Mordecai adjusted the cuff on his dark sleeve, "Secondly, if we didn't put stakes on sparring, no one would make the effort to train, and then Brighton would never win the war. This is how it has to be."

Mordecai turned toward Malcolm and me and continued, "The first one of you to yield loses. And the only rule is not to kill or seriously injure each other."

"Oh no, now this is going to be so much less entertaining," I muttered.

"Yeah, now you can't cheat," Malcolm cast a barbed look my way.

"Like you did in the gambling match."

"I didn't cheat. I played better."

Mordecai was already tapping his foot. "It's not a sparring match of words. One of you needs to take a swing eventually."

It felt like waiting for something to break, like watching it bend under the pressure before it snapped. He still didn't move, and neither did I.

Mordecai sighed, "You have five seconds, or neither one of you gets anything to eat until tomorrow."

We looked across the grass at each other.

Well, that settles it.

My hand flew up on its own and my knuckles glanced off

Malcolm's face. Not too hard, but hard enough. He took a step back, wincing as he smeared a small trickle of blood off his split lip.

Before I could smirk in satisfaction, he hit back, and a burning ache spread through my nose. I wiped my hand across my face, and it came away with a smear of red.

My grin fractured into a laugh, as I blinked through the burning in my nose and wiped what was left of the blood from my hand.

Malcolm wasn't laughing at all. "You think this is funny?"

"You don't?" I took a step toward him, blocking another punch with my arm, but he caught me in the stomach with his opposite hand instead. I doubled over coughing. He opened his mouth to make another remark, but before he could get a word out, I whirled my arm through the air and hit him across the face with the back of my hand, sending him a step sideways.

To my right, I heard Evander stifle a laugh, Taz cringed, and I saw Harris put his head in his palm.

Malcolm's blue eyes flicked back to me like icy flames.

The world spun into a tangle of limbs, grass, dirt, and the metallic taste of blood. Bruises sprouted into existence across my face, ribs, and hands as I dealt out hits of my own.

We split apart. I stood with my hands on my knees, spitting blood and wincing at the deep ache in my ribs. Malcolm was hunched over somewhere to my left growling out curses, one arm wrapped around where I had jammed my elbow into his side.

"Either one of you could yield," Mordecai reminded us. His arms were crossed as he observed the mess unfolding before him, and he wrinkled his nose at the scuffed ground between us.

"No." Malcolm and I said it at the same time.

Elysian pursed her lips and shook her head. It was times like that when she looked a lot like Mordecai, just without the pale scar.

I kicked Malcolm in the side of the knee, catching his arm as he swung a fist at me. He swept his opposite leg behind me, and we tumbled onto the grass again.

My vision was smeared with red and blinking did little to clear it.

The battle to fall, get up, and fall again through the endless parade of hits was as taxing as trying to wade through wet sand. The fight degraded into nothing more than an ugly display of clumsiness and swearing.

We both stumbled away, falling gracelessly to the ground, and stayed there.

Mordecai ran a hand down the side of his face, following the line of his scar. "I have a lot of work to do with both of you. That was pathetic."

"Who won?" Malcolm glanced his way.

I dragged my sleeve across my face, "Who cares?"

"I'm calling it a draw." Mordecai said it like the word left a bad taste in his mouth. "Neither of you yielded, neither of you won. But now I have a full understanding of how much you need to learn; bar and street fighting tactics lack the discipline a battlefield demands." He shrugged to himself, "Or, you both just lack discipline, period."

I nodded, "It's probably the second one."

"Pack up the attitude, lock it away in a box, and toss it off the end of the nearest pier, do you understand? I'm not dunking your head into a trough for a second time."

Together, we cleared out of the sparring area and took our places along the side. Taz and Evander went second, and Mordecai was disappointed again, only this time no blood was shed. Taz tried his best, cringing the whole time, but Evander seemed to think it was all a grand joke. He was laughing to himself by the time he swept Taz's legs for a third time, and Taz yielded.

Harris tried to convince Mordecai to let him spar with Evander or somebody else instead, to spare Nickolai, but Mordecai refused. And so, Harris ended the match after practically kneeling down for the lightest, most harmless punch I'd ever seen—after convincing Nickolai to *try* and hit him at all.

By the time that was all over, the sun had barely crawled past the highest point in the sky. My bruises were aching, my lungs were burning, and we were far, far from done.

Six men with loaded crossbows, one to keep a watchful eye on each of us, waited in a row as weapons training ensued. The blunted swords in our hands meant nothing if we couldn't move faster than the arrow aimed at us. Still, I weighed the metal in my hand; there were unrepaired dings in the edge and the balance was off. Made to function, not to last. If I were going to try and fight my way out, I wanted something lighter and sharper in my hands.

Harris' lip curled up from his teeth as he examined his own sword, and a single glance was all it took for me to know he agreed.

Still in the same pairings, we took turns attacking the wooden dummies.

Mordecai observed Malcolm and me out of the corner of his vision, even as he delegated notes and instructions to the whole group.

Nickolai was to my left as another rotation went. He cringed every time he lifted the sword. When Mordecai handed it to him, the point had landed in the grass, and he had to use both hands to hold it up in the air, leaning back to balance out the weight. But there was nothing lighter for him to use.

The loud crack of metal meeting wood split through my observations.

Malcolm had swung his blade into the dummy's neck, at an upward angle well suited to severing a head.

I felt myself flinch, and the corner of Mordecai's eye twitched as he watched.

Malcolm planted one foot on the round, wooden base to keep the dummy stable, wrenching the sword back and forth. I fought a grimace listening to the sound of wood splitting and cracking before he managed to pry the blade out.

Harris raised his eyebrows at the mark it left behind, and quickly returned to minding his own business, avoiding eye contact with either one of us. Taz blinked and looked away. At least Evander seemed entertained, arms crossed and a stupid grin plastered to his face.

Malcolm joined the row again as the next rotation started, using his shoulder to bump me out of his path. My teeth scraped together as several good remarks came to mind.

To my left, Evander had no issue swinging his sword straight down on the dummy's head, and beside him, Nickolai managed to wedge the point into its chest.

I swung the sword into my dummy's face. Using both hands, I twisted the blade until I was able to pry off a chunk of wood, about where a nose would be.

Mordecai planted his hands on his hips.

I silently ushered myself back into line, avoiding his stare by looking down at the grass.

Malcolm shoved past me again, and I bit back the reflex to reach out with my foot and trip him. Without hesitation, he swung the blade down on the dummy's right hand, cutting it clean off, and repeated his deadly attack on its neck. The square hunk of wood that comprised the head was now tilted, a few swings from falling off.

The rotation ended, and Malcolm moved to shove me again as he passed. But this time I kept my feet firmly planted, and braced so that the impact of his own petulance did more to him than me.

His gaze sparked like blue flame.

"We're supposed to be cooperating. Or have you forgotten that we have bigger problems?" I asked.

Malcolm's eyes narrowed. "You're the one who keeps harping on the other issue, and you can't seem to shut up about it."

"Pardon me if I don't give up so easily on something I've needed an answer to for my entire life. If any shred of what you've told me is the truth, then you'll probably understand."

"But that's not what this is about, is it." He pointed an accusatory finger at my chest, "You won't believe me no matter what I tell you. You're afraid that I really don't know anything."

"Whatever the two of you need to work out, do it at a time when I don't have to listen to it," Mordecai warned.

I ignored him entirely. "At least I can admit when I'm afraid. I won't ignore it like a coward who can't face the truth."

His hand tightened around the handle of his sword, and his eyes turned flinty. "Call me a coward again."

I set my jaw as I thought of all the hours I'd spent trying to piece together the unknown, what I would say if I ever met my parents, how I would ask them *why*. Malcolm had a part of something that I could use to find my way to some kind of answer—and he wouldn't let it go.

"You're a coward, and you're the worst liar I've ever seen."

I was acutely aware of my own pulse during the span of silence that followed, and of the open, waiting stares of everyone around us. Harris' was the kind that reminded me of someone trying to hold something broken together, that if they grasped the pieces tightly enough, it would mend itself.

Malcolm's hand tightened around the handle of his sword again until his knuckles turned white.

Evander's green eyes darted between us, like he expected a song and dance routine, and Taz's gaze rolled upward, "Mother of God..."

Mordecai could only take one step in our direction before the delicate balance of civility tilted completely on its side.

The rush of air that followed Malcolm's blade past my face made my heart punch into my ribs, and I swung after him.

Nickolai scurried out of our path.

The men with the crossbows followed us with steady aim, but Mordecai raised a hand, and they didn't fire.

Metal clanging into metal echoed off of the surrounding walls. I darted out of harm's way and stumbled into one of the dummies. The wooden beam that made up its left arm caught another wave of Malcolm's anger.

He cringed, tugging on the handle, and I kicked the mass of wood and straw forward, its weight forcing him backward. I drove the point of my weapon toward him, and he abandoned his sword. Instead, he picked up a rock and held it ready.

I secured my grip on my sword and lunged forward.

Harris threw his shoulder into me, steering me off course, and fought to stay in my way. "Stop it! That's enough!"

Mordecai stepped in front of Malcolm, cloaked in a blaze of anger. "Stand down *now*."

Malcolm still hadn't put the rock down, deaf to Mordecai's

demand. It was like he couldn't see him, as he pointed past. "I'm going to fix this stupid issue about the tattoos by burning yours off!"

"Get over here and try it!" I yelled.

"Did I sound like I was joking?"

I attempted to shove around Harris again, but he pushed me back, "You need to calm down. Give me the sword." He kept glancing at the men with crossbows.

Mordecai seethed, "I won't tell you a second time," and Malcolm finally cast the stone aside. Sighing through my teeth, I passed my weapon to Harris, who quickly threw it well out of reach toward Eric. But Eric was too busy watching Mordecai like a kid waiting for a firework to go off.

"Both of you," Mordecai barked, "get over here!"

He took us away from the main group, far enough that their chatter reduced to nothing. Malcolm and I followed with our heads down, like kicked dogs.

Mordecai started well before either of us could try to. "I don't give a shit what your problem is—that's the most important thing. Whatever it is, it doesn't matter."

I crossed my arms, cutting a scowl in Malcolm's direction. He didn't bother returning the gesture, instead locking his jaw and keeping his chest puffed out.

Mordecai snapped his fingers beside my ear, "Don't look at him, I'm talking to you."

Heat rushed down my arms, and Mordecai continued. "The only reason neither one of you was just shot, like your friend, was because I called them off. Because I need six people, not four. Take this as my *last* warning and pull it the fuck together!" His gaze had the weight of a boulder as he looked between us. He smoothed back his hair and left without another word.

It was dark and cold by the time training ended for the day. *One* day that felt like seven. If I hadn't seen the sun set only once for myself, I wouldn't have believed it.

Malcolm and I took to our separate corners of the barracks as everybody else tried to force some reason through our skulls.

"This is a delicate situation," Harris reminded me. "We're being trained to face war, and we still haven't come up with any solutions to escape. This is not the place or time for personal disputes."

I dragged my hand down the side of my face, "God dammit, I already know that. Can't you try to understand? I've spent my whole life wondering what that tattoo means, and I *know* there's something he won't tell me. He might know something about my parents—" my voice buckled, and so I shoved away the thought. "Do you get how terrifying that is? What happens if I never get Malcolm to crack, we all die, and I lose my one chance at getting some sort of closure?"

"To be fair," Harris said, "you don't have any real proof that he's lying to you."

Across the room, Taz was maintaining a calm tone as he spoke with Malcolm—something about how, "fighting will only make everything here worse."

I chewed on my lip as I considered. *Then I'll find proof.*

Harris clasped his hands. "You need to prioritize. The tattoos aren't going anywhere, and they can wait. Not to mention the fact that if we want to escape, you and Malcolm need to be able to work together."

I toed at the floorboard beneath me.

"You know I'm right."

"That doesn't mean I need to be happy about it."

Harris's brows lifted, "So you'll try to come to some sort of agreement?"

"It seems like we have to, at this point."

Once Taz had finished convincing Malcolm of the same thing, we met in the middle of the barracks.

He crossed his arms, and I mirrored the gesture.

"You want to call a truce?" he asked. "Neither one of us talks about the tattoos until we can find a way out of this mess. If we can. And until then, we act as if they don't exist."

Act as if they don't exist. The knowledge of its presence was like a pinprick, or a scratch, but I nodded anyway. "I think that would be for the best."

He pursed his lips, and I extended my hand.

"Truce."

"Truce." He accepted my hand, and we sealed the agreement with a firm shake.

Standing by the wall with Nickolai, Evander clapped. "Finally! Now we can actually get to working on a plan."

CHAPTER FOUR

T he smell of wet earth and stone was getting stronger, riding bursts of wind coming from the west, and there was a stirring, tingling sense of unease in the air so dense I could feel it close to my skin. There was going to be a storm.

I stood against the back wall, carefully working my way through my ration of chicken—which we all had for dinner. My stomach was growling at me by the end of the day, but now, strangely, I wasn't hungry at all. I only continued forcing down dry, flavorless bites because I knew I needed it.

Evander was sprawled out like a cat, his feet resting on a stool as he reclined in his chair. He bit a chunk out of an apple, which he'd managed to get his hands on after finishing his own dinner, and mused, "You know, the best meat pie I've ever had was actually in Arceos; I think it had lamb and cumin—or something like that. Either way, I'd gladly have it as every meal for the rest of my life."

"Isn't that south of Orvalia and Millfort?" Taz asked. "That's a long way to travel."

He nodded, "I've been to all five nations on the continent, actually. And I can tell you the best food from each of them—I'd kill for some apple cake from Millfort right now." He turned the half-eaten apple over in his hand and pursed his lips.

"What did you say you did for a living again?" Malcolm asked.

"I didn't," he grinned, his white teeth flashing. "Why? Don't you like a bit of mystery?"

Taz shrugged, "You told me when we were sparring that you '*deal in justice.*'"

"Are you some kind of lawyer?" Harris asked.

Evander scoffed, "*The law* and justice are two very different things, in my opinion."

"If we eventually guess right, will you tell us?" inquired Taz.

"Of course," Evander winked, "*if* you guess right." After a moment, he added, "On account of that dry chicken they gave us, I think I'd actually rather have a steak right about now—with garlic and pepper."

I slowly chewed another stale bite. With all this talk, the void of hunger was opening in my stomach once again.

"You ever had a waffle?" Harris chimed in. He twirled a now clean chicken bone in his hand. "I could use one of those right now."

"With syrup?" asked Evander.

"With strawberries and cream, you tasteless degenerate."

They both chuckled.

"How about you?" Harris asked, glancing toward Malcolm.

He was already gazing up at the roof above our heads in consideration, standing beside the door. "I'm struggling to decide, actually. Would you rather have custard pie or steak?"

Harris and Taz both said "pie" at the same time.

"No, no, no," Evander shook his head, "you had my attention at 'steak.'"

"He's right, there's no contest," I agreed.

Malcolm's eyes were still squinted in consideration, but he finally nodded, "Yeah, I think you're right. Custard doesn't pair well with confinement and impending war."

"I guess we can agree on *something.*"

He nodded, "*One* thing."

Harris shook his head slowly, but smiled anyway. "Progress is progress."

"My mom used to make baozi a lot; it's basically a steamed dumpling with meat filling. It sounds simple but it was actually really good," Taz added.

"Used to?" Evander asked.

Taz smiled, but it looked more like a cringe. "Yeah, before she and father-dearest disowned me." He cleared his throat, and did a snobby, deep-voiced impression of his father; "No son of mine plays with charcoal and paint all day, not when there's a bank to manage! If you can't take the business your great-grandfather started seriously, then I see no reason to take you seriously either!"

"Don't worry," Malcolm reassured, "he has a boat-load of karma coming his way if this war starts. The banks will be gutted."

Evander propped his chin on his knuckles and looked at Taz. "So, you're an artist?"

"A broke, struggling artist—but yes." He shrugged, "Better that than sorting files and being lectured on my own inadequacy every day by my family."

"You should do a brutally-honest chalk portrait of your father on the side of his bank someday," Evander suggested. "I've seen people do that to political figures in the south, and it's always a good laugh."

Taz nodded slowly, "Yeah, I should. Someday. If any of us make it out of here alive."

Nickolai was sitting on the ground to my right, hugging his knees to his chest like he wanted to take up less space than a deck of cards. His brown eyes never strayed from the floor.

My appetite vanished once again. *Poor kid.*

Malcolm followed my gaze and asked him, "You holding up okay?"

Nickolai looked up and nodded. Then he returned to his staring contest with the ground.

"How old are you?" Taz asked.

"I'm twelve."

Harris cursed under his breath, and the room plunged into silence. A pang of nausea bounced around below my ribs. Now the food I'd been forcing myself to eat tasted like charcoal, so I set the plate aside —next to the one Nickolai hadn't touched.

"None of you think I have a chance," the boy murmured. "I know I don't. I'm going to die here."

"Well, you certainly won't survive with a bleak attitude like that," Evander said, and Taz shot him a look that could have left a bruise— so Evander quickly added, "I mean, uh, you'll also have us. Mordecai will be too busy picking on us to worry about you, as long as you don't piss him off."

Nickolai chewed on his lower lip and asked, "Why are we all here again? To add us to an army getting ready for war?"

"Pretty much, yeah," I confirmed. "But we're all more useful to them and Mordecai alive. You have nothing to worry about."

"Even Mordecai doesn't always seem too happy about this," Malcolm added.

"Well, I can't imagine being employed by Brighton's King is all that fun," Evander tossed the core of the apple into a corner. "I've been to Brighton. And after all I've heard, I can't really blame him for that."

I asked, "So the King's a tyrant?"

"Absolutely, he is. Neither he nor his son were ever meant to take the throne, but they were the closest in relation after the rest of the original royal family was murdered twenty-two years ago. And it doesn't seem like he was particularly happy about taking up the workload."

Malcolm shrugged, "So he's bitter about his job?"

"Bitter about the effort it takes, maybe, but not about the title and the influence it gives him. They say that King Hector is a raging tyrant with a taste for violence, a power-hungry maniac, a heavy drinker with a general lack of good judgement—the list goes on. But I still can't understand why Mordecai would go along with this madness— he's highly ranked and obviously knows what he's doing; he has to know that Brighton will lose a war against Dale."

"Is Dale more powerful?" Taz asked.

Evander nodded, "You can see it before your boat hits shore— they're massive. Not to mention their navy is the finest in the world."

Malcolm wrinkled his nose, "Makes you wonder *why* Brighton is doing this, picking a fight they probably won't win."

"I hope I'm wrong," Taz said, "but maybe that's the whole reason we're here? They don't need soldiers with years of training and experience—their army already has that. But losing too many of them means they lose the war. They need people who can swarm a harbor and absorb projectiles, people who are dispensable like pawns in a game of chess."

Made to function, not to last.

I swallowed around the bubble in my throat. "An army that's half soldiers, half...what would you even call it?"

Taz shuddered, "Suicide runners and human shields."

Across the room, Nickolai's eyes widened as he stared endlessly at the floor, and his lower lip wobbled.

Harris crossed his arms, swiftly changing the subject as he asked Evander, "So, you've been to Dale?"

"I have. They make fabulous wine, if you ever get the chance to try it."

"Do you travel a lot for your job?" I asked.

Evander's sleeve was still securely pulled down to cover the brand on his arm. "I do."

Justice and travel, I considered; still, no guesses came to mind.

He must have seen that he still had us fooled, because a brief, satisfied smirk graced his lips.

We talked about odds and war for a while longer. It was a half-hour before Nickolai, who still rarely spoke, started turning pale and rocking where he sat. Taz saw it too, and found pieces of charcoal to scribble on the walls with; he encouraged Nickolai to join him.

"Drawing always helps me feel better," he'd explained.

Together they worked, and the rest of us shifted the conversation to the remaining time here.

"Sparring seems like it's the biggest influence on what happens. It determines how useful we actually are," Harris thought aloud. "No one needs to be *gotten rid of* if we all succeed the same amount. We fail if we lose more than one sparring match—at least that's one of the most important parts, according to Mordecai. But if we all agree to stage it, so everyone in each pairing wins and loses once, we all make it out."

"You mean throw a match on purpose?" Evander clarified.

"Yeah."

"That seems fair," Evander agreed.

"What if the first match was a draw? How does that balance out?" I asked, and Malcolm was already looking back at me, his arms crossed.

"Then I guess it'll have to be another draw," he said. "That is, *if* we can cooperate and not turn it into an actual fight. Again."

"That's only if we can't figure out a plan to escape, and soon," I clarified.

They all nodded, eyes drifting down to the floor between us.

I looked across the room at the wall that Taz and Nickolai were drawing on. The lines Taz was making with the charcoal wound together, like fabric, to create an image. It was rather good, actually. More than that, it was enough to coax a grainy laugh from my chest. "That's supposed to be Mordecai?"

Taz peeked over his shoulder as everybody else followed my gaze, and he smiled crookedly, "The man has very distinct expressions. I couldn't help myself."

Taking up most of the wall was Mordecai's stiff-jawed, serious expression. It looked remarkably realistic in some ways, but the vein in his neck and the downward turn of his mouth had been exaggerated just enough to be funny.

Softly, cautiously, the rest of the room chuckled, and Nickolai managed a smile. The lines he'd drawn were much more exact, like a diagram, and Evander was eyeing them as well.

"Is that…" he squinted, "is that the lock in the main gate?"

As soon as he said it, it made perfect sense.

Nickolai nodded, "I saw it when they led me in. I've seen some like it before, too. My dad is a locksmith."

Malcolm lifted his brows, "And you've obviously paid very close attention."

"They're fun," Nickolai explained. "Each one is a little puzzle; you just have to know the pieces—the rest is easy."

Harris pointed at the diagram, "So, do you know how that one works?"

"Well, it's big, so I can't break it. But the locking mechanism is really common, and if you can push the pins down to match the pattern of the key, it'll open." He underlined the section of the drawing with a row of seven vertical springs.

"Could you do that?" I asked.

"Maybe. I think I could try."

We all looked at each other as Nickolai continued drawing, and a spark of hope singed my fingertips.

We have a locksmith.

Evander patted Nickolai's messy brown hair. "Kid, you're a genius."

IT WASN'T long before we decided to throw every ounce of luck we had into our new plan. It was morning, but so early that the sun was still not going to rise for hours.

Nickolai sat cross-legged in front of the locked door to the barracks, his brow wrinkled as he worked a bent fork prong into the lock. Something faintly clicked, and he rotated the handle a fraction of an inch. The rest of us stood behind him and waited.

Nickolai had been working on the lock for less than a minute.

Another small click sounded, and he wrinkled his nose as he rotated the fork again. Each movement was nearly imperceptible; a millimeter left, right, a fraction-of-a-hair down. It was nothing like swinging a hammer into hot metal, where at least you could *see* progress taking shape.

I was shifting from one foot to another, holding a clenched fist in front of my mouth.

The lock clicked a third time, and then we all heard the bolt slide out of place. Nickolai turned the door handle and opened it a sliver. "Done," he announced.

"Already?" marveled Harris.

Nickolai got to his feet and smiled. "Door locks are the easy ones."

He retrieved the bent fork, and we exited into the night. We hid around the corner of our barracks, in shadow, and surveyed the main gate where six men with crossbows stood guard, three on each side. We were an even match as far as numbers, but we had no weapons. And with torches lighting up the area, there was no room for error before the rest of the minions within the walls heard the commotion and saw us trying to pick the main lock.

We retreated into the shadows and whispered until we devised another plan.

Carefully, we made our way behind the barracks and other structures, where we would all be the most out of sight as we tried to scale the twenty-foot wall.

Harris tilted back his head to stare all of the way to the top, whispering, "This is probably a really bad idea."

I nodded in agreement, as he, Malcolm and I took our places in a row at the base of the wall, linking arms.

"Nonsense," declared Evander, "this will be fun. Just don't drop us."

I cringed as he braced one foot on my calf, leveraging up until he was standing with one foot on my shoulder and one on Malcolm's beside me. Malcolm, thankfully, had agreed to take the middle spot, bearing the most weight.

Through gritted teeth, I bit out, "Can you reach the top from there?"

"If I jump—provided that doesn't kill you three."

Down the line from me, Harris and Malcolm both winced as Taz climbed onto their adjacent shoulders as well.

"I'm smaller than you," Taz said to Evander, once he was steady, "I'll jump."

Poised on top of the wall, he'd be able to help Evander up. We'd get Nickolai over the other side first, then Taz and Evander could help the rest of us over. If all went according to plan.

Nickolai was standing behind us, staring skyward at our wobbly tower. "This sounded easier when you were explaining it."

"Tell me about it," grunted Malcolm, with Taz on one shoulder and Evander on the other.

My own shoulder, with Evander, was aching, and my legs were burning as the weight constantly shifted.

Evander started the count of three, and I braced my free hand on the wall in front of me. I was already grimacing when the teetering balance above me lurched.

Taz leapt high enough to grip the top of the wall, using Evander's hip as a foothold. But the pressure was enough for Evander to start to lean, since he had nothing to steady himself with, try as he might to dig his fingertips into the section of wall in front of him.

The pressure on my shoulder became crushing. Drawing in air sent a stabbing pain through my rib as I tried to shift my feet and compensate for the instability.

Taz swore as his grip on the wall began to fail.

Nickolai took several long steps back to safety, beside the rear wall of the barracks.

The whole tower leaned my way. Harris, with the weight off his shoulder, tugged on Malcolm's arm as he tried to keep us all centered. His heels left deep scuffs on the ground as the weight dragged him forward—but he was just one man, and the momentum was already at work.

Our tower collapsed. The night swirled sideways, and cold hard ground greeted the side of my face. Malcolm and Harris were both sprawled across my legs, and Evander's ankle was caught under my arm as I lifted my head, surveying the damage. Taz was crumpled farther away, the bottom of his shoe dangerously close to Evander's nose. Outside the barracks, Nickolai's face was frozen into a grimace, and his eyes wandered again to the faraway top of the wall.

At least no alarms were sounding.

I began untangling myself from the pile as Evander stifled a laugh. "I'm rather fond of my nose; I would've been pissed if you broke it," he remarked at Taz.

Taz was still on the ground, and he didn't answer as Evander pushed away the foot that had nearly caved his face in.

It was then that we all noticed a narrow stream of blood trickle down Taz's brow.

"I'M GOING to change the bandage every few hours for the next day or so," the medic explained. "Head wounds bleed like a motherfucker."

Taz was lying down, a mass of cotton strips wrapped around his head. Some blood had already dotted through the layers of material above his right temple. "Oh great," he muttered. He cringed and squeezed his eyes shut, sinking his fingers into the material of the cot below him. "God! What the hell?"

The medic stopped half-way out the door to our barracks. "Feel like you're falling backwards out of a chair?"

Taz nodded.

"Well, meet vertigo. And it's probably going to stick around for a while, so exercise caution while on your feet. It'll sneak up on you."

Taz sighed, "Wonderful."

With that, the medic closed the door behind himself, and I could hear the three, newly instated men with crossbows shuffling back into their rightful places beyond the threshold.

After we'd dragged an unconscious Taz back into the barracks, and roused Eric to find a medic, we all seamlessly shifted into a lie when Mordecai asked what had happened. We blamed another fight that had simply gotten out of hand, but Mordecai still insisted on the new watchmen.

Nickolai was sitting cross-legged on a chair, staring down at his hands. "Maybe I should have been the one at the top. Even if I couldn't have pulled any of you up…"

Evander shook his head. "Kid, last night was a combination of errors, and none of them were yours."

"Is this the part where you tell me I should have done a tuck-and-roll?" Taz asked. "Because I don't think I can handle that right now."

"No, actually. I was just going to say, we can both be glad that bump on the head didn't damage that handsome face of yours," Evander winked.

Taz didn't notice, and clasped a hand over his eyes as he cursed through another wave of vertigo.

"You're not going to be able to walk in a straight line, let alone try to run out of this place," Harris pointed out. "So, what do we do now?"

I shrugged, "Pray to whatever Gods are willing? Cry? I'm open to suggestions."

"If we wait, maybe the vertigo and the headache will go away sooner than expected," Malcolm offered. "We can come up with a better plan then."

"Maybe? Hopefully," Evander shrugged.

"Don't forget the nausea," added Harris. "The medic said there would be nausea."

"Do you feel sick?" I asked Taz.

He was staring up at the ceiling like it was changing colors. "No."

I sighed, "Alright, at least that's a good sign." The rest of the room nodded.

Taz rolled away from us and immediately vomited onto the floor. Nickolai stood, put both hands over his nose and mouth, and retreated to the farthest corner of the barracks beside a window, where the sun had started to rise only minutes before.

"I'm so *tired* of throwing up," Taz wheezed.

I couldn't think of anything to say. Probably because that steaming, lumpy, misshapen splatter on the floor was in better shape than our odds of getting out of here.

CHAPTER FIVE

I was running behind on purpose the following morning.

After Taz's injury, training went on as usual for the rest of us; the long list of routines piled on until my limbs were soar and heavy. But that was the least of my concerns. We couldn't escape without leaving Taz behind—and that was out of the question. So instead of scheming ways to get past the main gate, my mind wandered to the truce I'd called with Malcolm and the words Harris said that kept bouncing around in my head: *you don't have any real proof that he's lying to you.*

That changed today.

I was slow to get up and slow to get my things in order. When Mordecai called for us, I deliberately forgot to put on a shoe—earning a snarl and a brief lecture on how much dust surely accumulated on the inside of my skull—before Mordecai ordered me out of line to go retrieve it.

Taz was the only one still in the barracks. The vertigo and nausea meant he spent most of his time sleeping, which the medic said would help him recover. So, as long as I was quiet, he'd have no idea I was rummaging through Malcolm's belongings.

I tugged on my forgotten shoe as I crossed the room, keeping an eye trained on the door everyone had left through moments before. Then, I sank to my knees and started digging. There wasn't much to go through, no one brought much with them when we'd decided to get into that armored carriage, so it wasn't going to take much time. Less than I thought, as a matter of fact.

A piece of paper crinkled when I lifted a shirt, and I rooted through the pockets until my fingers caught on the bent corner of a page. When I pulled it out, it didn't remind me of the papers I'd seen in school with sharp edges and a smooth, clean face. This paper had been folded and unfolded a hundred times; its corners were tapered and bent, one had even ripped off; it felt more like a piece of cloth than anything else, its texture velvety from wear.

I gingerly unfolded it. The page itself was no bigger than my hand, but it didn't need to be. My throat went dry as my eyes scanned a short section of slanted handwriting. But that didn't matter nearly as much as what was on the right side. The fast lines of a drawing, in red pen, interlocked to form an all-too-familiar star.

My teeth scraped together, and the paper bent in my tightening grasp. "I fucking knew it."

I glanced over my shoulder, remembering that I was trying to be quiet, but Taz was still soundly asleep. Better yet, he was still on his side facing away from me.

I scanned the writing again and refolded the page as I stood and crossed the room. There was no point in wasting another second. I pushed open the door, spied Malcolm's red hair amidst the group, and stormed across the grass.

He still had his back to me and his arms crossed by the time I bumped my shoulder into him. "Do you want to explain this?" I shoved the paper at him.

His eyes went wide. He snatched it from my hand, and he should have been thankful it didn't tear. "What the hell is wrong with you? You went through my stuff?"

"Explain," I demanded through my teeth.

Harris glanced over his shoulder, and Evander was already arching a brow in our direction. Mordecai was beyond them, discussing something with Eric.

Malcolm shook his head, "We called a truce."

"And you lied," I pointed at the slip of paper, "there's all the proof I need. Explain it."

He squinted and shook his head. "What do you mean *explain*? Didn't you read it?"

I pulled in a long breath through my nose and crossed my arms. Burning prickled my face.

Malcolm blinked. "You can't read?"

Escaping class nearly every day hadn't done me any favors. I recognized a handful of letters, but only if I saw them frequently enough. And saying that would have just made me feel worse.

Malcolm kept one eye on me as he stuffed the letter into his pocket. "Well, I guess that's your own fault."

"You're going to tell me what that paper says."

"Why should I?" he asked. "You invaded *my* privacy. Is it too soon to appreciate the irony that you can't read it yourself? But I guess you had that coming. I'm not giving up a single word of what's on it."

I wasn't sure why, but I could taste blood as I raised a fist, as I imagined spitting right between his eyes and launching myself at his throat.

Mordecai raised his voice mid conversation with Eric, enough for me to glance that way, and he was staring right back at us. He shook his head in warning and continued his discussion.

Our last fight, the one where Mordecai had called off the men with crossbows and given what he called his *last warning*, was the only thing that gave me the willpower to lower my fist.

"We're not done. I hope you realize that," I maintained.

Malcolm crossed his arms and walked away, to stand beside Evander. To my left, I caught Harris giving me one of his thin-lipped glances, and I sighed as I joined him in line.

"So, there's more?" he asked.

I shrugged one shoulder, "I won't say I told you so."

ON THE FINAL day of training we were set into the same pairings from before; Taz (now sufficiently healed) and Evander, Harris and Nickolai, Malcolm and me. As planned, the winner from the first sparring round would lose on the second, and everything would be balanced as precisely as a new blade.

Taz pinned Evander face-first to the ground, and he yielded.

Harris, after having spent at least an hour convincing Nickolai to really, honestly hit him the night before, yielded after a half-hearted strike to the jaw. Nickolai apologized profusely, but at least it had worked.

By the time it was our turn, Malcolm and I had already solidified our plan for another draw. Matching bloody noses came first—it wouldn't have been as convincing without bloodshed. Second, we acted through a seesaw, back and forth pattern of gaining and losing the upper hand. Finally, after maintaining a double choke-hold until our faces were the color of plums, Mordecai called for it to stop and declared another draw.

If Mordecai knew we had all staged it, which he almost certainly did, he didn't let it show.

Regardless of all that, the plan had worked, and the training was over.

The next morning, we were all awake and preparing to leave for the larger base, Fort Ketta. Sunlight was barely reaching into the sky, and looming to the north were rolling, black clouds. A tiny droplet landed on my skin, hinting at what might come spilling down at any moment.

Mordecai, Eric, and several other reinforcements stood facing us, the gate leading out of the camp at their backs. As usual, they each carried a crossbow. Short arrows were already into place, and at least a dozen more arrows were strapped across their backs. Elysian would be going with us, too. She was on the far end, carrying an absurdly overpacked bag on her shoulder—presumably full of other tools and supplies to keep us in order.

Mordecai drilled through his demands and instructions for what would hopefully be the last time.

"I expect you to all stay in a single file line. There will be no talking unless you are asked to, especially once we make it over the first ridgeline. And when or if you do talk, it will be as quiet as possible. You cannot carry anything with you—especially weapons."

He made sure that his look of warning crossed each of our faces.

"You stay in line, be silent, and do as you are told. You all understand by now what happens if you make a run for it."

The crossbow bolt protruding from the back of Everett's skull flitted through my mind, and I swallowed around a bubble in my throat. It made my insides churn...or maybe that was because I had already broken one of his most fundamental rules?

They already made sure that none of us were carrying anything we weren't allowed to have. And for the most part, that was true. But the feel of hard metal tucked safely into my shoe was an ever-present reminder that they had missed something. A throwing knife. One they would never miss because Mordecai had forgotten to count how many he had on the first day of training and how many he had now.

It was a calculated effort, one set into motion after our first failed escape attempt. These people needed to get us to Brighton somehow, and that span of travel—the biggest gap of weakness we would get—was our best bet at getting away from the war.

Harris stole the knife during training the following afternoon. From there, we all did our best to work out a strategy, planning for the day we left without fully knowing what they would do to keep us in line.

That day was here, and we had all agreed that I would be the one carrying the knife.

"The base in Brighton known as Fort Ketta is just north, and a little west of the border. If things all go according to plan—*and they will*—we will get there before the sun goes down. Have I made myself perfectly clear?" instructed Mordecai.

I didn't let myself falter under his gaze as he swept it across each of our faces again, still very much aware of the knife pressed against my foot, and nodded.

We walked through the gate and into the open wilderness. Mordecai led us out at a brisk pace, with Harris immediately behind him. Next was Malcolm, then Taz, Evander, me, and Nickolai. Eric was behind him with Elysian, and the other reinforcements scattered themselves along the line. They had us outnumbered by one; but given their weaponry, it was more than enough to ensure that our chance of escape was as narrow as possible.

Eric was charged with having to watch everything. I could feel his dark eyes burrowing holes into my back, and into the backs of everyone ahead of me. No twitch of a hand or shift of concentration would go unnoticed. Mordecai looked back periodically too, making sure all was still in order.

Evander glanced back with uneasy eyes as well. He was the one who suggested that I take our only weapon against our captors, but we'd underestimated the numbers they would be taking with us. Still, we agreed that I would have the best chance at reaching help because I had the best hope at outrunning Mordecai or one of his assistants. The pressure of that responsibility lodged itself into my chest.

I dismissed the nervous looks from Evander. We just needed to follow the plan. An opportunity would open up.

The slope of the mountainside steepened as we followed the narrow trail. Rocks and tree roots punched through the dirt in many places. The white trunks of aspens surrounded us, their leaves fluttering in the strengthening breeze.

We stayed close as the climb became steeper and more arduous, but I liked the dull burning in my lungs. I liked the smell of dirt and an approaching thunderstorm. Escape and freedom could signal for me at any moment.

"Pick up the pace, runt," I heard behind me.

I paused to look over my shoulder. One of Mordecai's assistants used a massive arm to shove Nickolai up the hill. He staggered forward, cheeks red and eyes wide.

I narrowed my eyes into slits, staying put long enough for the man to notice. He fixed me with an equally menacing stare, and I had no choice but to turn back around and continue forward.

A pang of nausea hit me. I could only imagine how hard this had to be for Nickolai. He'd probably never been away from his parents, his family, for this long, and certainly not under such harrowing circumstances.

I kept marching uphill, gaze aimed out at the trees and the ever-darkening sky, but at a considerably slower speed so that Nickolai could catch up to me. I allowed him to get close behind me and moved to the far side of the trail so that I could speak to him more directly.

"Remember what we all talked about? I'm going to bolt in a few minutes. When I do, Mordecai and some of his assistants will go after me, and you need to run the other way," I whispered.

He nodded—he already knew the plan. "Where do I go?" he asked.

"The other direction, as fast and as far as you can, and then try to find your way home."

"Okay." His voice shook a little.

"Do you know where home is?"

He nodded. "My parents told me not to wander too far. Hopefully I can tell them that I'll listen next time."

I wished I had a map to give him, or something to make sure he made it home. He was always looking around with those big, scared eyes like he expected shadows to lunge out at him and become monsters—and fear had a way of wreaking havoc on a decent plan.

"You're going to be okay." It was all I could think of saying, though I knew it didn't help.

We finally crested the ridgeline, following the trail through a clearing of tall, swaying grass speckled by white and yellow flowers. I could smell their bitter sweet fragrance drifting on the breeze.

Ahead, over the tops of the trees, I could see down into the sprawling valley on the other side. I stretched to view farther, toward the ocean, but there were too many branches in the way. Still, I could easily imagine the faded scattering of a town right at the edge of the water—or perhaps it was farther up the valley. Mordecai insisted that we were quiet once we passed the first ridgeline, and maybe that was because he knew there was a settlement close to our path. Within hearing distance.

My heart pounded into my ribs as we walked back into the tree line. The trail turned with the slope to the right, with a steep downhill on one side, and an even steeper uphill on the other. The same tall grass grew up around the trees, parted only by large rocks, stumps, or taller shrubs, and masking the dangerous tangle of loose stones and tree roots underneath.

I balled my hands into fists to keep my escalating nerves under control and to hide any slight shake from the eyes of the men behind me and Nickolai.

There were two options: up or down.

I could feel Nickolai watching me, walking so closely he should have been stepping on my heels.

Maybe that wouldn't matter. Like summer heat rising off the road, anticipation and fear rippled around all of us, and at some point they were going to notice.

Uphill, through all the grass, leaves, and tree branches, I could see the sky. The gray had shifted to an imposing shade of black, and a white flash of lightning cut through it. The thunder rolled past in a wave.

My pulse was so loud I could practically hear it.

The downhill side of the trail was just as unnerving as the uphill. The shadows of the trees clawed their way down. With every flash of lightning they turned as dark as ink, and the white bark lit up like the sun catching on metal.

An ear-splitting crack of thunder took us all off guard. Even Mordecai turned to look up at the raging sky.

A split second of misdirection.

Everything went numb as I bolted off the trail, running down through the trees. Sharp twigs hiding in the grass clawed at my legs, and the jagged rocks made my footing unstable.

I reached out, using the branch of a nearby tree to slow myself down and to keep myself steady. The rough bark raked across my palm, but I hardly felt it.

I heard Mordecai curse, and footfalls raced down the hill after me. I could also hear some of the other men yelling, their words jumbled by another clap of thunder.

I never bothered to look back. I knew Mordecai was the one chasing me—because of course he would.

Eric, who had been one of the people closest to me, was probably still gawking at the sky, and hopefully it would be enough for Nickolai to slip away. In the chaos, there was a small chance that they hadn't noticed him run at all. I hoped that I gave him enough of an advantage by making him take the uphill path.

I broke the silence we had maintained since leaving the camp, yelling for help in the hope that someone nearby, if anyone was nearby, might hear.

The battle to yell as loudly as possible, keep my footing, and outpace Mordecai was harder than I expected. Struggling to slow down, I ran my shoulder into the side of a tree. Ridges in the bark dug into my skin as I slid around its other side, leaving burning, stinging scratches that I quickly forgot about. Mordecai stumbled after me, crashing into the side of the tree with a grunt.

Icy droplets of rain pattered down through the leaves, accumulating into a loud roar of water and whipping tree branches. It soaked through my hair and my shirt, all the while making the descent more grueling.

Dirt turned to mud, and rocks became sharp, slippery death traps.

My feet kept sliding out from underneath me, forcing me to use my hands to keep myself off the ground. My hands slid through mud, and across saw-toothed rocks and tree roots. I was grateful that I couldn't feel my pain through the cold wash of panic.

My cries for help felt useless. I could barely hear my own voice through the downpour. But this was our *one* chance for help or escape. This was all we had. And it was my job to avoid *one* person. Even if the rest of the group continued toward Brighton, as long as I got away, there was hope that someone could be sent to stop them.

Mordecai's footsteps had gotten dangerously close. I wished I could sprout wings and fly out of reach.

Grabbing the trunk of a tree, I tried to swing myself out of his path as he lunged for me. His shoulder caught me in the chest, forcing the air out of my lungs, and the tree seemed to be wrenched out of my grasp.

The world spun into a swirl of gray, white, green, and black. Cold mud streaked across my face and roots dug into my arms. Jagged rocks scraped across by back. I rolled over something softer than the rest of the ground, quickly realizing that it was Mordecai, arms flailing out for something to grab to stop the fall.

We both plowed into a tree trunk, in a tangled, muddy heap of limbs and uprooted grass. The force knocked any breath I had regained straight back out of my chest, sandwiched between Mordecai and hard tree bark.

He began spewing curses, whirling around at me like a vicious animal. I curled into a ball, using my forearms to shield my face as his fists rained down.

His face was smeared with dark mud, like mine, making the whites of his eyes seem as bright and wicked as a bolt of lightning.

I kicked out at him, but it didn't achieve much.

He pried one of my arms away from my face, clawing out with incredible strength and fury. I could taste the mud on his hand as I bit into flesh.

"God damn it!" he roared, tearing his hand out of my teeth.

It had to have been painful; now all I tasted was blood. I spat it out at his face, struggling to escape his grasp.

"Let me go!" I screamed at him, reaching up and grabbing a clump of his hair. I slammed his head into the side of the tree with a resonant thud.

He retaliated quickly, swatting my arm away and plowing a fist into the side of my face. A streak of light split across my vision, and I almost mistook it for another lightning strike.

His grip tightened around my throat like a vice, clamping out any air. I hated the feeling—and the instinctive panic that came with it. My mind flickered back to the sight of the bottom of a water trough and the same horrible sensation of helplessness.

The knife in my boot screamed for my attention but I knew I couldn't reach it with Mordecai sitting on me.

I lashed out at his face, the training he gave me turning to bite the hand that fed it. I started to dig my thumb into the soft flesh that made up his right eye, but he grabbed my wrist before I could cause any damage. He tried to wrench it away from his face, but I ensnared my fingers into a lock of his hair and pulled hard, leaving him to struggle with keeping my fingers far enough away from his eyes, and close enough not to tear out a section of hair.

He bared his teeth, trying to fight through the pain that I knew I was inflicting.

Black dots pooled in my vision, slowly expanding out like ripples in water. I was trying to breathe, trying to pry his hand off my throat, but he was too strong.

I let go of his wrist, still using my other hand to pull his hair, and reached through the mud and grass for something I could use.

His eyes tracked my movements with scalding rage, but there was nothing he could do, not while he was using one hand to strangle me and the other to keep my fingers out of his eye sockets.

His grip tightened even more as he tried to get rid of me before I could find something, but it was too late for that.

I settled on a section of broken branch that must have been snapped off in our fall. The sharp edge caught my hand. I grasped it in a fist, and drove the sharp point into his side.

Mordecai screamed, but finally released his ironclad grip on my throat. Relief washed over me and I let go of his hair, pushing him back so that I could plant a kick in the center of his chest.

Through a blinding symphony of coughing, gasping, and hacking, I could at least see that Mordecai was still grasping the stick that I had stabbed into his side, just below the bottom of his rib cage.

He pulled it out with a pained yell, clutching at the bleeding hole it left behind.

I was disappointed to discover that only the top two inches of the stick were coated with blood. It wouldn't be a fatal wound, but it would certainly leave a scar.

I rolled over, slowly dragging myself away from him as the spots in my eyes began to fade. I used tree roots and rocks to pull myself up the hill as the pain from dozens of scrapes and bruises set in. My hands were bloody and scratched, radiating an unrelenting, stinging pain. Similar wounds laced my arms, sides, and back.

Mordecai forced himself to his feet, and staggered after me, one hand still grasping his side.

"You fucking piece of shit!" He grabbed my arm, forcing me to my feet and twisting my wrist up between my shoulder blades.

My head spun from the sudden motion and I felt like collapsing.

"You thought you could get away! After I warned you what would happen! That was a big mistake!" he seethed.

"Let me go." It sounded nothing like the demand I meant for it to be.

"After this bullshit? Not a chance."

He pushed me forward, straight back up the war-torn path we created on the way down. My head throbbed. I didn't have the energy to fight him anymore. The drenched soil made the ascent ten times more difficult than the trip down, and the ceaseless rain was only good for making everything cold and unpleasant.

I tried to use the time it would take to return to the trail to gather my energy back, and to fight off the fear of the inevitable consequences that awaited me—if I couldn't get away a second time. But wading through the thick sludge of failure made that possibility feel distant and unlikely.

I hope Nickolai got away.

Malcolm, Evander, Taz, and Harris were all sitting in a row on the muddy path, surrounded by the rest of the reinforcements, with crossbows aimed at them in case they tried to move. They were all drenched, waiting in silence as they watched the trail turn into a river of mud.

They looked up, and their eyes widened with some combination of horror and shock when Mordecai and I stumbled back onto the trail. Even Eric looked surprised, dark brows knitting together as he lowered the point of his crossbow. He had Nickolai by the scruff of the neck like a defenseless animal. But at least he was still alive.

Mordecai unceremoniously shoved me into the mud beside Taz, who did his best to shield himself from the resulting splatter. The jarring motion triggered another coughing fit from my aching lungs.

All eyes followed Mordecai as he marched toward Eric. He looked like more mud than man by now, clumps of grass still clinging to the thick sheet of sludge that covered him. I looked the same, weighed down by water and wet earth.

He tore the crossbow from Eric's hands and turned back toward me, marching forward with deadly intent. He smoothed his matted hair back, his eyes glazed over by unbridled rage.

I felt the color drain from my mud-painted face.

A flash of lightning gleamed off the tip of the arrow that was loaded into place, begging to kill.

All I could do was scoot backwards, fighting to get to my feet before it was too late. I knew I could never outrun that arrow once he set it free.

"It was my idea!" Nickolai squeaked, stopping Mordecai in his tracks.

He turned slowly to look over his shoulder, his expression somehow becoming even more lethal. "Excuse me?"

I stood slowly and quietly. Nickolai's face had gone pale as he cowered beside the slightly less ferocious monster that currently had a hold of him.

"It was my plan."

Mordecai wrinkled his nose into a sneer. "Is that so?"

"That's a lie and we all know it," I cautioned, glancing at Nickolai. "It was *my* idea, and I told him to run."

Everyone else kept their heads down, not saying a word—a wise choice for now, all things considered.

"That doesn't change that fact that you both ran."

I felt sick, but forced myself to plant my feet firmly, collecting the strength so sound as serious as I felt. "Don't touch him."

Mordecai had the gall to smirk, keeping his deadly gaze trained on

Nickolai. "And what can you do?" He turned the point of the crossbow back in my direction. "I can kill you before you take a single step."

"It's my fault—I told him to run. Don't kill him for something that wasn't his idea."

"That's not the issue! I don't give a shit who's plan it was, all I care about is the fact that *both of you* tried to escape! You're lucky that either one of you is still breathing right now."

I curled my fingers into fists, masking the shaking.

"And you think it didn't cross any of our minds either?" Malcolm asked. "Running?"

Mordecai sighed and looked up.

Harris seemed about ready to reveal that it had been a plan we all worked on, but I silenced him with a hard glance.

"At least leave the kid alone," Taz interjected.

"Are you an idiot? Do you really want in on this?" Mordecai snarled.

Taz's eyes drifted over to me, earnest, and trying to convey a point. It didn't take me long to figure out what it was.

He looked back to Mordecai. "Killing him would be wasteful, I'm sure he's learned his lesson."

"Insubordination from people I train reflects badly on me, not to mention it goes against the entire point of my job. I train soldiers not carrier pigeons."

I watched carefully, ready to reach for the knife in my shoe.

"He didn't know what he was doing," Taz gestured to Nickolai with his hand, snaring Mordecai's attention for a split second.

I stepped directly behind him, withdrawing the small blade from my boot, and pressed the knife tightly against Mordecai's throat.

Mordecai didn't flinch, but I could feel the escalating rage radiating off of him like heat from a fire. Eric scowled, visibly tightening his grip on Nickolai, but kept his feet planted in the mud.

I felt like I was juggling knives. We were still outnumbered, and I could feel the weight of the eyes around us. One misstep was all it was going to take to destroy our small edge. None of them could help

Mordecai without me having the chance to kill him first, and no one could help me without getting shot first.

My grip stayed tight. "Put the crossbow down," I demanded.

The deadly contraption of wood and metal splashed to the ground near the edge of the trail.

"Fine," Mordecai hissed. "Have it your way."

I barely had time to think before the world spun out of focus. He grabbed my arm, pulling the blade away from his neck, and hurled me over his shoulder like a useless sack of potatoes.

The mud was not soft, and the air got crushed out of my chest once again as I landed on my back. The dark sky and treetops loomed above me.

Shit.

Mordecai planted his knee on my neck to hold me down, making it nearly impossible to breathe. I managed to suck in one jagged breath as I hurled the knife up at him, hoping that my anger would be enough to save me. He caught my arm and used his other hand to start to pry my fingers off the handle.

"Let go," he demanded through gritted teeth.

I wanted to scream, but I didn't have enough air. Harris and Malcolm started to get up in the corner of my vision, to try to help, but stopped. I followed their gaze over Mordecai's shoulder where Eric had retrieved the crossbow, still dragging Nickolai with him, and aimed it at the rest of the group.

They couldn't rescue me.

I swung my leg up behind the back of Mordecai's neck and pulled down, forcing him to hunch over, but his grip on my arm didn't falter. By now, I only had two fingers left to keep my only weapon in hand.

Through the sound of the rain and swaying trees, I heard him begin to snicker. It started out as an amused chuckle, but escalated into full, hysterical laughter. His shoulders heaved beneath my leg.

All I could manage was an enraged growl as he finally pried the knife out of my hand. I clawed at him in hopeless rage, which only seemed to make it more comical to him.

Nickolai's face said it all; he had gone completely pale, his eyes were wide as he stared at Mordecai, both brows furrowed deeply. Like he was watching the sun explode.

"This fucking group never disappoints, does it? The fighting, the staged sparring matches, and now an escape attempt en route," Mordecai said through his laughter.

His deadly hold on the knife did not match his droll tone. In fact, it sent a cold shiver up my spine.

I'm not ready to die. Not like this.

I pried at the leg he was using to pin me down, struggling to release the pressure from my neck.

"You keep me on my toes, I'll give you all that." He peeled the back of my knee from where I had wrapped it over his shoulder, straightening his spine. "But you are so *fucking* lucky that I need to bring all six of you to comply with policy. Or you'd already be dead."

I snarled in outrage and slammed a fist into the side of his thigh, as his laughter started to taper off. And his knee was still pressed down on my throat.

He examined the hand I had bitten earlier, flexing his fingers to reveal a deep gash on his knuckles. The rich red of fresh blood stood out well against all of the sludge and grime.

He sighed once more to collect himself. "Eric, hand me the pack."

Elysian passed it to Eric, who slung the bag onto his shoulder, dreadlocks swaying, still keeping the crossbow aimed at the others. Then he tossed it to where Mordecai could reach it.

Every muscle in my body wanted to run. I thrashed around, watching him rummage through the bag in horror of what he might pull out.

A coil of rope emerged from the burlap.

I tried to curse at him, but his knee was still making it difficult to breathe, so all I got out were a series of pathetic yelps and growls.

Mordecai wrapped the ropes around my wrists tightly, coiling them into an intricate knot. I pulled against his grip, making it as hard as possible for him.

"Stop struggling," he grumbled, pulling the knot tight. "Bear in mind that a small government mandate is all that's keeping you alive right now. But if you pull any bullshit like this again, I won't care. I'll kill you anyway, and be happy to face the consequences."

He finally removed his knee from my throat, hauling me to my feet as another fit of coughing took over. A dull headache blossomed into existence across my forehead and I hunched over to try to get my breathing pattern back to normal.

Beside me, he beckoned Taz to his feet and tied him next to me, until all of us were connected by a chain of rope.

Mordecai held the front end of our leash, and Eric took his place at the back again.

"There. Good luck trying to run down a hill like this," Mordecai remarked.

Everything hurt. The cuts on my arms and hands, although they had stopped bleeding, still burned like fresh wounds. Moving my shoulders sent a ripple of pain down my back. My breathing had restored itself, but it sounded hoarse and tired. The right side of my face was blanketed in a deep ache, and I was fairly certain that most of my neck was bruised.

"Fuck you," Malcolm seethed.

Mordecai ignored him effortlessly. "The same rules apply. No talking, *no weapons*," I couldn't help but surrender to a smirk, glancing at the bloody wound on his side, blood soaking through, "*no running*, and now, since we are behind schedule, no stopping. Got it?"

None of us uttered a word.

"Good. Let's go."

Our pace was set slower than it had been before. Mordecai had a limp and was clutching his side. Nickolai was probably relieved—his shorter limbs could keep up now. I didn't mind it either. Every step was slow and achy.

If I possessed the effort, I would have kicked myself.

All I had to do was run. All I had to do was get to the nearest settlement; it probably wasn't that far down the hill. All we needed was for someone to hear those cries for help.

We walked with our heads down, quietly mourning our plan. Our last chance.

CHAPTER SIX

T he sun was beginning to go down when Fort Ketta, the strongest and oldest military base in Brighton, came into view. From the ridgeline we were walking down, the entirety of it could be seen, sprawled out like a deadly net waiting to close.

An old but impressively well-built stone wall enclosed the camp in a vast square. The oak forest had grown close to its ominous edge over time. A large brick building sat in the center of it, surrounded by a few shorter wooden structures. There were four stone towers built along the outer wall as well, atop far older cobblestone foundations, serving as benchmarks for the four directions. Tents of white canvas, varying in size, had been put up on the western half of the establishment—dozens upon dozens of them—and there wasn't a specific pattern in place. No grid system, and whatever rows had been formed all splayed in different directions.

"Keep walking," Eric complained from behind me.

I hadn't realized that I stopped, too busy planning a way out of it... or *if* there was a way. I bit back a remark and proceeded forward, doing my best to convince myself that the cold pit forming in my chest was the result of an injury from the fall, an inconveniently placed bruise, and nothing more.

To the west, above all of the treetops, was a faint strip of blue. The ocean. I could smell the aroma of salt if the wind blew a certain way. On the shoreline, clustered around a small bay, were distant buildings and streets, thin strands of smoke rising into the gloomy sky. I kept my gaze trained on that, thinking about the soreness in my feet and the ache of my bruises. I couldn't stand to look at my next cage, the next deadly trap we had to sit in.

And we were just their pawns. Their suicide runners and human shields.

No one spoke as we passed through the gate in the southern wall.

We were standing in a row still connected by a long section of rope by the time one of Mordecai's compatriots arrived to deal with us.

Mordecai stood in front of our line, but for once he wasn't the one doing the pacing. The strange man glaring each of us down wore a similar uniform to the one I'd first seen Mordecai wearing back in Orvalia. The only difference was that he had three red stripes on his sleeve, not four. His eyes were dark, contrasting his blonde hair and lighter skin. He had a shallow dent in his chin and an air of superiority that was already highly obnoxious.

The national seal embroidered into the shoulder of the uniform was clearly visible, flaunting itself. The sword crossed by twin axes and enclosed in a ring might as well have been an elaborate middle-finger.

He walked down the line slowly, eyeing each of us with indifference. He held his hands behind his back, puffing out his chest like a bird.

He stopped at the end of the line in front of me.

I sulked back, well aware of the fact that the only parts of my body that weren't covered in mud were my eyes. The rain had done its best to wash most of it away, slopping off the more prominent clumps of grass, mud, and weeds, but the rain had let up well before we made it here.

He sniffed, casting a disgusted glance over me before turning back around. Mordecai met his stare expertly, even though he was in a similarly muddy state. But with his hands free, he'd been able to wipe the worst of the sludge off his face and arms.

"I'm going to assume you didn't get caught in a flash flood on the way here?"

"No," Mordecai answered, tossing an irritated glance my way. "There was an escape attempt after the rain started."

The man nodded, and folded his arms across his chest. He was probably only a few years older than Mordecai—maybe thirty-five.

"So, we have an obedience problem."

Clearly.

Mordecai simply raised his eyebrows in response, as Elysian joined him on his right.

The man pressed his lips into a thin, false smile. "We'll take care of it."

"This group was especially tricky," Mordecai explained. "There was constant bickering and sarcasm—not to mention one of them tried to bolt the first chance they got."

"And which one was that?"

"The example," Mordecai said.

The man nodded once, "I see." He turned on his heel to look back at us. "Names?"

Go to hell.

At the opposite end of the rope from me, someone started.

"Harris."

"Nickolai."

"Malcolm."

"Evander."

"Taz."

I kept my face fixed into a well-practiced scowl, my gaze directed at our new captor. He matched my expression.

Eric turned to frown at me, probably debating if he should hit me over the head.

"That's Ignatius," Mordecai sighed.

"Fantastic." He spat the word, maintaining his glare before turning back to the rest of the group. "My name is Cedric Vernon. And unfortunately for all of you, my name is the only one that matters because I am the leader of your battalion. You will all be assigned a number that will serve as your name."

He resumed his pacing, taking note of the resentment rising to the surface in all of our expressions. "You will also be assigned to certain tasks, in addition to the ones that every soldier has to participate in like training routines. You will be under constant observation from the watchtowers, so try not to do anything stupid."

Mordecai directed a pointed glance at each of us as Cedric continued his speech.

"You will be up before dawn every day, and you will not be allowed to sleep until all of your jobs have been completed. That process will repeat until we tell you otherwise."

Until the war started, and they needed to throw us at their enemies like rocks.

"Cooperation and diligence will be rewarded; disobedience and spite will be met with severe repercussions. It's up to you how easy or difficult your time here will be, so try to think about what you are going to say or do *before* you actually say or do it. Keep in mind that this is your first and only warning of these rules. Your first offence will also be your last."

I toed at a clump of grass to distract myself from the steady ache spreading through my gut.

"Everything works around a strict hierarchy; you do what we tell you, no matter what." He paused to scowl down at me, dark eyes narrowed. "Does everyone understand?"

The weight of his stare made me want to shrink and cower away. His eyes could burn holes through my skin.

I clamped my jaw, burying my anger somewhere deep inside and meticulously replacing it with raw, life preserving fear. I nodded slowly, forcing myself to keep his gaze.

His face remained stern and motionless like chiseled stone. "Excellent."

After a moment more, Mordecai cleared his throat and asked, "Do you expect me and the rest of my group to return to the smaller camp today or wait until tomorrow so we don't have to navigate in the dark?"

"That won't be necessary, actually," Cedric revealed, "numbers have been increasing steadily, so there's no need for you to go back, unless it's to tell the rest that they should pack up and come here."

Elysian wrinkled her brow, the same way Mordecai would have. "You mean we're staying here?"

Beside her, Mordecai clenched his jaw, taking a regretful glance over his shoulder to the south at the main gate, which was closed, locked, and guarded by men in black uniforms on both sides.

Cedric nodded. "Yes. But with a war on its way, I should think here is the safest place to stay, wouldn't you agree?"

"Yeah," Mordecai turned back around and nodded stiffly, "Perfectly safe."

IT TOOK ten buckets of bone-chilling, cold water to wash away all the mud. And that was only the first link in the chain of nettling requirements.

Drenched and shivering, all of us were ushered to the front of the north watchtower, where a row of cross-looking officers tossed us uniforms and water canteens. Unlike the uniforms I had seen in Orvalia and the one Cedric was wearing, the fabric was red—easy to distinguish from the black that higher ranking individuals wore. Embroidered into the right shoulder was Brighton's national seal in ebony thread.

The fabric was thick and rough. Every fiber had been diligently woven into place with the intent to make it strong and durable—and it would have to be.

Red was the color for pawns. And pawns would have to bear the brunt of the fight.

Members of Brighton's original army were separated from us; they wore red uniforms as well, but a thick band of black crossed their left sleeves. Additionally, their tents were situated on the northwest corner of Fort Ketta, ours were to the southwest.

Regardless, the heavy material and stiff sleeves were a welcome relief from the lingering cold. I wanted this over with. A tight, constricting pain had wrapped itself around my shoulders and was slowly working its way down my spine. The incessant throb in the side of my face, a sure black eye, had only gotten worse now that I had the time to think about it. The sting from the cuts and scrapes had dulled at least, but faintly.

From there we were filed past a large open area in the northern portion of the base, where several clusters of about thirty were all working through training routines. Officers in black stood close by at all times.

By my count there were about a hundred and twenty in that field, maybe another hundred in or near the tents that took up most of the area beside it, and about seventy others working near the watchtowers and center edifice. That was only based upon what I had seen so far. Fort Ketta could easily hold thousands of people.

And there are still more on the way.

Cedric joined the band of officers as they began to lead us down a row of the disorganized tents. He spoke with one of the officers quietly, running through a list of mundane numbers.

The heavy canvas material that made up the tents was still wet from the storm, sagging and pulling down on their supports. They were all about the height of a shed, and rectangular to fit more people.

The grass between each tent, and especially in the lazily mapped rows, was worn to bare dirt from so much foot traffic.

We came to a stop in front of a tent near the middle of the row. The number 1028 had been painted into one of the front flaps, each number about the size of a hand.

"We are short on space, so all six of you will be staying in here," Cedric informed us, waving a hand at our glorified prison cell. It would be barely enough to fit us, but it would have to work.

"This should be interesting..." Harris muttered.

Malcolm's eyebrow twitched in agreement.

"You all start working before dawn tomorrow," Cedric added with a faint smirk, already turning to walk back toward the rest of the fort. The other two officers followed suit.

It was a test. He was leaving us out here with no immediate supervision to see who would try to run when they got the chance. But we had all seen this trick before.

Evander went in first, pushing through the tent flaps, and I followed second.

On both sides there were sets of wooden bunks, and at the back there was another, crammed into place to fit us all. On each sat a blanket, the only slight comfort that could be afforded. Brighton couldn't let all of their *soldiers* freeze to death in the middle of the night—I doubted that would happen until after the snow came, when a simple blanket wouldn't be enough.

"This is a nightmare," Harris declared, plopping down onto the bottom bunk on the left side of the tent. The wood creaked loudly in protest. "We're all going to be dead, or somewhere close to it before this war starts."

"Don't do that yet. There's still a possibility that we can find a weak point and get out of here," Malcolm said, skeptically eyeing the canvas above our heads as the evening light weakly shone through, like it was being filtered through murky water.

I walked around Evander, claiming the bottom bunk on the right as mine. I bit my tongue to stifle any depressing or unhelpful comments, choosing instead to frown up at the wooden underside of the bunk above me.

It looked weak. Just planks of wood held into place by supportive slats. If I was ever frustrated enough, I could probably kick a hole through it.

"Have you seen the wall?" Harris sighed, "There's no way anyone can get past that. This base has been here for nearly a century for a reason."

"If we play along with what they ask, they'll eventually let their guard down. They need to pay more attention to the people they think will escape anyway," Taz added.

I held up my hand as I listened, examining the jagged scrapes across my palm. They still stung, but the blood had already turned to scabs.

"Do you think we'll make it that far?" I asked numbly. "Do you think we're actually going to make it out of this alive? We're only here to catch arrows and swords so that their real soldiers have a chance against Dale."

Evander crossed his arms, leaning on one of the four bunk posts to look down at me. "Well, don't you just radiate positivity?"

Across the space, Taz asked, "All of this for what? Is it land Brighton wants from Dale? Their wealth? Power?"

"Maybe all of the above?" Malcolm tilted his head, "That's why most wars start, and that's what they'll get if they actually win. Sometimes kings and leaders are never happy to stop with what they already have. Sometimes it's never enough."

Harris gazed around as the sounds of work and misery continued outside. "Brighton's government is out of its mind. This fortress, the black armbands to distinguish the other soldiers, gathering up people like us just for numbers—things like this belong in the past, during the age when nations were still fighting over land."

Evander's jaw tightened. "Governments are shockingly good at fucking with people's lives, actually."

"You've witnessed it during your many travels?" Taz asked.

"I wasn't traveling then—but that's beside the point. They can all kiss my ass."

I returned to staring at the underside of the bunk above mine. "And consider it an honor and a privilege, I assume? Kissing your ass?"

Evander's white teeth flashed into a sarcastic grin, "I can't imagine who wouldn't."

Taz shook his head and rolled his eyes.

I must have fallen asleep after that, because I didn't remember much of the conversation that continued until after the sun was down. I'd hoped it would earn me a few extra hours of the rest I craved, but instead I found myself wide awake in the dark. It was quiet all around me, and I blamed the stinging bite of the cold for waking me up early.

Across the tent Harris was asleep. In the bunk above him, however, Nickolai was sitting in a tight ball, staring forward in thought. He had his arms wrapped around his knees and his dark brows scrunched.

I couldn't see who was in the bunk above me, but it was quiet enough that I knew everyone else was asleep. As long as I talked quietly, they wouldn't be bothered.

"Can't sleep?" I asked Nickolai.

He flinched at the sudden sound of my voice, turning to face me. He looked so out of place here.

"Yeah." He turned to frown at his feet. I could practically see him stuffing his fear into a distant corner of his mind. "I miss my family..."

A strangulating bubble rose into my throat. I asked, "Did you sleep at all?"

He just shrugged, staring ahead at nothing.

I wished there was something I could do other than *hope* he didn't die. I'd be able to share my food before he starved here, and so would everybody else, but as soon as the war started, as soon as we all needed to fight for our lives, he would be alone. It would be every man for himself.

"I'm sorry your life was stolen from you."

He blinked slowly, thinking, and gave me a sideways look. "They stole your life, too."

"Yeah, but I had already started to mess up my own life as it was. I was trying...I think this just sped up the inevitable for me. There was still hope for you."

After a pause, he asked, "What if you make it out of here? What if we all do?"

I half smiled. "I'll take it as a very serious warning from the universe. I'll pay Malcolm back his money, stop gambling, figure out what I really want to do, and straighten out my life."

It felt like wishful thinking now, like a faraway dream.

"And I'll start listening to my mom better—no more wandering off." Nickolai paused, then smirked in my direction, "And I'll remember to never start gambling."

I chuckled. "Smart kid. Learn from my mistakes—I'm a treasure trove of wisdom."

It was amazing what a smile could do for a face, even just a small one. He looked younger when he was scared. At least this way, it seemed like he had higher hopes.

"Try to get some sleep," I said.

"Only if you try, too."

"Fair enough." I rolled over, thinking again of the immense stone walls, the four towers rising into the sky, and the iron gate. Metal didn't usually look like my enemy. A little fire had always been enough to set things right.

This was different.

I wished I could complain to Harris, but he didn't deserve the disturbance. Waking him up wouldn't solve anything, not when I already knew my mind wasn't going to leave me alone.

Oh, please Ignatius, you never sleep.

CHAPTER SEVEN

All of us were up before the sun—not that it mattered. I hardly slept, and nobody else had done much better. After that, we stood through a brief and rather dull lecture on how the rest of our time here would be going; we had been sorted and assigned shifts for that day. Harris and Nickolai were placed in the training group, and the rest of us were in the labor group—I couldn't tell yet if that was good or bad news.

A group of officers, dressed in their cold, black uniforms, came to usher us off to our jobs for the day.

"Let's go, halfwits! Meet outside the east watchtower!" the one at the front yelled so that we could all hear.

"Wonder how many demoralizing terms they can use in a day?" Malcolm thought aloud.

"I'd say fifty," I shrugged.

"No, seventy at least," Evander countered. "We've got a long day to get through, and they're probably going to be shouting at us for most of it."

As we passed the brick building at the center of Fort Ketta, we saw a large sheet of parchment nailed to what was essentially a large sign post. There were other slips of paper pinned up as well—information, numbers, what looked like lists—but none as large as the one on the right. I couldn't read the large lettering, but the detailed sketch of a face was all I needed to know it was a wanted poster.

Evander nodded toward it, "That guy looks a bit like you, Malcolm."

"If you tack on a few decades," Malcolm squinted at the image, "and add a beard. But yeah, I can definitely see a resemblance."

As we passed it, Taz added, "I wonder what he did? The reward is 8,000 marks. Actually, that's a pretty sizeable chunk of Brighton's economy, now that I think about it."

The air vanished from my lungs, "How would anyone know what to do with that much money? You'd have to start sleeping on piles of it, just to put it to use."

Evander shrugged, "I'm just thankful I'm not that guy. You're in shit up to your eyebrows if any government has put that much on your head—especially if it's Brighton's government."

Malcolm's brows lifted in agreement. "Best of luck to him...I suppose."

We continued across the grass at a brisk pace, packed into a tight swarm of almost a hundred people. The large training group, including Harris and Nickolai, joined us as well. All of us descended into silence. Officers trailed after us on all sides, their black uniforms slicing through the sea of red soldiers.

Nickolai was on my heels, occasionally stepping on the back of my shoe.

I began fidgeting with my sleeve as I considered the fact that half of the people walking alongside us had black armbands. They knew how things worked. They already knew how to kill. The separation in the masses was a deeply carved gash because they avoided new soldiers like a disease, and I had already seen some of them harassing people. Just this morning, before the sun had come up, one of them shoved in front of Harris in line for food and used a racial slur. It was the kind of word that shot a cold spike through my chest and made me hope I'd simply misheard. But there was no mistaking it.

Harris had clenched his jaw and looked down at his feet. Malcolm was standing beside him, and his nostrils flared. Before I could, before any of us could—Malcolm marched directly up to the other soldier, wrenched him around by the shoulder, and knocked him flat out. A tooth had gone sailing through the crisp morning air, and no one dared stray too close to our segment of the line after that.

Needless to say, breakfast had been tense and quiet as we observed the people walking near us.

It would be so easy for things to turn south. I had my speed I could rely on to save myself, Malcolm had his strength, Evander had his wit, Harris and Taz were both too smart to be caught in that kind of mess, but Nickolai had nothing. He was small, so he could hide easily, but he would have to get away from an immediate threat first.

We were herded into two groups; new and old soldiers. Cedric joined the row of officers standing in front of us as they continued to bark out commands, and eventually they achieved some level of silence from us.

"You all need to be assigned numbers before you can return to your designated shift for the day. After you have been numbered, the training group will meet on the left side of the tower, and the labor group will meet on the right."

Cedric's voice carried over the horde easily. He sounded bored. Shouting over the heads of a crowd had been his job for a while now.

Nickolai was still behind me, practically hidden altogether as he continued to glance left and right.

"Form four lines, each one starting at one of us," Cedric instructed, gesturing to the other officers with him.

All at once, we shuffled into disorganized lines. We stood in clumps, inching toward where one of the officers designated us numbers, and either tossed a blunted sword into our hands, or filed us into groups for certain labor tasks.

I glared around the clusters of heads in front of me toward the east watchtower. The wall connected to it on both sides, branching out. The interlaced beams that made up its walls plus the tightly stacked cobblestones and mortar that served as a foundation were just tall enough to be disquieting. I felt miniscule and helpless walking into its shadow, which was disturbingly intentional. The top of the watchtower loomed even higher. The roof was supported by thick, wooden posts over the top of a landing, where several black uniforms could be seen peering down. Watching always for any sign of rebellion.

I would spit at them from here if I could.

Apparently, the line was moving faster than I had guessed. I was still scowling up at the tower when Taz cautiously pushed me ahead of him, to the front of the line.

A grim looking officer stood in front of me, clipboard and papers in hand. He scribbled something down with quick, violent motions, not even bothering to look up as he ground out a question he'd already repeated at least twenty times before.

"Tent number?"

I sifted through my memory, wincing at my own mindless compliance as I answered, "1028."

More scribbling.

The less stern officer who stood beside him grabbed my arm, scratching down the numbers 1028-1 on the inside of my wrist with dark, sour smelling ink that dried on my skin quickly. I curled my lip at it, glancing back to the other officer, who still hadn't looked up.

"Until we have a more permanent way to keep track of you all."

Oh great, another irreversible marking will be just what I need...

"If you're in training go left. Labor go right." He waved at me to leave, like I was merely a fly. I did before I had the chance to say something I would regret, attempting to rub off one of the numbers. The ink smelled strongly, and it stuck surprisingly well, much to my aggravation.

I walked in silence toward the rest of the labor group to the right, taking my place on the edge where I didn't have to speak to anyone. We were all too busy trying to scrape the markings off of our arms with little success. Even soldiers from the original army seemed disgusted by it, turning the skin around the sloppy numbering red and raw.

Nickolai followed Harris over to the training group, glancing at me anxiously. I had to turn away.

Taz, Malcolm, and Evander joined me in silence.

Like me, Malcolm attempted in vain to rub off the numbers on his skin; 1028-5. Evander was 1028-4, and Taz was 1028-2.

The officers began to yell at us again, herding us like cattle across the camp and delegating out jobs. We broke off in clusters, dispersing out to all corners of Fort Ketta, with belligerent supervisors close by.

Tasks for the day would range from carrying materials, putting up more tents, and repairing various things.

It occurred to me now that we were the lucky ones—being in the labor group. Mind numbing tasks were a thousand times better than a never-ending flood of routines, exercises, and tests where failure wasn't an option.

***

THE INSIDE of the east watchtower was cold and damp, and smelled like fresh rain. If I paid careful attention, I could smell the tangy undertone of metal too. The walls of the lowest level were thick, made of the same materials as the outer wall and the foundation, with no windows and no light.

I walked behind Malcolm, Evander, and Taz as an officer led us and half a dozen others from the labor group into the dark enclosure. Large wooden crates were stacked against the outer wall, along with bundles of spears as wide as a person, which left only a small space in the center of the room for people to stand.

The officer carried a single oil lamp that barely illuminated the murky darkness. Dull, copper colored light bent across the walls and over some of the farthest storage bins as I tried to count them in my head. I eyeballed them in fives, and I was somewhere past fifty when his voice interrupted my concentration.

"You are moving all of these supplies to the west tower so we can make room for more weapons. Two of you carry one crate at a time, and don't stop until this space," he gestured around, "is empty. Got it?"

I thought of dragging crates back up a mountainside, one of the first tests Mordecai had given. At least this time the ground would be level.

Without a word, two by two, people began hoisting the crates up by their rope handholds and carrying them out the door. Evander and Taz were just about to take up the closest one when another officer came up and whispered something to the man with the lamp, and he called the four of us out by our designated numbers. "You have been summoned to the main building," was the only explanation he offered, as he waved us out the door. "You will await instructions outside, where the rest of your tent group will be joining you."

The other officer led us back toward the middle of the fortress, scarcely looking over his shoulder to ensure that we followed. A good thing, I assured myself, because it meant he wouldn't see the color rapidly leaching from our faces.

The sky was still a pale shade of gray that didn't seem all that much more vibrant than the inside of the watchtower. It reminded me more of the dirty, cloudy water that would pool in the streets after a heavy rain.

"What could we possibly be in trouble for now?" Malcolm grumbled, looking over his shoulder as the rest of our labor group continued hauling out crates, receding behind us.

"But we haven't done anything," Taz pointed out.

Malcolm shrugged, "Maybe that's it?"

"Whatever it is, hopefully it's better than training," I added. "Unless we're just being added to that group for the day?"

"If the instructors here are more stringent than Mordecai, I think we're all fucked. Nickolai especially," observed Evander.

"I'd prefer not to think about that." I glanced over at the edge of the training field.

Malcolm followed my gaze. "I hate to say it, but now that we're here, there isn't much that anyone can do to help him."

"Doesn't 'not much' still count as more than nothing?"

The corner of Malcolm's mouth angled down. "Not enough to save him."

The overwhelming urge to kick something crossed my mind; the surrounding wall would be a good target, but I'd certainly prefer landing a boot in the King's ass.

"What kind of a tyrant does Brighton's king have to be to support this?" asked Taz. "Half of the people here are *meant* to be killed and trampled."

Malcolm grimaced, "I guess that's just how greed works. It blinds."

"Maybe he imagines all the gold and ships and fields he'll own, just so he can sleep at night. Forget all the blood that will be on the monarchy's hands," I added.

Another reason to kick the king in the ass.

We were nearly half-way across camp. The structure that sat at the center of it all was made of red bricks and a dark, wooden roof. It looked like it belonged on a crowded street in Salona, not here in the middle of a desolate portion of Brighton.

There was a cluster of self-important looking people standing outside of it near the board with the wanted poster, talking quietly and occasionally glancing out at their dismal surroundings. I recognized the black uniforms of two of the officers, Mordecai and Cedric among them, but the rest weren't wearing ranks or insignia that were obvious. They dressed like they were above that altogether, with fine stitchwork adorning their clothes and clean boots that didn't look like they had ever seen mud.

I bit my tongue to keep myself focused on the topic at hand, not on how my frustration was escalating like a fire surrounded by nothing but dry tinder.

Malcolm arched one brow, taking note of my increasingly bitter expression.

"I wonder how any of them sleep too, with this going on all around them," I seethed, fighting my gaze away from the group of men.

Evander winced, "The more rested they are, the more worried we should be?"

"Probably," I said. "I think I lose a little more of my faith in humanity every day."

"You're not alone in that, but what can anybody do about it?" Malcolm asked.

It wasn't really a question. It was a matter of fact. Brighton had harnessed the power of a weapon far different from all the spears, swords, knives, shields, and clubs in the crates being moved; it was fear that they used, drawing invisible lines in the sand that no one in their right mind would dare to cross. Some might try like Everett had, but what happened to them for it, whatever the government came up with as punishment, would scare whomever was left into compliance.

At last, the officer signaled for us to stop near the main building—within earshot of the group of finely dressed men—and lingered nearby as we awaited an explanation and for Harris and Nickolai to join us.

"Nothing can be done to stop it," I said hopelessly. "At least, nothing that would be enough to change what is coming."

"If you're going to be scheming amongst yourselves, at least do it quietly enough that we don't have to hear." The voice came from the group of men, who I'd purposefully turned my back to. I followed Malcolm's gaze, like the trajectory of an arrow, over to one of the more finely dressed men in the group. He probably wasn't all that much older than I was, maybe twenty-four or twenty-five, but he had a pristine face. His combed hair was a light shade of brown that caught a hint of gold in the light as he looked back at us, and he stood like he had something to be proud of, with his head high.

I bit down the taste of a cutting remark forming on my tongue, tightening my hands into fists and wrenching my gaze away to keep from lashing out.

He turned back to the rest of the people he was with. "If only they realized how much work there is to be done before the war. Then perhaps they'd be grateful that they don't have to carry around little boxes all day."

"I'd pay good money to see you try and lift one of those *little* boxes." Did I say that out loud? I couldn't tell. It felt like the words were only in my head, something that I would debate saying, but never set free.

Malcolm hunched, stifling a laugh, and trying to disguise it as a cough. He looked back at the man with widened eyes, and my heart fell straight into my stomach. An aching rush of dread poured down my back, and I sealed my lips tightly, but it was too late.

Oh God. I really said it.

I looked back at them, in time to see Mordecai clap a hand over his eyes and turn away, shaking his head. The man I'd just insulted stayed where he was and raised his brows, his jaw already slack, and he tilted his ear toward me.

"Tell me you did *not* just say that."

I wish I could.

He glanced at the rest of the people with him, like he was still in disbelief.

Mordecai slowly straightened himself, looking at me with the kind of warning that had weight; it settled on my shoulders until my back felt like it was going to bend and snap.

I looked away, back at the other man as he turned to face me again.

"I've never seen so much nerve in all my life," he gibed.

I think you meant to say stupidity.

My mouth kept running off anyway. "Clearly you've never walked down the common streets in any of the bigger cities—you'd be insulted worse than that. And by far more than just me."

"What makes you think I'm not common?" he asked incredulously.

"Your face." I said it plainly, but inside I felt like I was being ripped to pieces. "Anyone can wear fancy clothes, but only certain people can make it this far in life without scars on their face or a broken nose."

He pressed his brows together, and his eyes squinted. "I'm choosing to take that as a compliment?" He waved a hand at the distance between us. "Come closer."

I looked at Malcolm, and he looked at me. His nose was wrinkled slightly, and his brows were pinched. I didn't dare glance at Evander (who was probably struggling not to collapse into hysterics), or worse, at Taz (who might look as horrified as I felt). My face was blank, what little of it I could feel, as the color drained from it completely. But we did as we were told.

When we stopped, he stared me dead in the eyes. I was barely taller, yet I felt incredibly small.

"Do you know who I am?" he asked.

I glanced past his shoulder to Mordecai, whose eyes were wide and stern, and the vein in his neck—the one that usually only became visible when he was angry—was plain to see.

"No," I confessed, turning back to him. "I don't."

His mouth curled into a sneer. "Then there's hope for you and that feral tongue of yours."

"Does who you are make a difference to what I said?"

A blaze of color started to creep up his neck, but his gaze remained firm. "It does if you recall where you are, and what your job is."

"Doing dirty work for pigs and snakes." I grinned falsely. "Yeah, I know exactly why I'm here. I just can't quite tell if you're a pig, or a snake."

His eyes turned flinty. "I could have you beaten or killed with the snap of my fingers. Do you want to test my authority?"

I was debating spitting on one of his shining boots; I was certainly close enough. But a glance at Cedric's stiff-jawed expression made me reconsider.

Malcolm was completely silent beside me, and in the corner of my vision, Mordecai seemed as if he might faint. He came forward, hands ready, like he planned on having to separate us like a pair of fighting dogs.

"Gentlemen, let's not resort to throwing hands," he grabbed the back of my shirt, roughly pulling me a step away, "I'm sure you didn't mean any offense, *right?*"

Malcolm raised his eyebrows, giving the ground a sidelong glance rather than actually rolling his eyes. Evander snickered quietly. Taz was going paler by the second.

I turned my stare on Mordecai. "Have you met me?"

He held up one hand, "Ignatius—for God's sake, I'm trying to help you—"

"You can't be serious," the man interrupted, as he dusted a nonexistent speck of dust from his sleeve. "He's one of the ones you were just telling us about in our meeting?"

Mordecai sighed, releasing me from his bone-shattering grasp. "Yes, your Highness, he is."

My stomach lurched as I tried to tell myself that I'd misheard. The dry piece of bread I had eaten first thing in the morning threatened to escape, but luckily, I forced it back down.

Cedric, who had released a long, relieved exhale, now said "I think we should sort the rest of this out in my office. The remaining two from their tent group will be here shortly; they can meet us inside. Get this taken care of in one fell swoop."

"I think that would be best," Mordecai agreed, nodding toward the main building. His eyes still held the same heavy warning, and before I could fully comprehend everything, we were reluctantly following him, and Brighton's future King, toward whatever god-awful plans they had in store for us.

Walking beside me, Malcolm quietly asked, "You were going to spit on his shoe, weren't you? A *prince's* shoe."

I nodded as I stared blankly ahead. "It did cross my mind, yes."

He chuckled tentatively, "There may be hope for us to be friends after all."

"If I don't get myself executed first," I said, glancing around at Fort Ketta's imposing walls, the same walls that had been standing through long past wars and disputes and would probably still be here after this one. "If we aren't already on the way there."

CHAPTER EIGHT

The air in Cedric's office smelled like wood and new paper, which would have been welcoming, maybe even calming, if I had actually been able to focus on it. Instead, as I stared at the floor in front of my feet, I tried to suppress the feeling that a cold, aching void had ripped itself through my chest.

Cedric stood behind his desk, keeping an eye on us while Brighton's prince, Kassian, gazed out the window that faced the main gate. Mordecai, for once, wasn't doing the same; he stood in the main portion of the room with his back to the door like the rest of us, now that Harris and Nickolai had joined the meeting.

"Your judgement is more reliable than most, Mordecai," the prince droned, glancing over his shoulder, "and I can understand the rest of this group being candidates—just not that one." He aimed his chin at me.

The edge of my lip curled.

Holding me in the corner of his eye, Mordecai answered. "He's out of sorts at the moment."

"Wouldn't it be safer to nominate someone who *doesn't* get out of sorts?" Cedric asked.

"Nominated for what?" Evander interjected, looking back and forth between them.

The prince barely spared him a glance, "That's not important for you to know yet," he turned to nod at Cedric, "But, yes, I agree; it would be a terrible mistake to use someone so unruly."

Evander scrunched his brow, keeping a skeptical green eye trained on them both as Mordecai argued.

"We will need people who aren't a substantial loss, if things go south—and as of today they are the newest group here, with the least number of hours invested in their training. If they get caught, it will hurt us less than if we send over people that have spent more time here."

"And these six are the only ones you'll suggest?" Cedric wrinkled his nose, as if the very idea gave off a smell he didn't like.

"Would you rather have your thumb cut off, or your pinky?" asked Mordecai. "Because they are our pinky finger right now."

Biting down on my tongue to keep quiet was becoming more painful by the second. Nickolai was silently examining the floorboards near where he stood, beside Malcolm.

I shook my head. "You plan on sending us, and a kid, out to do your dirty work?"

Once again, Mordecai gave me a silencing look that was nearly pleading. "You don't understand all that we intend—"

"Then explain it. I'm *dying* to know."

The prince walked away from the window, his hands behind his back as he crossed the width of the room. His clean shoes and the sound they made with each methodical step was like a stabbing drum beat across the floor that I could feel in my stomach, and all eyes turned to him.

"At a certain point, the war effort needs observation on its enemy. It would be considerably easier if they were a part of the main continent, of course, but traveling to their land—to note how they do things, who they align themselves with, and *who's* in their capital—is essential. We have one spy there already, but it's not enough."

"You mean in Dale."

He continued without pause. "It would be a tradeoff, simply taking a small number of soldiers out of the ranks and placing them in Dale as additional spies. No more than ten, that would be enough to cause suspicion, and no less than five. But Mordecai makes a good point; if things were to go wrong, we'd want them to be the most dispensable."

I looked at Mordecai again, the way his face seemed tense underneath, like a sheet lain over a cage of tightly wound metal. His stare was nearly unblinking. The warning underneath was plain to see; *don't fuck this up.*

"We have nearly as many soldiers as we planned for," Mordecai looked to Cedric. "And we don't have the time to wait for any more options. They have sufficient combat training, and they are the least problematic if we have to cut our losses. Personally, I see it as the safest bet."

Cedric said nothing, only turning to the prince as he stood by the desk in silent consideration. His brows were still squeezed together as he looked to Mordecai. "You're certain, after all your years working for the crown, that this is how we should proceed if we want to gain the upper hand?"

Mordecai nodded slowly, refocusing his drifted stare. "Yes."

The prince nodded once. "Alright. I'll be back momentarily, after I have a word with my advisors."

I didn't look up as the prince walked by, nor as he closed the office door after leaving. The more I watched everything, the more I felt like I shouldn't be seeing it at all. This was the kind of conversation that belonged in a grossly over-decorated conference room in the capital, at a table surrounded by rich lords and the King's court. Not me. Not any of us; a blacksmith, an engineer, an artist, a stonebreaker, whatever Evander was, and a child.

The room fell into a deep stretch of silence, with time dragging its heels. At least Cedric was able to busy himself with the papers at his desk. The rest of us only stood. Waiting.

I considered what would have happened if I truly lost my temper with the prince, where this would have ended if I spat on his shoe. The future king's pride mattered too much for him not to react, I knew that. And it would have gotten me killed.

In an odd way, I was grateful to Mordecai for stopping me. Yet it seemed that it would be in vain. If this went the way that I feared, we would be walking into a new country with orders to help destroy it from the inside out. Failure to stay discrete, or failure to bring Brighton the information it needed, would both end the same way. I could have saved myself the trouble if I had been executed today.

Looking down the line didn't soothe my nerves; Nickolai appeared to be holding his breath, Harris was chewing on his own lip, Taz was shifting his weight from foot to foot, Malcolm's arms were crossed tightly, and Evander had no sly remarks to lighten the mood.

After several minutes, the clink of the doorknob cut through my thoughts, and I looked carefully over my shoulder as the prince returned.

"You all have only a few hours remaining here today," the prince announced. "Then, after some arrangements, you'll all be leaving for Dale in the morning."

The air in my chest went cold as his words settled. *So, this is it,* I thought, feeling oddly calm and resigned. *This is what it feels like to have my own life ripped from my hands.*

The tension in Mordecai's shoulders loosened, like he was letting out a breath of air. "Thank you for trusting my recommendation. The six of them should be able to get the job done."

"Seven," Kassian corrected. "You're going with them."

All the color washed out of Mordecai's face, and for a moment he only stood. His jaw was hanging, and he blinked. "Me? Why?"

The prince tilted his head, and creases formed at the corners of his eyes. "Do you think we'd send these gutter snipes into the belly of the beast without supervision? They may be dispensable, but we need someone who knows what they're doing to keep an eye on them, make sure things go according to plan. I figured you would be the best person, since you've worked with them before; you know them better than any of our other generals. Not to mention you were the one to recommend them in the first place."

Now it was like a ball of lead had landed in my stomach. If Mordecai was reluctant to go, shouldn't the rest of us be as well?

"But—wouldn't I be of better use here?" he asked. "We still need to gather and train more people. And Elysian, my sister—"

"Your sister will be fine. Fort Ketta is one of the safest places to be during times of war." The prince dismissed his concern with such ease that it was sickening.

At that moment, it dawned on me that Mordecai wasn't afraid to go to Dale, to face Brighton's enemy, or to brave the tasks of a spy. He was afraid to leave his sister here. Without him. He had to worry about keeping himself and Elysian alive; we were probably the last people he wanted to look after and keep out of harm's way.

Unfortunately, it seemed that now he would have to do it all.

The prince turned to the rest of us, "You will prepare to leave immediately."

Mordecai's hands were in fists at his sides. "I'm just one man. How do I keep six people under control in the enemy's capital?"

"I thought about that as well," the prince clicked his tongue as he returned to staring out the office window. "You need something you can hold over them."

I swallowed hard. Every heartbeat was like a punch to the chest.

"The kid stays here," Kassian decided. "If things go wrong in Dale, he dies."

Malcolm uncrossed his arms. "You can't do that—"

"What the *hell* is wrong with you? You'd use a twelve-year-old as leverage?" Evander interrupted, his stare dripping with disgust as it shifted between Kassian and Cedric.

Still holding Mordecai's gaze, the prince pointed. "See? They care. If they try to sabotage anything, it's his blood on their hands."

Nickolai blanched.

The color had returned to Mordecai's face, and the additional flare of anger had risen in his cheeks, but he nodded sharply anyway. "Do you mind if I have a quick word with our new spies?"

"Go ahead," Cedric waved a hand, still behind his desk.

The prince flashed a thin smile and went to leave. As he passed

Mordecai, he patted him on the shoulder. Mordecai, I thought, must not have even noticed. Once Kassian was gone, Mordecai nodded for us to follow him out the door into the hallway.

"You wait in here." He put a hand out to stop Nickolai, who blinked his wide eyes and silently returned to where he had been standing.

The hallway was empty by the time all of us were out of Cedric's office, and the door was closed. I placed myself with my back against the wall, using it like an anchor as my nerves rolled and crashed like the waves of a storm. Malcolm and Evander were on either side of me as Mordecai started to pace, cracking the knuckles in both of his hands as he did.

"Why did you do that?" Taz asked.

"Lower your voice," Mordecai hissed. It was said in a whisper, but with the tone of a yell. "I'm not going to bother painting a nice picture of this because I can't. This is not going to be easy for any of you but it's what needed to be done. I endorsed you because you are, in fact, the newest people here that Brighton has invested the least amount of time in; I wouldn't be doing *my job* if I didn't suggest it. And you," he pointed at me, "you weren't fucking helping when you got in the prince's face. You're lucky I was there."

I sighed and looked down.

Taz flopped against the wall, placing a hand over his eyes as he usually did when the vertigo showed up. Still, he managed to ask, "What's the real reason? Did they offer you a higher rank if you can pull off this spying mission for them? All you ever talk about is your precious job."

Mordecai's teeth flashed into an angry grimace. "Believe me, vying for rank is the least of my concerns."

"Because you didn't plan on going with us," I finished for him.

"All that matters now is that it's become my responsibility," grumbled Mordecai. "But first I'm going to make absolutely certain that you know what happens if you do something stupid while we're there. If any one of you tries to sabotage the plan, or gets us caught, we are all as good as dead—and so is Nickolai. Got it?"

Reluctantly, we all nodded.

"Good. Now go pack your things. We leave for Dale first thing in the morning."

<hr />

THAT NIGHT in the tent was worse than the first night, by far, and we were up past midnight discussing our fate.

Harris was drumming his fingers on his chin as he quietly considered, "It would have been one thing if we could flag somebody down in Dale and tell them all that Brighton intends; but if we did that, it wouldn't be long before the people here knew. We wouldn't be able to rush back before they acted on their threats..."

Nickolai was curled into a ball on his bunk. He hadn't spoken since before that meeting with the prince.

Evander nodded in agreement, "And there's no guarantee anyone in Dale would believe us if we came forward anyway."

I raised my shoulders and crossed my arms to fight the nighttime chill. "We're there for three weeks before they send a boat over to bring us back. That's a lot of time where things can go wrong, and they'll assume that it's our fault if it does."

The minute any bad news arrived, that would be it. No one here would give us the chance to return, let alone explain, before they killed Nickolai.

Mordecai's sister, Elysian, was to supervise him while we were gone. Because Nickolai was Brighton's lever to use against us, our ultimatum was that they separate him from the daily onslaught; Elysian would watch over him and keep him away from the hordes, and he'd be exempt from training and labor rotations until we returned. A fancy way of saying, 'imprisonment,' basically. But it was better than having him thrown to the wolves—because if none of us could be sure he'd survive daily life in Fort Ketta, then how could they expect us to cooperate? By the end of it, everyone agreed. We would do Brighton's dirty work so long as they kept Nickolai alive.

All we had to do was make sure things went smoothly in Dale, and in three weeks, we'd return to find Nickolai unharmed with Elysian hovering nearby.

"Nothing's going to go wrong," Taz asserted. "We can handle this. And when we make it back, after we've learned more about Brighton and Dale, we can find a way to destroy what little edge Brighton has—in a way where we all survive."

"It's a tall order, but I like it," mused Evander, and he grinned sidelong at Taz. "*Almost* as much as I like you."

Taz barely managed a smile before flushing scarlet.

Harris shook his head. "Shameless flirting aside, I think we're in agreement. We keep playing Brighton's games until we have leverage of our own."

Malcolm nodded. "If it helps, I'm feeling pretty lucky."

"You're always lucky," I pointed out.

"Well, of course he is," Evander grinned. "Everybody knows redheads are good luck—Malcolm is our own walking, talking rabbit's foot."

"We should hope so," added Taz. "We're going to need it."

CHAPTER NINE

I had gotten used to the weight of the uniform they made us wear at Fort Ketta, so it was refreshingly unfamiliar to wear street clothes. Something that made me look less like a military pawn and more like a typical, inconspicuous civilian. They took the time to scrub the numbers off of our forearms as well, leaving red, frustrated skin in their place; though, not nearly as frustrated as Mordecai.

He stood with his arms crossed and his jaw set; his feet were planted apart in a wide stance on a dock that was more packed than the inside of a shipping container. Regardless, the townspeople gave our entire group a wide berth, bumping into each other as they made their way past.

I ignored Mordecai and squinted out at the expanse of gray water, where a ferry could be seen in the distance returning from its trip to Dale. The white sails looked small from here, as did the rest of the boat.

Endless clusters of people continued wandering past, their feet clumping across the wooden planks that made up the dock in Amphitrite, Brighton's westernmost city.

"Maybe if you stopped scowling like that, we would be a little less conspicuous." Evander commented, raising both dark eyebrows past me at Mordecai.

"Perhaps," Mordecai grunted, still gazing out at the slow-moving ferry.

Evander clamped his jaw, turning to do the same thing with a sigh.

I eyed the sloshing water, debating, for just a second, if throwing myself in and trying to swim away would be worth it.

The cold wind coming in from the sea was grating on my already tense nerves, and the fabric of my clothes didn't do much to stop it from soaring through me. The sun itself hadn't climbed high enough to offer any warmth yet. The sky was still a deep shade of blue, and the few darkened clouds to the east were rimmed by pink and orange. It would be a while before the light could hit the dock—and that would probably be after the ferry arrived anyway.

"He has a point," Taz added. "We should at least try to seem a little more cheerful." He was standing on Evander's right, keeping a hand on one of the dock-posts for support; staring across the ebbing and flowing water, I imagined, wouldn't make the occasional vertigo easy to deal with.

"For all these people know, we're going to a funeral," Harris suggested with a shrug.

Yeah, our own. I didn't let myself say it. No one needed that, especially in the middle of what had been such a *pleasant* morning. We packed in a rush, went over details with Cedric in a hurry, and then Mordecai had said goodbye to Elysian. The latter seemed to be the biggest influence on the atmosphere.

Nickolai had been there too, pale and unnervingly quiet, as we left.

We silently agreed to stop talking, and stayed that way until the ferry finally pulled in.

We shouldered our way onto the boat, through the surging crowd of people getting off, along with many others and shuffled our way across to stand on the port side in tightly packed rows. Then came more waiting.

As we sailed away from the dock, I watched the water shift from murky gray, like the last remnants of a bruise, to a dark blue hue that mirrored the color of the sky. My skin crawled with unease. I tried not to imagine how deep the water went, or what might be waiting down there, somewhere below the layers of cold, pitch black.

The channel between Brighton and Dale was only fifty miles. But still, the short span of time where the coast of Brighton was no longer visible and where Dale's coast could not yet be seen was the most unnerving.

"You look a little anxious," Malcolm remarked, eyeing my white-knuckled fists.

I feigned a smile. "I don't like the ocean. I never have."

Harris was on my right, watching other people on the ferry as they chatted.

"Have you been on a boat before?" Malcolm asked.

I looked east, to where Brighton's craggy shore should have been, where Amphitrite's clustered buildings had been visible minutes before. Now, there was only more water. "Not this far out."

Malcolm shrugged, "Then I guess that's fair."

On his other side, Evander was looking out at the endless blue with a relaxed smile on his face. The wind raked through his dark hair, but it didn't seem to bother him one bit. Meanwhile, I went back to concentrating on my own breathing. Forgetting to do it usually didn't end well.

No sooner had I begun to question my ability to contain my nerves, standing in the cold wind for what felt like a lifetime (when it was actually only two hours), did Dale's western coast come into view.

From what I had been told, Dale was only slightly smaller than Brighton as far as land. But clearly that didn't matter. Dale's capital city, Angel's Landing, spanned from end to end of the peninsula. A colorful blend of houses and greenery crawled up the steep hillside of the island country. The earth tapered into the ocean, turning to a skirt of white sand around the front where the crowded port sat. It boasted long stretches of dock and ships of many sizes, with sails like the pages from old books. There were tall, jagged white cliffs on the north side, and some shorter ones to the south. Atop it all, perched on the highest point like a glittering crown, was a palace. Towers of ghostly marble clawed into the sky, seeming too tall and too grand to be real. The lower half of it was constructed of intimidating walls, glass domes, and curved outcroppings, each littered with gleaming windows and arches.

It was beautiful in a way that made it seem deadly, like a well-designed blade. And it was deadly. This was war, only they didn't know it yet, and I decided I would rather be anywhere but here once they figured it out.

Brighton was picking a fight with a much stronger nation. Why Brighton wanted to go to war with Dale was still foggy to us, but now it was clear that we had been right; Dale's wealth was something Brighton wanted. A quick glance at their shoreline made that abundantly clear. If nothing else, Brighton's king was after their wealth and the power that it could give him.

Stepping off the boat and out of the tight confines of the crowd was like a breath of fresh air. The wooden dock, one of at least a dozen, connected to an elevated section of road made out of smooth pale stone. The smell of clean salt and churned sand carried on the wind, which had finally calmed.

Centered above the docks, on a higher platform of the white stone, stood the massive statue of an angel. It was made entirely out of shining, smooth white marble. Her hands were clasped around the hilt of a sword, and her head was lowered. Waves of hair poured over her shoulders and down her back, nearly fading into her billowing robes. Her feathered wings rose behind her, so detailed, so realistic, arching and curving out wider than some houses I had seen back in Salona. The shrieking white birds flying overhead were as small as mice compared to her. Below her bare feet, on the face of the raised platform, Dale's national crest had been chiseled out with as much care and detail as the feathers on the angel's wings; it was a curved tree with sprawling limbs, enclosed by twin olive branches.

We paused on the far side of the road in the angel's shadow, below one of the two green-and-gold flags that flew on either side of her.

Beyond the statue, neat rows of houses with copper shingles swept uphill. I stared, marveling at the sheer size of everything and the fact that this was only one hillside.

"This place is like a different world," Harris observed, as Mordecai passed him.

Mordecai looked up at our surroundings, and all eyes followed his to the serene, resting face of the statue. He made a noise in the back of his throat. "It's certainly much bigger than I expected."

"Personally, I don't mind it here at all," Evander said to himself, half smiling out at the ocean.

"It is much less depressing than that camp," I agreed, noting that the water here was not nearly as murky as the water off of Brighton's coast; in fact, its greens and blues could rival the sky and the trees.

We followed the crowds down a short section of stairs that connected to the rest of the cobblestone road, arching upward toward the houses, where the waves of people dispersed.

Naturally, Mordecai was in charge of all the money Brighton's prince sent with us, and it wasn't long before he decided on an inn. It sat about halfway up the bustling hillside between the ocean and the palace, overlooking a sloping portion of the street. We would stay there until things were solidified and the plan was set in stone. And Mordecai wasn't going to waste any time on that either.

We congregated at a table on the main floor of the inn, in a secluded corner beside a window and close to the white-plaster walls. Evander had insisted on food as well, and Mordecai begrudgingly handed over enough money for what now sat in front of us: flat disks of soft bread, peppers, cheese, white fish, and strange green and brown orbs that were bitter and salty, but in a good way. They were called *olives*, as Evander had informed me.

"We need to get as close to the palace as possible, if we can," Mordecai explained. "It'll work best if we can get jobs that allow us onto the grounds; the spy Brighton has had here for six months can help us with that, though. From there, sneaking in and collecting information will be our priority. We have three weeks to find as much as we can before we have to go back to Brighton and bring them everything we've found."

"And what are we looking for, exactly?" Malcolm asked.

"Three things," Mordecai held up three fingers. "First: anything that indicates what nations Dale works closely with. Knowing who their allies are is crucial. If you find any correspondence, notice shipping containers marked by specific countries coming here, things like that."

If they even need allies, I thought to myself. You don't call upon friends to swat a fly, and it was hard to imagine Dale struggling to squash Brighton.

Mordecai continued, "Second: we want to pay attention to where they station the bulk of their military. We know they keep their warships on the northern end of the city and that guards regularly patrol busy areas like the docks. But we need to know how many soldiers are in the palace at any given time, and where."

I asked, "Is Brighton planning to storm the inside of the palace, then?"

"What do you think?" Mordecai squinted, "It's war, isn't it?"

"You could've just said 'yes.'"

Beside me, Taz sat back in his chair, "What's the third thing?"

"This," Mordecai extracted a slip of paper from his pocket and unfolded it across the table. It was the wanted poster we had seen before in Fort Ketta.

Evander chuckled, "You want us to find Malcolm's twin?"

Mordecai ignored him, and pointed at the drawing of the face. "If you see this man here—I don't care where or when—*get him*."

Harris' brows lowered, "You want us to *kill* someone?"

"No, I want you to apprehend someone. Killing is a last resort, in this case."

Malcolm leaned forward, resting his forearms on the table. "Why? What did that guy do?"

Mordecai refolded the paper and tucked it away. "He messed up. Badly. He was once the captain of Brighton's royal guard, meaning it was his job to keep the king, queen, and their children safe. But when assassins broke into the capital twenty-two years ago, he did nothing to stop them. He abandoned his post altogether, and let them go on their killing spree, let them light the fires; the bastard was probably colluding with the radicals for years before it happened, too. He's the reason Brighton's original royal family is dead."

MORDECAI WAS up hours before the rest of us the next morning. In that time, he tracked down Brighton's other spy who'd been in the city long enough to have connections and a foundation of trust; after six months working in the palace fields to the west, he was able to put in a good word, securing each of us a job that allowed us into the palace. We would be starting the next day.

Apparently, Brighton's other spy and Mordecai had been in training together nearly a decade ago. It made sense; they were both in their late thirties. But that was all we learned about him, because he was quick to part ways. He couldn't risk being around us too long because it meant risking the six months of progress he'd made undercover. The less connected we were, the better.

Mordecai insisted on filling out all of the paperwork himself. We sat around the table on the main floor of the inn again in silent observation as he swiped a pen on page after page, scarcely looking up as we ate breakfast. A few hours later, we cleared out of the inn and met with Jurian, the man in charge of the vineyards in the city, and followed him to where all of the workers resided; we moved into a separate building from the palace with all of the other workers, but Jurian insisted on leading us through the palace so that we could get our bearings first.

It was a good thing Mordecai was doing most of the talking. Approaching the palace from the streets was like walking up to the base of a cliff—a vast, layered assembly of cliffs, actually; I regularly needed to remind myself to close my own jaw. But once we were inside, I doubted I would have been able to remember my name, if someone had asked.

White marble walls towered above us. Sounds bounced across the high ceilings. Doorways weren't doorways, but smooth stone archways with carvings wrapping up their height; some were open and some had massive wooden doors attached. Everything was bright, and huge, and smelled like an open quarry of salt and stone.

Harris walked beside me. I felt less ridiculous watching him, too, gape at everything we passed.

"So, you're all from Millfort?" asked Jurian. He adjusted one of the brass buttons on his plum-colored sleeve as we rounded the corner into a wider, longer hallway.

That was another thing; everyone here wore so many colors. I'd never seen so many different shades of violet, red, blue, and green in my whole life. We'd passed a woman earlier wearing a flowing dress that was somehow the *exact* shade of blue in the sky, as if they'd plucked the yards of fabric right out of the air to make it.

"Yes, we're from Millfort," answered Mordecai. He was a better actor than I expected, because the gruff tiredness in his tone from this morning was nowhere to be found as he carried on with Jurian. He actually sounded *pleasant*, as he stuck to the falsified backstory Cedric had instructed us to use in conversation. A backstory that didn't have a single connection or mention of Brighton.

They carried on about the climate and Millfort's economy for a bit before Jurian asked, "Do you plan on staying here, or will you all eventually return home?"

"We'll see. It depends on what happens with Millfort's labor strikes," said Mordecai.

He was still talking politics as he turned right, through a massive set of open wooden doors; each one was nearly three people tall and almost a foot thick, donning carvings of the national crest on each side.

They guarded what was probably the largest room I had ever seen. Granite pillars lined either side of the space, covered by ornate designs and highlighted by embossed rings of gold. To the left were long, colorful tapestries, and to the right were arching rows of windows that looked out over most of the hillside and the ocean. The light poured through them, casting long shadows and making the smooth marble floor glow. The guards, servants, and civilians already inside were like small decorations, their voices drowned out by the sheer size of everything.

Now even Evander looked around with wide eyes and an open mouth.

I didn't hear a word of Mordecai and Jurian's conversation as we made our way through the space. On the right, three guards were chatting near one of the massive windows. One of them was over a head taller than everyone else in the room and had a wide, dignified stance. His skin was dark, maybe even more than Harris'. There was an array of medals pinned across his chest, glinting against the green uniform as he stood with the immense authority of a mountain.

I fought back a smile after I pictured the tall, foreboding guard picking up Mordecai and hurling him into one of the pillars like a ragdoll, and the prince of Brighton, too.

"That's the Navy-captain, Banor," explained Jurian, since all of us had apparently been staring toward the impossible-to-miss man.

"I've never seen anybody so tall," observed Taz, as he peeked around Harris.

Jurian chuckled as we continued, "And you probably never will again. He's a delight—one of the nicest people I've ever met. But he's also the captain for a reason."

"Yeah, the enemy would shit themselves into oblivion if they saw him coming," remarked Evander.

Mordecai shot a tight-lipped, scathing glare of warning across our ranks.

We were shown down many flights of stairs and many other hallways in the palace (the basics, according to Jurian) before we crossed a section of the palace grounds to the workers quarters. The separate building extended out from the main grounds like a giant arm toward the vast patchwork of green and tawny fields. After being designated into rooms, Jurian gave us a cheerful "welcome to Angel's Landing" and encouraged us to start wandering around. He emphasized, "This palace takes some getting used to, so you may as well start now. Getting lost a few times is par for the course."

"Thank you," Mordecai had replied with an easy smile. One that didn't match the dark shadows already forming beneath his eyes.

We had made it through two days in Angel's Landing without messing up. But this had been the easy part, and I could feel the balancing act beginning. The unsteady sway of my nerves was just the same as if I'd stepped up to the edge of a balcony without a rail.

IT WAS a rare thing to see Mordecai, the poised, expert soldier, the steady, unyielding teacher, look afraid.

After a short quest to learn some more of our surroundings, the shadows below his eyes had darkened by a few shades. Maybe it was the fact that he wouldn't let us out of his sight for a second, or perhaps it was the unshakeable presence of Dale's power that was crushing him bit by bit. Probably both. Regardless, he insisted we all go for a short walk just before the sun started setting. It had the illusion of calm, the same way a diplomatic meeting over a clean table with a platter of cheese had the illusion of civility.

We followed one of the wide, turning paths that cut through the palace grounds toward the coliseum and the neatly groomed training fields where soldiers were still working tirelessly.

Mordecai's eyes did not stop moving for a second, scanning every wall, every reaching tree, every green flag, and every wandering sentinel as we pressed onward.

"So, you're trying to tell us that we're all in over our heads?" Malcolm chided, holding Mordecai in the corner of his vision. "You remember that it was *your* idea to come here, right?"

"We aren't in over our heads," Mordecai replied, "this is merely a well-deserved reality check. Now I'm doing my job and ensuring that you all recognize that fact as well."

Evander's green eyes narrowed. "Any other moron in the world could have told you that. Haven't any of the leaders in Brighton had their heads out of their asses long enough to know that Dale could crush their army like a bug? I'm surprised it took this long for you to see that."

"We aren't completely helpless," Mordecai insisted, with a firm glance over his shoulder.

"Aren't you?" Harris nodded ahead at the training fields and the ranks of trainees, all of them with grins on their faces and determination in their hearts—something Brighton's army was severely lacking. "The best soldier at Fort Ketta wouldn't last a second against one of them."

"Well then it's a good thing half of the people at Fort Ketta are mostly for numbers, not necessarily for skill," replied Mordecai.

I wrinkled my nose as I repressed a grimace.

"We're meant to be mowed down and trampled so that the rest of Brighton's army has a chance; yes, we know," Taz remarked.

Mordecai's eyes narrowed. "Nothing about what's happening is that simple. I can assure you Brighton is *well* aware of what they're up against. We may not have soldiers like Dale's, but we have other resources on the way."

I asked, "Like what?"

"I'm not at liberty to say," Mordecai bit out.

The training soldiers were closer now, as the path straightened out past the wall that guarded the edge of the gardens. The clang of swords and shields echoed up the arching, elaborate white walls of the coliseum.

Armor glinted in the fading light as one of the sparring soldiers reached out with one massive arm, lifting their opponent easily, and cast them across the grass like a bag of rice. They were both laughing as he staggered back to his feet and twirled his sword.

Nearly all of them were like that; tall, wide, built like statues, and trained to have the strength of giants. The kind of men and women who could crush a skull by accident, or rip a door off its frame with their bare hands.

"You see how strong this place is?" Mordecai continued, this time more quietly, and with a precautionary glance all around. "We need to be more careful than we ever planned to be. One misstep is all it's going to take to destroy what little advantage Brighton has, at least until there's been more time."

Time for what, I wondered. Time could mend things, but I wasn't sure it could conjure raw power from thin air.

Over the edge of the hillside, above more white, rocky cliffs on the northern side of Angel's Landing, the ends of several long docks could be seen. A few ships steadily crossed through the waves beyond them. They were relatively small, with plain white sails and long oars fitted through the sides. As they moved, despite the distance, I could see the gleam of metal carving through the ocean in front of the bow, and the darkened shape of something continuing below the water.

"That's where they keep their military ships?" I asked, nodding in their direction. "In a separate harbor on the north side?"

"Yeah," Mordecai said, "They can steer them into caves down there so they don't get beaten up in storms."

My eyes were still squinted against the evening glare as I pressed, "Their ships seem different. Is there something added to the front?"

"Oh, you didn't know," Mordecai shook his head, turning toward the sight of the palace walls. "They have metal battering rams on the bow; all they have to do is steer that thing into an enemy ship, and it will tear a hole through the framework and sink it."

Evander nodded, "It's true. That's why practically the whole world knows about their navy."

Malcolm peered at the distant ships and shook his head. "Then this war is going to be worse than we thought."

From the glint in Mordecai's eye and his mention of some *other resources* I figured we didn't even know the half of it.

CHAPTER TEN

A blanket of cold hovered close to the ground. Pale sunlight had only just cut across the sky, birds chirped, and milky drifts of fog slowly retreated toward the sea.

I didn't mind the early hour—I'd hardly slept as it was. I spent most of the night contemplating the delicate balance happening all around us, staring up at the pristine white ceiling above my bed. Each room was large enough to hold the essentials—which felt shockingly excessive and grand after spending several days packed into a tent with five other people, and then an inn with rooms the size of a horse stall. But now I had the luxury of a bed that didn't make my bones ache, a small table, and much needed space to clear my mind.

All six of our rooms neighbored each other in a hallway on the first level of the worker's quarters, along with all the other field workers.

There were about a hundred of us as we walked out into the clear, cold morning air. Two dozen, including Mordecai, went west to the far side of the fields where they would sort and organize the crops that the rest of us collected throughout the day.

We would work six days out of every seven, and we were designated specific sections of the fields that we needed to cover. The sooner we finished, the sooner we could get to dealing with our real, slightly more pressing job.

Harris, Malcolm, Taz, Evander, and I followed the wide dirt path around the palace as it curved south, where a long swath of earth had been groomed into neat rows of grapevines. It was easily the largest vineyard I had ever seen—even larger than some of the ones in Salona, where the supply of wine was always somehow in need of restocking.

The long rows of green ended near the edge of the large hill that the palace sat on, butting up to part of the wall that surrounded the palace and its gardens, and overlooking some of the smaller towns farther inland.

Workers split off in clusters, walking down between rows of crops to their designated sections for the day.

"This is quite a lot," Evander commented. He put up his hand to shield his eyes from the rising sun. "Are the five of us going to be enough to get it done?"

Taz shrugged, "It can't be that bad. We have most of the day to do it." He was pulling a large wheelbarrow behind him made of wood and molded metal. In it were the small knives we would all use to cut the bundles of grapes from their vines.

"I'd take this over doing Brighton's dirty work any day," I resolved.

Harris nodded. "The only question is, if we finish ahead of schedule, will they let us have some of the wine?"

Malcolm picked up one of the knives, approaching the nearest section of vines. "It's possible. But wouldn't drunkenness and spying not be the safest combination?"

Evander was already eating the grapes. "You never know—maybe it would help."

I chose a knife of my own. "It's probably for the best. Too much wine gives me a headache anyway."

Some of the clusters of grapes were small and green; the ones we needed to cut down were all rich purples and crimson red. It was almost a shame to think that they were going to be crushed up.

Work progressed at a decent speed throughout the morning. We split into two teams, and raced each other to the end of the next section of grapevines; so far it was a tie. Harris, Taz, and I just started a new row.

Harris noted, "You and Malcolm are getting along better than when we were at the smaller camp."

"Yeah, I think we are," I agreed.

"The truce is holding strong?" Taz asked.

I ran my tongue around the outside of my teeth. The writing on that scrap of paper flashed through my mind, and the sketch of the star in red ink. I hadn't known about it when we made that agreement; I only wished I'd shown it to someone who could actually read before I decided to confront Malcolm about it. But I simply answered, "So far."

Harris tossed a bundle of grapes past me and into the wheelbarrow. "At least there hasn't been another fight." The glance from the corner of his eye carried the reminder of what had nearly happened the first time, how Mordecai had chosen to give us a warning instead of using us as another example, like Everett.

"I haven't forgotten how serious the situation is here, don't worry." I went back to work, shook my head, and added, "It's better if we both avoid losing our tempers over it again."

"I'M BUSY," Mordecai growled, not looking up from the long wooden table that was buried underneath piles of different crops. "You take it to the kitchen."

I sulked at him over the bushel of apples he'd shoved into my hands. "This isn't my job, just send someone else to do it." Taz was waiting behind me with the now-empty wheelbarrow we'd hauled over. The first of what would probably be many. The two of us had just finished emptying it at the appropriate sorting table, about to return to our designated jobs in the vineyard, when Mordecai had seen his chance to dump some of his work onto our shoulders.

Long wooden tables stretched the length of the fence beside the palace, with about ten people working at each one to organize the mountains of crops and put them into baskets. Many were walking past, either carrying something or returning from dropping something off at speedy paces.

Mordecai paused his task of shuffling apples to one side of the table, and what appeared to be corn to the other, to shoot me a stern look. "In case you can't tell, everyone else is also busy at the moment. The kitchen isn't that far, just take the damn basket!"

The older woman working to his right looked over, a questioning eyebrow raised.

Well, aren't you in a lovely mood?

I smiled through the urge to say it out loud, keeping up the act of a harmless worker. "Of course."

The woman blinked once and went back to her work. Mordecai was maintaining his stern glare, nodding for me to go. I curled my lip at him as I lifted the full weight of the basket from the corner of the table where it had been resting.

The faintest ache bit into my still-healing shoulders and back. Bruises from that fateful brawl on the mountainside, when we first left for Fort Ketta, lingered.

"Should I go too?" offered Taz.

"Don't worry about it. This won't take long."

He shrugged, walking back through the crowd and doing his best not to run over any toes with the wheelbarrow. I fell into stride behind several others who were carrying things. I had no idea where the kitchen was, but I assumed they did.

There was a door situated into the outer wall of the palace that I followed them through, and I recognized it from our first walk-through with Jurian. I kept pace down a long corridor and a flight of stairs before the set of doors that guarded the kitchen came into view.

The kitchen was not nearly as big as the great hall, but it was still sprawling. The wall opposite the door was made of large bricks, rising all of the way above the heads of workers to where short windows lined up with the level of the ground outside. They opened on hinges and had been left open to allow in more fresh air. From the floor, only the pale blue sky was visible through the glass. In the center of the room was a fireplace that towered all of the way up to the ceiling, and long tables were set up in rows on either side. It was just as bustling as the station outside, if not more.

I weaved my way around people to one of the nearest tables, wanting the heavy basket out of my hands sooner than later. I heaved the mass of apples onto an empty section and waited for my shoulders to adjust.

Some of the other carriers stretched their arms above their heads and chatted briefly before they went back to collect more.

The muscle connecting my neck to my left shoulder was furious with me, and I tilted my head as the ache dissipated.

A glimpse of light blonde hair in the corner of my eye snared my attention; not just blonde, but a golden white that reminded me of rays of sunlight. A girl walked through the large wooden doors, a bright, beaming smile on her face and a bundle of herbs in her hand.

One by one, I started taking apples out of the basket. If I was here, I might as well make use of the time.

She made elegant work of ducking between people and out of the paths of busy workers. Her willowy frame certainly helped with that, slipping through some of the narrower gaps in the crowd.

"Elise, I got the basil and mint that you needed," she announced to a servant working at one of the far tables, as she handed her the bundles of greenery. The other girl had light brown hair, and her arms were coated with flour as she worked to knead a lump of dough.

"Thank you so much," the brunette—Elise—said as she accepted them. "I would have gotten it myself but I just knew I wasn't going to have the chance." She dusted off one of her hands on her apron, "Sorry for pestering you."

"Don't be silly," the girl with sunlight hair dismissed it with the wave of a hand, "I know you're busy. I just happened to be less busy."

Elise rolled her eyes. "Oh please. Don't pretend that what you do isn't far more important than baking bread."

Why am I still piling apples? Procrastinating? What does it matter?

"I should get going," said the blonde girl as she started walking back along the row of tables, "and bring me a piece of that bread when it's done."

"Will do, madam!" exclaimed Elise, making a salute with one hand and leaving a streak of flour across her forehead.

She laughed at her friend, a beautiful sound as she continued to the doors.

I directed my attention back to the task at hand, surprised to find that I was nearly done. I took out the last four apples and set them atop the pile, picking up the now easy-to-carry basket. I'd save someone the trouble of having to tote it back outside for another round.

I made my way through throngs of people going in and out of the kitchen, back into the hallway that led out to the fields. As I turned right, I was unable to stop myself from looking back. It would be difficult to miss the cascading waves of light blonde hair going the other direction. She made everyone around her look dull and dim, like a shining glass amidst tarnished pots and pans.

I bumped into a man carrying a full basket, and apologized as he shoved past me, working hard not to drop any of the contents. I quickly decided that I should probably pay more attention to where I was going.

I handed off the empty basket to another organizer and returned to the vineyard, where the rest of the afternoon went by in a blur. The sun had moved the vast shadow of the palace enough so that we could work in warmth—which was helpful as we finished the last row of grapevines.

From there, I returned to my room to take a break and try to sort out my thoughts, grateful for the door that I could put between me and the rest of the world. Lying on my back, I stared up at the plain ceiling above my bed, frowning through the storm in my mind. The presence of Brighton's leverage, their threats on Nickolai's life, hovered over my shoulder like the cold shadow of a dead man; I could feel it lingering there no matter where I went. And the reminder of the tattoos—the agreement I made with Malcolm—it was like a burn, or a scratch that was just deep enough to leave a red mark. If I could wash it off, I would. If I could dismiss it as a coincidence, I would. If there was some way I could train myself not to notice the nauseating sensation that washed over me every time I considered what it was, I would. But I could not. The tattoos were far too deliberate for that. And Malcolm had to know...

AFTER OUR FIRST day in the vineyards was done, we started simple: by walking. We wandered down hallways and climbed stairs until the air was heavy with the fact that we were somewhere we didn't belong. Brighton demanded information on Dale, and there was only one way to get it.

Harris led the way as Evander and I followed close behind. The hallway curved with the outer edge of one of the palace's enormous towers, windows gaping out at the distant waves.

Most of the higher-ups were out somewhere running a nation, leaving some important places unattended. The few people we did pass, either servants or guards making rounds, didn't bother to stop us. We didn't seem threatening. A smile with an extra ounce of effort could work wonders.

I paused beside a set of wooden double doors that, unlike the rest we had passed in the hallway, were open. The fragrance of paper would be difficult to miss in the expanses of muted, white stone. There was no sound coming from inside. It was empty.

I nodded, and we slipped through the doors before closing them in our wake. The soft click of the latch was reassuring. Stealing behind a closed door would be far easier than sneaking things out from underneath people's noses.

A long table ran the length of the room, coated by organized stacks of papers and files. It sat atop a pale green rug with flowering designs. On the farthest wall there was a tapestry depicting the view of the palace from the ocean with a fade of sunset behind it.

I turned back to the papers on the table, biting my lip.

Harris was already rooting through a stack of folders across from me. "This is a lot scarier than stealing pies."

I chuckled, and started browsing through the nearest collection of papers. "I actually miss that." The onerous lessons I took at the orphanage were faded and far back in my memory. I recognized the shapes of a few letters, especially the ones I was used to seeing on signs in Salona, as I frowned at the words.

I quickly gave up with the stack I'd started with, sighing as I surveyed the rest of the orderly papers. It all had to be sorted somehow? There had to be something that *looked* more important than the rest of it?

Evander walked along the side of the table, thumbing over some of the closer piles. "Let's not forget that a kid dies if we get caught."

With that, the quiet shuffle of pages sped up.

I crossed to the far end of the table, closest to the doors, and searched through a pile of letters. That was the first order of business Mordecai had outlined; correspondence. *Anything that indicates what nations Dale works closely with.*

After all, wax seals were easier to read than words.

I made my way close to the bottom of the stack, flopping letters to the side since nothing appeared to be worth my attention. There were about six letters from the Orvalian government, which would make sense because they had a trade agreement, and one or two from some other countries farther south.

The sight of red wax jarred my frustrations. There, plain as day, was Brighton's menacing national seal stamped into crimson wax. The paper was of a good quality, with a smooth texture and no evident tares.

I picked it up. There was nothing written on it, no sweeping signatures or stamps on the back side or any of the corners. It looked plain and unimportant.

But why is it here?

"This doesn't seem right," I thought aloud, as Harris and Evander joined me.

Evander frowned and pointed at the wax. "That seal is something only specific people can use. Only someone with some degree of importance could use it on a letter."

"But why would anyone in Brighton send something to Dale?" asked Harris, as he rearranged the rest of the stack that I'd disturbed. "Especially since they know war is coming. Mail ships cross once a week, so it has to be recent..."

I shrugged, "Maybe it's an act, or something like that?"

After another moment of staring at the letter, Evander jutted a thumb to the closed office doors. "I say it's enough to start. Let's get out of here."

I tucked the letter from Brighton into my shirt as we opened the doors, leaving everything almost exactly as it had been before.

We took a brisk pace down the hallway, and by the time we were halfway to the turn, distant bits of conversation made their way around the corner ahead.

Evander cursed under his breath.

I worked my nerves down, leveling my breathing so that I looked and sounded as innocent as possible. A calm demeanor and an even tone were the best ways to mask a lie.

We silently agreed that we were far enough from the doors that we wouldn't seem incriminating, and slowed to a natural pace.

A pair of guards rounded the corner, I assumed in a rotation of shifts, and squinted across the length of the hallway at us.

"What are you doing up here?" the taller one asked.

An easy smile shifted onto Evander's face as he said, "I know, I know—we shouldn't be here. We took a wrong turn somewhere and started going in circles."

"Oh," the guard conceded, his shoulders relaxing. They were probably used to seeing people get lost in this maze of a palace. "Well, keep going down this hallway, take a left, and the first stairs on the right will take you back to one of the main levels."

"Thanks," I replied as they continued past us.

I couldn't resist a little bit of a smile as we rounded the corner, listening to their boots clunking across the stone farther and farther away. They didn't even bother to ensure that we actually left this level.

The three of us shared a glance, and I knew we were all thinking the same thing; Dale was a strong nation, but they were overly relaxed about it. Enough for it to count as a crack in their heavy, gold-accented armor. If they weren't actively keeping an eye out for trouble, then it would make getting away with things so much easier.

Stealing pies, in fact, had been more challenging than this.

CHAPTER ELEVEN

After assembling the rest of our crew in Harris' room, with the exception of Mordecai, we explained the strange letter to Malcolm and Taz. All we had left to decide was whether or not to open it.

Evander shrugged, saying, "How bad could it be? Mordecai can notify Brighton to send another one if it turns out to be nothing—but if it is, then we're doing exactly what we're supposed to, and we already have something to bring back to them."

I stood with my back to the door, twirling the letter around in my hand. "And they can't hurt us if we're doing our job." Or Nickolai.

Taz's arms were crossed as he stood beside Evander, but he nodded. "Then let's open it."

I pulled the wax seal, freeing the outer flap, and unfolded it to reveal a short group of words. I blinked at it, not bothering to try to decipher the sweeping, frantically scrolled letters. I could at least see that there were only three sentences, which was unusually brief, and that there was no signature at the bottom.

"Well?" Harris pried, elbowing me.

I passed the paper to him, and waited as he read it aloud.

"This is an urgent warning to everyone living and working in Dale.

There is an attack being planned for a month from now to disable a large portion of your naval fleet," he said. "The king and other leaders in Brighton are planning a full-scale invasion—and they have a new weapon called Nightfire."

I stood motionless as the words slowly took hold.

Malcolm cringed. "Thank god you guys found that thing before anyone saw it."

"Yeah, the people back in Brighton would have assumed we were the ones to deliver a warning. They wouldn't wait to learn details or the fact that it came from a letter," I agreed. "Three days here, and we all would have been…"

"*Unequivocally fucked* is the phrase you're looking for," remarked Evander, but his face was dead-serious.

Taz was gnawing on his lip and shaking his head. "Well, maybe there's a rat back in Brighton who sent it, or someone here knows what's happening and disguised the letter to be from Brighton in order to protect themselves."

"That, and maybe the writer knows we're here?" Harris suggested. "They could be using us to take the blame for them."

Cold spread through my guts at the thought.

"Could their existing spy have done this?" Evander crossed his arms.

Taz shook his head. "Why would he? Other than us, he's the most obvious one to blame—he'd be a fool to do something like this."

Malcolm took the letter from Harris and frowned at the words. He flipped the paper over for good measure, ensuring that the other side was blank. "It seems authentic. It would take a lot of time and effort to carve out such a detailed stamp for the wax. We don't have the time or the tools for that, and neither does their other spy."

"So hopefully it's a rat? Someone who already had an official stamp?" It was my own wishful thinking, but it made enough sense to soothe my nerves. As long as it wasn't somebody in Angel's Landing, we had a chance.

"It's definitely real," Taz agreed. "Look at it. No one could create such an accurate forgery here."

Malcolm's brows furrowed as he gazed at the floor. "But who would have the time for it in Brighton? Everyone close to the war effort is in Fort Ketta, constantly being watched by the people in the towers."

"Unless it's someone who doesn't need to be watched—someone higher up." It seemed so simple, and yet it made everything ten times worse. More importantly, it meant that we needed to be very careful of who we showed it to once we got back; *if* we made it back. It could be anyone. Hell, it could even be Mordecai. Maybe he was so resistant to coming here because he was the one who sent it and didn't want to be on the scene of the crime when it was found?

Harris sighed. "Well, what do we do with it?"

"This is the kind of leverage we need—to show Dale what's coming and stop Brighton," reminded Taz. "We can take it to one of the high-ranking guards and stop this before it gets any worse. As long as we explain the threats hanging over us—"

"It's too much of a risk," Malcolm argued. "If the people at Fort Ketta even get an inkling that something's wrong on our end, they'll kill Nickolai. They won't wait to learn details if news arrives that Dale received a warning—leaving it up to Brighton's interpretation will end badly. We also broke the seal," he tapped on the split, bent dot of wax. "In theory, we could have tampered with the writing before showing it to anyone here. And how we found it to begin with isn't exactly honorable—that's assuming they believe us at all."

I was already massaging my brow and wishing away the early signs of a headache.

Harris cut in, "We can't reverse opening it, but we can find a place to keep it until we figure out what to do. Maybe it isn't a total loss..."

"I'll find a place for the letter. I saw it first, so it's only fair," I grumbled.

Without a word, Malcolm passed the paper into my hand.

"Where are you going to hide it?" asked Evander.

"I'll keep it on me until I figure that out."

Taz jutted a thumb toward the closed door, "What about Mordecai? Do we tell him?"

The silence, as we stared around at each other, was answer enough.

"What he doesn't know can't hurt us," I tucked the paper into my shirt, right next to the tattoo.

DESPITE THE FACT that the sun had nearly disappeared below the edge of the ocean, it was still warm outside. The long shadows of trees and other greenery in the palace gardens, just beyond the north wing, made for easy concealment as I tried to outwalk my thoughts. I needed to put as much distance between myself and the looming palace as possible.

But the letter, tucked safely into my shirt, wasn't letting me gain much of a lead.

Mordecai had joined us not long after we finished discussing it, and the first *spying conference* had gone as expected; we would be compiling all of our findings after each bi-weekly meeting under a floorboard in Mordecai's room that he'd managed to pry up. In the time between said meetings, we were to hide the information we collected on us—in pockets, shoes, and so forth. If we eventually decided to tell Mordecai about the letter, we could hide it amongst the other things we gathered.

I followed one of the many dirt paths through the gardens that curved around clusters of trees and flowers, savoring the smell of fresh soil. Checking over my shoulder, I was pleased to find that the towering white walls of the palace's northern face, at last, were blocked from view by the greenery.

The path straightened out, lined on either side by short trees. Their dark leaves were beginning to fall, and moats of them had gathered on the dirt. Ahead, the organized ranks of shrubs stopped as the path split in two, arching around where a larger, elegantly curved tree sat. Its branches reached across the space to form a natural dome that blocked out the sky. Small, pink flowers clung to the branches. A ring of stones had been placed into a neat circle, marking where the tree's tangle of roots clawed their way below the ground so that no one tripped over them.

The flowers gave off a sweet smell that wasn't overpowering, but faint and soothing. The branches acted as a natural roof, trapping the warmth from earlier in the day underneath.

I wouldn't mind hiding from the world out here, I decided.

After one final glance at my surroundings, I ventured along the far edge of the path, looking through the neat rows of trees that continued beyond. Hedges grew just high enough to obscure the view of what was on the other side, making the idea of wandering around in a tranquil bliss tempting. Maybe I would wander for a while longer. *Why not?*

As I came around to the opposite side of the tree, I noticed someone sitting below it. I startled and a curse slipped off my tongue.

It was the girl I'd seen bringing herbs into the kitchen earlier today, neatly perched on a rock that the roots diverted around, an open book resting on her knees. Her golden-white hair was swept over one shoulder as she glanced up at me, the corners of her mouth tilting up into a soft smile.

I took a deep breath as a cold rush faded down my back and laughed a little at my own stupidity. "Sorry—you scared me."

"Well, in your defense, I do blend in quite well," she kicked out a section of her green dress which would, in fact, be easy to lose in the shrubs of the garden.

"Is that on purpose?"

"Occasionally." She smiled and tilted her head, "But not today."

It may have been the first time I genuinely laughed since being in Dale—even since being a part of Brighton's schemes, for that matter. "I'll keep that in mind, assuming I see you again?"

"I think you will."

It had been years since I'd had to pause and think about what to say to a girl. Usually, I just went with whatever came to mind first— but that was because things came to mind. My thoughts went joyfully blank when I looked at her.

"Well, I'll let you get back to your reading, in the meantime."

She gave a nod of her head, and a gracious smile. "Thank you."

With a smile of my own, I continued down the path toward the rest of the garden.

"Goodnight," I said over my shoulder.

"Goodnight," she answered.

THE MINUTE the sun sank below the line where water met the sky, the cold took over. The ground turned hard and frigid, and the trees on the far end of the garden did their best to break apart the icy breeze that had picked up.

I hadn't been out for more than an hour, but I figured Mordecai was already scheming to tear my head off the second he tracked me down. Any time he couldn't keep an eye on us a little bit more of him frayed apart. A lot could go wrong in an hour. And he was bound to assume that I was up to no good.

I should probably get back, before he has the chance to get even angrier...

I'd walked the north side of the garden, which ran three quarters the length of the palace. The northeast corner looked out over the bustling hillside, down to where the docks were. A few small ships sat on the water, and the closer streets were slowly becoming quieter. It was a far cry from the streets in Salona where, if anything, things became louder after the sun was down.

In this part of the garden, trees stood in clusters, allowing for more open space where people could stand and look out at the world, what little of it they could see. Stone benches had been placed to look out over the top of the surrounding wall, which stood low enough down the hill so as not to obstruct the view. One of them was occupied.

Lounging across the presumably uncomfortable bench was Malcolm, frowning up at the sky.

I stopped, folding my arms to shield myself from the cold. "Well, at least I'm not going to be the only one in trouble when Mordecai interrogates me about where I've been. What are you doing out here?"

He half sat up, looking over, but quickly laid back down like a lazy cat. "I couldn't sleep."

"You didn't strike me as the somber, contemplating type."

He scoffed. "Do I look that somber?"

I gave a shrug, "It would be worse if you were fanning yourself."

We stared toward the east for a moment, toward Brighton and all of the people that wanted us to do their bidding.

"I've been meaning to ask you something," I revealed, looking down toward my feet.

He glanced my way, one eyebrow raised at the difference in my tone.

"I know we agreed not to talk about them..."

He sighed loudly, "And the one time I actually wasn't worried about it, you decide to bring them up."

"I don't know what else to do."

"We called a truce."

"I'm not going to fight you over them, I just want to talk," I insisted.

"Look, there's nothing for us to talk about," he maintained steadily. "I can't help you."

You're lying. You aren't doing it to hurt me, I know that now, you're just doing it to protect yourself from whatever it is you're afraid of.

I wanted to say it, and I wasn't completely sure why I didn't. I toed at the ground as I thought, chewing the inside of my cheek, struggling to decide which path to take next.

"I asked the woman who ran the orphanage about how I ended up there *once*—the day before I was old enough to leave," I finally said, and Malcolm continued to look up at the sky, acting like he wasn't listening. "She told me it was the first day it snowed that year, and I was left on the front doorstep in the middle of the night. My *obnoxious* screaming and crying woke her up. All I came with was a blanket and a slip of paper with my name on it. And a tattoo."

Malcolm kept his expression forcefully blank.

"That's all I know. I don't remember anything about that night. I have no idea who the people who left me were or why. They abandoned me there, giving her no choice but to *deal with me*, as she put it. So please, if you know anything, I would appreciate hearing it," I pleaded.

Malcolm spared one second to look at me before he stood up and walked down the path back toward the palace. "We're done talking about this."

He could have punched me in the stomach for the same effect. So, I took his place on the bench.

The mere thought of Mistress Helena, that mean, angry woman who ran the orphanage, opened up a void in my chest.

I was grateful that I didn't remember being planted on the cold stone step that sat in front of the main door. Or that I didn't remember waiting in the icy wind, watching someone, maybe my mom, turn their back and leave. It would have proved that wretched woman right; every time she lost her temper, she never failed to remind me that I was a hopeless cause.

CHAPTER TWELVE

E arly morning, with its cold, white-wine rays of light, arrived far too soon. I hadn't gone to bed until long after I should have, and now I was going to pay for it. A lack of sleep, unfortunately, did not count as a valid excuse to waste a day—especially if Mordecai had any say in the matter. Last night, he'd thoroughly questioned me about where I vanished to after our shifts ended, and this morning, he'd already gotten the chance to harangue me for moving sluggishly in the hallway.

I was happy when we went our separate ways to work for the morning. He was still stranded at the sorting tables, and the rest of us had been moved one plot over to the cotton fields. I made it a point to start at the far end, away from Malcolm and the lack of sleep that was also etched into his face; shadows hung below his eyes like stains. I concentrated on work instead, tearing off clumps of white fluff and throwing them into a bag. It ate away at the hours efficiently until, before I knew it, I was working side by side with the person I least wanted to talk to.

"I understand why you are angry," he finally conceded, after a while of listening to the wind.

Now it was my turn to pretend I was ignoring him.

"You can't expect me to tell you everything you think you need to know," Malcolm pressed on, "But it's my past, and it's up to me to decide what to do with it."

Everything I *thought* I needed to know? I pulled off a wad of cotton too forcefully, snapping a twig. "Did I ask you to hand over your entire life? No. I've only asked *one* question."

"And I don't have an answer."

I ground my teeth together. My temper thrashed in its cage, on the verge of tearing through the iron bars that I had carefully placed around it, and I was tempted to let it out.

His face tightened into a warning as he watched me.

"I'm running out of patience with you," I hissed. "You're kidding yourself if you think I can't recognize a lie when I see one—I don't care how good your gambling face is."

He pressed his brows together and turned his attention back to the cotton plants. "Keep this up and I'm definitely not going to tell you what I know."

My jaw fell down despite my best attempts to keep it shut. "You admit it!"

It was a blind reach at best, but it was something, a frail strand of the truth. I knew it when I saw his jaw clamp, too late to catch what was already said. And now I was going to hold on for all it was worth.

A few rows away, Harris, Evander, and Taz peeked cautiously over the top of their section of cotton plants.

"No, I did not!" he argued, a muscle in his neck pulling tight.

"Yes, you did! I just saw it—you practically went pale!"

"You're jumping to conclusions!"

"No, you're just lying to yourself."

His fist flew and struck me across the face. It sent me a step sideways, and I blinked as my head took a moment to make sense of what happened.

Now Malcolm actually was pale, standing rigidly as he watched me, like a guilty child who had just broken an expensive jar.

I tasted blood, and I wiped some of the red off of my lips, laughing at it a little, at the twisting, writhing sensation trapped in my chest. I tossed my half-full bag of cotton into the dirt and whirled my hand through the air, striking him. He cursed and wiped the blood from his lip onto the back of his hand.

"There," I contended. "Matching bloody lips to go with the matching tattoos."

He managed a short breath of laughter. "You just can't be persuaded, can you? You asshole!"

I put up a hand as I secured my grip on my anger, perhaps a bit too tightly, but it was better than nothing.

I'm not going to lose my temper.

Malcolm shoved me back a step, "Go on! Hit me again!"

I clamped my teeth together as I forced my hands to remain at my sides.

I'm not going to do it.

"You said it yourself, we need to settle this, so let's settle it!" He pushed me again. "Or are you too cowardly to finish the things you start!"

His words and my silence exploded into a tangle of punches and shoving before another second could pass, and we were both a thrashing heap in the dirt by the time Taz and Harris tried to pry us apart.

Taz used my own arm like a leash to hold me back while Harris stepped into the narrow gap between us and shoved us apart.

"That's enough, both of you!" Harris shouted, keeping both arms extended in case one of us decided to lunge forward.

I spat past his head, aiming for Malcolm, but missed by a considerable margin.

Malcolm cracked a condescending smile at my poor attempt.

"I thought you both were past this!" scolded Harris.

There was a sharp, burning sensation from a scrape on my left cheek that I didn't appreciate, as the anger retreated back into its cage. Malcolm had a small, bleeding cut on his forehead.

The heads of other workers that had been in hearing distance peered over the tops of the lines of cotton plants. Most were too far to discern an expression, but I could imagine each one regardless.

Taz looked to Evander. "Take them inside while we try to clean up this mess. We don't need them getting blood all over everything." He kicked my bag that I had thrown to the ground, and small balls of cotton tumbled across the dirt, riding on the breeze.

Evander rolled his green eyes, but complied anyway, shoving Malcolm ahead of him. I wrenched my arm free of Taz's grasp and trailed behind them, wiping my hand across my face, not surprised to see it come away streaked red.

Great. Fantastic. Could today possibly get any better?

"You're lucky Mordecai didn't see that. He'd strangle both of you to death," Evander commented.

"Yeah, yeah, I guess we should just start digging our graves now, right?" Malcolm remarked. "Cut out the middleman?"

The ache of a fresh bruise was slowly spreading across my right shoulder. Fortunately, most of the damage had been isolated to my face. Shallow scrapes would mend faster.

I sighed. "That's certainly one way to settle it."

None of us spoke for the rest of the walk back to the palace. I trailed behind Malcolm and Evander down the long corridor that passed the kitchen, where we earned quite a few solicitous glances from the people that we passed. Evander paused to ask for directions to the infirmary. From there we took a right, climbed a set of stairs, and went down another long hallway to the farthest set of doors on the right.

They opened to a long room with high ceilings. Lined on either side were cots, most of which were unoccupied. The few people that were there looked ill beyond repair, with pale skin and rings of darkness hanging below their eyes. Across the length of the room, on the far side, there were tall, arched windows looking out over the top of the white cliffs. Beyond that, the view was miles of blue water extending south.

"Is this really necessary?" I asked. "I can fix my own wounds with a washcloth, without taking up space in an infirmary."

Evander looked over his shoulder to respond before Malcolm

could. "If this humiliates you both enough, maybe you won't do it again, yeah?"

Malcolm scoffed and sat down on the closest cot. I crossed to the opposite side of the room, with Evander still trailing between us, and plopped myself down as well.

"*Humiliation?* Interesting choice."

"Would you rather Mordecai found out about that scene you two caused?" he retaliated.

I bit my tongue to stop myself from making another remark and grimaced.

I caught sight of the girl I talked to the night before as she rounded the corner into the room, a sizable stack of papers in her hands, and her light blonde hair tied up neatly on the back of her head. She set the papers down on the end of the nearest cot and shook out her wrists from the strain.

I busied myself with attempting to wipe some of the blood off of my hands, and it did nothing except spread it around even more.

When I glanced up again, she was raising an inquisitive eyebrow at me and the streaks of blood that, I'm sure, were getting everywhere.

I shrugged, offering a guilty, blood smeared grin.

She narrowed her eyes at me in comical skepticism as she continued across the room, casting a brief, inquiring glance at Malcolm as she passed him.

Evander explained the altercation to an aid in a white apron before leaving us. I also noted that Evander was still wearing his sleeves long enough to cover the brand on his arm. I had only glimpsed it the one time, and he hadn't allowed for a second so far.

The girl from yesterday retrieved a cloth and a bowl of water as she walked, still eyeing me questioningly. "Seems like you've had an interesting start to the day."

"That's an understatement," I smirked.

She dipped the cloth into the water and held it out to me. "Are you in a lot of pain?"

"No," I took the cloth and shook my head. "It's just a scratch...or two."

She raised her eyebrows, smiling with one side of her mouth. "Or four, or five."

One pass over the side of my face with the cloth already left a smear of red across it. But the bleeding had mostly stopped, so that was an improvement, at least.

"The trick is to not keep count on that sort of thing. It makes it easier to salvage my dignity afterwards," I added.

She blinked stoically, a peaceful smile resting on her face. She had gray eyes, I noticed. They weren't cold or dark like steel, but more like the pastel gray on the inside of a seashell.

"I'll have to remember that, assuming this sort of thing happens often?" she asked.

I folded the cloth over, using a fresh side to clear away the remainder of the blood, and I couldn't resist a sly grin. "That all depends on what you call often." I winced through the final, faintly stinging pass of the washcloth and balled it up, since no more blood seemed to be coming off. "I think that's the last of it."

She took the bloody rag from me and nodded. "You got all of it. There is a small gash," she touched my cheek and squinted to examine the mark, "but it doesn't look like it will need stitches. So, you're all set to clobber someone else in the next few days," she remarked with a smile.

"Knowing my luck, it'll be the same person." I cast a peeved look across the room at Malcolm, who was busy cleaning his own face. "But it's better than punching a stranger in the fields. I've known him since when—" I caught the truth in my hands before it could fly away, "since when he cut the line on the dock back in Amphitrite."

Because that made perfect sense?

"Well, it's only polite to know someone's name before you punch them in the face," she winked.

As I looked at her, half of my thoughts were busy reviewing the lies I was supposed to stick to, the ones designed to divert attention away from the fact that I was here to help incite war. But the rest were wandering aimlessly, somewhere between her hair and her eyes.

"What's your name?" I inquired. "I just realized I didn't ask earlier

—not that I plan on getting into an altercation with you any time soon."

I could have slapped myself for that one.

She didn't seem to mind, because she extended a hand to me with a kind smile. "I'm Ithaca."

"Ignatius," I accepted her hand, giving it a gentle shake.

THE LONG HALLWAYS and arched ceilings of the palace were not as unsettling as they were on the first day. The expanses of cold marble and white stone felt much less foreign, but I was still miles away from being at ease. It was worse on the upper levels. Unfortunately, that was still precisely where we needed to go on the hunt for information.

Taz was with me this time, since Evander, Harris, and Malcolm were already far away scouring part of the north wing.

Most of the guards, as stern as they seemed, were more like decorations in the hallways. Their leniency could be earned with a smile and a simple excuse—and that was exactly how we found ourselves slinking through the same hallway past the conference room where I'd found the warning letter the day before.

It was busier than it had been that day; I could hear voices behind some of the doors that we passed. I was conscious of every breath and every beat of my heart as we continued onward. And all that stood between us and certain disaster were some wood and hinges.

I tried not to think about it. All we needed was another empty room, and some moderately useful papers that we could take back to Brighton—to prove that we had done as they instructed.

It didn't take long before we found an open door.

A glance down the rest of the hallway on either side confirmed that no one had seen us yet, so I figured it would be worth a try.

The room was cold, but not particularly large compared to the rest of the palace. It was enough to fit a table in the center, and each of the walls were lined with shelves of books. Most of them had old worn-out spines with dilapidated lettering, accompanied by the occasional stack of papers, which had perfumed the stuffy air.

The click of the door closing made it that much easier to breathe.

"You start on that wall," Taz said in a hushed tone, pointing to the left. "I'll start on this one and we can meet in the middle?"

"Seems fair," I agreed, and we started searching.

We could make the argument that this was purely for the sake of the job, that this was solely a means of collecting information for Brighton, but that was only part of the truth. But *part of the truth* was all Brighton had given us, even as spies. And nothing was stopping us from looking for answers. War always had a motive, and there were only so many places I could think to look for answers. This guarded, isolated room stuffed with books was one of them.

Any record of past quarrels between Brighton and Dale, or any other country, could be in here somewhere among the treaties and history records.

I perused the rows of books, doing my best to read the words scrolled across each of the dusty, worn spines. Taz, thankfully, was a more proficient reader than I was.

It could hardly be considered a gamble to think the impending war had something to do with the two royal families. Something personal. I would be the first to admit that I was nowhere close to a military expert, but I had enough sense to know that wars didn't usually start unless blood had already been spilled.

Gold lettering on a vermillion cover caught my eye. I assumed if it looked important, chances were that it was. I plucked the book off of its shelf and examined the front side where Dale's national seal sat proudly, embossed in the same gold as the words.

"Can you tell me what this says?" I asked, holding out the book for Taz.

He crossed the room and narrowed his eyes at the wording. "A history of the royal family."

I eyed the cover again, and opened it enough to flip through a few of the front pages. There were sections of normal text with large chunks of words running the width of the page, and other sections where there were neat rows of what looked to be names and then years or dates on corresponding rows.

"That could work," I decided, while Taz took the book and set it on the table.

"Have you seen anything worthwhile yet?" I asked as I turned my attention back to the shelves. I had almost scanned over half of the wall already.

"Not really...except..."

The sound of a heavy book being pulled off of its ledge filled in the answer to my question.

He swatted away a layer of dust as he read over the cover. "It looks like a book of death records." He flipped through a few of the pages, "There's a map of Dale and the main continent in the front, so I think it has things from different countries, which would also explain why it is so heavy." He lugged it over to the table and set it down.

"Do you want to start reading through it while I finish looking at the shelves?" I asked.

"And miss out on inhaling more dust?" he joked. "How could I resist?"

"I don't mind breathing in the rest of it on my own."

As I worked my way around the room, I placed a few other books of interest on the center table for Taz to skim through. He made much faster work of the pages than I could have, and by the time I reached the opposite side of the room, we had four that were of interest; one on death records, one on the history of the royal family, marriage, and family records, and a history book on the nation. The latter proved to be the least helpful. It only explained that Dale had no outstanding feuds with other countries, nor had it ever been in a complete war. It lived up to its reputation of isolated, strong, yet peaceful.

The book on the royal family, as well as the documentation of marriages, was also a dead end after some perusal. There were no marital connections between Brighton and Dale, which ruled out a lot of things as far as a motive for war.

The book of death records mainly covered the deaths of people from Dale, which made perfect sense. There were much shorter sections for other nations, consolidating things down to only the most noteworthy deaths. Brighton's section was near the back, and slightly longer than the others—for good reason.

I knew that Brighton's original royal family had been murdered twenty-two years ago, and that the current prince and his father had been the closest in line for the throne as replacements. I did not realize, however, how brutal the deaths had been. It was a mess of knives and fire dealt out by a small band of revolutionaries with an axe to grind. Taz skipped over the worst of the details as he read aloud.

All of the people who broke into the palace that night, who hadn't already been killed by guards, were hanged. So, they were irrelevant now. Brighton's new king was crowned, and a long stretch of peace followed. But the fact that Brighton had decided to attack Dale *now* meant some connection must have come up.

Taz stopped at the bottom of the page and aimed a searching look my way. "Nothing has changed recently that we know of, right?"

"Maybe the only thing that's changed is what Brighton knows?" I drummed my fingers on the table as I mulled over the instructions Mordecai had detailed for us at the inn, and one of the three items stood far above the rest. "Brighton must think that guy from the wanted poster—the former captain of their royal guard—is here in Dale. Mordecai said he's the one they hold responsible for the deaths of the royal family; and since all of the revolutionaries who initially attacked are dead..." I eyed the spread of open books in front of me. "He's the last piece. If they think he's here, then they must also think that Dale knows about it. They'd have to; a man with a reputation like that doesn't hide easily."

Taz closed the book, "You realize what that means?"

I nodded. "If we're right, then we've figured out why Brighton is going to war." I tore out a few pages from the history book, focusing on what Taz had indicated to be explanations of Dale's allies. Brighton could make use of that, to know who would be working against them when they did wage war. "We should go tell everybody else."

We returned the books to their rightful places, clearing the table, and went back out to the hallway.

I peered down the longer corridor, which was still inactive. The discussions happening in the conference rooms were continuing to drag on. Taz tucked the torn-out pages into his shoe as we started back from the way we came. If we were lucky, we would be on the main level again before the guards did their hourly rotation.

I sped up, thinking through our line of logic again for good measure, but the pieces fit together like a lock and key. The renegade revolutionaries who actually committed the murders were all dead, and the man who let them pass was still at large. And Mordecai did say it was possible he'd been working for the rebels for a long time, using his position and leverage to help them pull off the murders. Either way, there was no one left for Brighton's king to blame. A nation like Dale harboring the former captain spelled war no matter what angle you looked at it from.

The slight shift in my pulse came a moment too late, as my thoughts were interrupted by the sound of a door opening, footsteps, and two different voices making their way down the hallway toward us.

I swallowed down a wave of panic and searched for a place to hide. Taz halted and the color fell from his face like a heavy curtain.

I quickly crossed to the other side of the hallway and put my ear to the closest door. There were no voices on the other side, or none loud enough for me to hear. But it was better than barging into a busy conference room.

I tried the handle, jarred by the fact that it wasn't going to open. The lock held firm.

There was no time to curse at our rapidly declining luck. I rushed to the second closest door on the left. The handle didn't budge, all I did was create a loud thud as I rammed the door into its own frame.

My heart was beating in my throat. The footsteps were getting closer. I crossed to the last available door, rummaging through the few excuses I could think of.

Lost? No.

Looking for someone? Stupid.

What else? What else?

I twisted the handle and pulled harder than I probably should have, but this time the door gave way and opened.

I barely spared a second to look into the room. Somehow Taz managed to rush in before me, leaving me to do my best at closing the door without slamming it. Slow, careful movements were a difficult thing to accomplish in such a hurry.

I held my breath and waited, keeping a cautious ear close to the door. A secondary glance at the room, to my relief, confirmed that it was empty. The latch below the handle that controlled the lock was tempting, but the bolt sliding into place would cause too much of a sound, and I could already hear that the guards, ambassadors, whoever they were, had rounded the corner. It would be better to wait until they passed.

As the footsteps came dangerously close, I realized I should have started to hold my breath later. The need for air was clouding over my already tangled thoughts. Time felt like it was moving forward at an impatiently slow crawl, and the strangulating sensation became more like the grip of a hand.

The footsteps were calm, even, and noticeably heavy, indicating them as guards because of the boots that they all wore. Their voices had quieted slightly out of consideration for the other discussions happening in this hallway, but the sound of casual conversation still carried through the doors.

I clamped my jaw, still holding my breath, feeling as though my existence alone was loud enough to get their attention. Taz kept his distance from the door, watching it like he expected it to spring to life and attack.

One second spanned the length of thirty, but eventually it passed. The heavy footsteps moved by and continued across the expanse of echoing marble down the rest of the hallway. I slowly released the breath I was holding, still trying to be quiet as I waited for them to disappear.

I carefully pushed the door open after the hallway returned to silence.

"Well, that was fun," I whispered.

Taz winced, "Don't. That's not even funny."

From there, it was an unencumbered—if not slightly nerve-wracking—trek back to the main level. Mordecai had arranged our second meeting to discuss everything we'd found so far, and being late wasn't going to help anyone.

LIKE A DOG that had broken free of its tie, my mind had plans of its own. And none of them involved sleep.

Taz and I told everyone about Brighton's former captain of the guard, and why we believed he was the central reason for the impending war. They all agreed. Minutes later, Mordecai joined us, and the second meeting went about the same as the first; we handed over what we'd gathered and tucked it under the floorboard with the rest of our findings. Taz offered up the pages he and I had gathered; Malcolm, Taz, Evander, and Harris handed over the little information they'd collected from the north wing as well, including a map of old escape tunnels beneath the palace foundations that Harris discovered. But that was that. We were dismissed for the night.

Once again, I took a walk and let my thoughts run amok, only this time it was through the darkened halls. I paid just enough attention to where I was going not to run into a cold, white wall.

I was vaguely aware of rounding a corner into a stretch of hallway with tall windows on the left side. Pale moonlight streamed through the glass onto the floor, causing sparce particles of dust in the air to glint like stars. It wasn't until at least halfway to the other side that I caught sight of a shape standing in front of one of the windows.

I blinked myself back into focus, nearly expecting a threat, but I was relieved to see only Ithaca staring out at the night. Her eyes lifted over to me. Her arms were folded to secure a white shawl around her shoulders and her hair was pulled back into a braid, with a few loose strands sweeping down to frame her face.

"Trouble sleeping?" she asked.

"Something like that," I stopped beside her to look out the window at part of the gardens. "You can't either?"

The corner of her mouth twitched, "It's a bad habit of mine."

"Us night owls are a strange brand, aren't we?"

The leaves on the shrubs beyond the window fluttered with the breeze. More and more leaves had accumulated on the visible section of a pathway. Any day now, it wouldn't be surprising if snow began to fall.

She angled her chin up at the healing scuff on my cheek. "How's your scratch holding up?"

The corner of my mouth pulled into a smirk. "Oh, it's excruciating. I'm not sure how I'll ever manage to recover."

She chuckled as she turned back to the window, "Good to hear."

I wasn't sure how someone could have such a perfect smile. It was radiant somehow, and contagious. "Not that I have much room to complain—I've seen papercuts worse than this."

She nodded, staring into the trees with a faraway look. "I have seen much, *much* worse."

"Do you work in the infirmary a lot?"

She nodded, "I do, yes. I spend more time there than I probably should, actually." Reading my next question off of my face, she added, "I'm the physician's daughter, so I was a bit of an automatic choice as an apprentice."

Oh wow. She's way too smart for me. Even the way she *spoke* sounded clean and intelligent. *God, what do I do if she uses a word I don't understand?*

"Do you like it?" I asked.

She smiled, "Yes, I like it very much. There are bad days, of course, but helping people makes it worthwhile. The blood and carnage haven't ever bothered me either—not very ladylike, I know—but I was never fond of sewing and cooking anyway."

I grinned, as I remembered a select few women I had encountered in the past. Some of them would almost certainly faint at the sight of a drop of blood—or pretend to. But not Ithaca.

"The world could use some more people like you."

She turned her head to look at me, a serene half smile resting on her face. "You think?"

It was her gray eyes that added to her beauty the most. Not because they were brimmed by long lashes, or because of their warmth, or even because they would be as easy to drown in as a pool of water, but because they were kind.

"Definitely."

Her smile widened a little, and a hint of color appeared in her cheeks as her eyes roamed my face. The weight of her gaze was light, like the brush of a soft feather.

"Tell me something about you," she said. "What do you do for a living?"

I smirked out the window, where the midnight sky had the slightest hints of daylight. I sorted through the things that were real, and not part of a recited backstory. Something I could say that was honest. It was the least I could do, considering her country was going to be at war soon.

"Well, before I came here, I was a blacksmith, making and fixing knives for people."

"Is that where all the scars are from?" she nodded at my hands.

I held one up, looking at all the whitened lines on my knuckles and wrists. "Yeah," I laughed a little. "I was a bit clumsy when I was first learning. Not to mention all the stupid fights I've gotten into."

She tilted her head, "So what brought you all the way out here?"

"More work." Half a lie, half a truth. "I was given an opportunity, and I needed to take it."

"I see," she looked back out the window at the trees and shrubs.

"What about you?" I asked, eager to steer the topic away from myself.

Her smile gleamed as she gazed back out at the trees, thinking for a moment. "What do you want to know about me?"

Everything.

I chewed the inside of my cheek as I considered. "Oh, I don't know...what's your family like?"

"Well," she explained, "it's rather small. No siblings, cousins, aunts and uncles, or anything of that sort. Just me and my father." She fidgeted with a piece of fringe on the edge of her shawl. "We don't travel to the main continent much either. My mother died when I was young, when a ferry sank out in the channel."

"I'm sorry."

"It's okay, you had no way of knowing." She turned to look at me again, her face still kind, "I suppose I should apologize for the depressing turn in conversation."

"It's not depressing, it's genuine."

After a moment she said, "Your turn. What's your family like?"

I pursed my lips. "I hardly know anything, actually. Whoever orphaned me didn't even have the nerve to do it in person. I was just tossed onto a doorstep with a name and unanswered questions."

Her brows pinched together out of solace, but her face lightened as an idea crossed her mind. "Then it seems we both have something in common."

"And what's that?"

"Missing pieces."

I couldn't help but smile, thinking of it like that. And she was right; we both had to carry around old wounds and act as if they weren't there. Something about knowing that I wasn't alone, even if I already knew it, was like having a weight lifted from my shoulders.

We carried on like that for some time. It could have been hours for all I knew, but the minutes passed quickly and without notice. The continual exchange of questions was a good way to get my mind off the task at hand, and it was refreshing to talk to someone without constantly rehearsing lies in my head for Brighton's cause.

I learned that she feared the water because of her mother's death; she learned that I feared it because of a near drowning.

She was good at gardening; her mother taught her. I was good at starting fights and losing card games.

Her favorite color was purple; mine was green.

We talked until orange and gold had seeped across the sky, and we both realized that the day had nearly started without us. Honestly, I probably wouldn't have cared if it did.

CHAPTER THIRTEEN

I t was still early. The sky was a pale wash of violet and blue as I made my way toward my room in light, gleeful strides. For a night without sleep I was surprisingly alert and certainly in a finer mood than I had been in for days.

I was only mildly irritated to see Malcolm standing near the edge of the hallway ahead of me. I kept my gaze directed at the floor, hoping I could pass him without having to get into another argument that led to nowhere, but I found that he had deliberately placed himself between me and my door.

I stopped to look at him out of the corner of my eye.

He returned the gesture, keeping his arms folded. "I should apologize."

I cast a look over my shoulder. No one was there. "To me?"

His face remained fixed. "Well, I'm not talking to the wall."

"Apologize for what?" I crossed my own arms.

"For yesterday morning," he bit out, leaning against the wall like he needed the support.

I tried not to look as blatantly suspicious as I felt. The faint burn of the scratch on my cheek from our latest quarrel lingered, and he still had one on his forehead.

"I may have overreacted," he continued. "You tried to be honest with me about what little you know, and I didn't exactly return the favor."

I tried to come up with something to say, but my mind was blank.

He examined the bruises on his hand from the other morning, avoiding my gaze. "Your story about how you were abandoned has been bothering me. It's similar to mine, actually."

"It's not that uncommon of a thing to happen. Babies get left on doorsteps all the time," I murmured.

He chewed the inside of his cheek, still frowning down at his hand as he mulled over a thought.

"I never talk about it," Malcolm offered, filling the silence. "Taz has known me for ages, and even he doesn't know everything. I avoid thinking about it as much as I can without allowing myself to completely forget." His voice was oddly calm. "I don't trust people with my story because I can't even trust myself with it. Do you understand? It hurts that much."

I nodded. The past, the truth, did hurt; it wasn't quite like a stab or a burn, but more an ache that could move and change as it pleased. It could sneak around and hide away until sometimes I could forget it was there, but then it would find its way back home and invade the quietest, safest places I could ever hope to carve out for myself.

"I'm going to tell you what I know, which means I'm going to have to trust you," he continued, this time with more effort. "Not because I want to, but because you trusted me by reaching out, and I acted poorly in return. I only ask that you keep everything I say to yourself."

I nodded again. "I can do that."

He took a careful breath, looking back down at the bluish bruising on his knuckles. "That scrap of paper you found in my belongings was the letter I came with when I was abandoned. Half of it doesn't really mean much; it has my name and simple things like that." He narrowed his eyes, piecing together words. "The management at my orphanage didn't tell me about it for a long time. They didn't want me to know, but eventually they had to come clean about what it said."

Anxiety tied itself into a tight knot in my stomach. It twisted around, bunching up all of my questions and concerns.

"Whoever left me on that doorstep wanted to explain why their baby had a tattoo on its back."

"What does it say?"

"Well, it explains that getting rid of me was *for my own good*, whatever that means. And the tattoo is a way for me to 'find my way back.'"

"Back to where?" I pressed.

"Delphi. It's the capital city of Valanhurst. And it mentions the name Lourna Karabian; I think she's supposed to be my mother, but I'm not sure."

I blinked at the new shreds of a broken, still very unclear image. It was absurdly vague. A cruel joke, more than anything else. "That's it?"

He nodded gravely.

All of that bickering and fighting, for something that didn't put a single dent in the larger problem. I could not deny being disappointed —mostly in myself, for being so hell-bent and blinded. The past weeks could have been so much easier if we hadn't been fighting and stuffing secrets into dark corners.

The only silver lining, if nothing else, was that this could end the conflict between us. If there was nothing more for us to do, no way to find any more answers, then at least that was some closure, some finality to help put it away.

"Thank you for telling me."

He nodded once, "You're welcome. Just remember that this stays between us."

"I won't say a word," I promised, "but only if you let me get past you." I nodded to my door, which he was still standing in front of.

Half smirking, he said, "Fine," and stepped out of my way to continue down the hallway toward his own room.

Delphi. Valanhurst. The surname Karabian. I shrugged and went back to getting ready for another day.

FOR THE REST of the morning, I got through the difficult things first; work in the fields came earliest—unavoidable—and after that I made my spying rounds, which today meant I struggled through a stack of papers in a different office and eavesdropped to no avail.

But it didn't take long for spying to slip my mind, because I crossed paths with Ithaca again; considering the immense size of the palace and the number of people constantly moving through it, it was a marvel that we kept bumping into each other. Maybe it was luck, or a series of happy accidents steering us into the same hallways, but it truly didn't matter to me. I was too busy dealing with the rush of terror and joy that swept over me every time I saw her.

"Hang on," her eyes twinkled as we spoke, "you've never had *chocolate* before?"

"I don't think so," I bit my lip as I tried to remember some of the more unique food items I had stolen in the past, "if I have, I must not remember it."

"Oh, trust me, you'd remember." She took my arm and pulled, "Come on; this is an emergency. It's unacceptable and I won't stand for it."

I couldn't resist a laugh as she led me along, "So, has chocolate always been this important, or is it just a Dale thing?"

We took a right turn, down a flight of wide stairs. "I should hope it's everywhere—but no one can make it as good as they do here," she said. "And clearly I'm unbiased about it."

"Clearly, yes."

When she grinned over her shoulder, I understood why people like Taz dedicated countless hours to laying paint on a canvas. That smile deserved to last forever. It was the kind of smile I'd put in a gilded frame and hang on a mantlepiece, the kind of smile that would make me smile every time I passed it.

When we made another right turn, I recognized the corridor and the set of double doors leading to the kitchen.

"Elise keeps a stash of chocolate by her work station," Ithaca peeked through the oak doors, at the quiet room beyond, "but you can never tell her that I showed you where it is. She'd hang us both outside the palace wall by our toes."

I nodded, "Got it."

We shut the doors behind us, and Ithaca led the way to the far wall of cabinetry. She pulled out one of the lower drawers and emptied the contents—stacks of recipes, measurement notes—and fiddled with the back corner.

"She put in a false bottom so no one would know she had it," she explained, and the wooden slat gave way with a hearty *thunk.*

"She takes her chocolate very seriously then?"

"More seriously than she takes most people, if we're being honest."

She retrieved two small brown squares from the disorganized storage compartment and plopped one onto my hand. As she reset the false bottom and the rest of the drawer back into place, I lifted it toward my eye.

"So, what's in it?" I asked.

"It's a blend of cacao, sugar and milk basically. And a bit of magic." She stood and held up her own piece. "Ready?"

I nodded, and mirrored her as she set the piece on her tongue and chewed.

It snapped when I first bit into it, but then the smaller shards quickly melted. It was sweet, but not in the same way plain sugar was sweet; it was smoother, like the difference between cotton and silk, or juice and wine. My mouth pulled into a smile, and she nodded.

"You're right, I would have remembered this," I concluded.

"You like it?"

"I think it's probably the best thing I've ever tasted." And that wasn't just because of all the overcooked meat and stale bread that Brighton had been giving out as rations lately.

"Good. I'm glad."

I kept forgetting why I was in Dale. I worked on finding information, observed high ranking guards, and eavesdropped where I could, but I'd throw it all out one of the palace's high windows for a minute with her.

We made plans to meet again after she finished her shift in the infirmary, and we spent several hours talking later that afternoon; she sat perched on a windowsill overlooking part of the gardens as I stood leaning by the opposite side. It had become damp and foggy outside, and the air coming in from the open window smelled like an approaching storm.

When she talked about her work, her eyes sparkled like freshly fallen snow in the sun. The light would shimmer off them when I tilted my head. She told me how one of the women from the kitchen had broken her hand, and that two of her fingers had lost the ability to curl down.

"So how did you fix it?"

"Look," she held out her arm, "when you curl each finger, you can see where the tendon runs in your wrist," and sure enough, with each finger, there was a small ripple just below her hand. I copied the motion, and she pointed. "Those farthest two tendons were the ones that had healed wrong—but as soon as I was able to repair the area that had torn, it would be hard to tell that anything had ever happened, except for the scar. It's not perfect by any means, but it's an improvement."

"How did you know what to do?" I asked.

"An ungodly amount of reading," she explained, "and practice too. My father once did a similar repair for one of the field workers after he injured his hand years ago, and I helped—so at least I could say I've seen it done."

"Is it difficult to read up on all there is to know?"

"At times," she nodded, and turned her face toward the cool breeze drifting in, "but I like it. Knowing I can make myself better by helping people is, well...I'm not sure exactly what to call it. You understand what I'm trying to say?"

"I think so," I thought for a moment, "I probably threw away dozens of failures before I ever made a half-decent blade. But making myself and my work better was enough encouragement to keep me going; the hard work doesn't feel so bad that way."

She chuckled to herself and turned back to me, "Elise often accuses me of being too 'shoulder to the wheel' in that way. I'm not so bad now, but she used to struggle just prying me away from my father's office for a break. Apparently, I'm a fun-hating curmudgeon."

"I'm positive that's not true—and trust me, I'm an expert in the troublesome, rule-breaking kind of fun. Tomfoolery is my calling."

She tapped her chin in mock consideration, "You? A troublemaker? Surely not."

"I used to climb up into the roof of the orphanage and toss baby tomatoes—the ones I refused to eat—onto people walking in the street," I recalled, and then snickered. "They never did figure out how I kept getting up there."

"No fear of heights, clearly."

"Yeah, and the fact that I have yet to develop one probably doesn't bode well for my intellect."

She laughed, and we carried on until she needed to get back to work, and I needed to go sit through another one of Mordecai's bi-weekly lectures on the delicacy of our mission. The mission I kept forgetting about.

THERE WAS tension throughout the entire palace the following morning. I could feel it from the instant I opened my eyes. It balled up in corners and hovered over heads, hiding in the archways and beams far above—waiting to pounce.

Something felt wrong.

The day started with everyone trying to create the illusion of normalcy, going about breakfast and other preparations for the day as if nothing was amiss. I exchanged concerned glances with Mordecai, Malcolm, and Taz in passing. Each return of the same tense expression only strengthened the guttural ache of anxiety.

No one was talking. It was nauseating; the shuffle of feet and soft clatter of dishes were all drowned out by the vast silence.

Just as all of us workers were about ready to disperse to the fields, the severity of the situation, whatever it was, escalated. A forum had been called by the king and queen of Dale. It wasn't for select people either; everyone living or working in the palace had been ordered to attend.

The weight of my purpose here pulled far more heavily on my shoulders. These people didn't deserve to be harmed by an impending war; they were only ever kind, generous, and welcoming, even to strangers from faraway places.

And here I was, with five other spies, taking advantage of that kindness to aid a far less deserving nation; and all stemming from selfishness, the false promise of money. *A hundred pieces in six months.*

Guards ushered people down hallways as politely as possible. Some of them seemed just as confused as I was, talking quietly with people nearby. It was a good sign. It meant that this wasn't a way to search through the crowd and find us. If they knew there were spies here, chances were, we would all be in a cell already.

It was too late for me to wish I wasn't involved, too late to turn my back and let the two nations fight out their issues. Too late, because a side had already been chosen for me, and I wasn't okay with it anymore.

The great hall seemed smaller than it did on the day we arrived. The steadily increasing crowd made sure of that. The cold, unyielding marble floor was almost completely hidden underneath clusters of people. The only blank space was at the front of the room, on the platform where the thrones sat.

I really don't like this, I decided, scanning the room for a familiar face.

Inching my way along the left side of the room, I got away from the steady pour of people filing through the set of double doors.

I spotted Malcolm's red hair farther onward near the edge of the room. He and Harris were talking quietly, keeping a suspicious eye trained on the rest of the crowd at all times. I did my best at politely shoving my way around others toward them.

"Do you know what this is about?" I asked once I made it through the horde.

Malcolm shook his head, "Not a clue."

"It must not be too dire," added Harris, "otherwise there would be more chaos."

"Unless they are trying to prevent a panic," Malcolm countered. "This could be their way of trying to keep everyone calm."

The reality that this could be a way to hunt all of us out continued to loom overhead. And if that were true, it meant Nickolai was facing certain death.

The guards standing near the heavy doors and trailing on the far edges of the room stood out like beacons. The green uniforms sliced through the crowd like knives.

I recognized the tall, hulking guard closest to the thrones as the navy captain, Banor. Standing beside him, however, was an unusual scene. A man with patches of blood streaking up his sleeves was talking with him, having an oddly calm demeanor for someone who looked like they had been rummaging through a carcass. He was still working to wipe his hands clean with a rag.

I stared on, doing my best to keep down a gag fueled by fear.

Malcolm raised an eyebrow at my colorless expression, and I nodded toward the front of the room.

He furrowed his brows, squinting through the gaps between people. "That doesn't look like a good sign."

Harris followed his gaze.

"Someone's dead. They wouldn't call everyone here for anything else—"

One of the other guards near the thrones drummed the base of his spear against the cold floor, cutting me off, and a deafening silence fell across the room.

The entire crowd looked on as someone who could only be the king marched across the front of the room, wearing a grim, deeply lined expression. Trailing on his heels, with far more elegance in her stride, was the queen. She grimaced at the man with blood on his sleeves as she passed him. But to his credit, he did not so much as blink at her repulsion.

Both of them looked the part of royals. They stood apart from the crowd in their dark, richly colored clothes. The queen's dress was a deep blue, pairing well with her mahogany waves of hair. She was tall, possibly even slightly taller than her husband—though he looked like the sort of man who would never admit to it. He made a noticeable effort to stand straight, to the point where it looked uncomfortable. A twinge of pain rippled down my back out of sympathy.

Additional guards planted themselves close by. Many of them, including the navy captain, wore gold insignia over their hearts that marked them as members of the royal family's personal guard. They carried tall spears, with gilded shields held firmly across their arms— the makings of a solid wall of metal and muscle. They did not need to stand in ranks to demonstrate their strength. Their added armor and concentrated numbers were a show of power that people in the palace weren't used to seeing.

The queen folded her hands neatly and looked out at the tightly packed room. She spoke with poised clarity, her voice carrying across the space easily. "Good morning, and thank you all for agreeing to meet here."

It was hardly a choice. One look at the guards lining the room made that fact freakishly obvious.

"I must be frank," she continued, "this is not the time to dance around an issue. A teenage boy from Brighton managed to make it onto a ferry yesterday evening, but unfortunately, he had been followed, and was stabbed several times shortly before landfall. He died from those injuries not much more than an hour ago."

I exchanged a horrified glance with Malcolm. We could both see where this was headed.

I felt the pinprick of one of Mordecai's glares from across the room and hunted him out of the crowd. He was closer to the middle of the room, arms folded, and looking more concerned than I had probably ever seen him. His brows were knit together as he continued to aim a cautioning look our way.

"Before he died, he was able to explain that he had escaped from a military camp somewhere in Brighton. The people who attacked him were higher ranking officers that had followed him in an attempt to stop him from getting here. They killed him because he was aware of plans for war, and of half a dozen spies from Brighton already being here."

A murmur slowly spread through the room. Concern started to boil over into fear.

"We do not yet know why Brighton would want to attack, and we don't know when. Of course, none of this has been confirmed yet, but if it is true, we will be at war for the first time in our nation's history." She exchanged a look with the king, before adding, "Our most trusted guards are already combing through every room and hallway of this palace, in addition to the worker's quarters. And until they are finished, no one will be leaving this room."

I looked around me at all of the frightened, shocked faces. This was news to them, but not to me. I should have seen this coming. We should have climbed our way out of this shit when we had the chance.

I glanced at the set of heavy wooden doors that we'd all walked through, noting that they were securely shut, with guards now standing in front of them.

This forum wasn't called simply to let everyone know what was going on. They needed everyone out of the way, so they could turn this whole place upside down. For what? Everything. Anything that had been moved, stolen, misplaced, and hidden.

Maybe they already got our names? Maybe the boy who'd escaped knew who we were?

My mind raced to the letter I still had hidden on me. Relief came just as quickly, with the knowledge that I could drop it among the masses of people if they decided to search everyone. With the right timing, it could never be traced back to us. But barely a second later, the crushing blow of our own foolishness struck. It left a dark, painful bruise that burrowed all the way down to my bones. The papers we'd stolen, everything the seven of us had compiled, was hidden under a floorboard in Mordecai's room. A *floorboard* was all that stood between us, a world of hurt, and cause for the prince of Brighton to act on his threats.

What would they do if they found them? All they needed to do was inadvertently step on that loose, wobbly plank. We would be questioned and then killed, that was obvious. But how long would that take?

Harris, Malcolm, and I all exchanged looks of terror as the queen continued her speech.

"What are we going to do?" I asked hopelessly.

Malcolm shook his head, "I don't know."

We both looked at Harris, who had a barely noticeable bead of sweat resting on his forehead. He said, "It's only been two weeks; the boat that was scheduled to take us back to Brighton doesn't come for another seven days."

I cast a cautious look around at the people closest to us, who were all too busy muttering amongst themselves or listening to the queen. "So, we're stuck, unless we can think of a way to escape the city without anyone noticing. But security is *not* going to be lenient after this."

Malcolm shook his head as he looked back at the doors. "We are so monumentally—"

"Fucked? Yeah, I know."

"The worker's living quarters are probably going to be the first damn place they look," Harris added.

"Want to bet they don't even bother interrogating all of us, and just shoot one of us from a distance to make a point?" I remarked as I surveyed some of the closest guards, half serious.

"How did someone manage to escape?" Malcolm questioned. He eyed the queen, an eyebrow raised, as she continued to weave one polished sentence after the next.

"Maybe he climbed the wall in the middle of the night? Or just happened to be passing the front gate at the right time and made a run for it," Harris answered with a shrug, keeping his eyes on the royal guards near the front of the room. They stood like sculptures of stone, but underneath their gold-plated helmets and armor, their eyes were hunting.

For Harris's sake, I hoped that miniscule bead of sweat didn't become too incriminating.

"What if it was Nickolai?" Malcolm suddenly asked, face going pale. "What if he's the boy who escaped? Because if he's dead..."

If I didn't feel nauseous before, I certainly did now. "Oh god..."

Harris cringed, eyes scanning the crowd. "Not now—not around this many eyes and ears."

Warm rage spread through my core. "If they killed him, we need to sink this fucking ship before it can get any farther, Harris. Their leverage over us is gone—"

"I'm still clinging to the possibility that he's alive," argued Harris in a whisper. "Until we know for certain, we should act as if nothing's changed. We can regroup after they let us out of here."

"He's right," agreed Malcolm. "We need to be sure."

I took a deep breath, steeling my nerves. Even if waiting felt like letting Brighton get away with murder, I could do it long enough to be sure of Nickolai's fate. "How long do you think it will take them to search the entire palace?" I asked.

"Hours, at least," Harris murmured.

The temperature in the room was steadily rising. It hung over all of us like a thick fog. It was too crowded. I didn't even want to try to imagine what a few sweltering hours would do to my sanity as we waited to be singled out for our crimes.

THE WALLS of the room seemed to be inching inward. With every passing minute, it was more difficult to ignore the temptation of sitting down on the cool marble floor.

At least make myself a harder target to shoot at...

Mordecai hadn't bothered to come close enough to talk to us. But he stood within hearing distance, keeping an ear directed our way. An extremely blatant warning not to do anything to sabotage what was left of the plan. Because *if* Nickolai was alive, there was still a chance he wouldn't be harmed—as long as nothing was found, and as long as we kept quiet.

As the royal family waited amongst their guards on the dais, I kept myself occupied by observing the other people near the front of the room.

The navy captain, Banor, and the man with the blood on his sleeves were both calm with unruffled expressions on their faces as they talked. I was not nearly close enough to decipher any of their words, but I didn't need to. Blood and gore clearly didn't get on their nerves; the man with blood on his sleeves, in particular, hardly seemed to notice the varying shades of red streaking his clothes. His eyes moved methodically and with a keen accuracy that few people could ever hope to match.

The impassable clusters of people converged into a tightly packed clump, and I resisted the urge to push out an elbow to clear room for myself.

I looked over my shoulder at the guards standing watch in front of the doors. They weren't scanning the crowd like the ones near the front, but rather discussing amongst themselves quietly.

Their conversation looked severe, all of them wearing expressions of intense concentration; brows drawn together and stern lines for mouths. It hadn't been very long at all, but they had to be onto something already. They wouldn't be discussing so seriously if they weren't. Had one of the guards helping with the search come by with evidence already?

If they knew that there were at least six spies here, killing one of us to make a point wouldn't cost them anything. A death like that would be a demonstration for them to use against Brighton. They could interrogate everyone else on their own time.

I had scrutinized half of the room and found nothing. No suspicious looks from guards nor the glint of the tip of an arrow. It was just radiant sunlight pouring through the windows, warm rays shining onto a mass of frightened people.

I had nearly perused down the final side of the room when something ensnared my attention. It was like walking through the trees and catching a sleeve on a small branch, it pulled everything to an abrupt, yet gentle stop.

As usual, her hair set her apart from the masses. Ithaca stood facing the right side of the room across from Banor and the man with the bloodied sleeves.

I could not believe I had missed such an obvious connection before. She and the other man—who was now obviously the lead physician and her father—had astoundingly similar features, although his hair was several shades darker because of age. Even from a distance, certain details of their faces matched, like the angle of their noses.

If I squinted across the distance, I could see that there were faint smears of blood on Ithaca's sleeves as well.

She was composed, holding her shoulders in a relaxed yet poised manner. She hardly cared to note the rising tension throughout the room, much like her father and the navy captain. She handled the situation with far more grace than anyone else I had seen so far.

I hardly noticed myself cracking a smile. I would do well to try to be more like her at a time like this; a level head would certainly be more useful than a self-inflicted haze of fear.

Her eyes carried the same, precise watchfulness as the physician. It was different from the quiet kindness I had seen. It was a completely different mode of thought, one that she had clearly mastered.

The sharp prod of another stare broke my trance. I eyed Malcolm as he observed me, an eyebrow arched with amusement. He had been scanning the rest of the room, too, and had taken note of my gawking.

I narrowed my eyes. "What?"

He shrugged and directed his gaze past Harris at the guards on the far side of the room, failing to stifle a smirk. "Nothing, nothing at all… you just aren't very subtle."

"Did it look like I was trying to be?" I retorted, to counteract the singe of embarrassment.

He shook his head, ironing the corners of his mouth down to contain a grin, but with very little success.

I forced a frown onto my face, but I couldn't keep a mild laugh from boiling over. He chuckled back at me.

Harris was ignoring us, too absorbed by his intense scrutiny of the guards near the door to care. I spotted Evander and Taz near the center of the room, but they were still close enough to cast perturbed scowls over the tops of heads at us. It was Mordecai's stabbing glare that silenced our laughter immediately, as if he had brought an axe down on the necks of two squawking chickens.

This was no place for humor.

We returned to observing the rest of the room in silence.

The creak of the wooden doors at the back of the room cut through the muttering, and the great hall descended into silence again.

A dozen or so guards filed into the room, too far away for me to hear what they were saying. While most of them talked quietly, the rest pushed the doors all of the way open.

One of the guards crossed the room and spoke with the navy captain briefly. Keeping his face unreadable, the captain then turned to the king and queen, relaying something to them in a few quiet sentences.

Projecting her voice across the space once more, the queen addressed the crowd. "As soon as we know more, you will be notified immediately. All travel in and out of the country will be halted for the time being, but otherwise, you can all go back to your normal lives. There is no immediate threat here." After a moment, she quickly added, "And if, in fact, there are spies among us that wish to come forward and face minimal repercussions, they should do so now."

There was a low murmur of questions spreading as the people closest to the doors began to spill back out into the adjoining hallway.

I could sense Mordecai's gaze honed on us, daring us to so much as take a step toward the dais and admit to everything. See if we could get a word out before he snapped our necks.

If Nickolai was dead, it would be worth the shot. But if not...we could do nothing until we knew for sure.

I exchanged a look with Harris and Malcolm. Staying silent was the clear, unspoken agreement. But there was also a question; surely the guards had found something during the search?

There was no way to stay put. The crowd was too dense to try to shoulder out of it, so I didn't bother trying.

Malcolm's eyes never strayed from the guards near the doors as we flanked Harris.

I held my breath as we approached the exit. My thoughts spinning. These people didn't deserve this; this country needed an edge against Brighton. But there was nothing we could do yet—*unless?*

I didn't hesitate, keeping my movements casual and smooth as we moved with the crowd, passing through into the hallway. At the threshold, I extracted the warning letter and let it slip from my grasp. As soon as the horde dispersed, the guards would find it on the ground. It wasn't much, but it might still help.

The guards did not falter. We continued forward without being stopped among the surging crowd.

I curled my hands into fists, like I could hold on to the hope that we hadn't been found out. But the only thing that could tell either way, was whether or not those papers were still under that floorboard.

CHAPTER FOURTEEN

I never thought I would be so happy to see a few measly slips of paper. But there they were, safe, and right where Mordecai left them under the floorboard near the back wall of his room.

I reached for them, and held them up for Malcolm and Harris to see.

Harris's brows remained pressed together, forming a crease in his forehead. "Did they look like they were moved? Do you remember how Mordecai left them?"

"I don't think they were moved—"

Mordecai shoved the door open, narrowly missing Malcolm. He scowled at the papers in my hand for only a second.

I got to my feet as Taz and Evander followed him into the room.

"I don't think I need to explain how close of a call that was," Mordecai pushed his door closed again, with more force than was necessary. Taz flinched. "The timing could not possibly have been worse."

As I waited for Mordecai to explain, he snatched the collection of papers from my hand. "These were unmoved?" he asked, as he shuffled through them.

"As far as we can tell," answered Harris.

Malcolm crossed his arms. "What are we going to do? We aren't scheduled to return to Brighton for another week, and staying here while Dale's government tightens security is only going to make this more dangerous."

"Doesn't Brighton have some sort of a plan in place?" asked Taz. "Is there no emergency protocol we should be trying to follow?"

"We're in deeper shit than that," Mordecai pronounced, as he replaced the stolen papers and set the floorboard back into its rightful spot above them. "We are completely on our own. The boat that was scheduled to retrieve us in a week was all we had, and now even that's uncertain. Brighton may not send it at all."

Well, we were meant to be dispensable; the least problematic, if Brighton had to cut its losses...

The corner of Evander's eye twitched. "If they kill Nickolai over this—"

"Relax, they know this was their mistake," Mordecai growled. "And that kid is the only thing keeping you idiots from squealing now that everything's fallen apart."

If he's alive.

I shared a glance with Harris and Malcolm. We needed to discuss with Evander and Taz as soon as possible, as soon as Mordecai left us alone.

Changing the subject, I said, "We can't be expected to hide *here* now that Dale knows there are spies in the city. Not for a whole week, and not without being sure that the boat is coming for us." I chewed on the inside of my lip. "This spying campaign of yours is going to be a total disaster."

"Of *mine?*" Mordecai's eyes flashed in warning.

Evander raised his hand before any argument could ensue. "We just need to think for a minute. Can we at least agree that we need to get the hell out of here, as soon as possible? We can bring Brighton everything we have so far and leave it at that."

Mordecai dragged a hand down the side of his face. "Any suggestions on *how* we do that?"

"Actually, I was hoping you had a few." Evander shrugged, "You're one of the higher-ups; aren't you trained to handle situations like this?"

"I'm not a *spymaster*." Mordecai shook his head. "Look; we have to get across the straight somehow, and it's only fifty miles. Commandeering a ship from any of the docks here would be a mistake, so we have to figure out where we can get a small boat in a less populated area. We'll probably need to bolt for a neighboring town."

"And we'd want to leave at night," elaborated Harris. "That's less chance of being seen, and no one will notice that we're gone until morning, when none of us arrive at our designated shifts in the fields."

I swallowed around the lump in my throat. "So that's our plan? Leave at night and steal a boat to get back?"

Taz shrugged, "In theory. But getting past the city's guards is going to be a nightmare after today. They'll be everywhere."

"I found that schedule in the north wing," Malcolm cut in, pointing at the floorboard. "It details the guard rotations by the hour. There may be more guards around after what's happened, but their rotations will probably stay the same. Getting out of the city-center is going to be the hardest part, but as long as we have the right timing, we'll be fine."

Mordecai massaged his chin as he considered. "Get the schedule out. We have a lot of work to do."

IT WAS ages before our plan was established; broken down hour by hour and beginning just after sunset. We would be returning to Brighton near the middle of the following night. The extra day in between gave us time to adjust, in case the guard rotations were different than we planned for.

If Nickolai was still alive—that would be the plan *if* we could confirm that he hadn't broken out of Fort Ketta and been stabbed to death.

By the time our meeting ended and Mordecai finally dismissed us, the clocks had barely reached the smallest morning hours. But there was no time for sleep. Harris, Malcolm, and I immediately pulled Taz and Evander aside. We went as far from Mordecai's room as we could, down to the end of the hall, into Harris's room.

Malcolm did most of the explaining—how Nickolai might have been the boy who escaped, that him being dead meant Brighton's leash on us had snapped, and that we needed to be sure of his fate before we considered doing anything. Only now, we had less than a day to figure it out. After sundown *today*, we needed to know whether we'd be following Mordecai's prescribed escape plan or hurtling into a revenge mission for an innocent child.

I also informed them of what I did with the warning letter we discovered. Because at this point, Dale's leaders would make much better use of it than we ever could.

"How can we know for sure?" asked Taz, steering the conversation back to Nickolai. "This palace is fucking huge; we can't exactly track down a body, not when he's—" he winced, "whoever it was—has probably been buried or cremated by now."

"So, we wait until we're back in the confines of that fortress? Surrounded by hundreds of Brighton's soldiers?" I shook my head. "It would accomplish nothing. Nickolai would have *died* for nothing. We need to act now while we can still do some damage."

Malcolm stood across from me with his arms folded. Poised to argue—as he had been since this conversation started. "As soon as we can be sure it was him—"

"Malcolm, I don't see how there's *time* for that now. We only have until sundown—"

"The risks should be calculated." He frowned. "Getting ourselves killed by doing something stupid isn't going to help—"

"And doing *nothing* will?"

Malcolm had already opened his mouth to fire off a rebuttal, but Harris cut in. "We're all going to be here until sundown if this doesn't stop. What we need are more ideas on how to confirm who died yesterday morning."

Evander, pacing a short line with his hands on his hips, said, "If people saw him before he died, on the streets or at the harbor, we could ask them what he looked like?"

"We'd need to track a witness down—but that could take ages," pointed out Taz. "And who's to say what they saw would be reliable? Depending on how far away they were and what they were doing at the time, their word could be meaningless."

"Surely there's a reliable set of eyes somewhere in this damn city —" as soon as I said it, the idea struck me across the forehead like a brick. "*Ithaca.*"

The crease between Harris's brows deepened. "Who?"

"The physician's daughter; she works with him. She had blood on her sleeves earlier so she obviously got a very good look at whoever died." I shook my head to stop myself from rambling. "Never mind that—just don't worry about it. I'll figure it out before the end of the day; I just need to ask her about it."

Then the cold pit started to form.

Find her, talk to her—but don't let slip that I'm leaving tonight. Forever.

CHAPTER FIFTEEN

The rest of the morning passed about as smoothly as I expected. Mordecai was teetering on the edge of a mental breakdown, studying the schedule of guard rotations during every spare second he had.

I spent most of our morning shift wrestling down my nerves. I'd bitten my lip hard enough to taste blood. My hands couldn't stay still, and I was grateful to be working in the vineyard once again to keep them busy. To be keeping up the facade of normalcy for a few more hours. But even that felt like it was over too quickly.

Harris checked the time every five minutes. He was practically counting the seconds until ten-and-a-half chimes—the time when we would begin our escape, one way or another.

Evander had gotten his hands on some wine, and he was unnaturally pleasant by the time he emptied the bottle and during the additional meetings Mordecai arranged.

Taz suffered three episodes of vertigo in a matter of hours.

Malcolm found his way to the nearest gambling table, among some other disquieted workers on their break, where his never-fleeting luck had apparently taken a leave of absence. He lost. And if there had even been such a thing as a bad omen, I suspected that was about as bad as it could get.

By then, it was only mid-afternoon.

I was acutely aware of my remaining composure slipping and of the reckless abandon taking its place. I felt like doing something bold and stupid—because what if the escape failed? Or what if Nickolai really was dead? Did it matter? Would it end in a bloodbath either way?

When Ithaca rounded the corner ahead of me, part of me fractured like glass under pressure when I saw her, and I didn't feel the usual spark of delight; it dawned on me that I'd been *hoping* to avoid her, to avoid learning the truth about Nickolai and run out the hours on the clock during this last day in Angel's Landing. A cold, sick panic knotted in my chest.

Just ask her a few questions, and this can all be over.

This is goodbye. I'm going to have to leave. Tonight.

I did my best to hide it under a smile and pretended as if this afternoon was no different from any other.

Ithaca was eating a tangerine and tossed me a slice, "Someone looks like they've had a busy morning. Did you finish your shift early?"

I shrugged, falling into step beside her. "I work fast under pressure; and I think everyone is still feeling the pressure of what happened yesterday. Completely immersing into the job seemed like a good escape—until it was over."

Her hair was coiled into a bun at the nape of her neck, but sections of fly-aways were swept out at all angles like she'd been standing in the wind. She also wore a simple white and gray dress that I remembered seeing aids wearing in the infirmary. "You also look like you've been busy," I bit into the orange, "What are you up to?"

"I was fortunate enough to help deliver a baby for most of the morning," she explained, as she ate another section of the tangerine, "My father and some of the aids took care of final reports on the boy who died and arranging a proper burial."

"How old do you think he was?" I asked. "I know they mentioned he was young…"

"He couldn't possibly have been more than fifteen, poor thing."

Fifteen. Not twelve.

I waited a moment before pressing further. "It's hard to imagine someone so young going through all that. What did he look like?"

She finished the last segment of the orange. Dusted off her hands. "It was hard to tell when he first arrived because there was so much blood, and then there was the chaos of trying to save him. I didn't even realize his hair was blonde until after we'd soaked through at least half a dozen rags cleaning up—"

I stopped listening, and it was an effort not to instantly sag with relief. Blonde hair, not brown.

It wasn't Nickolai.

The tightness in my chest released. But a second later, my thoughts steered right back to the fact that since he was alive, Brighton's power over us held firm. They could still hurt him. And we had to follow Mordecai's plan to escape Angels Landing tonight.

"If there had been more time, I think he could have been saved," lamented Ithaca, as she frowned down at her shoes.

I put my hands in my pockets as we rounded a corner. "If there was nothing *you* could do, then there was nothing *anyone* could do. I'm sure of it."

She looked at me like I'd given her an overflowing basket of flowers. "You think so?"

"If it were me bleeding to death, I'd want you in charge."

"Hm," she smiled and gazed ahead, "thank you. But I'd appreciate it if you didn't find yourself on the wrong end of a knife anytime soon."

We walked and talked like that for a little while, until we passed through one of the open-aired passageways above the north wing. A tower rose high into the sky at the other end of it, taller than every building I had seen in Salona and reaching higher than the lofty ceilings in the great hall.

Ithaca followed the direction of my stare, "That's the bell tower, but people hardly ever go up there—in fact, I think only guards are allowed up. That bell is for emergencies, and we haven't had any of those for a very long time."

"You think people don't sneak up there?"

"Well, I don't know…" she paused when she saw the mischievous grin inching across my face. "No. Absolutely not. We'd be in so much trouble—"

"That's what makes it so much fun."

A smile blossomed onto her face, as she peered down the corridor in both directions. "You're absolutely serious?"

The arched doorway into the tower was only steps away.

"Tomfoolery is my calling, remember?" I winked.

"Well, what do we do if somebody sees us going in?" she asked.

I tried the handle on the door and it opened, "Better start running then."

After one final pause and another glance around for good measure, she took off ahead of me, giggling, and we started rushing up the stairs.

The stone steps climbed higher in a seemingly endless loop around the inside of the tower. We raced upward, taking two by two, until we were both so out of breath that we needed to stop.

"Apparently it's taller than it looks," I commented in between pants.

Ithaca nodded, "Can you imagine having to run up all of this in the case of a real emergency? Just to ring a bell?"

"I don't think I *want* to imagine," I wiped my brow. "My lungs probably won't be able to stand the thought."

Once we recovered, we continued the climb until the steps ended with a wide platform. Four columns on the corners supported a high, domed top from where the massive bell hung, and a comforting balustrade ran along the outside edge. It was the same design that I had seen on several terraces far below.

I leaned on one of the columns, relishing the fresh air and the strange, vast quiet that surrounded us.

Ithaca's dress fluttered around her as she peered over the edge of the rail at the city far below. She smoothed a stray section of her hair behind her ear. "I've never seen the world from so high up."

I joined her, and my stomach rolled a little at how small everything was. The tiny, dark specks on the roads were people, but they looked more like flecks of pepper.

"Reminds you of climbing up to places you don't belong?" she asked with a smile.

"A bit, yeah. But I'll admit, the view from here is much better." Except I wasn't looking at the winding streets, the copper roofs, or the ocean.

She rested her chin in her hand, "Are you always this charming?"

"I try my best. But you are rather intimidating, so I've been a tad clumsy lately."

Her eyebrows rose, "*I'm* intimidating?"

I nodded, "Wits and beauty can scare a lot of men. It's a formidable combination."

"Well, personally, I'd say you have an advantage; you're extremely handsome. It's unfair, really."

I grinned and my nerves crackled, as I reminded myself not to say or do anything stupid.

Her hand brushed my cheek, and her thumb traced the healing cut from before. The one that was nearly gone.

An ache filled my chest—a good ache, like my heart was stretching its arms and legs—and I let myself relax into the touch, trailing my fingers up her arm, her slender wrist, her hand.

Her gray eyes were unshifting as strands of her sunlight hair blew across her face. A face I didn't realize I was taking into my hands until I had already done it.

Should I?

The air caught in her throat. I could barely hear it over my heart drumming in my ears, and I wondered if she could hear it too. The quiet around us felt like it stretched for miles, the world was small and far away, even the birds didn't seem like they were in the mood to bother us.

No. I found a way to ruin it all by myself. My own thoughts cut a hard line between us.

You can't. Not if you really care.

Carefully, fighting a grimace, I lowered my hands, resting them on her arms, and she brought her forehead to meet mine.

Far away or not, I hid from the world by shutting my eyes and holding onto her. Her hands rested just below my elbows. Her hair tickled my cheek and my neck, and she smelled sweet, like tangerine and lavender.

"Something's weighing on you, I can tell," she murmured.

I smiled, "You do have a knack for that."

I didn't let go, and neither did she. My thumbs brushed against her skin.

"You can tell me, if you'd like," she offered. "Sometimes it helps. But only if you want to."

I do want to. I really, really want to.

But if I told her any of the truth, she'd tell Dale's leaders—she'd have to, and I couldn't blame her; this was her home. Then Brighton would inevitably figure out one of us had broken cover. They wouldn't hesitate for a second before killing Nickolai.

"It's nothing you deserve to have hoisted onto your shoulders. It'll pass."

FORCING Ithaca out of my thoughts was harder than I had expected, as our crew followed a sloping street toward the outskirts of Angel's Landing. I'd taken several healthy swigs of another bottle of wine Evander stole, fully expecting the headache it would give me, but even that wasn't helping.

Mordecai led the way through the dark streets, with all of the papers we'd amassed during our weeks here tucked into a bag across his shoulder—save for one; the letter I'd left in the great hall for palace guards to find. Hopefully it was proving useful in some way...

We crested a hill and stopped in the shadow of the building on the corner, where the streetlamps couldn't reach. But we could see all the way to where a stone wall marked the city's edge; the gaps in it, where main roads crossed through, were lit up brighter than the main platform back at the docks. Soldiers swarmed each gap. The once lenient checkpoints were now heavily guarded and impassible.

Harris glanced sidelong at where Mordecai was already brooding, "I thought you said there would be a way around?"

"That's because I thought they wouldn't have concentrated so much of their force *there*." His scar shimmered in the dim streetlight. "I'd assumed the docks and all the ships would be their biggest concern."

"You knew the roadways were going to be protected regardless," Malcolm noted.

Evander scoffed, "Either way, *that* isn't going to work. We have to come up with another way out of the city before dawn."

"Like what?" I asked. "The roads are blocked, the harbor is guarded too well for us to steal a boat. There's nothing left."

As soon as the words were out of my mouth, I remembered the old map Harris discovered in the north wing; a map that detailed a labyrinth of old escape tunnels under the palace's foundations. Some of them let out below the cliffs to the south, meaning we'd be able to bypass the city's checkpoints. When I looked at Mordecai's stiff jawed expression, I knew he remembered too.

He was already turning on his heel as he decided, "We're using the tunnels—it's going to take a little longer, but they'll work."

"Haven't they been sealed off for half a century?" asked Harris, as we all fell into stride behind Mordecai.

"Who's to say that they haven't caved in already—or that they won't cave in on us?" Evander agreed. "And we have to go back into the palace to access them."

Mordecai didn't bother commenting. We continued back down the street toward the ghostly palace of marble and granite, the minutes already slipping away and accumulating against us.

The headache began pounding against my skull, as I shared a worried glance with Malcolm and Taz. It didn't let up, and it had escalated into a pulsing drum-beat by the time we'd passed the workers' quarters and snuck through an unlocked window on the palace's main level; trying to pass the guards stationed near all of the doors would be too risky.

Mordecai insisted he knew where the closest entrance was, and his stride never faltered as we passed through the darkened halls. But each turn was nearly enough to make me hurl. Each blind corner was a game of roulette hinging on whether or not Ithaca had decided she didn't feel like fighting sleep. And if it wasn't her we crossed paths with, then maybe it would be a keen-eyed guard, or perhaps the navy captain himself; one look at us and he'd probably see right through the lies we'd spun for weeks—the lies we'd prepared if we happened to bump into anybody now.

"Have you ever been this close to death?" I asked Mordecai, as we rounded another turn leading to a dead end. "One slip and..."

Mordecai's eyes traced the walls as he answered, "I've been closer. Believe me, it can get much worse than this." He stopped at a tapestry and shoved aside the heavy fabric, revealing a smooth lip carved into the stone. It was just enough to curl his fingertips under, and he pulled.

Scraping stone grated against my ears as a vertical dark line appeared. *A hidden door.*

Mordecai summoned Malcolm forward, and with the two of them working together they could pry the door wide enough for someone to fit through. But the sound—the echoing screech of the stone slab that hadn't been moved in half a century set my teeth on edge, and the headache pulsed behind my eyes.

Somewhere beyond the end of the hallway, the rustle of movement turned our heads. Then footsteps.

"Precisely how *much* worse, would you say?" It was hard to tell if Evander was kidding. But I didn't hesitate shoving him toward the open door, where we all darted into the abyss.

As the last one through, I quickly asked, "Close it?"

"No time, too loud" answered Mordecai. He was already descending the steep stairs ahead of us.

So, I didn't.

CHAPTER SIXTEEN

The air was bone-chilling, and a draft was blowing toward us from the unknown emptiness of the passageways, bringing with it the smell of earth and water. By the time we reached the bottom of the stairs, the light streaming in from the door was all but gone. Vague planes of gray stone were all I could discern as Mordecai forged ahead.

"We need light," Harris whispered. He was on my left as the light faded farther and farther behind us, and I held out one arm ahead of me to keep from running into anything.

"And make ourselves a beacon for guards to chase? Absolutely not." Mordecai spoke so quickly and quietly that I was impressed I understood.

We paused at an intersection between three other passageways when I realized how much my eyes had adjusted to the dark, but the question still remained: "How do we find our way out then?"

"I know this long corridor goes for a mile in each direction from here," Mordecai said to himself, "and there are thirty more passageways branching off of it." The map we had was useless if it was too dark to read. "There are two exits below the south cliffs— and south is that way," he pointed left, and then decided, "If we go south far enough, we should be able to hear the ocean when we're close."

"How much of the map do you actually remember, aside from what you've already said?" asked Malcolm.

"Enough," Mordecai grumbled, as he led the way around the turn.

I dared a final glance at the ribbon of dim light reaching down the stairs at the other end of the corridor behind us, and I told myself it was the headache that sent a shadow rippling through it. If anyone discovered that the door was open, they would call into the void or the commotion would be obvious. It was nothing.

The walk to the next intersection was not long—only a few hundred feet. Curtains of spider web accumulated near the ceiling, trapping particles of dirt and shreds of dead moss. We paused again as Mordecai decided that we would be continuing straight forward.

With the little light from the stairway now long gone and my eyes as adjusted as they were going to get, I returned to keeping an arm out in front of myself as a precaution. Harris was doing the same beside me, occasionally bumping my elbow. My unblinking gaze was met with near emptiness, almost no different than if I kept my eyes closed.

Finally, we stopped at another intersection where five corridors met. This time, we all listened for the waves, and maybe I would have been able to imagine them, but the ancient stone above our heads creaked and groaned like a sleeping monster. I pretended not to notice, just like I pretended not to notice that there were more loose chunks of rock under my feet, broken from the walls with time and decay.

Maybe it was a good thing we couldn't see the deep fractures and crumbling patches in the ceiling above us.

Evander sighed, "Well, at least nobody's taken a rock to the head—"

"Be quiet," Mordecai interrupted. He ambled down the corridor to the next intersection and paused again, waiting for the rest of us to join him.

Somewhere in the distance, past the darkness and stone, we could hear the faint sound of waves crashing on rocks. But it was far away and distorted, making it nearly impossible to distinguish which way to go. The reverberations traveling through all of the passageways made it sound as if every way was the right way.

Down the corridor to my left, the faint echo of movement caught my attention. It was far away, and if I hadn't been listening so intently to the ocean, I might not have heard it at all. It was like someone had stepped on a loose rock and slipped a little.

A stab of nausea hit me hard, like a fist.

"We're being trailed," Mordecai concluded, and he swiftly decided on the passageway to the right, adding, "from now on, no one speak unless it's absolutely necessary."

To my left, Harris elbowed me and whispered, "If it was a guard that followed us, they would have alerted others rather than following on their own."

I elbowed him back. "Then who else could it be?"

"Shh!" Mordecai snapped back at us. My head throbbed.

We turned right again at the next intersection, veering away from where the sound had originated. That corridor only led to two other passageways. The distant purr of the waves was louder now as we paused to listen.

I watched as Mordecai went to go right again, but reached out to stop him. Before he had the chance to snap at me, I explained, "It sounds closer to the left. Going right again is going to turn us around."

"It's the echo," he countered. "We go right."

I stopped him again. "I'm telling you; we should go the other way."

"I agree," said Malcolm. Harris and Taz parroted him.

If only to keep us from making any more noise, Mordecai silently gave in, and we took the left passageway. It was a matter of minutes before the sound of the waves grew louder. After one final turn, moonlight sliced into the darkness, and I took my first full breath since the night started; an arched opening looked out over the southern shore of Dale, obstructed only by a series of metal bars. One by one, we all stepped through them.

The wind rushing off of the water stung my face as we crossed the rocky section of shoreline below the cliffs, heading southwest toward the neighboring town. We continued until we were well past the farthest gate into Angel's Landing before we climbed the hillside and followed a road the rest of the way. But each of us kept glancing over our shoulders to see if anybody was still trailing us; even as we entered the quiet cobblestone streets of the other town, I couldn't stop searching the darkness at our backs.

The shadows cast by the streetlamps were still jumbling my thoughts as we hurried to the end of the nearest dock. Our feet clumping on the wood was too loud; the adjacent lamps were too bright; the wind had gone too quiet.

We stopped where the farthest of two boats had been moored. The sail was neatly tied away, and the oars were stacked on either side where they could be fitted through.

Crates sat near the back of the other boat, covered by a canvas tarp. Though it was of the same design, it would be heavier and harder to set into motion. Not to mention it was much closer to shore —much easier for someone to witness us stealing it.

"Forget the sail, take care of the oars," instructed Mordecai. He gestured to where the front and back of the boat had been tied to the dock, "And somebody help me cut it loose." After extracting a blade from his belt, he held out his secondary knife to whoever was closest —to me.

It was like my hands were numb as I took my place by the back of the boat and began sawing at the rope. My heartbeat was hollow and low in my chest, and I eyed the rolling water beneath the dock, as black as ink.

It had been bad enough crossing the straight during the day on a ferry, but like this?

My knuckles were white around the oak handle when the shouting started. In a quick glance, I saw that we had apparently not been the only ones at the end of the dock. Five men exited a larger ship tied at the farthest end of the wharf. And since we were obviously in the middle of stealing—

I had to abandon the rope, with only a quarter of it left to cut through; one of the five men launched at me. Narrowly avoiding him, I stumbled to the other side of the walkway.

They drove us away from the boat, toward the middle of the dock. Mordecai barely exchanged a few words with them, a short, clipped warning, before firsts and blades started flying.

It was over quickly. Mordecai handled the first; Evander and Taz injured the second one's leg bad enough to keep him down, Malcolm knocked the third clean out, and Harris helped me shove the fourth into the water.

People who'd heard the commotion now filed into the streets, and a few had started down the dock toward us. Trapping us.

The fifth man was still standing, planting himself between us and the lighter boat we'd been cutting loose. He lifted his arms wide in challenge, a blade in each hand.

All Mordecai had to do was point. We rushed toward the second small boat, the one with the crates, and hacked into its ties. Better to deal with the extra weight than run out of time fighting a sailor and the townsmen closing in from shore.

This time I finished cutting through the rope. We hopped the short gap over the water onboard, and by the time Mordecai finished barking our few orders, the boat was already moving. I helped Taz, Harris, and Malcolm with the oars. Evander unfurled the small sail and angled it against the wind, the fabric snapping taught.

I only noticed the blood dripping from my nose and the ache of a new bruise by the time we passed the end of the dock, as the rest of that small town stirred awake and watched us disappear. Lanterns bobbed down the road heading east, toward Angel's Landing where they would alert the nation's leaders and the navy.

Taz was sporting a split lip and winced like he, too, was just noticing it existed. Malcolm curled and uncurled his hand, knuckles already darkened with bruises. Mordecai, unscathed, sheathed his knife and snatched his spare blade from my numb grasp. He said, "Keep the sail up, keep the oars moving; we don't stop until we hit land."

Wind ruffled the tarp over the few crates in the back of the boat, and Mordecai's eyes narrowed. He pushed Harris out of his path and marched toward them.

I pinched the bridge of my nose, spitting the blood that had coated my lips over the side of the boat, and asked, "What happens if they send one of their warships after us? They're fast, and with the battering rams—"

This was a nightmare. It had to be. As I turned, I saw Mordecai wrench a hooded figure out from beneath the tarps. And when the hood fell away, Ithaca was staring back at me.

CHAPTER SEVENTEEN

"There's no point," insisted Mordecai. "She's an obstacle that none of us have time for."

"We're almost back!" A steely calm settled over me as I argued. I expected my thoughts to spiral out of control, or catch fire, or both—but I sorted through ideas and angles without flinching. And I couldn't find the courage to glance at Ithaca as I decided on a plan.

Mordecai heaved a sigh, "She *followed* us. And hostages are useless—"

"Her father is the lead physician in Angel's Landing, and probably the most respected one in Dale; she's *valuable*, and killing her—" a bitter taste closed around the back of my throat, but I forced through it. "Killing her means wasting a very useful bargaining chip we didn't know we had."

Mordecai's chin jutted forward as he considered. Harris, Malcolm, and Taz were continuing to work the oars and keep the boat moving without my help. Evander was maintaining the sail. But they all became the least of my concerns as Ithaca's stare settled on me; it was so cold it burned.

She twisted in Mordecai's grasp, trying to wrench free. "If you had any balls, you'd try and say that while looking me in the eye."

And she was right. I couldn't. In fact, I'd rather squeeze my eyes shut and deal with the rest of this completely blind.

Ignoring her, Mordecai asked me, "You're sure? She told you about her job and her training herself?"

I couldn't hold back a cringe as I said, "She did. I'm positive." But I knew it had worked. And at least this way she wouldn't be dead.

Mordecai shoved her back to the crates and ordered her to sit and stay, like a dog, unless she wanted to be discarded into the water. Her face paled at that—the threat of suffering the same fate as her mother. I cringed again.

And when Mordecai turned to give more orders at the front of the boat, I took the opportunity to move closer and ask Ithaca, "What the hell were you doing back there?"

"I believe I could ask *you* the same thing," she snarled. Her eyes gleamed silver in the darkness. "You lied..."

"Why did you follow us?"

I got the distinct impression that she wanted to wrap her hands around my neck. It was something about the wrathful glimmer in her eyes. But her hands remained fisted in her lap. "Because I saw *you* going through that door, you prick! I thought maybe you were the one in trouble! But now I see how *stupid* that was. I didn't even believe what I was seeing until I saw you working with them to cut loose the boat, until I got close enough and overheard you obeying commands, but by then people were coming down the dock from shore and I needed to hide from them too—and the tarp on this boat was the closest thing."

I massaged my brow with my thumb and forefinger.

Before I could think of anything to say, Ithaca added, "I really should applaud your performance, you know? Whatever they're paying you, they should double it. Because I never suspected you for a second."

That cut deep—enough that my breaths hitched, and the invisible barb sank between my ribs like physical, honed steel.

And I deserved it.

SHE DIDN'T SPEAK to me again until long after our boat scraped onto the rocky shoreline south of Amphitrite and we were approaching the gate leading into Fort Ketta. Though, I was impressed we'd made it that far.

In the process of getting Ithaca out of the boat, she'd kicked Evander between the legs (which he was still limping from), scratched Harris across the jaw (the nail marks still bleeding), and slapped me hard enough that I'd seen stars—the lingering handprint was like a glowing brand against my skin.

It was still pulsing and burning when she turned to me and asked, "Why?"

Evander and Taz flanked us, and pretended that they weren't listening. Mordecai only spared a glance over his shoulder as I whispered, "He would have killed you if I didn't say—"

"No. Why did you lie to me? Why bother speaking to me at all if you were in Angel's Landing to spy? Or maybe this is just how you keep yourself entertained."

I opened my mouth to try to explain, but it was like the air had vanished from my lungs. The words I needed were nowhere to be found.

She shook her head and looked away, like that was exactly what she'd been expecting.

Mordecai spoke with the guards at the gate briefly, and then the massive iron hinges swung open.

As it closed behind us, with the pale morning light just beginning to rise, it was clear things had changed in the last two weeks since we'd been in Dale; the tents, now placed in organized rows along the west side of the camp, butted up surprisingly close to the center structure. There had to be at least eighty more of them. In addition, two wooden structures had been set up on either side of the east watchtower—and stretching from there to the main gate was a line of armored carriages. Each one was stacked high with barrels, and the men unloading them were filling up the tower and the new storage buildings.

I kept my face blank through the wave of nausea that washed over me. The prince and his cronies were starting to get things under control.

Instead of going into the center building, we passed it and approached a large round tent that had been set up to the north. Before any of us could share more than an apprehensive glance, we were already inside.

Four long tables had been set up to form a square, and all four sides were crowded with men in imposing black attire. I recognized Cedric and the other battalion leaders on the front and left sides. Everyone on the right side was unfamiliar; but they weren't wearing military uniforms, so I assumed they had traveled here from Brighton's capital. The farthest table, however, was the one that sent a cold rush down my back.

I knew the older man in the middle was the king, not because Kassian was seated beside him, but because of the silver and black-diamond crown on his head. Standing on his other side was a woman who I thought might be the queen, but she was *far* too young, probably only twenty-five. She didn't have a crown either. Her black hair was swept into a low bun, and she wore a long white dress with a neckline that cut straight across the base of her throat. She had her arms rested on the back of her chair, and her hands—I had to blink to make sure I was seeing right—at first I thought it was blood, and then possibly some kind of tattoo, but her hands were *stained* red nearly up to her elbows. It was faded and patchy in some spots, especially above her wrists, but her fingertips were nearly black from the concentration of color.

"Ah, look," Kassian nodded toward us, "all of our spies made it out alive." He reached into his pocket and set two silver coins onto the table, adding, "That's the last time I make any bets for a while."

All around the tables, many others joined him in emptying their pockets until the inside of the tent was glittering with money, and I could smell the coppery tang in the air.

Cedric, one of the few who didn't place forward any money, gave Mordecai a subtle nod.

"I see we're just in time to interrupt a council meeting," Mordecai crossed his wrists behind his back and stood taller. "Shall we come back later, your majesty?"

I swallowed around the lump in my throat as King Hector shook his head, crown glinting. Gray had faded through his curls of hair, which had to have once been a rich black. "Now is as good a time as any. I'm interested to hear what you found." His brows lowered, and he pointed at Ithaca. "What's this?"

"She's the daughter of Dale's lead physician, and a useful bargaining tool," explained Mordecai. "That, and she followed us onto the boat we used to escape; we didn't realize she was there until we were already offshore."

Ithaca leveled a glare his way. "I can speak for myself, you know?"

As if not hearing her, Kassian asked, "Do you have proof she's really who she says she is?"

Mordecai had barely turned to look at me from the corner of his eye when Harris interrupted. "Where's the kid?"

"We did everything you asked, and we kept our mouths shut," Evander agreed. "We never gave you a reason to kill him"

Kassian gave Cedric a nod, who silently stood and exited the tent. He was back moments later with Elysian and Nickolai—who was completely unharmed. As Cedric returned to his seat, Nickolai and Elysian took their places on the opposite side of the tent door from us, and Kassian simply asked, "Happy now?"

None of us deigned to comment.

Ithaca was silent as well, but I watched her glance between Nickolai and the prince several times as Mordecai set the papers we'd stolen before the king.

"Before we get to this," the king held up a hand, "I still want to know who *she* is. We need to know how valuable she really is—if at all."

My heart plummeted out of my ribs, but Ithaca didn't flinch from the many eyes that turned her way. She lifted her chin, scrutinizing the far table.

"And how do you suggest we do that?" asked the prince.

The king stood, prowling around the table to get a closer look. Mordecai swiftly stepped out of his path.

Ithaca met his gaze, her own eyes shining like iron. If anything, she was the one appraising the king in his entirety, and not the other way around. In one measured glance, from his silver crown to his polished boots, she seemed to have him figured out.

"Tell me, girl," the king droned, stopping no more than an arm's length from her, "how am I expected to believe that *you* are a physician?"

A man seated at the far table spoke up, like a puppet of the king's own thoughts. "It's improper for a woman to train in the medical field. They're too prone to hysterics. Surely the government in Dale doesn't allow it?"

Ithaca smirked faintly. Still not breaking the king's stare, she said, "You have a limp; favoring the right leg. You hide it remarkably well, I must say, but I suspect that's because you've been masking it for a very long time." His majesty blanched, and Ithaca continued. "It could be an old fighting injury, sustained in training or a battle—but it would be considered improper for a king to fight alongside his soldiers by Brighton's social standards, correct?" She didn't wait for an answer, and instead she nodded down at the king's right leg. "Now that you're closer, I can see that your ankle is swollen, and slightly bent. Not a poorly healed break but more likely a club foot that you've been hiding since childhood and trying to fix with painful, archaic casting techniques."

The king swallowed, already working to school his features back into pompous neutrality.

As the killing blow, Ithaca added, "You've become so good at hiding it because you knew people would talk. Brighton's new king, a cripple? No—that was a scandal you certainly couldn't afford."

The whole room winced as the king struck her across the face with the back of his hand.

"You are mistaken," he seethed, face tinged red. "But your vigor and arrogance are both dearly noted. Only someone trained in Dale's senseless practices could have gotten it so wrong, so congratulations; you've proved yourself to be just the miseducated bargaining chip we needed." He turned and summoned Eric, who was standing near the far table. "You. Keep her here, and don't let her out of your sight until I decide what to do with her." With that, the king marched back to his seat with rigidly poised strides.

Ithaca glared after him while Eric marched up to her side and assumed his new role as jailor. Pride swelled in my heart, even as Ithaca brushed her fingers over the bright welts rising on her cheek. I'd pay all the money in the world just to see her *dismember* the fool like that again.

The other men at the tables were all silent, all looking down so as to avoid an accidental moment of eye contact with their red-faced king as he took his seat.

Mordecai cleared his throat, gesturing back to the spread of papers we'd amassed in Dale, and explained each piece, one by one, before the silence could drag on into any more awkwardness.

He started with the guard rotation schedule and ended with the map of the hidden tunnels—accompanied by a detailed description of how we'd used them to escape. Everything else we found wasn't nearly as useful as those. Mordecai was just about done when a man in a red uniform with a black armband entered the tent. He mumbled an apology as he approached the king's table and held out a clipboard and a pen. He explained, "We just need you to sign off on this latest shipment, your majesty."

The king obliged without so much as a blink, scribbling down a signature, and waved the man away. To his right, he quietly asked, "That was the last of them, correct?"

The woman with the red hands gave the workman a nod as he hurried past, answering the king without even looking his way. "Indeed, your majesty. A full quarter of the supply is here, the warships back in Northgate are prepared, and our numbers are up to what we needed, at last."

My mind wandered back to the armored carriages full of barrels, and the fully stocked east tower. Then, how the warning letter back in Dale had mentioned some kind of new weapon. I glanced down the line, only to find that the rest of us were squinting and straining to overhear as well. Harris caught my gaze and shrugged.

Ithaca didn't so much as blink as the workman slipped past her out of the tent.

Before I allowed my nerves to get the better of me, I spoke up and asked, "What are all of the barrels for? The last time we were here, the east tower was being used to store weapons."

"Unless the barrels *are* the weapons?" Malcolm added pointedly.

The corner of Mordecai's eye twitched as he surveyed us, but he didn't say anything as his king rolled his eyes. "Yes, how very observant."

Evander crossed his arms. "It's something new, then? Something you've made?"

Mordecai pursed his lips. The king didn't seem to care. Kassian twirled a pen in his hand.

The woman in white explained anyway. "It's an explosive of my design, yes. We are storing some of it in the east tower, in case we need it here. Most of it is still in Northgate, in my lab. It's too dangerous to transport in large amounts; an accident would be enormously lethal because even one barrel alone…it's more powerful than we thought." She smiled a little at that.

I considered for a moment, taking the few shards of truth we had and fitting them together. My stomach rolled as I asked, "Is that why there are so many of us here?" I looked down the line of faces beside me; I watched each one of them realize that we had been right from the beginning.

They don't need soldiers with years of training and experience. They need people who can swarm a harbor and absorb projectiles, people who are dispensable like pawns in a game of chess.

Only it was worse than that. My hands curled into fists. "You need people to handle your new explosive, and die doing it."

One of the men on the right table shrugged, "We can't afford to face Dale without enough numbers to accommodate losses."

"Then don't use the explosive," Malcolm countered. "Find a way to weaken it—don't send hundreds of people to their death."

None of them were listening; if they weren't shaking their heads, they were sharing joking glances with the people beside them.

"I hope it blows up in your faces first," I decided. "The east tower is an accident waiting to happen."

Mordecai raised his eyebrows, and the king sat forward. "Is that a threat?"

"What do you think?" I pointed to the tent flaps behind me. "There are almost a thousand people out there, and you still haven't disclosed why they were brought here. How long do you think you can hide a bomb?"

Kassian shook his head. "Going out there and spreading hearsay about what's in the barrels isn't going to help you."

"Accidents happen," I forced a smile onto my lips and added, "your highness."

Watching Mordecai repress a cringe as the king stood unnerved me more than I expected. Kassian stood as well. All the other men at the tables were silent.

The lady with the red hands was practically beaming as she nodded at Kassian and asked, "Are you going to allow this pawn to make threats?"

"No one gets away with making a mockery of this war campaign," the king answered for him, nudging his son forward. "Go on. You have a point to make."

Putting on the cold, dignified mask of a future ruler was easy for Kassian as he rounded the tables of onlookers and stopped less than a step in front of me. "You see what needs to happen now?" he asked.

I was glad Harris was beside me; it kept me calm to imagine the way he'd ask me what the fuck I'd been thinking later.

Kassian waved a hand at the far table. "Cedric, you know what to do."

As Cedric got to his feet once again, he asked, "How many?"

"Twenty," resolved Kassian. "But leave the rest of them here; don't let them get in the way. There are still things we need to hear from their time in Dale."

Harris and Malcolm both gave me looks that instantly sent nausea rolling through my gut, and Cedric and I left the meeting tent in silence. I didn't waste my time looking back; Kassian was still acting smug, and Ithaca looked like she was about ready to flip one of the tables or kick Eric between the legs as Mordecai resumed his discussion with the king.

As we walked, Cedric flagged over a few other men in black uniforms, and he was still quietly talking with them as we rounded the south end of the center building to where four posts stuck out of the ground. Each one was taller than a person and as wide as a tree trunk. They were new; the dirt around them was darker and freshly turned.

One of the other men in a black uniform gestured for me to continue forward, "Go stand by one of those."

I squinted at him, taking slow steps toward the nearest post.

Cedric went into the main building for a moment, returning with a short coil of rope and—

Oh shit.

It was a leather whip, coiled up like a black, poisonous snake.

I could feel my pulse thudding in my wrists. The number twenty bounced around in my head; *twenty lashes.* And just like that, all the nerve I'd gathered to make those threats vanished.

"I'll be needing that." Cedric pointed to my shirt.

The walls of Fort Ketta loomed in every direction. There was nowhere to run.

My heartbeat was thrumming in my ears, and I clenched my fists. "Come and get it."

I glanced to the big tent where Harris, Malcolm, Evander, and Taz were, willing a silent message toward them; *stay out of it.* It only took a second, but by the time that was done, a burly man in a black uniform had marched up to me. He shoved me toward the post with a massive arm, and my cheek scraped the rough wood. Another one of them was already on the opposite side, looping the rope through a metal ring and around my wrists. As he finished the knot and walked away, I spat on the side of his face. He raised a single finger in response. The other one used a knife to slice open the back of my shirt, and cold air bristled across my skin.

I stared ahead, as if I could pretend none of this existed. But instead of a momentary escape, I only caught the uneasy looks of other soldiers that weren't in training as they passed.

I craned my head back around to see Cedric rolling his shoulders, like he was getting ready to throw something.

I tried to brace myself for what was coming, locking my teeth together and staring at the rough dirt near the bottom of the post. There was no warning. No chance to be ready. Searing pain sliced through my thoughts, like a stripe of fire had been lit across my back. Somehow, I kept my mouth shut, my teeth gritted together so hard it seemed like they could shatter. But it wasn't enough to take away from the pain. The burning didn't go away, it just sank deeper like the blade of a knife.

A second lash came like an explosion. Cold pinpricks formed along the edge of its path. I could imagine deep bruises already forming, like droplets of ink landing on paper. I forced my eyes shut to ease the burning in them.

And that's only two...

I hardly noticed my own scream as the third slash landed. Then there was an odd, warm trickle running down my spine. Blood. I almost gagged, but another streak of fiery pain cut across my left shoulder.

I wanted to collapse, to curl up and try to hide, but the ropes wouldn't let me.

I lost count somewhere around eight or nine. Each lash got worse, cutting across two, three, four others. The snaking coil of leather could just as well have been a finely sharpened blade. The damage it left behind would be no different. The streams of blood were proof of that; I didn't have to see any of it to know.

Black seeped across my vision like spilled ink, and loud ringing shot through my left ear. My hands were numb from being pulled on.

Eventually, despite the continuing assaults, my head drooped, and the darkness took over.

CHAPTER EIGHTEEN

Groggy awareness and immense pain came into light. I kept my eyes closed, afraid to move. I felt like I was adrift at sea, yet the side of my face was pressed against something hard. I heaved my eyelids open enough to get a peek at my surroundings. There were bricks. Lots of red bricks, and they were moving? No, I was moving. I was lying face down on something. Maybe a tabletop, or part of what had once been a crate?

Maybe I'm dead? No, that can't be it.

Voices were coming from everywhere, and it was enough for a headache to bloom across my forehead. I couldn't keep my eyes open.

"What do you mean you didn't see it!" bellowed Kassian.

"He didn't cooperate," argued Cedric, "we needed to cut the shirt off him—there was no way for me to see the tattoo until after we untied him!"

Somewhere in the distance, Harris, Evander, and Malcolm were shouting at someone. I could barely hear Taz trying to convince them to stand down.

"Find a medic now!" Mordecai barked, and feet scuffed the ground as people followed the order.

A door creaked open, and the sunlight beyond my eyelids dimmed.

The air got colder and smelled like clay. The wood beneath me lurched as the men holding it began descending stairs.

Kassian went on, "We need him alive—he can't answer questions if—"

"Let me help! You're wasting time." Ithaca's voice was far away, past the top of the stairs.

"Don't be ridiculous—" began Cedric.

Mordecai interrupted him. "She can be our last resort. Besides our medic, she's the only other person here who knows what they're doing in regard to this."

Cedric wasn't convinced. "Why does she give a shit?"

From the stairway, still barely on the edge of my hearing, Ithaca explained. "It's against my hippocratic oath not to help! And if you don't hurry, that bleeding isn't going to stop. You idiots are killing him as we speak." I could hear her arguing with Eric, since he was no-doubt doing his job and keeping her away.

"Is he still breathing?" asked a different voice, much closer than Ithaca. Maybe the king.

"So far, yes," answered Kassian.

I am?

The simple, miniscule movement of taking in a breath sent twinges of pain down my back. I tried to take shallow breaths, and absorb them into my stomach instead, but it was too taxing on my mind.

Kassian added, "Keep that bitch out of this. We don't need her in the way."

To my left, Mordecai huffed, "For fuck's sake, put him down!"

I winced as the wood beneath me scraped onto a cold stone floor, and the dizzying movement finally stopped. But it didn't take long for the headache to send my head spinning.

People kept talking, and movement rushed around me until someone found the medic. "Move," he instructed, and people got out of his way. A box clanged against the ground by my head, and he rummaged through it.

I forced my eyes open enough to get a glance at my

surroundings; a crowd that included Mordecai, Cedric, Kassian, and the king was standing by the far wall; we were underground, the walls and floor made of stone bricks; other strangers were still rushing up and down the stairs; there were rows of iron bars mapping out empty cells. That was all I could take before my eyes closed again on their own.

The weight of a rag, to soak up the blood, was enough to make me cringe. A thumb tugged open my right eyelid, and a grizzled man was staring back at me. He didn't look pleased.

"Well?" demanded the king.

"Not good," answered the medic. He let my eyelid go.

I was cold. I was hot. I might throw up. I wanted to punch whoever the fuck just started dabbing at the gashes on my back, but I pounded my fist against the cold ground instead. White dots flashed in my eyes.

"I'm not convinced there's much I can do," the medic explained. "Stitches could take too long, and without a way to effectively stem the bleeding, it would be futile." He continued listing all the reasons I would die, and I stopped paying attention.

"He needs to survive, at least long enough to answer questions," reiterated Cedric.

Mordecai's aggressive steps crossed to the other end of the cell. "Someone fetch the girl from Dale." Quickly, he added, "it's worth a try," because I was positive the king and the medic both took some kind of personal offense to that.

Right on que, the medic scoffed. "No *woman* is going to step in here and take my job. Not when she'll probably just make it worse."

Kassian dismissed him. "If there's nothing you can do, what's the harm?"

After a few moments, Ithaca descended the stairway, still accompanied by Eric. Her light footsteps sped up as she crossed the room. "*Shit.*"

Now it was her rummaging through the box of supplies. She peeled the first rag from my back and tossed it aside. It landed with a saturated slap somewhere across the cell. Two, three more rags took its place. She told someone to find more and to bring alcohol, a bowl, and water.

I sensed her movements instantly becoming more methodical as she took a deep breath. The clatter of supplies quieted as she found the things she needed.

She paused suddenly and asked, "What's this?"

The medic scoffed—nearly laughed, actually. "It's a needle, obviously."

"Have you been giving stitches with a standard *sewing* needle?"

There was a short pause, and I felt the whole room turn to look at the medic.

Ithaca didn't wait for him to explain himself. "I need a leather needle. The point is flattened on three sides, creating three sharp edges that are easier to pierce skin with. If you actually know what you're doing, you should have one somewhere." Then she unwound a section of the spool of thread that was in her other hand. "And this thread is weak." She snapped it easily, tossing it to Cedric. "I need something stronger."

Feet shuffled up the stairs as people went to get the proper tools. Those who remained in the room were silent as the medic, his dignity in tatters, joined them. It was almost enough to make me smile.

I tried to concentrate on breathing instead. The ringing in my ear wasn't going away, and the headache was stabbing. Even the bruising on my wrists had begun to ache, and the skin scratched by the ropes burned.

A cool palm on my forehead made me flinch, but then it was soothing. I forgot about the headache—or maybe it actually went away. The weight of her hand somehow made everything a little better. But it was gone again in a second.

"When was the last time you had water?" she asked, and it took me a moment to realize she was talking to me.

"Early yesterday...I think?" My voice was weak and grainy. I would have hardly recognized it as my own if it hadn't taken so much effort to force the words out of my mouth.

"Do you think you can sit up?"

Sit up. When had something so simple become so daunting. My limbs were dead weight that had been fused to the ground beneath me. There was no obvious point where I ended and it began. But more than anything, I wanted to get away from the sensation of being submerged and drowned in a pool of my own blood.

I nodded stiffly.

With a grimace, I dragged my arms to my sides, folding at the elbow. I took a few deep breaths, filling my lungs despite the pain, and pushed myself up. It would have been easier if I opened my eyes, but the pain was less difficult to ignore when I couldn't see where my blood had pooled on the floor. I kept a gag trapped near the back of my throat.

The people who'd left before returned, marching down the stairs with a new spool of thread, a new needle, a cloth, a bowl, and two flasks, one full of something that smelled strongly. Even from a distance, I recognized the sharp scent as alcohol, and I could almost feel the stinging already. The other flask had water in it, and I was shocked that I smelled it too.

I grabbed the water, not caring that it sent pain ripping down my shoulder, tore out the cork, and started gulping it down. The cool soothed everything, and breathing no longer seemed so important. I downed most of it before finally setting it aside, sucking in breaths of air.

My vision went white with stinging pain. "God *DAMMIT!*"

"Sorry," Ithaca said. I looked over my shoulder to see her dumping more alcohol onto my wounds. "I should have warned you."

I was cringing too hard to reply.

She pressed her lips together, holding up the alcohol-drenched cloth for me to see better, "And unfortunately it gets worse."

I locked my eyes back on the floor in front of me, bracing for the inevitable.

"Ready?"

I gave a slight nod.

The texture of the cloth felt more like the serrated edge of a saw. I clamped my teeth together and planted a hand on the bars to my right, squeezing my eyes shut and waiting for it all to end.

The crowd that had formed exited the cell and congregated at the base of the stairs, discussing in whispers. Only Eric remained at the open cell door, brooding, but continuing to do his job—an overbearing shadow to hover around Ithaca at all times.

It felt like years before Ithaca crossed to the front of the room and retrieved the new needle and thread. "This may take a while," she unwound a long strand, using her teeth to sever it off, "would you rather sit, or lie back down?"

"I'll sit." Any extra movement seemed impossible.

She eyed the tattoo on my chest as she walked back around me, threading the needle without looking. The rest of the bystanders were already staring. Cedric, Kassian, Mordecai, and the king were now in a tight circle, lowering their whispers further.

Ithaca said, "I didn't know you had a tattoo."

I would have shrugged, but it would be too painful.

She gingerly prodded the start of a gash near my shoulder, "This will hurt." The sharp stab of the needle made me suck air through my teeth, and my hands tightened until my knuckles were white. Somehow, I kept myself from cursing again.

"Do you need something to bite down on?"

"I don't think so," I glanced over my blood-tinted and bruised shoulder. The odd movement of the thread through my skin didn't hurt as much as it made me uneasy.

Ithaca finished pulling the first stitch tight and angled her ear toward the hushed conversation with the king. She held still as she focused on listening for a moment. Before they had time to notice, she went back to work.

The needle pierced my skin again, and a shaking groan escaped the back of my throat.

"Tell me what the tattoo means," she murmured, so that none of the people by the stairway might hear.

It was supposed to be a distraction from the pain. It was certainly an attempt to understand why they wouldn't just let me die from my injuries—and that hurt worse than the stitches. Still, I tried to pay attention to her words.

"I don't know what it means. I don't even know who gave it to me." I was ready for the next pass of the needle, but it made me dizzy and nauseous anyway.

"You've had it forever?"

"Pretty much."

She was silent for a moment. The pressure of her hands alone was enough to make me wince. "They all seem pretty interested in it."

"I'd rather not think about that right now."

As she finished a stitch, she said, "Then tell me how long you've been working for them, if *working for them* is what you want to call it."

I turned to look at her, asking quietly, "After all you've seen and heard, you still think any of this was a choice?"

Without pausing her work, or meeting my eyes, she answered, "I never said I did. Not anymore."

Having the needle driven through raw flesh was becoming more and more familiar each time. Ithaca worked fast, and for whatever reason, I felt like that helped.

I winced through a fresh stab from the needle. "If it weren't for your oath, would you have volunteered to help me?"

She shrugged, pulling the last part of the stitch tight. "I don't know."

Her lingering handprint on my cheek flared with warmth, enough to make me cringe.

I nodded and turned back around. "Fair enough."

I WAS LYING on the cold, unforgiving floor when I stumbled out of the hazy confines of sleep. Instantly, I was struck by the pain, and I growled through my teeth.

The hours it had taken for Ithaca to sew me back into one piece were painstakingly fresh in my memory. At some point, she'd been ushered above ground again. Those who remained tried to question me about the tattoo, but it got them nowhere; I was too exhausted to keep my head up for more than a minute. They gave up after about an hour and left me alone to recover enough so that when they returned I could give them answers.

I used the iron bars to my right to pull myself up, wincing and grumbling the whole way. Only once I was stable did I notice Malcolm and Harris standing outside my cell. A locked door separated us, but that was hardly a surprise.

"Well," I asked, dusting dried blood and dirt from my face, "how do I look?"

Malcolm looked at Harris, who took a moment to decide that "spectacular" was a good answer. But the smile he added at the end was more like a cringe.

A single breath of laughter escaped me. I didn't feel spectacular at all. "What are you doing here?"

"Trying not to get caught, first of all," explained Malcolm, with a precautionary glance back at the stairway and the closed door beyond. "Second, to make sure you weren't dead. They refused to tell us anything and...well, it sounded pretty bad."

Gingerly, I leaned my shoulder against the bars beside me. My chest was unnaturally heavy, and my bottom lip had a crack deep enough that I could taste blood. "Are things getting worse up there? Now that they have an example of what happens to people who make threats?"

"Actually, I think the balance has shifted a little," Harris offered. "All of us without a black armband are getting antsy. Everyone knows what happened to you and why; and almost everyone believes the *rumors* that those barrels are full of explosives now."

"Not to mention the stunt they pulled a few hours ago," Malcolm reached into his pocket, retrieving a small silver coin, "they gave out two of these to everyone here as part of the supposed one-hundred pieces we were all promised. They're trying to keep everyone compliant."

My thoughts had already wandered. "I think they recognize my tattoo from somewhere. They were talking about it when I first woke up, and they asked me about it before they left. It's probably why they haven't let me wither away and die yet."

I strained to keep my eyes from wandering to the reddish stain in the middle of my cell.

Malcolm's brows lowered, "Have they told you why they want to know about it?"

"No. And I'm afraid to find out."

Crossing his arms, Malcolm asserted, "Then let's not give them the chance to get that far. We're in a better position to escape than we have been in weeks; we're all in the same place."

"They aren't going to let you down here, and you can't keep sneaking around them. What they did to me will look like mercy if they catch you." I gestured around. The movement was painful enough to make my vision spotty. "Not to mention I'm locked in a cell. How would we ever communicate and plan?"

"Because they want to keep you alive," Harris cut in. "Whatever information they want out of you, it's valuable enough that they're going to use Dale's beautiful physician to make sure you're well enough to answer them. We were all still in the meeting tent when they talked with Ithaca again. She insisted she could keep you from dying and that her training is better than the current physician's. They've agreed to let her."

"And she wants to ruin Brighton's war campaign as much as anybody," added Malcolm. "She knows we can help her escape. That means she's on our team. And since she will be down here to make sure you survive, we can talk back and forth through her."

My headache returned in full force, and I rested my brow against one of the iron bars. "Do they know you have the same tattoo?" I asked Malcolm.

He shook his head. "No."

"I don't think they should ever find out," I decided. "We have no way of knowing what they really want."

"That tattoo essentially just saved your life. It might help us if they knew about Malcolm's too," Harris pointed out.

"Or it could get so, so much worse," I argued. A chill poured over me, but I masked it by shaking my head. "That's not a risk I'm willing so see play out. If I figure out *why* it's such a big concern to them, I'll let you know. Until then, it would be safer to hide it."

"I agree," said Malcolm. "Better not to show our hand."

The conversation steered back to escape, and a rough outline of our plan began to form. But I kept losing focus, feeling worse by the minute. I concentrated on drawing air into my lungs, hoping I didn't feel a sudden pinch, making sure the steady drumming in my chest didn't hollow out and stop without warning. I was going to be afraid to close my eyes. To fall asleep.

After about five minutes, with the noises above ground coming too close for comfort, Malcolm and Harris decided it would be best for them to sneak back out. I couldn't agree more. Every muscle in my body was tense, waiting for something horrible to happen, until the door at the top of the stairway finally clicked shut and silence descended.

Another chill scraped against my bones.

I tried to appreciate the quiet as I sat in the dark, waiting for Kassian and his entourage to return. Being questioned, even about the tattoo, was still better than being alone.

CHAPTER NINETEEN

T he lady with the red hands, the chemist, joined Kassian, the king, and Mordecai when they arrived to ask more questions. She stood just beyond the bars of my cell and had decided to wear red this time; her dress had a high collar and sleeves that tapered to a point on top of her hands, blending perfectly with the stains.

Behind them, Ithaca sat on the bottom step leading from above ground, watching everybody with that razor sharp glint in her eyes and her jaw set. Eric stood a few steps above her to keep an eye on the door; apparently, he was still in charge of her constant supervision.

"Do you recognize this man?" asked the king, setting forward a crisp paper.

"It's the wanted poster that's been put up in the middle of camp since I got here, and the one Mordecai showed us in Dale," I observed. "Other than that, I've never seen him before."

"Have you seen the hollowed-out red star anywhere else before?" Mordecai folded his arms. "How much of Brighton have you traveled to?"

I sighed through a pang of nausea. "I've lived in Orvalia my whole life. I'd never been to Brighton before you dragged us out here from that smaller camp."

Cedric cut in. "Are you lying about any of this?"

"I don't have the energy to lie—"

"You probably don't have time either," warned the king. "Maybe days."

I resisted a shiver. The chills had gotten worse, and they reminded me of the times I had been sick as a child. They signified a fever; I remembered that too.

Kassian repeated a question he had already asked before. "You say you don't know who put it there, but you must recall something? Tattoos can be painful."

"Well, I don't. It's been there as long as I can remember."

The questioning went on like that for a while, in circles, until I couldn't mask my shivering anymore and they grew tired of listening to the same responses.

The only time the chemist spoke was as they were leaving, when she vowed, "We'll be back again when your mortality is clearer to you. Perhaps then you will see there's no point in taking things like this to the grave."

Once they were gone, Eric unlocked my cell for Ithaca, allowing her to carry in the med-kit unencumbered, and locked the door behind her. Then, he returned to his post at the bottom of the stairs to brood.

As Ithaca sorted through the med kit, I quietly asked, "Am I going to die? Be honest."

Ithaca picked up a small vial of translucent yellow liquid, squinting at it, "Well, there's always the risk of things not healing properly, or the wounds going bad."

"I'm sure I'll sleep so much better knowing that."

She sighed, glancing over at Eric—who was scraping dirt out from beneath his fingernails with a small blade. "Don't worry. The only reason they're so pessimistic is because they don't understand wounds. It looks bad now, but I've seen people survive worse." She stood up, walking toward me as she opened the vial and dumped some of the liquid onto her fingers. As she reached toward my face, I flinched away. It was like a blink, and I hardly noticed that I had done it until she lowered her hand to look at me.

"Sorry," I said. "Old habit."

"It's alright. You've been through a lot." She raised her hand again, "May I?"

I nodded.

She gingerly smeared the liquid onto my temples, wrinkling her brow as she concentrated on her work.

I eyed the vial in her hand, "What is that? It smells good."

"This," she handed it to me, "is lavender oil."

"What does it do?"

She worked it into my skin meticulously, pressing with just enough force to relieve the worst of the headache. "I have found that it works beautifully on nausea—which I figured you would need. But it can also help with headaches and nerves."

"How did you know I had a headache?"

She smiled lightly, "I can see the outline of the iron bars on your forehead. You weren't standing down here with your face pressed into cold metal because it was comfortable, were you?"

My headache was nearly gone. She said it was the oils that helped, but I wondered if it was just *her* that eased the pain so effortlessly.

"There are tonics that are more effective, but they don't have any of them here. This was the best I could come up with." She took the small vial back from me, closing it, and returned it to the kit she'd set down by the cell door.

No, don't stop.

"How's your back?"

"It hurts. A lot," I blinked through the warm, tingling sensation that lingered around my eyes.

She left the basket again, carefully putting the back of her hand to my forehead. "You have a bit of a fever, but that's fairly normal. You don't have an infection as long as it doesn't get too high."

I closed my eyes, relaxing into her hand.

"But a big part of the problem is that you haven't had enough water. That probably started the headache in the first place," she removed her hand, examining my eyes keenly.

How was it that even in a dark cell those gray eyes were still so dazzling? They radiated a mesmerizing, gentle warmth, like the sun.

"Have you been feeling light headed or faint?"

Only around you...

"No."

"Good."

She stepped around me to look at the sutures, "I know it hasn't even been a day, but it looks like things are holding together." She lightly touched the gash closest to my shoulder, sending a twinge of pain straight down to the bone.

"Ow."

"Sorry," she eased the pressure as much as she could, turning to Eric. "I need some clean gauze and water."

The only indication he gave that he heard was a slight lift of his dark eyebrows.

She sighed. "Unless *you'd* like to take the blame for a fatal infection that could have easily been avoided? I don't imagine your king taking kindly to that."

"My orders are to not let you leave my sight," he answered dryly.

"I can't *leave* this cell," she rattled the locked door for emphasis. "Please. It will only take you a moment."

Grunting, he snapped closed his small knife, and trudged up the stairs. "Don't get any bright ideas—because my orders are also to kill you if you try something stupid," he reminded her, right before he slammed the door leading above ground.

"As I was saying," Ithaca acted like he'd never been there to begin with, "if you don't move too extensively, your sutures should be fine. Just try to be careful."

"So, trying to throw myself over the surrounding wall is out of the question?"

Her lips disappeared into a narrow dash. "I hope you're joking."

Actually, tumbling through the trees on the other side sounded rather appealing.

"Speaking of the surrounding wall," Ithaca added quietly, "I talked with the rest of your companions, and I've agreed to work with you. In fact, I think I've come up with a plan that might work."

"As in all seven of us escaping?" I cringed as she poked at another gash.

She walked back into my field of vision, dusted off her hands, and then folded her arms. "The people who have died here are placed outside the wall; the current medic explained that to me. And since the higher ups are so positive your injuries are fatal, it wouldn't be impossible to convince them that you died."

When I tried to take a deep breath, my chest felt heavy. "I can play dead, but I can't hide my own pulse, Ithaca."

"You wouldn't have to," she smiled a little as she went back to her basket, rummaging through it, "I can fix that."

I blinked, tilting my head as I wondered if I'd heard her right. "You're going to kill me?"

"Well, not exactly."

"What do you mean?"

Ithaca paused, "It would wear off after a few hours. I just have to make it. It's like a sedative, and it slows your heart rate enough that if someone checks for a pulse, they won't feel anything."

"Have you ever made it before?"

I saw a muscle in her jaw feather, and she eventually admitted, "No. I haven't."

I ran my hand down the side of my face, "Alright, so you're going to sedate me and throw me outside. Then what? How do I help the rest of you still inside?"

"We will steal one of the officer's black uniforms. Then one of us can find a way to get into a tower and throw it over the wall. You'd have to impersonate one of *them*, come back in through the main gate, and get the rest of us out. As long as no one recognizes you, it should work."

I chewed on my lip and considered. "Playing dead is clever, I guess. As long as I don't end up like that permanently..."

"For what it's worth, I promise to do everything in my power *not* to kill you." She went back to rummaging through her basket, "And as much as I would have considered it when I first learned why you were in Angel's Landing, I think it's been made clear that you didn't exactly sign up to be a part of this—especially not after they threatened a child to keep you quiet."

"So, we're all planning to do this sooner than later?" I asked.

"Within reason," she cautioned, "Your back needs time to heal more before you can be gallivanting around."

"How long until then do you think?"

She shrugged one shoulder, "It depends on the wounds, honestly. They may heal quickly, or they may not."

The door at the top of the stairs creaked and Eric returned. Ithaca silently gathered her things and stood. She watched him through the bars with an effortlessly neutral expression as he unlocked the cell door.

"I'll be back early tomorrow to check on you again," Ithaca said over her shoulder, with a pointed look behind her eyes as Eric closed and locked the door again.

I gave a small nod. And when they were both gone, I tried not to think of all the ways things could go wrong.

THE WAY my heart used to thud in my chest when I worked up the nerve to start sneaking in and out of the orphanage, causing mischief, was eerily similar to how I felt in the days that followed. Sneaking in conversations, rushing back and forth with details, it all made me feel like an on-edge, inexperienced little kid again.

Ithaca checked my wounds twice a day. In the mornings, Kassian and his entourage usually joined her so that while she worked, they asked me the same questions they had a dozen times before.

"I'm getting the feeling you know something I don't?" I finally asked one day. "It's like you're all trying to get me to say what you want to hear."

Ithaca silently eyed the king as he replied, "You truly don't know, do you? About how the previous king and his family were assassinated, and that the palace in Northgate was practically left in ruins? Most of it is still in ruins today—"

"What does that have to do with me and my tattoo?"

Ignoring me, Cedric turned to the king. "He's too young to have been alive when it happened, let alone to be involved."

Mordecai was drumming his fingers on his chin. "Then how do you explain it? Coincidence?"

Kassian shrugged, "What could it be if it isn't? Based on the report we received from our first spy in Dale—very recently, I might add—maybe this could be a way of sending some kind of message? There must be something we aren't seeing."

With that, they left once again to discuss amongst themselves.

When Ithaca wasn't tending to my injuries or I wasn't being interrogated, Malcolm or Harris would try and sneak down to meet with me to work on the plan. When they couldn't see me, they would talk to Ithaca. The information and ideas wandered back and forth like that, like little paper boats in a pond, bumping into each other, but making slow progress anyway.

"The king is the biggest jackass I've ever seen," Malcolm told me one day, after sneaking down to the cells once again. "He's started allowing fights for people to let off steam, and now they've practically become gladiator matches; two people were killed yesterday, and I think the sick bastard finds it entertaining."

"Isn't half the point of keeping people here for the numbers?" I asked.

He shrugged, "He must not care too much, I guess, or he just sees them as useless if they can't win a fight. Ithaca tried to help the guy who was stabbed, but the bleeding wouldn't stop."

When she visited me later that evening, she'd been unusually quiet. She communicated with vague shrugs and nods as she examined my rows of stitches. Everything she did was in a daze, and I had gently grabbed her wrist to make her pause.

"It isn't your fault," I told her.

She knew what I meant, and lowered her eyes. "It's the second stabbing death I've witnessed. I tried to focus and stay calm, but I couldn't stop thinking about the first one. If I had just been able to think—if there wasn't so much blood—"

"There are some injuries that just can't be mended," I insisted. "Don't blame yourself."

She'd nodded weakly, and continued her work until Eric decided he had enough and they both left.

It wasn't long after that when I noticed that the pain was fading. I would catch myself moving more without wincing, sitting down and standing back up without gritting my teeth and swearing. The bruises had shifted from grotesque purple to dull green-and-gray splotches. I'd even been allowed to take a bath.

It hadn't mattered that the water was cold. I didn't realize how much I needed to feel clean, how much I needed to clear my head. It was the same when we had first arrived and needed to wash away the mud from the storm; there were dozens of other people around, cleaning off dirt, blood, and sweat, only this time they made sure to stay as far away from me as they could. The sutures were far from pretty, and some people could barely bring themselves to glance in my direction, while others would stare outright, cringing, looking cold and worried.

I tried not to let myself care.

"The scars seem to be forming well," Ithaca had told me later that day.

Nickolai nodded, "They look like bolts of lightning." He'd been following her around lately, like a little assistant, dutifully fetching this and that, even agreeing to carry her basket of supplies.

"Lightning, huh?" I smirked. "It sounds so much more valiant that way."

Ithaca asked him to get more water, and watching him scurry away on a mission, past Eric, was the first time I had seen her smile in days.

"How are you feeling?" I asked.

"I believe it's my job to be asking you that question," she said, as she continued to examine one of the more persistent wounds on my shoulder.

"Well then, I feel better than I have in a long time. All thanks to you."

"You don't need to keep thanking me."

"But I will," I grinned, "And you can't stop me."

She smiled again. Just a little. "Keep in mind that I'm making a sedative for you—so don't be too sure about that."

The bruising on my shoulder was sore when she pressed on it, and it was still darker than most of the other areas. Nevertheless, the cloudy yellow and gray was making a sure retreat. The gashes themselves had mostly fused into pinkish scars that no longer qualified as open wounds.

"So, how are you really?" I asked again.

"Living one moment at a time," she sighed, "avoiding crossing paths with the king as much as I can. When he's not in the center building, he's out making people's lives as difficult as he can. I've never seen someone who looks so grim all the time, so mean and foreboding. Making eye contact with him is like looking an angry bull in the eye."

"Does he target you?"

"No more or less than anybody else," she set her jaw. "And knowing what he's planning to do to my home makes me angrier than I care to admit."

"In all fairness, you have more cause to be angry than anyone else here."

Before Eric ushered her upstairs again, we had enough time to agree that I had healed sufficiently: Whispering so quietly that it barely qualified as speaking, we decided that the plan would be set into motion that next night.

That morning, Malcolm snuck past the early guard shift to meet outside my cell one final time. We listed through the steps of the plan first, triple checking each twist and turn. All seven of us, including Ithaca and Nickolai, knew it by heart.

Then came the other pressing issue.

"Still no word on why the tattoo is such a big concern?" Malcolm inquired. "I've tried asking around where I can, but nothing's come of it."

"They talk about their capital, Northgate, that man from the wanted posters, and the deaths of their first royal family; each time they question me, those things come up," I explained. "It doesn't make any sense. I don't see how any of it is connected to me. To us."

"But they think the star means something important, obviously. Why not tell you?"

I shrugged. "I've asked. Several times. And they just carry on as if they didn't hear me."

After a moment, Malcolm sighed. "Well, after tonight, it won't matter anymore."

"And good riddance," I agreed. *Assuming the plan works.*

The rest of that day went by in a blur, and at long last, darkness fell across Fort Ketta's ancient walls.

Ithaca and Eric came down the stairs; I had been good about putting on an act every time he or someone else higher up saw me. They needed to think my wounds were killing me, and so I pretended to slump against the back wall like a bag of rice, breathing shallowly, and staring out at the space in a trance.

Eric crossed the room and claimed his usual spot at the bottom of the stairs. I was surprised he hadn't started bringing a book or something to keep him occupied; each visit, he paid less and less attention to us. His fingernails had to be immaculate after all the time I'd seen him cleaning them with that small knife, which he extracted from his pocket yet again.

Ithaca was already rummaging through the basket, securing a dark gray shawl around herself with one hand.

Even with Eric as uninterested as ever, I kept up the sickly façade.

Quietly, carefully, I asked, "Did Harris manage to toss an officer's uniform into the hedges on the other side of the wall?"

"It took some impeccable timing," Ithaca explained, whispering just as inaudibly, "but yes, he managed. It's on the eastern side—so you should be near it when we leave you out there." She retrieved a vial made of indigo colored glass, slightly larger than the one that the lavender oil had been in. She carried it over, tilting her head to the side to observe it as she sloshed it around.

"I have to warn you, it will probably taste terrible; it's mostly valerian and saffron." She tugged the cork out of place, kneeling down and holding the vial out to me. Keeping it out of Eric's line of sight.

I took it from her, squinting through the opening at the liquid inside. "Just down the whole thing?"

She nodded, still keeping her head turned to the side, but not enough to prevent a brief glimpse of something on her right cheek, close to her eye.

"What is that?" I asked, gesturing to the mark on her face.

"It's nothing."

I lowered the vial, observing her skeptically. "Then look at me."

She didn't move her head, just glanced at me out of the corner of her eye. I stared back, sitting up straighter. Near-death act be damned.

After a moment of consideration, she sighed, and turned to face me, revealing a small, purple bruise near her eye.

"Who did that?"

"It's not important—"

"Was it him?" I nodded toward Eric.

"No."

"Then who?"

She turned away again, looking at the floor. "It was the king."

That pompous, vindictive, wretch—I shouldn't have been nearly as surprised as I was. The way he'd backhanded her on that first day streaked through my memory. It had taken days for those welts to fade—and now this?

"Why?" I pressed.

"I dealt with it. It's not important." Her voice was firm. "He won't be doing it again." Then she pointed at the vial, "Now hurry up and drink before that brute over there gets wise."

I forced myself back into the act, letting my posture sink as I peered across the room, beyond the metal bars. Eric still hadn't so much as looked in our direction. Then I eyed the indigo glass hesitantly. "It'll work that fast?"

"It should," she nodded.

It probably won't kill me, right?

"It will be just like drifting off into a peaceful sleep," she assured me. "You'd have to drink a lot more than that to die from it."

I nodded, forcing a bit of a smile. "Well, in that case..." After squinting into the vial one last time, I barricaded through the wall of hesitation I'd built up, and chugged through the whole thing. It was bitter like raw ginger root, searing through my senses. The impulse to spit it back out came after I had already swallowed it, thankfully, leaving me to struggle with the lingering, burning taste that made my eyes water. "God, that's absolutely disgusting," I tried not to gasp.

A faint smirk tugged at the corner of her mouth. "I did warn you." She took the bottle, tucked it away instantly. No evidence of anything amiss.

"Yeah, but my sense of taste may never be the same again," I laughed, noting of the wave of lightheadedness and the blur in my vision. Then there was a cascading downpour of tiredness that made my limbs heavy. But still, I managed to stay sitting up.

"I guess the next time I see you, we will either be free, or headed for an execution..."

"Hopefully it's the first option," she agreed.

I nodded weakly. A dense fog was building up around my thoughts, sending all of them stumbling around with their hands out in search of guidance. Most of them just tripped and fell over, while others carelessly bumped into each other.

The floor seemed closer. Probably because it was. The cold, packed ground was like lying in a grassy field.

"You're like the sun..."

She looked down at me quizzically. "I am?"

I nodded, "You make pain go away..."

She tilted her head. "You mean *what I do* makes it go away?"

"Nope. Just you."

I remembered seeing her soft smile before my eyelids were too heavy to keep open. I felt like I was sinking slowly into the ground. My mind retreated into sleep, slipping through my fingers like fine sand until there was nothing left but peace.

CHAPTER TWENTY

The air was cold, and it smelled like grass and pine needles. Short bursts of wind rushed over me. My limbs were strangely heavy. Falling back asleep would have been absurdly easy, but there was something in the back of my mind that kept prodding at me.

When I opened my eyes, it was still night, and I could see the trees and their swaying shadows through the grass.

I can see the trees? Where's the wall?

I turned my head, scanning the starry sky that abruptly ended in an expanse of black. The towering mass of bricks loomed behind me, allowing only faint echoes of sound and dim torchlight to travel over it.

Oh, there it is.

And I was outside it. The plan was working.

Pushing myself off the ground, I stared at my surroundings in momentary puzzlement. I thought I'd been placed next to a mound of dirt or rocks as my eyes adjusted to the dark; whatever it was, its peak was about a third of the way up the wall. Then I looked closer, right in front of me. Milky, unblinking eyes were staring back at me.

I vaulted to my feet and stumbled backward into the wall. Pain laced across my tender scars, but I was already scooting sideways. I finally noticed the hum of the flies around the pile of bodies, and the smell—

My stomach knotted. My knees crashed into the ground and I nearly threw up. Covering my nose with my sleeve, I tried to blink through the watering in my eyes, as the reason I was out here came back to me—find the uniform Harris threw over the wall.

I didn't look too closely at any of the bloated corpses in varying stages of decay, and I did everything I could not to touch them, even if it meant prodding limbs aside with a broken branch. My vision rippled and no amount of blinking cleared it. It felt like a lifetime before I found a bundle of black fabric on the opposite side of the pile, caught next to a bush toward the northeast corner.

As I shrugged into the disguise, I told myself I'd thank Harris later for having enough aim not to land it among the corpses.

With that, I wiped my eyes, smoothed back my hair, and marched around the corner to the main gate. I stopped on the opposite side of the sturdy metal bars and sulked at one of the skinny, on-edge looking guards that waited there.

"Hey, open the gate."

The one on the left blinked at me, "What are you doing out there?"

He had two red stripes on his sleeve, as did the other guard. Quickly, I glanced down at my own uniform; I had three.

I sighed, and channeled my best impersonation of Mordecai. "I had too much to drink, now open the door."

"I never saw you leave," the one on the right said.

"Well, it's not my fault that you must be fucking blind. Open this damn door!"

They both flinched and, with eyes averted to the ground, fumbled with the keys and the oversized lock. The one on the right used his set of keys, and I could see a matching set hanging from the belt of the one on the left. The lock clinked, and they pulled the heavy gate open.

I shouldered through, sneering down the end of my nose at both of them. "Was that so difficult?"

I bumped into the one on the left, continuing on a meandering course to match my nonexistent drinking problem. The keys that had been secured to his belt fit into my palm, and I undid the clasp without a sound. Both of them stared after me, none the wiser.

I stayed off toward the left, aiming for the orderly rows of tents. Despite my deliberately clumsy steps, I made sure to tread lightly and quietly.

The few red uniforms that were still awake barely looked at me. They would glance up, then shrink away with heads down.

I found the row I wanted and followed my memory to our tent. I carefully edged myself through the two flaps serving as a door and found everyone in the same, basic arrangement as when we had first arrived, all awake.

Nickolai saw me first. His eyes darted to me, going wide, and all color fell from his face. He sat up quickly, reaching for something to his right. I opened my mouth to announce myself, but he'd already sent a metal water canteen flying straight at me.

"Mother of—"

I ducked to one side, feeling the rush of air as the canteen sailed past my face.

"Stop! It's me!"

Nickolai froze mid throw with a shoe in hand, eyes still wide.

I pointed to my face, which thankfully hadn't been dented inward. "Remember the plan?"

"Hey, at least we know the disguise really works," Evander chuckled. The rest of the room nodded in agreement, but I could still see that split-second of terror fading from their faces.

"Right." I tossed the stolen set of keys to Nickolai and winked reassuringly. "Let's go cheat death."

IT WAS JUST after midnight as I stalked back down the rows of tents, alone. My breaths fogged the cold air.

Ithaca was supposed to meet us at the tent once she managed to sneak out, but when she still hadn't arrived, I decided to look for her and try to help if things were already going wrong. As the only one in a uniform, I was the only one who could. The disguise would work as long as I didn't cross paths with Mordecai, Eric, or anyone who knew my face.

Passing the end of the rows of tents, I paused. Another officer in a black uniform was approaching—but upon a second glance, the fabric didn't fit right and was too big, and then I spotted a section of sun-white hair wisping out from beneath their hat.

"I had to improvise," was the only explanation Ithaca offered as she stopped beside me. The loose strands of hair blew across her cheek, and she tucked them back into the hat with the rest of her hair.

When I looked back at the center building, the path was clear, and no one was following her. "That's brilliant."

"Only until they notice I'm gone." She led the way back into the lines of tents, gently touching the bruise on her cheek, like she was disappointed the cold wasn't numbing it.

"Are you ready?" I asked in a low voice, in case anyone was still awake to hear us.

"I've been ready to see this place go up in flames since the minute I got here." She straightened the front of her coat and shrugged her shoulders, tugging the uniform into place until it looked like a better fit than it was. "Are you?'

I nodded. "But if things fall apart—"

"Don't start down that road," her gray eyes glinted, "I won't entertain the thought."

"I'm trying to apologize again, *and* thank you." I stopped. "I would have died if you didn't sew me back together—even if you were only keeping your oath."

She stopped too, her hands fisted and holding onto the ends of her sleeves. When she sighed, the little white cloud drifted away with the breeze. "I would have done it regardless, oath or not. I was furious with you at the time, yes, but to die like that...I wouldn't have let it happen."

I took a step closer and carefully fitted my hand through hers. Her cold fingers curled tighter. "I owe you one, my dear partner-in-crime."

"I didn't do it so you'd owe me," she shook her head.

"That's how the whole life-saving thing works," I said as we started walking again, hand in hand. "And *if* things go awry, you can be positive I'll have your back too."

THE TIRED, but constantly present eyes of the guards in the watchtowers carried a different kind of weight when they weren't scanning a crowd, but tracking one group. I could almost imagine the weight of a target on my back. But I kept my eyes trained on the goal, taking confident steps toward the east tower.

Ithaca was on my left, still in uniform. Malcolm, Nickolai, Harris, Taz, and Evander walked in front of us in a cluster. They played their part well, with a hunch to their shoulders, and eyes directed at the ground as we herded them forward.

A pair of other officers were walking from the opposite direction, eyeing our odd-looking group suspectedly, with a noticeable lull in their conversation.

I cleared my throat, forcing a scowl onto my face. "My god, would you idiots hurry up," I swung my leg out, kicking Harris on the backside.

He stumbled forward a few steps, glaring over his shoulder at me. I watched the other officers out of the corner of my eye. They snickered at his expression and continued past us on their way.

I released a slow breath and turned back to the fast-approaching tower.

"That was uncalled for," Harris whispered.

"That was necessary, and I apologize."

He smirked over his shoulder, "Do you?"

I grinned back, "I never said I didn't enjoy it."

"Shh," warned Evander, since the guards outside the tower were already squinting at us.

I let all emotion fall from my face as we approached, taking out the set of keys I had stolen and swinging them around my finger. Nickolai had taken the main gate key off the ring earlier; he was our locksmith, after all, and the means to our escape once we destroyed the cache of Nightfire that Brighton had in Fort Ketta.

"We need to move some of the barrels around; there's another shipment arriving tomorrow, and we need to clear more room," I droned.

Like the guards at the main gate, these men only had two stripes on their sleeves, and they stepped aside once they spotted the three I wore. Even though Ithaca was staying near the back of the group, she also had three stripes, and the other officers didn't miss them as we passed.

The first thing I noticed as Ithaca shut the door behind us was the sheer lack of space remaining; the storage area that had once been filled with crates was now packed with barrels, leaving only a narrow gap of floor down the middle. The unusual smell hit me second. It was like smoke, but with a sour undertone that reminded me of some kind of salt.

"Did these all used to be wine barrels?" asked Evander. He motioned to the blocked openings on the sides of the barrels, each rimmed with red stains.

"Maybe," Taz shrugged.

Malcolm cut in, "Or it could be the stains from the explosive itself —like it stained the chemist's hands?"

Ithaca kneeled by the closest one and, after planting a boot on the side of the barrel, managed to yank the plug out of place, and red powder streamed onto the stone floor. It hissed like falling sand, and she backed away. "What are we waiting for? Open as many as you can."

Starting in the middle of the room, we opened barrel after barrel, letting the crimson powder spill out into drifts and moats until there was more than enough to ignite a disaster. In fact, it already looked like a bad dream as red dust hovered in the corners, swallowing the air until it felt like trying to breathe through a dry rag.

As we made our way back to the door, Nickolai etched a lopsided smile into the powder with the toe of his shoe. That alone was enough to make me forget the plan for a second. I grinned as I opened the door, and we filed back into the night. But it didn't last long.

A bolt of frigid cold shot through my chest as we lurched to a stop. Mordecai was standing directly in front of us with his hands planted on his hips. The two guards that had let us pass were watching from a safe distance behind him—and farther behind them I could see the chemist storming in our direction with an entourage of other officers, including Cedric and Kassian.

Mordecai forced a smile that was closer to a sneer. "Care to explain? Or shall we skip the bullshit?"

Behind me, I heard the scratch and hiss of a match being struck. Mordecai's gaze flew over my shoulder, and he turned a shade of white I'd never seen from him. I followed his stare. Malcolm was holding a tiny flame in one hand, and the door to the east tower in the other. He tugged it open, revealing the spilled powder beyond.

Mordecai shook his head and choked out a single word; "DON'T—"

The two officer's who'd been guarding the tower were already fleeing in the opposite direction. Kassian, Cedric, and the other men who'd been following the chemist turned and did the same, some already shouting for anyone who could hear to run, leaving *her* alone as she practically stumbled to a halt, mouth hanging open. She clutched the front of her white-fur coat with one of her red hands.

Malcolm met their eyes, both of them, before delivering a brutal, finalizing, "Fuck you." Then he tossed the match through the doorway and slammed it shut.

By the time I turned back around, the chemist was running the other way too. Mordecai's throat bobbed, and before he also turned and ran, he pointed a shaking finger at us and declared, "You just killed us all."

And if *Mordecai* was running away, that meant—

Nickolai already had the gate key in his hand, and sped away toward the main gate faster than someone with such small legs should have been able to go, but we all followed his lead regardless.

Now it felt like a bad dream too, the kind where no matter how hard I tried to run, it seemed like my legs weren't working hard or fast enough, like struggling through waist-deep water.

To the west, people were waking up and stepping out of their tents to investigate the shouts escalating all across Fort Ketta. The soldiers with the black armbands were all talking amongst themselves; the ones without were watching the men in the black uniforms, paying attention as all their control was completely and obviously lost.

I felt the explosion before I heard it. A ripple of force shot through the ground, like some immense demon tried to punch up through it, disrupting our balance. A flaming red glow shot through the darkness, stretching and bending pitch-black shadows into long, clawing shapes. Then, above all the sounds—the officers shouting, soldiers yelling—thunder and fire split the air, swallowing the rest of the noise entirely. The searing heat of flames spread across my back; I could imagine strands of fire nipping at my heels, but I didn't turn around.

A wave of people, the people who'd been trapped here, surged toward the main gate.

Another explosion lit up the night sky. This time, when the ground lurched, we all went with it and tumbled sideways. Chunks of what had once been the east tower rained down. A blistering hot chunk of stone bounced off the arm I raised to shield my face. Others peppered my side and legs. My left ear was muffled and ringing. My throat and lungs burned as smoke clouded the air.

As we stumbled back onto our feet and began the final sprint for the gate, I dared a look behind us. A column of sheer black rose into the sky where the east tower once stood, and flame bloomed within as it stretched wider, moving too fast. It was going to eat this place alive.

The two officers remaining at the main gate were staring past us. One was white in the face and clutching the metal bars that he stood with his back against; his eyes shimmered with unshed tears and a dark patch soaked through the front of his pants. The other one had a spear in his hands, and white-hot hatred in his eyes. He gripped the wooden length of the weapon, leveling the iron point in our direction.

"Open the door!" shouted Evander.

The first officer didn't move. We were upon him in seconds, and I yanked him out of our way by the collar, shouting in his face, "If you want to live open the gate!" Only it wasn't a threat, not from me, but from the stampede of fire and ash behind us. Nickolai ducked past me and stabbed the key into the lock as Malcolm dodged the tip of the other officer's spear, gripped the wooden pole, and snapped off the killing end. He flipped it into his other hand, holding it like a knife. He looked ready to eviscerate the officer, who raised his fists, but Harris sped at him from the side and punched the guard in the jaw before practically tossing him aside.

The officer in my grasp shook his head and sank to the ground, and I let him. I wasn't about to try and drag him through the main gate with us.

Ithaca and I both looked toward the stampede of people rushing toward us. They were so close I could read their faces.

"Any second now!" Ithaca gasped.

In answer, the lock gave, and Nickolai threw the gate open wide. By the time we were through it, the black cloud had blocked out all the stars above us. We swerved left, avoiding the horde of prisoners launching themselves through the main gate behind us as a blast of hot, smokey air spilled over the south wall. Somewhere, I could hear stone breaking and falling. The black cloud reached the south wall in the same moment, and the ancient expanse of stone bricks shook, buckled, and bowed outward, sending spiderwebs of cracks across its face.

The hot air continued to surge as we ran away from the wall, until we were out of its reach if it fell. The air was stinging my eyes, and it felt like trying to breathe through sand.

We didn't stop running for a long time, until my chest heaved from fatigue instead of the smoke and ash. I could taste blood underneath my tongue by the time we stopped to look back.

Fort Ketta was an uneven, distant pile of embers in our wake.

Black, velvety clouds rolled into the sky above it, bursting and sparking with flames. Falling stone echoed across the expanse.

Our faces were gray and smeared with soot, like a bunch of chimney sweeps as we all glanced at one another. Everything looked bad enough in the dark, and I was actually afraid to see what dawn would reveal—if it could pierce through the smoke at all.

CHAPTER TWENTY-ONE

B y the time I'd washed the ash and soot off my face with water
from a stream, my hands were too cold to feel. Too cold to
rip the insignias from the stolen uniform. So, I settled for
turning the much-needed coat inside out.

Ithaca came up with the idea as everyone else finished scrubbing
their faces and hands clean, having already done the same with her
stolen uniform. Her nose and cheeks were bright pink from the frigid
water, and some coal had splashed into her hair, forming streaks of
gray around her face.

We were walking at the back of the pack as we followed a road
farther south. I appreciated the dark, because it meant she couldn't see
me warring with myself on whether or not to reach out and touch one
of those strands.

As the first signs of dawn arrived, we came to a town stirring
awake on the coast. People were already standing in the streets as they
stared north, pointing at the distant black cloud in the sky that grew
clearer and starker with each passing minute of sunrise.

None of us paused to do the same as we trudged down the main
streets, weaving through the gathering crowds. In fact, I only looked
back once to eye the black plume in the sky, and that was enough.

As we rounded a corner onto a narrower street, one facing west toward the foggy shoreline, a short, lean woman caught my arm. Her grip—it was like iron, and I winced despite myself. When I glanced down, I recognized the snake tattoos wrapping around her wrist and up her arm. Then I recognized her dark hair and her cunning, elegant face.

Of all days, of course, *today* would be when another one of my monetary debts hunted me down.

Before I could get a word out, and before everyone had noticed her at all, the card counter announced, "I can help you."

"I don't want to owe you any more money," I said automatically.

Her grip tightened. "This isn't cards, and it was never about the money. I'm not who you think I am."

When I breathed in, I couldn't smell any alcohol. But there had to be something that could explain her. How was she this far north of Salona and beyond Orvalia's borders altogether? And how did she find me?

"Now isn't a good time," Malcolm answered for me.

Her jaw edged forward, and she turned to him with fuming eyes. She opened her mouth like she was about to tell him to mind his own business, but no sound ever came out. She released my arm.

"You..." she trailed off, face paling. "How have you managed to stay so young?"

Evander took a generous step away from Malcolm, like he expected the woman's stare to cut a path through him.

Malcolm shook his head, "We've never met. I don't know you."

After a moment, I watched as her eyes widened with some sort of realization, and she took a step back from all of us. Just as I started to hope she'd leave and disappear into the crowd forming up the street, our eyes met again.

She asked, "Does this change your mind?" She turned her back to us and swept her curtain of dark hair aside.

I felt like I was going to be violently sick.

On the back of her neck, the blood-red star was plain to see. I wanted to ask Ithaca if I was hallucinating, if I had a fever that had scrambled my mind, or if the explosion had somehow turned my thoughts into rubble too.

And this near-stranger was—she was my—

The card counter turned back around, putting up one hand. "We should talk."

"You lied to me." I barely heard myself say it.

She nodded, "I can explain."

She'd been in Salona practically my whole life; I knew her reputation as the city's best card counter well before I'd ever set foot in a gambling hall. She'd dragged me out of the waves that day I nearly drowned when I was nine. She had been *walking distance* from me. But worse, she'd known the truth and never said a word—all for what?

Reading my face, she added, "You have a right to be angry, but you'll want to hear what I have to say. The game has gone on long enough."

I quickly decided that *that* might just be the only time I allowed myself to agree with her.

THE WAXY, dented surface of the table blurred in my vision as I stared at it. Through it. The hum of the dim parlor was far away in my ears as townspeople speculated about the deathly plume of smoke to the north. I didn't let myself truly hear any of them.

Malcolm sat on my left, and across the small round table from us the card counter was drumming her fingers on the edge. Ithaca, Harris, Evander, Taz, and Nickolai were across the room near the doors, watching from a distance as we talked—as *she* talked, actually.

"I knew as soon as I heard the boom, and then when I saw the smoke," she said, having just explained why she was here at all. Apparently, after I'd gone missing from Salona, she'd gone on a mission to track me down; and once she discovered the existence of Fort Ketta a week ago, the dots were easy to connect. Even more so when it erupted into flames.

"How considerate of you, *mother*," I bit out.

Her eyes—*my* dark brown eyes—glinted briefly. "Give me a chance. Anger is one of the five stages of grief, and you have every right to be grieving right now."

I returned to staring at the table and sighed. "Why now? After twenty-one years of being in Salona and *keeping an eye on me*, for my entire life, why did you finally decide to stop lurking and introduce yourself?"

She leaned forward, tapping a finger on the center of the table. "Because I was afraid of this. Because anyone would be furious if they were in your shoes." Her rings flashed in the low light; the widest one on her middle finger tapered to a blunted point, designed to hurt. "I was still convinced my presence would do more harm than good."

"You were convinced?" I wrinkled my nose.

She swallowed, leaning back into her seat. Her hand clenched into a fist on the table. "Your father was a good man—or I like to think he was. Ever the charmer. But I know he was in trouble for something, because he was the one who told me to hide you...before he left." It was hard to tell, but her eyes seemed to shimmer like water. "I wouldn't have done it if I didn't trust him. All he said was that I needed to hide you, and leaving you there was the only way I could think..." Her knuckles faded to white, and a tendon rippled beneath the snake tattoos on her wrist. "He never told me why. I trusted his word and his fears for a long time, but I could never truly walk away. I was a fool."

A tendril of anger sank its claws into my side. "You think?"

She blinked as if I had thrown something at her.

I sighed at myself, averting my eyes back to the table. "I'm sorry. I just...I don't know you," I stammered as I glanced back up at her. "For my whole life, I've been telling myself that I don't want to know you and that it doesn't matter. This is going to take some patience."

"I understand," she nodded slowly. "I never thought I would find myself telling you the truth," she glanced over at Malcolm, then down at her hands. "And it's apparently a little more complicated than I thought."

Malcolm hadn't spoken since she insisted he join us for our

conversation, and based on the set of his jaw, I knew he wasn't about to start.

I asked, "What do you mean?"

She traced a hand over the back of her neck. "It appears your father was right about the stupid tattoos, if nothing else. He insisted they would help bring things back together. That's why we each have one, him included."

My hand instinctively moved over my heart, like it was trying to block a gaping red wound.

Looking at Malcolm, she added, "But you probably never needed one."

"How do you know I have it?" he asked. "What if I said I didn't?"

Her brows lowered with what looked like pity, and she shook her head. The pointed edges of the scarlet star on the back of her neck could barely be seen peeking around like talons. "Your face alone is a better maker's mark than that tattoo; you would not believe how uncanny—how eerie it was to look at you, because for a second I thought..."

"So that's what you meant when you asked me how I'd stayed so young," his jaw feathered. "You thought I was him."

She fussed with one of her rings, then nodded.

"But I'm not your..."

"No," she confirmed. "I only ever had one child."

Resting my chin on my knuckles, I gazed blankly at the far reaches of the room and tried not to grind my teeth.

Brothers by half.

"You didn't know, did you?" asked Malcolm. And when the card counter couldn't find an answer, he added, "I'm sorry you had to find out *like this.*"

She waved one of her glinting hands. "There's no need to apologize; none of this was your doing. I'd rather know the truth."

When I ended my scrutiny of the far wall and sat back in my chair, I couldn't help but stare. It was still Malcolm, it always would be, but suddenly his face seemed as foreign as my mother's. Everything about him was cast in a darker kind of light.

That's the face that started all of this. That's the face that left me, and my mother, and Malcolm, and whoever Malcolm's mom was too. That's the face that branded all of us with an irreversible red mark, and a now ever-present reminder of him.

"You mentioned that he was in some kind of trouble," I pressed. "He's a wanted man?"

Her smile was sad and restrained, and somehow she knew where I was going because she asked, "You've seen the posters then? The reward of 8,000 marks?"

"We joked that he looked like Malcolm," I recalled. It felt like the air was being vacuumed out of my chest. "He's the reason Brighton is going to war with Dale; they think Dale is harboring him. They say he let the radicals who killed their royal family do as they pleased, and that he was probably working for them all along."

"It's a waste of their time," she muttered, "they'll never find him."

Malcolm's brows furrowed. "What makes you say that?"

She shrugged one shoulder. "You can't hunt down a ghost, especially not one that's been gone for so long."

"He's dead?" I clarified.

When she nodded, I didn't feel anything. Maybe because nothing had truly changed. That man had been dead to me from the minute I arrived on the orphanage doorstep.

No one spoke for what had to be several minutes. All three of us were staring at the table by the time the card counter said, "I guess this is the part where I ask if you have any questions."

I didn't need to think for long. "What's your name?"

"Serafina," she answered.

Malcolm's blue eyes were a shade darker than normal, like the sea before a storm, when he asked, "What was *his* name?"

"Full name?"

I have a last name? I glanced over at Malcolm. *We have a last name?* We nodded.

"His name was Xavier Karabian."

My head was already pounding when I stood from the table and went back outside. I remembered mumbling that I needed to go for a walk. Malcolm stayed behind and was continuing to come up with questions for Serafina, while also filling in the rest of our group on *everything*.

I rounded the corner, following the road toward the coast. The wind stung my face, numbing my hands and the tip of my nose. Some people on the streets were still staring north at the curtains of smoke fanning across the sky, and flecks of ash had begun to fall. Even so, nothing about it reminded me of a normal fire. If I breathed deeply enough, I could faintly smell the dry, chemical fetor that had clouded the inside of the east tower.

I ran a hand over my face and blinked my eyes back into focus, clearing my senses.

That's when I saw him—on the street corner ahead of me. The physician from Angel's Landing was holding open a map and asking a local man for directions. Just like Ithaca, he stood out because he was tall and lean. The breeze ruffled his light hair, in contrast to the unyielding, sharp set to his jaw as he frowned at the map.

I didn't think twice before rushing down the remainder of the street and interrupting them. "I know who you're looking for."

His eyes, gray just like his daughter's, narrowed. "You what?"

"I know where she is."

His face paled a shade. He refolded the map without looking, gesturing back up the street behind me in silent question. When I nodded, we both started walking that way. His strides were long and fast, enough that I nearly had to jog to keep up as he asked, "And who are you, exactly?"

"My name is Ignatius," I explained, "and the rest is a bit of a long story."

"She mentioned you before; I recognize you name." He extended a hand for me to shake as we turned back up the narrower street. "I'm Tobias."

CHAPTER TWENTY-TWO

When Ithaca saw her father walking up the street, she practically shoved Harris out of her way. Her feet were near silent on the ground, like each step barely touched the cobblestones. "Da? How in the world did you get here?"

Tobias picked Ithaca up off the ground when he hugged her. "How do you think? I was on the first boat I could find out of Angel's Landing after you vanished—just in time too, because the people I paid to make the illegal crossing got caught just after I made it off the docks." He laughed a little. "I would've had to swim."

Only it wasn't a joke. The way he said it, like a promise, and the way he still hadn't let go of his daughter—if all else failed, if there was no other way, he would have swum to get to her.

Ithaca peeked at me over her father's shoulder. "Where did you find him?"

I shrugged, "Just around the corner and down a few streets. I wasn't even paying attention, but there was no way to miss him." I had to step closer to the buildings and away from the street. More and more people were headed for the main road, nearly swallowing us with them, and the jumble of voices all shared a common word; *ships.* I gestured at the crowd and asked, "What's going on?"

"People are saying they can see ships from Dale," Malcolm answered, "I think they're here to investigate where all the smoke is coming from; they can probably see it from Angel's Landing by now."

"There's one from Northgate, too," added a passing woman, "a warship." And as she disappeared into the growing crowds, we all watched each other's faces go pale.

"Brighton's leaders knew Dale would see the smoke," Harris pointed out. "Could they really get ready to fight that fast?"

"The chemist said they had more Nightfire in the capital," I thought aloud.

Malcolm nodded, "And if they already had some loaded onto a warship..."

The chill that went down my spine wasn't from the cold.

Taz was the first to begin following the waves of people back down the street, and I wasn't far behind. An ache was expanding through my gut by the time we rounded the corner, and I was straining to see over people's heads toward the sea. Behind us, I could hear Serafina asking "what's Nightfire?" and Harris trying to explain, but once I'd shouldered my way through the crowd and stopped at the short stone wall above the quay, I knew he wouldn't need to.

Three of Dale's ships were cutting through the waves, white sails curved like crescent moons. They were close enough that I could see the long oars moving. And coming from the north, a brig painted black for winter and donning a blood-red sail was crawling to meet them.

Ithaca planted her hands on the short stone wall beside me, standing on the tips of her toes. The salty wind tugged at her hair.

I wasn't sure why, but the pile of bodies that had been outside the east wall of Fort Ketta flashed through my mind, and watching the distance between the ships narrow felt like staring into the white, foggy eyes of a dead man.

Dale's ships turned to avoid the unwavering course of Brighton's, but by then it was too late. When they crashed together, the dark body of Brighton's ship vanished into a burst of fire that ate up the red sail. Black smoke poured outward. Chunks of wood, metal, and what I prayed weren't people speckled the water as an expanding ring of force flattened the waves.

I would have kept staring like a fool, but Ithaca tugged my arm as she ducked behind the short wall. I'd barely made it down, too, when that blast ripped through the air. The crowds tumbled backward. Glass windows erupted into falling waves of glass. The sound blended with the screams and the delayed roar of the explosion, and maybe it was my imagination, but the wind coming from offshore was suddenly as hot as if I was next to a forge.

Ithaca and I stood slowly, eyes locked, before we both turned to look at the sinking, wounded ships in the distance.

"They're not going to put an end to this," Ithaca shook her head, "It's like they've developed a taste for it."

The time to stop Brighton, to stop what they could do with their new weapon, was running thin. That fact settled over me in a wave. If anyone was going to do something before Brighton amassed all of the power Nightfire could give them, then they needed to do something *now*.

But worse than that, far heavier than that, I realized we might be the only ones who stood a chance at filling that gap.

———

"IF WE DON'T DO something, Brighton will win the war against Dale and wipe them from the map with that shit. When they get bored of that, they'll come for the rest of the main continent, and after that, they will set out to find new land they can burn to the ground and take over." My heart was beating low in my chest. If it sank any farther down, I was worried it might make me sick. "It will never end."

"Think of all the people who would die," agreed Malcolm. "Both the ones they use to handle the explosive and the ones who are killed when it's set off."

Ithaca was sitting on the opposite side of the table beside her father and was cringing with doubt. We'd all returned to the parlor to discuss what to do after the initial panic from the boat attack had died down, and the streets had cleared enough to walk through. Ithaca asked, "Why can't we return to Angel's Landing? We don't have an army, a navy, or anything it would take to stand against Brighton—but they do. We could pass everything we know into far more capable hands."

Now Tobias was cringing too. "About that...I've been meaning to explain why returning home isn't an option, at least for now."

Ithaca's brow wrinkled. "Because of the travel routes being closed down?"

"No," he shook his head. "You vanished at the same time that six of Brighton's spies did. It wasn't hard for the higher-ups to draw conclusions about your loyalty," he sighed, "regardless of how much I insisted they were wrong. And now that I've come here, without warning and without permission, they won't be apt to trust me either."

"They think we're *traitors*?" Her eyes shimmered.

"All the more reason to go to Northgate and fight this ourselves," Evander cut in. "You can prove the leaders of Dale wrong—even if you shouldn't have to."

Harris added, "We know more than anyone else involved; we've seen both sides of the war up close. If anybody has a chance at stopping this, it's us."

Serafina didn't look convinced, leaning back in her chair with her arms crossed. "So, what's your plan? Other than going to the capital?"

"That's where the rest of the explosives are stored," Taz explained. "Their chemist mentioned it before; it's in her lab somewhere in the city, and there's not enough time for them to move it. They've said it themselves; they aren't strong enough to fight Dale without it. If we destroy all the Nightfire they have left, then they can't go to war."

"We need to destroy their recipe for it too," I pointed out. "So that they can't make more once it's gone."

"How do we do that?" asked Nickolai. He was hugging his knees to his chest. "Unless we're going to use the explosive to destroy the explosive—but we'd have to rig some kind of timer if we want to survive that."

Malcolm shrugged, "That could work, actually. We could divide into teams; one to rig the explosion where the Nightfire is stored, and one to kill the chemist and destroy her formula."

"That's only three things," Evander grinned. "We can handle a to-do list three items long, for the good of the world?"

"Provided nothing goes wrong," mumbled Tobias. "Nothing is ever that simple."

"A little extra optimism does wonders for the complexion. Notice," Evander gestured to his own face, "not a wrinkle in sight. I highly recommend it."

Ithaca, who'd been frowning at the surface of the table for a few moments, finally asked, "So it's a heist? Because every good heist needs a truly, absolutely solid plan."

Malcolm pursed his lips. "Before we get to that, how many of us are actually in? Because this could easily end up going to hell in a handbasket."

Ithaca's hand was the first to go up, and upon the questioning look from her father, she said, "That explosive should never have been made. They are not going to use it on my home, not if I have a say."

With a single nod, Tobias rose his hand too.

So did I, and Malcolm, and Harris, and Evander, and Taz, and Nickolai.

Serafina's jaw angled forward as she considered, and she twirled one of the rings on her hand. Unlike the rest, it didn't have a sharp edge or a winking jewel. It was a plain band of gold, and my stomach hollowed out when I realized what finger it was on.

It may not have been a wedding ring, not truly, but it was still a vow. It was a promise from the former captain of Brighton's royal guard. An unkept promise, as hollow as the ring itself.

She ceased twirling. "The last time that city burned, it was at the hands of your father," she said to Malcolm and me. "I can't think of a better way to end it this time. We might even be able to count it as a family tradition."

A grin broke across my face; an unexpected one, but somehow it felt right. "Then let's get to work on that plan."

CHAPTER TWENTY-THREE

orthgate reeked of ash and soot. The city was under a perpetual blanket of smog that had tinged its stone buildings and canals with shades of gray and green. Barely two days had passed since we arrived, and I still wasn't used to it. It clung to my hair. It wove itself into the fabric of my clothes. Given enough time, I wondered if it would become permanent, if I'd ever be able to scrub the city air from my skin and wash it away.

Perched atop a slanted, frost-dusted rooftop, I watched as a group of kids played in the square below, chasing each other around the mossy fountain in the center. I almost envied their joy, and the fact that their biggest concern was who could race to the other end of the plaza the fastest.

Most of the city was quiet, staying indoors, some already calling their children inside for the night well before sunset. But the northern reaches of the city, where the king's cabinet and wealthy merchants lived in estates along the main canals and the coastline, were cheering, drinking, and setting off fireworks. Even with the sun still out, the distant pop of firecrackers echoed up the streets. Faded red, blue, and green dotted the skyline to the north.

From the minute we arrived, we knew it could all be over in an instant. The time to act could run out at any second. And the festivities meant it was worse than we thought. Brighton's wealthiest all believed they had already won.

Tomorrow was the word on the street. *Tomorrow* and *dawn*.

We had until then to end it. To stop the attack that would destroy everything.

In the middle of the premature celebrations, I looked to where the hulking forms of the old and the new palace loomed. They were like sleeping giants, barely more than dark shapes through the haze. The new palace was larger, made of a lighter stone, and far simpler in design. But the old palace, the one that had once burned and was still damaged from that night when the first royal family was assassinated, looked like an old church—with green, domed roofs and steep, sharp details crawling up its walls. All the copper detailing had faded to pale green a long time ago, blending with the moss that was slowly covering the tan and gray stone exterior. When we'd gone closer, we'd sized up the brick wall that separated it from the rest of the city. Beyond that wall, a moat sectioned off the old palace on its own small island, and that moat had a canal that connected it with Northgate's main port.

It only took a matter of hours for us to confirm that the old palace was the location of the lab where Nightfire was made. We'd already observed a few barrels being carefully transported on the grounds, and the charred, blackened remnants of where a few had accidentally gone off.

Our plan to invade the old palace, destroy the formula for Nightfire, and kill the chemist who designed it *had* to happen tonight. We had no other option; dozens and dozens of Brighton's warships were anchored in the north harbor, and tomorrow morning—perhaps as soon as midnight—workmen would begin loading the barrels of Nightfire out of the old palace where they were stored, down the canal, and onto the ships as they prepared to attack Angel's Landing. Many of the sails were dyed crimson, distinguishing which ships were to be stocked with the explosive—to be floating coffins for every man and woman on board.

The nearby window slid open, glass winking in the dim afternoon light. "I thought you might be up here," Ithaca climbed over the sill, carefully navigating the thatching before sitting on the flat section of the inn's rooftop beside me. "Hiding?" she asked.

"Maybe a little," I admitted.

Ithaca rested her elbows on her knees and gazed across the square. "Taz just finished drawing out the map of the old palace's main layout. Based on the records we've been referencing, I think it's as accurate as we're going to get it," she explained. "I'll never understand how he can take all that information and make it make sense visually."

I smiled, "Especially not with Evander's *help*; they get more flirting done than anything else."

Over the last day and a half, they were perhaps the only one's who'd had any fun. Then again, that was just the way Evander faced stress and danger. The rest of us had been too afraid to stand still for more than a minute. Hoarding every spare second, in case it might help later and keep the plan from falling apart like a house of cards in the wind.

Harris had engineered a timer that would strike a match when the seconds ran out.

Taz had drawn up a map to guide us through the old palace.

Serafina had extensively scouted the grounds, climbing up trees, walls, and nearby buildings to get a scope of how to break in; Nickolai had gone with her, using a stolen spyglass to see details like the types of doors we'd have to get past.

Tobias did research, reading up on notes and maps of the old palace that had been shoved into a dusty corner of a library near the center of Northgate, confirming Serafina's observations and Nickolai's accounts on what types of doors stood between us and our goal.

Malcolm had practiced throwing the grappling hook until he could do it blindfolded.

Ithaca had planned for dealing with life-threatening wounds—which would almost certainly occur, even if the plan went well.

Yesterday, she'd also removed the stitches from my back, since the scars were fully formed.

"They're not as bad as you think," she'd told me, as she worked with a small pair of scissors.

I had glanced over my bare shoulder. "You say that—and I know you're probably right—I'm just dreading the part where I have to *explain* them to people." We were in a separate room for that reason. So that no one had to glimpse the crisscrossing, pink-and-white stripes that Ithaca insisted would fade over time. I also chose to have the stitches removed while Serafina was out scouting, because she still didn't know about them or what had happened. Telling her was something I knew I didn't have the courage for just yet. Not until we'd acclimated to each other's company more.

And, naturally, Ithaca somehow understood all of that without me voicing a word of it. "You're under no obligation to reveal your scars, not unless you want to," she asserted. "And you know I'd never say anything to her."

"I know. I've never doubted that for a second." I turned back around as she finished removing the last few stitches. "You're too good for this world, Ithaca. It doesn't deserve you."

I felt her smile before she said, "Well, I happen to like this world a lot. And I think it deserves more credit."

With that, my stitches were gone, and I'd stood up feeling like a weight had been removed from my shoulders. Still, nearly a whole day later, breathing was noticeably easier with the tight rows of black string finally gone.

Lastly, I'd done my part in preparing for the heist by forging an assortment of long, sharp lockpicking tools for Nickolai with scraps of metal, in addition to sharpening everyone's knives—which reminded me…

I took out the knife I'd made, its shine reflecting onto the rooftop beneath us, and extended it handle-first to Ithaca.

She blinked at the bone handle. "What's this?"

"Well, you didn't have a knife—I figured you might need one for this."

She took it like she thought it was made of glass.

I'd started over three times while making it, but it was worth it. The steel blade was simple, with a fuller running two-thirds of its length, starting just below the brass guard. It was long without being unwieldy, and slender without being weak. And I'd made sure it was sharp—sharp enough to shave a patch of hair from my arm without feeling it, and sharp enough to match that gleam in her eyes when she was truly furious.

"I know you've sworn an oath to do no harm, but... just in case you have to," I added.

Her eyes were as bright as the moon, and her chin wobbled slightly. "It's the most beautiful gift I've ever received." She put her hand out, "Thank you."

I laced our fingers together. That was how I'd measured for the handle; I knew precisely how the size of her palm fit against mine.

She held up her knife and looked at her own reflection in the blade. And the handle—it was a perfect fit.

Flecks of snow began falling. With no wind, they floated straight down, dotting the rooftop and the streets far below. The children in the square shrieked and giggled as they tried to catch snowflakes in their hands.

Ithaca was staring north at the old palace. "This is going to be the fight of our lives, isn't it?"

I nodded, not sure if she saw me do it, and squeezed her chilled hand.

———

MY HANDS WERE numb with cold and clenched into fists at my sides, though nobody could tell in the dark.

It was certainly the longest any of us had gone without talking. After two days of constant planning and communication, the silence felt like a knife to the gut as we inched along the northwest portion of wall that surrounded the old palace. The moat on the other side lapped against the stones. On our side, the snow that had accumulated through the afternoon reached just above my ankles and crunched softly with each stride.

I was second in line, behind Serafina. Clad in all black, with one guiding hand brushing the brick wall, she stopped at a corner where the main surrounding wall met with a slightly shorter wall that protected the canal. On the other side, a gate would allow the small transport boats to take barrels of Nightfire to the warships in the main port.

And shining from far away, beyond the wall, dim torchlight from the first of those boats inched closer.

Serafina extended one hand, snake tattoos on her wrists and arms standing out even darker than the night around us. With the other, she adjusted the small crossbow that was strapped across her back. A single bolt was already loaded into place—but she carried others if needed. The tip of each had been wrapped with oil-soaked cord, but not low enough to dull the point. They would stay put when they hit their mark.

I passed the matches into her open hand as Malcolm threw the grappling hook up, sinking its talons into the crook between the two walls. He tugged on the rope to secure it, then held it out to Serafina.

She nodded once, gripping the matches between her teeth, and climbed. The soles of her shoes scraped the face of the wall, but she made steady progress, arm over arm, until she laid flat along the top of the wall.

Spiders might have been a more well-suited tattoo choice than the snakes. She wasn't a tall woman, and like a spider, she could climb to any vantage point she needed. People might see her, turn their back for a moment to prepare themselves for a fight, but she'd already be gone when they looked back.

When I asked her where she learned it, she'd simply answered, "You learn to hide before you learn to fight. That means this won't be the first time I've needed to scale a wall. I've been chased down by sore losers after a game of cards and men blinded by alcohol—and sometimes a wall is what it takes to get away. It's cleaner than knocking out teeth. Most of the time it's just plain easier."

The tightness in my chest was making it hard to breathe. The golden torchlight of the transport boat wobbled as it passed through that gate on the other side, and Serafina unstrapped the small crossbow in one smooth motion. She struck a single match, the light casting her face in bronze. The flame took to the tip crossbow bolt easily, and before anyone would have seen its glow, she aimed and let it fly.

She watched it for only a second. We all heard the distant thunk of the arrow striking the side of a barrel. Serafina ducked back over our side of the wall, clinging to the rope, just in time for the night sky to flash with red light. The boom echoed up the walls and across Northgate's streets. A cloud of smoke drifted overhead, blocking out the stars.

My feet were moving on their own. Malcolm had the second grappling hook ready, and Serafina landed quietly behind me as we hurried back along the wall. Behind us, shouts escalated from the nearby port and a bell clanged in the old palace. It was a deep and hollow ring. It should have sent an icy bolt of fear down my back, but instead those three tolls cast a net of steely calm.

No turning back.

We stopped at the far end of the west wall, where the moat was narrowest on the other side. Malcolm threw the second grappling hook. Harris was the first to climb, the pack with the timer and rig strapped over his shoulder and across his chest. He unfurled the additional rope down the other side and began the descent toward the moat. The layer of snow from on top of the wall spilled down on us, some of it landing in my hair, but I barely felt the chill.

Taz climbed next, and one by one, we made our way over the wall.

Malcolm and I were the last two on the outside when I gave a tight smile and extended a hand as a silent 'good luck.' He clasped my arm, blue eyes reflecting the black smoke overhead, and nodded.

This was the part I'd been dreading. This was the part that had kept me up last night and made it hard to eat anything all day. Not just the knowledge that any of these moments might be final goodbyes—because that was worse than all of this together—but also the fact that there was only one way to get past the moat. The single bridge across was heavily guarded and currently being used to evacuate the old palace; with an explosion so close to its walls and so much more Nightfire stored within, they had to.

Which meant we had to swim.

The water was so cold that it stung, the shallowest part rising just above my knees as I finished climbing down the other side of the wall. I would have sworn, but the people evacuating on the bridge to the east might hear me, so I settled for clenching my teeth instead, bracing myself for having to wade all the way into the deeper water.

Snow ran along the outer edge of the moat like lace. It had dusted the walls of the old palace too, collecting on the green, domed rooftops and on the sills of arched windows. This close, the ironwork and masonry made its walls look like a rack of weapons—swords, spears, and knives big enough for giants to use, all lined up like teeth. Even the frozen, blackened vines growing up its levels seemed poised to kill. And if I looked closer, toward the tallest of the green domes in the center, I could see evidence of the fire. Some of the stones were newer and lighter than the rest, laid next to old brickwork permanently singed black.

I'm going to walk the same halls my father did twenty-two years ago. The thought struck like a fist, and I turned my attention back to the freezing water before it could truly sink in.

Harris was already halfway across, paddling steady through the deepest middle portion of the moat. Taz, Ithaca, Evander, and the rest were close behind, each trying to get out of the water as fast as possible. I couldn't blame them as I forced myself to take a few steps deeper, the water now climbing to my waist. My feet and hands were already numb. But the memory of that stormy day at the end of the dock when I was nine made my throat tight and my chest heavy.

By the time Malcolm had finished climbing over the wall and was wading into the water, I'd decided that my new life-motto was 'fuck the ocean.' That was enough for me to finally gather the courage and plunge all the way in.

There was something about swimming that felt painfully slow.

The frigid water made my skin ache as I paddled out, and I found myself biting back more and more curses. Especially once the thought of how deep the moat probably got crossed my mind. The black water was too dark and too clouded with ancient dirt to see through, and I couldn't decide if that was helpful or not; which was worse—not being able to see at all, or knowing precisely what was down there?

Everything was numb or shooting with pins and needles by the time I hauled myself over the frosted shoreline and onto solid ground again. My breaths were short and fast. They dispersed into tiny puffs of fog as I smoothed back my wet hair and got to my feet. It was harder than I expected; my joints stiffened and barked. My clothes were heavy with water and still, of course, freezing fucking cold.

Malcolm had actually beaten me across, as he was already trudging along the outer side of the snow-dusted hedge wall heading north. We all followed him, teeth chattering, shivering, and dripping muddied water onto the clean snow.

The hedge maze wasn't so much a maze, but more like decorative patterns and shapes meant to be admired from the higher windows of the old palace. Decades ago, it might have been beautiful. But now the hedges had been left to grow over the neatly mapped lines.

A granite sculpture of a woman holding a vase marked where a natural break between hedges used to be, but now her whole left side was being consumed by the plants, with frozen vines clinging to her arm and wrapping up her hip. But her right side still had enough space for each of us to slip through. We emerged into a curved alley, one that stretched closer to the old palace in a sweeping arc.

Ithaca wrung out her hair with shaking hands and kept checking over her shoulder as we walked. Tobias was beside her, and his eyes never left the walls of the building we planned to destroy.

Staying low, hugging close to the overgrown hedges, we passed two more granite statues and crossed three more barriers between rows before we arrived at the exterior wall of the old palace.

I couldn't help it. I placed a hand on the rough stone of the north wall. But I drew back sharply, leaving a damp handprint amongst the frost because something about it—I wasn't sure why—but it felt like touching a gravestone.

Harris gave me a concerned look as I dusted off my hand and held it close to my chest, but I dismissed him with a shake of my head. Even if we weren't sticking to the plan and being completely silent, I wasn't sure I would have had the words to explain.

After migrating left, around another statue, we found the cellar door Serafina had spotted when she went scouting for ways to break in. Old vines had grown across it after years without use, and Malcolm tugged the frozen plants from where they'd attached to the wood, iron, and stone. Frost scattered in the breeze when he tossed them aside. And unsurprisingly, when Malcolm twisted the handle, it was locked.

Nickolai already had a lockpicking tool in hand and stepped forward, silently going to work while the rest of us kept a watchful eye on the darkness. Dawn was far away, yet I still found myself checking to make sure that the horizon wasn't brightening.

The rusted lock made a clicking sound that nearly had me jumping out of my skin. Nickolai stood, tucking away the lockpick, and opened the door.

For a moment, we all just stared at the darkness beyond. The wind hummed past the doorway, blowing white frost over the threshold and scattering the dust on the smooth stone floor.

I decided to go first—before I lost my nerve; if swimming back across that godforsaken moat was starting to sound appealing, then I was already losing a battle with myself.

And the real fight hadn't even started yet.

The darkness was so consuming that becoming a part of it felt like being submerged in water. I could taste the old stone all around when I breathed. There was a little bit of salt there too, trapped from the ocean. I focused on that as Tobias closed the door behind us all, and I allowed my eyes to adjust.

It felt like forever before the basic shapes of our surroundings became visible. We were in a cavernous, empty room that was probably once like a cellar. Now, I'd say it was a tomb. The ceilings were arched between each support post, and a curved stairway sat against the far wall to our left.

This time, I was more than happy to let Malcolm lead the way.

The stone steps were sloped inward and worn down where foot traffic used to go. Our shoes left smudges in the dust as we climbed, up and up, until my thighs burned and the chill of the water in my clothes didn't bother me nearly as much. We passed a few empty, dark levels of the old palace until we arrived on what was clearly a main floor. One that was still in use, and not utterly abandoned. Arched windows lined either side of a wide corridor, and a swath of red granite ran down the center of the floor. I was admiring the small cracks and fractures in the stone as we crossed through into a much larger room.

The walls joined to form an octagon, and I immediately recognized that we were standing beneath that main green dome in the center of the old palace. Each doorway was arched. Battle-hardened broadswords were mounted on the walls like torches. The dais where the thrones once sat was empty. The red marble continued from the hallway, forming a vast diamond in the center of the floor. Traces of moonlight filtered in from high above through stained glass, casting a muted red glow across the dark walls.

I wished I hadn't looked up.

My feet scraped to a stop beneath me, and my eyes stung as if there was smoke wafting into my face. Maybe it was the ghost of that fire, because I could see traces of black creeping along the highest parts of the walls and tinging the edges of the massive stained-glass dome with soot. Still, I never expected to see the eight-pointed star hovering above me. Without sunlight, the red glass was dim and looked like dry blood, but the shape was unmistakable.

Malcolm stopped too and followed my gaze. I'd never seen his eyes so wide.

He did it on purpose, I realized. *Of all the symbols he could have chosen, our father decided to mark us with the crown jewel of his crime.*

Now it made sense why Kassian, Brighton's king, and everyone else had been so concerned by the tattoo; they'd all seen a symbol of power that was deliberately placed above the throne room eaten by flames while their royal bloodline came to an end. Even now, it was still looming over them. I was shocked it was still here and hadn't been torn down after that night.

Serafina's eyes practically glowed with rage as she stared up, one hand moving to trace the back of her neck.

I had no idea how long it was before Harris quietly said, "We should do this before the evacuation ends. If we're still here when any guards return, we're done for."

I tore my gaze away from the dome, straight back to the floor. This place didn't just deserve to burn again, it needed to be leveled. And if my father could still see anything that happened in this world, from wherever souls went after death, I hoped he had the best seat in the house.

CHAPTER TWENTY-FOUR

W e were in the right hallway. I knew because the hair on the back of my neck stood on end and because the air didn't feel right this far down into the old palace's sleeping heart. Didn't smell right. But by now, I could recognize that ashy, salty aroma of Nightfire anywhere.

Evander and Taz led the way, sharing the copy of the map Taz traced from one Tobias found during his research of the old palace, guiding us down stairs and through hallways in search of the storage room and the lab.

We divided into two teams, each walking side by side down the corridor. Taz, Harris, Nickolai, Ithaca, and Tobias were going to enter a room on the right, rig a timer in the storage room, and destroy the remaining stock of Nightfire. Evander, Malcolm, Serafina, and I were going to a different room across the hall on the left, the lab, to destroy any notes or recipes that detailed how to make it. To be sure the papers were destroyed, even before the palace burned. Once both were gone, the war would be over before it started.

We stopped at a set of oak doors. Evander nodded.

Taz folded the map back up and tucked it away, leading the other team a little farther to a set of double doors: the storeroom.

This is it. My stomach ached with dread and hope. Serafina was standing on the balls of her feet, like she was ready to run, as I tried the handle. *Locked.*

Nickolai was already busy with the other door. "This one is going to take me a minute," he explained, brows furrowed in concentration. "They invested in better locks for these particular rooms. If you can break open that one, it'll save time."

And at this point, every second mattered.

There was only one other way—only one of us strong enough to break past the door. I stepped aside as Malcolm tried the handle again. He discerned the sturdiness of the door and frowned. But we all knew from the beginning that we weren't going to get through this without a few bruises.

Malcolm took a few steps back before running his shoulder into the door. The lock bashed into the doorframe like the strike of a hammer, and the sound echoed down the empty hallways. It made me cringe. He did it twice more, cursing each time, until a crack split through the wood beside the handle. He rubbed his aching shoulder before planting a heel right next to the lock, kicking the door wide open. Splinters of wood skidded across the floor into the lab beyond.

At the same moment, Nickolai finally got the other lock to yield and opened the storeroom's double doors.

Without another word, our two teams filed into the darkened rooms.

A map had been painted onto the smooth stone floor of the lab. As we crossed into the room, sea-green and shades of parchment yellow spanned before us; the main continent, Dale, and the oceans stretched from wall to wall. Moonlight streamed across the map, coming from the tall windows that looked out at the eastern portion of the hedge maze and the moat beyond. Six long tables covered with decanters, files, mortar and pestles, and jars of dried herbs were beside them.

I could feel my heartbeat in my throat, and I grabbed the nearest papers I could find. I didn't care what they were. I tossed them onto the floor. Serafina, Malcolm, and Evander did the same, piling up all of the folders and sheets of paper into one big mound.

By the time that was done, my hands were shaking. I prodded through the glass bottles and jars nearest me, wondering if we should smash all of them against the walls too—turn the place upside down, just to be certain there was nothing left they could save.

Serafina struck one of her matches, lighting a slip of paper. The page withered and curled, turning black, as she set it on the pile. Then she lit a few more. Evander took a match too, and with his help, they turned the mound into a small bonfire in the middle of the room.

I found a small bottle labeled 'alcohol' and poured it over the flames. The blaze climbed higher, and smoke blackened the ceiling directly above it.

It was like a weight had been lifted from my chest, and I took a deep breath. The smell of charred paper and burning paint stung the back of my throat, but I didn't mind at all, because we were going to win. All we needed to do was reconvene with the rest of our crew in the hall and sneak out the way we came in. The rigged timer would already be started by now, and in fifteen minutes, the old palace would be a pile of ash and stone.

"If only we could see the look on their faces after this," I lamented.

"Wish granted."

As one, we turned toward the honey-sweet voice in the doorway.

The chemist placed her black fur coat on the end of the farthest table. Her dress was as dark as the night outside, with accents of crimson embroidery and a collar rising to below her jaw. She traced a blood-red hand over a blank space on the second table as she inched closer before eyeing the burning pages.

I couldn't believe it. She actually *smiled*. With the firelight catching in her eyes, she looked like a monster that was burning from the inside out. She clicked her tongue, "Clever trick—setting off a transport boat so close that we needed to evacuate. And destroying the formula was certainly a good plan."

"Why do you sound happy about it?" I couldn't help asking. It was making me want to make a break for one of the windows rather than go past her to get to the door.

Her lips curled upward. She swept her black hair over her

shoulder and tapped her brow. "Darling, it's all up here. You can't burn memory."

I was taking stock of my knife, the distance between us all, and how many glass objects I might throw at her when four more figures came through the busted door. The king's face turned red when he saw the burning papers, and Kassian's chin jutted forward as he surveyed the rest of the room. Two personal guards accompanied them, and both had hands on their swords.

I tried to be subtle about glancing into the hallway behind them, to see if they knew that the storeroom was being invaded too. As far as I could tell, they hadn't checked yet. And no more guards trailed them.

The king didn't bother addressing us, turning to his chemist. "Leave now," he waved a hand at one of the guards, "and you go with her. She's the only one who's memorized what was on those pages. And alert the rest of the city patrols to come here."

I could imagine it already; an army storming through the main gate and across the bridge to the old palace. Coming for us. When my vision cleared again, the chemist and the first guard were both already rounding the corner into the hallway. The formula, their ability to simply make more Nightfire, was walking away.

I thought that was the worst of our problems until one last person emerged into the room.

The explosion at Fort Ketta left raw, still-healing wounds on Mordecai's right brow and cheek. They trailed down his neck and below his coat, continuing onto his shoulder no doubt. As if he wasn't intimidating enough before, now he looked like he'd walked through hell and survived.

He kicked the broken door shut without looking back, sending chips of wood spinning across the floor. The king, Kassian, and even their remaining personal guard seemed to cower away as Mordecai pointed at Malcolm and me. His hand was unnaturally steady, directing a promise straight through the flames as his eyes glowed orange. "I'm going to kill you," he vowed.

I believed him.

CHAPTER TWENTY-FIVE

I had not known it was possible to miss the days of spying in Dale, but I certainly missed them now. I missed the delicate balance, keeping up a front, and even the life-or-death stakes that hinged on our every move. At least then Mordecai wasn't working against us.

Now with him marching around the fire, eyes blazing, knife drawn —it felt like due time to get on my knees and start praying.

Malcolm and I edged around the fire, keeping it between us and Mordecai. Serafina and Evander were right with us, but Kassian and his personal guard were coming from the other way to meet us as the king backed away toward the door.

Mordecai lunged, and the steel of his knife sang past my ear, barely grazing my neck like a papercut. Then all hell broke loose.

My fist throbbed with pain as I whirled it into Mordecai's jaw. Malcolm launched at Kassian as the prince made to draw his blade. The guard and Evander were already in a tangle of fists, bashing into one of the tables and spilling glass tubes across the floor. Serafina ducked out of their way before lending a blade; she wedged the steel through a gap in the guard's armor just beside his clavicle. Blood sprayed across the map. A scream echoed up the walls. The king wrenched the broken door open and vanished into the hallway.

I realized I was too close to Mordecai a second too late. His skull crashed against mine and my vision went dark. I only realized I was flat on my ass as the flashing dots began to clear, and I could see Mordecai, silhouetted by the flames, marching straight for me. The headbutt didn't seem to have affected him at all.

I was uncomfortably aware of my own teeth, which were tingling and achy, as I scrambled to my feet again. I lobbed a crystal decanter at Mordecai's head, and he ducked out of its way. It shattered somewhere across the room.

My focus reduced to the feel of my knife in my hand and the silvery glint of the one Mordecai held. Dodging it sent waves of hot and cold down my back. Even while radiating enough fury to burn my hands, even with his jaw set sharply like the blade of an ax, his maneuvers were deliberate, steady, and as polished as a choreography practiced a thousand times over. I kept up my retreat, bashing into tables and crunching through fallen glass. I noticed the hot trickle of blood before I felt the sting of the cuts he made—one on my arm, my wrist, and my thigh so far. The latter hurt the most, and I knew from the persistent itch creeping along the side of my throat that the first gash had started to bleed too.

Across the room, beyond the smoldering ashes of the papers, Kassian fled for the open doors. His personal guard was sprawled across the painted floors in an expanding pool of crimson. Serafina slipped in it, barely keeping her footing, as she tried to follow the runaway prince. Evander was prying the sword out from underneath its fallen owner.

Mordecai noticed Malcolm was coming to help before I did and kept him back with a swift kick to the side of the knee. Malcolm swore, gripping the nearby table to keep from completely falling. Mordecai switched his grip on the knife, catching it blade-down—ready to make deeper wounds. He raised it.

Sweat dampened my brow and I snatched up the nearest thing—a tall, brown-glass bottle—and swung it like a club against the back of

Mordecai's head. He stumbled sideways, shielding his eyes with an arm. When I went to step closer, he kicked my feet out from beneath me. Malcolm grasped for his knife-wielding hand, and Mordecai sent him sprawling with a punch so fast I barely saw it.

Luckily, I had already been moving, and my knife glided through the tissue of Mordecai's left leg in a smooth pass. He hissed through his teeth and planted a hand over the bleeding. It spilled between his fingers.

I stumbled back onto my feet and out of Mordecai's reach before he had the opportunity to slash back. Malcolm did the same, and in a shared glance, we agreed to make for the door.

Evander had the newly acquired sword in hand and was already helping Serafina with the door Kassian had slammed shut. With the lock already broken, the remaining slat of metal had lodged into the frame hard enough that it took two people to tear it open again. It screeched across the floor and was dangling by one hinge.

Mordecai snarled through bared teeth after us, perhaps more out of frustration than pain. He used one arm on the nearest table to begin hauling himself up. "You're going to fucking regret that!" he shouted, and the noise pulsed through my head and my chest like an explosion.

I didn't look back or meet his gaze as we left.

The dark hallway leading back the way we came from was empty. Farther into the shadows, the double doors to the storeroom were shut; nothing looked out of place because we hadn't broken that lock. The shattered door to the lab had drawn all the attention.

I was trying not to swear, trying to think; Kassian was probably already on the massive, curved stairway by now, maybe even farther. As for the chemist and the other guard, they might be beyond our reach, with too much of a lead.

One of the storeroom's double doors opened. Nickolai peeked his head out, and after a brief assessment of the blood, he waved everyone else out and immediately jammed the lock behind them, to keep anyone from getting back in.

"We heard the commotion—" began Taz, but I cut him off.

"We don't have much time." As we all practically ran for the stairway that connected back to the main levels, beginning to climb it, I explained that the chemist had the formula for Nightfire memorized —that for it to die, she needed to die with it. Her death was no longer just an accessory to the plan, but the keystone of it.

Mordecai's distant cursing echoed behind us.

Serafina elaborated, "The king and his son were with her, but they don't matter anymore. We might still be able to catch her if we try—"

A horrific sound blared in the distance. All of us paused. A horn screamed into the night, deep and low, echoing across the city. Goosebumps rose on my skin.

"That must be how they alert the city guard the king mentioned earlier," murmured Evander. He wiped the last of the guard's blood from the blade of the sword onto his sleeve.

Bruising already shadowed the left side of Malcolm's face as he peered through the darkness, as if he could somehow see into the night beyond the walls. "They'll be here in a matter of minutes—if we're lucky." He led the way up to the next landing of the stairs. "We're screwed."

I shook my head, "There still has to be something we can do; all of this will be for nothing—" The wind was practically knocked out of me as I realized one other thing. "Do you think she guessed the rest of our plan, about blowing up the explosives? She'd want to protect those barrels rather than run."

As if in answer, a crashing sound echoed from the levels below us, down the hallway from the storeroom and lab.

Of course, she knew. And she'd waited until we were out of her way to get to the storeroom. I only hoped that the jammed lock would hold until we could race back down.

Evander cursed under his breath. "We have to go back—"

"How long ago did you set the timer?" asked Serafina.

"Just before we heard the commotion start. Plus, however long it took us to get here, so not long," answered Harris. A deep crease appeared between his brows, "Why?"

"The timer only runs for fifteen minutes, which was supposed to be long enough for us to get out. If you've already set it, how much time do we have left?" asked Malcolm.

Ithaca shook her head slowly, "By now? Ten if we're lucky."

"Can you reset it?" I asked Harris.

His dark eyes were impossibly wide and he choked out a whispered, "No."

Ten minutes—to kill Brighton's chemist and get out of the old palace; not just out, but far enough away not to die in the explosion. And if we failed, the world burned.

Up the curved stairway, far into the main levels of the old palace, wooden doors groaned open and bashed into the walls they stood within. Then came the thunder of boots and armor. Men were shouting—something about different wings of the palace and varying teams of soldiers.

I was going to be sick. I clasped a hand over my throat, to soothe the burning cut, to keep from vomiting, or to hold back a scream—I wasn't sure which.

The city guard had arrived.

MY LEGS BURNED by the time we descended back to the correct level.

The storeroom of Nightfire was separate from the main catacombs we had entered through, but the structure was virtually the same; there were support pillars and arched ceilings, only these had red stains dotting the stonework like blood. Timber storage racks rose from floor to ceiling, all crowded with barrels of the explosive. More were arranged on the floor like pieces of a chess set running down either side of the long room.

The timer was right in the middle, next to a barrel that had been pried open. Red powder ran around it like a skirt, poised for destruction when the match struck.

It was a delicate contraption, but solid in the fact that Harris had put it together. He'd split a ten-minute sand timer at its weak point, allowing the fine grains to fall through open air onto the plate of a scale.

When that ran out, it would be just enough weight to send the red arm ticking past the line where the match was anchored. When the flame struck, with less than an inch between it and the spilled explosives, the Nightfire was sure to take. We'd seen it demonstrated before; we knew the lighting mechanism worked. That's what had me breaking a cold sweat as Malcolm and Tobias slammed the doors shut behind us.

Worse than that, the doors had already been open when we arrived.

The chemist and her guard made it into the storeroom first, only by a few moments. They were already half way to the timer. The chemist only looked at us over her shoulder for a second before running for the contraption; she knew that if she so much as kicked it, our plan would be a failure.

Taz, Harris, and Serafina chased after them, and I was about to join, but a thunderous crash from behind had me turning around. The set of double oak doors bashed against the lock Tobias and Malcolm were trying to secure.

I threw my weight into one of the doors to help keep it shut, and Ithaca joined me. Evander was helping with the other door. City guards were shouting on the other side. Malcolm shoved the iron bolt into place, but still the doors leapt against their frames.

"That lock won't hold," Nickolai pointed out. He was backing away, scanning the shelved bombs for a place to hide.

In the center of the room, Harris dragged a hand through the spilled powder and flung it into the guard's face as he drew his sword. The man dropped his weapon, clawing at his own eyes as he yelped in pain and fell back against more of the barrels. Taz and Serafina had stopped Brighton's chemist only feet away from the delicate timer; she was keeping a sensible distance, backing farther and farther out of their reach, inching along the wall of storage toward us—toward the only way in and out.

Kill her. It was my only thought. *Even if all else fails, as long as she can't help Brighton make any more Nightfire.*

Before I could take a step, the massive doors burst open, sending us staggering out of their way. Five city guards donning iron armor spilled into the room, along with Kassian.

The numbness started low in my gut and ended in my fingertips. By that time, barrels of red powder were knocking over as fights ran into them, clashing metal was echoing through the archways, voices blended and tangled, and Kassian decided that I was going to be his opponent.

I barely had time to right my stance before he struck, and my teeth flared with pain. Some of my own blood speckled the floor, hiding among the red powder and stains. I drove my elbow back at him. My bones rattled from the force, and the prince's head snapped sideways as fresh spit and blood dotted the wall nearest us.

I could feel each second ticking by, one by one. Just like I was acutely aware of the bomb looming—too close. How much time was left? Eight minutes? Maybe less?

Nickolai scaled two levels of the storage racks and sent a barrel of Nightfire crashing down. Wood splintered. Fine crimson dust fogged the air. One of the city guards began to cough. Somehow, even from a distance, I already had grit crunching between my teeth as the dust settled.

I shoved Kassian's head into the wall. He drove his knee into my stomach. The air went thick, and it was painful to breathe. Dry air chafed my throat as I watched the chemist, black gown billowing behind her, slip around where Evander and a city guard were fighting, back through the open doors.

Nickolai kicked down another barrel, and it broke over the head and shoulders of the city guard trying to pass Serafina and Taz toward the timer. The dust burned my eyes and I threw up an arm to shield myself from it. Everywhere I looked, I saw shapes fighting through the red haze. Maybe I was the only one lucky enough to notice the chemist leave.

Stop her—kill her.

I tried to slip past Kassian. He brought his boot down on my foot and clawed for my throat. We crashed into the wall and part of the oak door. I craned to see into the dark passageway beyond, but it was useless as the red fog spilled out from the doors.

Something violent took hold of me. I wrenched the prince's hands from my throat and shoved him over my own outstretched foot, throwing us both sideways and onto the floor. The swirling patterns of dust parted around us.

Before he had the chance, I snatched his knife from his own belt. With lethal accuracy I never knew I was capable of, I shoved the point between his ribs. It punched through, crunching faintly, and the jeweled hilt cracked against his bones. I twisted the blade and ripped it back out; the metal scraping against a rib reminded me of the rough drag of a file, and I nearly gaged. Blood spilled from the wound, drenching my sleeve and arm. I raised the weapon and buried it in his chest again. Blood bubbled from his mouth and trickled onto the ground. His eyes glazed, and his stare drifted emptily to the arched ceiling.

I left his knife with him, my mind already fuzzing at the edges as I stumbled back onto my feet and through the open doors. The prince, the fact that I had *killed* him, vanished to the back of my mind as I hunted the darkness for Brighton's chemist.

I followed a current of air, a wisp of red dust curling up the stairway from where she ran. I left smeared blood where I gripped the balustrade. It was dark enough that I could pretend it was ink or oil that soaked my arms, and by the time I followed the traces of fine crimson powder toward the old throne room, the liquid had turned cold.

My footsteps echoed through the chasm of the large room while I scanned from dais to doorways; all of them were shut. The red glow from the star overhead rippled as clouds passed outside. I let the image burn itself into my memory; the space in all its empty glory, the red marble and stone slabs, the ghost of a fire long since put out.

More than a ghost—a shadow fluttered over my shoulder and I barely turned in time to see one of the ancient broadswords that had been mounted to the wall in mid-swing. I ducked out of its path. The sting of a fresh cut ripped across my shoulder. The chemist whirled the blade again, and lunging out of its path sent me off balance and sprawling. My bloody palms stuck to the marble, and I tried to crawl away from her.

Her shadow twisted behind me. She would never give me enough time to stand.

I rolled onto my back. The point of the sword was shooting down at me, and I had no other option except to catch the blade with my hands. My palms burned as the uneven edges slid through them, and the tip of the sword came to a painful stop digging into the center of my chest. Blood trickled through my fingers and down the length of the blade. My hands stung. My vision blurred. My grip was weakening, slipping through my white-knuckled grasp because of my own blood.

Strands of the chemist's black hair clung to her cheeks as she gritted her teeth and leveraged her weight down on the sword. The edges sliced deeper into my palms, and the point of the sword sank into my chest until warm blood trickled and pooled next to my collarbone. My arms shook from effort. I couldn't gulp down enough air to scream, because each inhale sent the blade just a hair deeper.

She pushed down more, and each point of my spine dug against the red marble below me. The same marble I was afraid would shatter and explode at any minute, any second. I squeezed my eyes shut, because it was better than watching the blade of the sword slip through my grasp coated in blood. Numbness sparked in my fingertips.

Something hot splattered my face and neck, and then there was a gurgling, choking sound. The weight on the other end of the sword vanished. The ancient weapon fell and clattered against the stone to my right.

For a second, I didn't know what I was looking at. A heavy stream of blood poured down the front of the chemist's dress, dripping from her lips and nose. Most of it coursed from a wound at her throat. The tip of a knife gleamed in the moonlight, wedged straight through her neck.

Her stained hands grasped at it, fumbling around the blade as it twisted. She staggered, a choked, bubbling wheeze escaping her as she sank to her knees. The blade retracted. Blood pumped freely onto the ground.

Ithaca stood behind her, both hands clasped around the bone handle of her knife. Her wide eyes never blinked as the chemist, in a pool of black silk and blood, rasped out uneven breaths and clutched her throat. Her obsidian eyes glowed with hate, and she looked over her shoulder, baring her blood-smeared teeth.

Ithaca took a step back as the chemist lunged and clawed after her. Red hands snatched at her legs, but that was as far as they got. Brighton's chemist slumped against the floor, fingers curled like talons, as her gaze rolled upward. Blood stopped pulsing from her wounds and merely seeped, like syrup expanding across the ground.

I hauled myself onto my feet, wincing at the gash across my shoulder and the twin cuts through each palm. Ithaca lowered her knife, hands trembling.

Our eyes met, and it was like the world around us no longer existed. All that mattered now was the explosion, perhaps moments from going off, and we were too far apart. If there was a chance that this could be the end, I needed to do one thing first.

Careful not to slip, I stepped around the pool of blood. I used my sleeve to wipe the worst of the splatter from my face. The space between us disappeared, and I kissed her. It was a question at first, light and easy to pull away from—but she didn't.

If the world had exploded all around us, I wouldn't have noticed. All I knew was the soft press of her lips, the fluttering stampede of her heartbeat—or was it mine?—the smell of lavender, then the gentle curve of her neck and her waist as I drew her nearer.

Commotion rumbled in the passageway we both came from, and we broke apart. We turned to see seven people rushing out of the darkness, each dusted with a layer of red powder, splattered with blood, and two of them were practically being carried.

Blood was dripping from a deep gash along the back of Evander's left calf, and his arm was slung over Taz's shoulder as he tried to walk. Malcolm was much worse off. With Tobias on one side and Harris on the other, it was easy to see the handle of a knife protruding from below his right clavicle.

"What the fuck happened?" I asked as I limped toward them.

Tobias stopped me with an outstretched arm, seeing my intent before I realized it myself. "Leave the knife, it might be the only thing keeping him from bleeding to death."

Malcolm winced and spat blood onto the floor. "Mordecai made it to the doorway of the lab," he explained tightly. Each breath had to be agony. "So, he threw the knife."

"We need to go; the timer had maybe three minutes remaining when we killed the last of that group of city guards and left the storeroom," explained Taz. "We jammed the doors again, so no one's getting in there to stop it now."

Nickolai was nodding fast as he added, "On the map, the main door is closer. We might still be able to make it out if we go that way instead of the cellars like we planned."

"Which way?" Ithaca asked.

Taz, knowing the maps he'd drawn up better than all of us, pointed to the corridor on the left, on the opposite end of the room from the dais.

We had barely taken a step when Harris yelped and dropped to one knee, another small knife wedged to the hilt in the back of his thigh. Tobias and Malcolm both stumbled without his support.

Braced against the doorway behind them, Mordecai stood twirling another knife. He'd shredded off a sleeve and tied it around the gash on his leg, the fabric already dark and soaked with blood. The healing burns trailing down his neck and onto his shoulder were flushed red.

"Every last one of you is going to burn in here with the rest of us." His voice echoed up the high walls. "And any of you I manage to kill before that happens, consider yourselves fucking lucky." With that, he lurched off of the doorway and limped like some monster from a nightmare toward us. Slow yet unwavering.

Ithaca was helping Harris back into his feet, bending under his weight, and Serafina rushed to his other side to help.

I dashed to the sword the chemist had tried to use to kill me, its tip still wet with my blood, and picked it up with my wounded hands. Pain swelled up into my wrists and arms as I struggled to wield it properly.

Mordecai's lurching gait steered in my direction, and he switched his grip on the small knife—not to throw but to kill. His eyes were so dark that I couldn't tell that they were blue anymore, so full of wrath.

Dripping blood and red powder, our crew scrambled for the passageway that led to the main door. I trailed behind them, following nothing but the sound of their movement as I kept my eyes on Mordecai, backing away from him.

I was wishing that I had hurt him worse, because he forced through the pain of walking on a wounded leg like he'd been through far more terrible things—and maybe he had.

In a blink, he was too close. He sent the tip of his knife swinging up below my right arm for my ribs. I let the weight of the old broadsword swing down and bite into his shoulder. Grunting through the pain, he swung the back of his fist across my face. My vision flashed with stars. I'd bit my tongue, and blood pooled in my mouth tasting of salt and copper. Mordecai lunged again. My back hit the wall. The slices through my palms seared with pain as I leveraged up the heavy blade—not quite high enough to stop his arm.

The hilt of the sword thudded against my chest, my palms slippery and on fire, as Mordecai overcommitted to his swing and marched right into the end of the blade. I *felt* it punch through. His knife fell from his grasp and clattered at our feet. I thought I heard water, but it was just blood dripping, pouring onto the ground.

Mordecai's face went ash white, but he still bared his teeth and reached out, gripping my face hard enough to leave bruises. "If you make it out," he choked, "I hope you get to watch the rest of them die for what you've done."

I felt like I was suffocating, out of breath. I set my jaw and twisted the blade, my vision rippling from the deep sting in my hands. Mordecai screamed and sank to his knees in the vast lake of blood around us.

"And if I don't, if none of us do," I braced one hand on his shoulder, twisting the sword just a little more, earning a snarl of agony, "then I guess we'll all see you in hell."

I stepped away, wrenching the sword out of his chest, and watched him slump to the ground. I didn't wait for a reply, if he could have gasped one out at all, and ran down the passageway to where the rest of our group had gathered, my footsteps echoing off the cold stone.

Nickolai was already kneeling before the massive lock on the main doors, hands shaking as he tried to work it open. Ithaca and Serafina were still holding Harris upright. I picked up Malcolm's free arm, throwing it over my shoulders to help Tobias keep him from collapsing.

The lock clanged. Nickolai threw his weight into the left door, pushing it open. Taz and Evander, who was still bleeding from his leg, worked together to force the right one open. The stone bridge that crossed the moat yawned before us—two hundred feet had never seemed so far.

The ground rumbled, and we all staggered forward into the night.

Shouts escalated from inside the old palace behind us. I craned to look over my shoulder as we ran, seeing a cluster of city guards charging down the main passageway, vaulting over Mordecai's body, some skidding and slipping in his blood.

Not after us, I realized. *Away from the explosion.*

Dawn was just braking over the city as we raced across the bridge. I felt my heart trying to run away without me. I pushed to make each stride count—each one just a little farther and a little longer.

We had barely made the turn around the main gate, around the exterior stone wall on the outside edge of the moat, when the ancient foundations of the old palace shook and groaned. We threw our shoulders and backs into the wall, sinking down and curling into its shadow. People in nearby streets stared, pointed, and some began to scream.

A flash of light, as bright as the sun, shot across the city. A giant, hulking bloom of black smoke and fire sprung up, visible even from where we cowered next to the outer wall. A ring of gray ash and dust flew over us. The blast of grainy air stung my eyes. In the same instant, the loudest sound I ever could have imagined stabbed through my ears. It ripped through me like I was a flag in the wind. The wall pulsed outward behind us.

Heat. Ears ringing. Chunks of stone falling like hail. Then bigger rocks.

The air was enough to make me choke. My senses reduced to the pressure of the wall next to me, the stinging downpour of debris, and trying not to breathe too deeply.

The ring of gray air dispersed, leaving the black smoke in its place, climbing higher.

The windows on the buildings nearby, and for as far down the roads as I could see through the haze, were all shattered.

Somewhere across the city, a bell began to ring—though it seemed unusually muffled to my ears. Then the bell of the new palace chimed frantically. A horn, the same one used to summon the city guard, screamed across Northgate as shouts and screams and yelling escalated on every street and corner.

We were buried in rubble up to our knees, and so covered with soot and dirt that we could blend in with the gray stones. It clumped with the fresh blood that half of us were drenched in.

The old palace was reduced to nothing, and yet we were still alive.

CHAPTER TWENTY-SIX

S and. It was like I had swallowed sand, my throat dry and grainy by the time we'd made it around the southern edge of where the old palace once sat. The coughing ached in my chest. And everything was muffled, like I had two pillows strapped over my ears.

At least it made the screaming less obvious. The entire city of Northgate was stepping outdoors to get a glimpse of the damage.

As we had scrambled out of the rubble and followed the edge of what was left of the old north wall, we'd gotten a painfully clear look at the crater left behind. The island that the old palace's foundations were built into was simply gone. Mud, ash, and broken stone were all that remained, nearly submerged in the now black water that used to be the moat. It all looked like that, the whole grounds reduced to something like a trampled road on a rainy day. Anything else was too clouded with smoke to see.

Like the entire city, we were in shambles. Stumbling over fallen rocks and debris, we rushed toward Northgate's main port, shouldering through small crowds that were slowly becoming bigger, dragging Harris, Malcolm, and Evander with us. They all struggled not to swear with each bump and obstacle in our path. The trail of blood we leaked unfurled like a narrow ribbon in our wake.

It was a miracle more people didn't see the knives protruding from Malcolm and Harris, but they were all staring at the black plume in the sky. Their eyes all glinted copper when the flames blossomed. They stared without blinking, as city guards and other commonfolk rushed around them like a current.

The sun had climbed all the way over the horizon by the time we made it to the end of one of the long, cobblestone quays that stretched into the half-frozen water.

A small merchant ship, with a single mast and a hull painted dark green, was what we settled on. I left Tobias to keep Malcolm upright, while Serafina, Taz, and I scrambled over the ramp and onto the deck. The crew that had been tending to it were all on the main roads to get a better look at the chaos, and the one man left, who'd been sleeping in a hammock below deck and smelled of booze, was more than willing to leave after a few shouted threats and a drawn knife. At least it felt like I'd been shouting—and my throat burned enough that it had to be true; my voice was just as muted as everything else I should have been able to hear clearly.

We got everyone else onboard, and Evander bellowed directions while Taz tugged his arm back over his shoulders, helping him walk as blood dripped onto the polished deck.

Malcolm was propped against some barrels near the mast, and Harris was clutching the rail nearby, his other hand hovering over his wounded leg where one of Mordecai's knives still protruded.

It was a relief to simply put my head down and do as I was told— untie that rope, help Ithaca with the mast, move that crate over there and step on it to reach that other thing that does something else but Evander knows what he's doing so I won't ask—and eventually we were moving. Winter air stung my skin as we picked up speed and crossed farther out into the waves. Somehow, the fact that we were on the damn ocean barely presented as a clear thought.

Instead, I found myself standing over Tobias's shoulder asking questions as he dealt with Harris and Malcolm.

"There's no way to be sure what it's cut into," Tobias explained as he unwound a section of gauze. "The fact that you haven't passed out is a good sign though."

Malcolm wrinkled his nose. "And what if it has gone through something important?"

"I'll be honest," Tobias gestured to the protruding knife below Malcolm's clavicle, "if we can't stop the bleeding once it's out, you're likely going to die."

"Then fucking leave it in!" My stomach had gone cold and dense, and I waved an arm at the expanding ocean around us. "Do we really have to tear that thing out *now*? *Here*?"

"The longer he has a knife in his chest, the more likely it is to be moved and cause even more damage," Tobias maintained.

Ithaca stopped on Tobias's other side and began unwinding a section of bandage from the pack of supplies they'd brought. Then she went to Harris and instructed him to sit carefully, keeping the wounded leg propped up so she could examine the protruding knife. She also handed off a section of bandages to Taz and told him how to wrap it to stall Evander's bleeding.

Tobias began, "If there's a bottle of something strong somewhere on this ship, that will help—"

"Don't waste the time," interrupted Malcolm, "just get it out."

"It's going to hurt worse without alcohol," noted Tobias, but he gathered another section of bandage anyway and folded it over into a thick pad. "Bite down on this."

Malcolm took it and nodded.

"Is there anything I can do?" I offered.

Tobias shook his head. "I need you to stay out of the way. You aren't going to want to once the blood starts, understandably, but panicking and interfering will only make it worse."

I must have gone alarmingly pale, because Tobias looked at me over his shoulder, then at the ship's decking—like he was gauging the distance of my fall if I fainted. Ithaca glanced over too, eyes wide. Her hands kept working on cleaning the wound on the back of Harris's thigh, and he hissed through his teeth.

I looked around at the rest of the ship as if that was going to help. Nickolai and Serafina were working together to man the sail, steering us in a clumsy, jagged arc to the west. Evander was helping wherever he could reach, wherever he could limp to, as Taz continued to keep him upright with a temporary bandage knotted around his calf.

More gently, Tobias added, "You're not going to want to watch this. Go over there—"

"Like hell." I steeled my nerves by taking a deep breath of the ashy air. I could feel my heartbeat in my forearms and in my throat, but I managed to kneel at Malcolm's side and extend a hand. "I'm not going anywhere."

Malcolm gave me a look that seemed to say, *you stubborn ass*, but clasped my hand anyway and nodded once.

Tobias nodded at the dried blood caking my wrists. "Those cuts on your hands are going to need stitches later. Remind me."

As if he wasn't too busy struggling to keep Malcolm alive. Some vital passageway running down the back of Harris' leg could be in jeopardy too; it was hard to guess from the way Ithaca was examining the knife wedged there, her brows tilted up in the middle of her face.

Tobias eyed the protruding knife's handle, already piling up more cloth, ready to catch the spray of blood.

"If you die, I swear to god—" for my sanity, I decided it was better not to finish that sentence. "Try to think blood-retaining thoughts."

"I'll do my best," Malcolm said. Then he stuffed the wad of fabric into his mouth and braced himself.

Carefully, Tobias closed his fingers around the knife's handle. It didn't wobble or move like I expected. It seemed more rooted into place.

"Count of three," warned Tobias.

Already wincing, Malcolm waved him on as a silent 'hurry up.'

The back of my throat was tight, painfully so, and I was holding my breath by the time Tobias reached the end of the countdown. He gripped the handle, knuckles flashing white, and pulled.

Tobias was already stopping the blood, already working diligently in the same instant that he cast aside the knife and it clattered onto the deck. I was cringing hard enough my teeth ached, doing everything in my power not to gag, or scream, or cry, or something in between.

Malcolm was very close to shattering my hand in his grasp.

With Harris apparently stable, Ithaca joined her father. Calmly, quietly, she was already asking what he needed. Thread. Needle. More cloth, more pressure.

Unintentionally, I looked over at the bloody knife. Even a glimpse of the thing was enough to summon a wave of nausea.

Never in my life had I felt so *useless*. I could barely stand to watch Ithaca and Tobias at work. *More capable hands don't exist anywhere in the world*, I kept repeating in my head. I knew it as surely that I knew the sky was blue. But still, I had the mindless urge to scream at them to do whatever it was they were doing faster, better, cleaner—because it looked like a mess of blood and fabric and agony to my untrained eyes.

Fresh blood leaked from the cut down my palm, dripping between me and Malcolm's joined hands. I cringed harder, trying to convince myself that I could bear it a little longer, even as my fingers turned purple.

Ithaca met my eyes, and nodded for me to go.

I couldn't see any more white gauze or fabric. Everywhere I looked —as much as I tried not to—all of it was soaked with blood. Bright red.

No—I should stay.

My hand began throbbing. It was like I could feel my bones slowly bending. Malcolm was strong enough to break it. Not on purpose, but he would. *He was.*

Ithaca looked at me again, more insistently.

"Please—my hand—" somehow, those three words that I barely choked out were enough for Malcolm to release me. I lurched to my feet, retreating from the mast.

I should have listened to Tobias.

"Give me something to do." I stumbled over to Taz and Evander, my vision spotted with neon and black orbs. "I need something to do, just tell me anything."

Evander pointed, directing me to take up Nickolai's place on the starboard side of the sail because he was barely tall enough to reach it. Then he instructed Nickolai to go do something else, and I barely had enough sense to hear a word of it.

For the first time, I welcomed the sight of the endless waves in every direction. The whitecaps rolling along with the ship kept my head from spinning because I counted them. I counted them faster than they appeared until I was just spiraling down the list of numbers. At least it felt like doing something. I could pretend it helped.

What felt like ages later, when Ithaca tapped my shoulder, I spun and nearly clocked her in the head. I barely heard her saying a word to me—though I did recall detecting a muffled, distant voice. I'd been too hell-bent on not hearing what was going on at the base of the mast.

"He's going to be fine." She put her hands on my shoulders, watching my eyes to make sure I'd heard and understood.

The tension in my chest whooshed out of me.

Malcolm was still sitting where I'd left him and was saying something to Tobias. He had a hand gingerly lain over the thoroughly bandaged wound and was a little pale—but alive.

"What about Harris?" I asked.

"I think he'll be alright, too." She looked over her shoulder, and I followed her gaze as Tobias crossed the decking and began working with Harris. She added, "He might have a limp after it's healed. That's all."

Evander talked Serafina and me through tying up a few things so that we didn't have to physically maintain the sail now that we were on a steady course. Then Ithaca made him sit on one of the crates near Malcolm so she could clean and stitch the wound on his calf. Nickolai volunteered to help. Tobias was doing the same for Harris, with the knife finally removed from his leg.

With the waves rocking the floor beneath us, blood streaked and pooled up and down the length of the deck, and a dark shadow looming through the haze behind us, I went on a mission to find the aforementioned bottle of something strong.

CHAPTER TWENTY-SEVEN

I knew every nook and cranny of the flagstone floor in that meeting chamber, tucked into the north wing of the palace in Angel's Landing. I'd paced it until every inch was cemented into my memory.

Patrol ships from Dale did not hesitate to swarm us and take us back to their capital when our blood-soaked vessel steered too far into their waters ten days ago. It was deliberate, on our part. There was a black plume in the distance and a lot of explaining to do.

Each of us had still been dusted with red powder and dry blood when we first set foot in that room, with its lengthy oak table and windows looking over the coliseum and the northmost reaches of the city. Then Dale's king and queen arrived, along with a small army of advisors and generals. The navy men who'd captured us explained the situation, and from there we essentially spilled our guts; the initial scam, Fort Ketta, spying, Nickolai's life used as leverage to keep us in line, Nightfire, the murder of Brighton's chemist, destroying the formula, leveling the old palace—all of it came tumbling out as the men and women at the table blinked, scrolled notes, and stared.

Ithaca explained how she ended up stuck on that small ship the night Mordecai had us flee the city. Tobias made his case for abandoning his post, his career, everything—to look for his missing daughter. An accident and an act of love. Not the actions of two traitors.

The committee was still skeptical about every word, so Harris insisted they scrape as much of the remaining red powder off us as they could. They could test and examine it, as proof that what we said was true.

I also brought up the warning letter we found, with Brighton's official seal, and detailed how I left it in the great hall for them to find. I described it, everything from how we broke the seal to what was scrawled inside, as further proof that we were sincere. All attention then shifted to a man at the far end of the table, and sure enough, he retrieved the letter from a folder he'd brought with him. A folder they'd been storing it in since the day it was discovered by guards at the entrance to the great hall. The paper was a little worse for wear after being trampled by the masses exiting through the doorway where I dropped it, but it was still legible.

When they pressed us for theories on who must have written it, we suggested Brighton's first, existing spy who'd been in the city; but he'd already been captured, imprisoned, and questioned. He wasn't to blame. For now, with nothing more for them to go off of, the author remained at large.

Then came the death tallies; Kassian, Brighton's prince, Mordecai —their finest and most ruthless puppet—and the chemist were all dead. Brighton's king had slipped out, and none of us could be certain if he'd escaped or died in the final explosion. They could use that information as proof of our honesty as well, once they gathered intel from across the strait. Once the smoke cleared.

Ithaca stitched the gashes through each of my palms as soon as she could. The rest of the cuts I'd sustained weren't as bad. We sat in the back corner of that room while discussions continued. Time crawled while she diligently put me back together; it hurt enough that my eyes burned, that was part of it, but also because I wanted nothing more than to hold her beautiful face without leaking blood onto her cheeks or her hair.

That was only the first day. Hours of questions, explanations, pacing, and a lot of stitches. But it was enough for Dale's government to deem us worthy of keeping our heads for the time being.

The next four days were consumed by long walks from our cells back to the meeting room, more questioning, and dealing with our wounds. For Malcolm and Harris, it was pain; a knife to the chest and the back of the leg weren't healing fast. And like Harris, Evander had to adopt a crutch in order to walk. The rest of us tended to scabbed cuts, scrapes, and bruises. And we all pretended we knew what we were doing about the deeper, hidden injuries.

Before that fateful day, almost none of us had ever killed before. Now we all had. I knew what a knife and a sword felt like when they punched through a human torso; Ithaca knew the searing spray of blood that came with stabbing another woman in the throat; Evander had cracked a city guard's skull against the floor of that lab; Nickolai crushed one of them with a barrel of Nightfire; Harris had snapped a neck; Taz had been left no choice but to crush a windpipe before that same city guard could turn about and strangle him among the barrels; Serafina knew where to cut to end things fast; Malcolm took up a fallen spear during the beginning of the fight, forced to wield it until it broke; Tobias, with his medical knowledge, was the most merciful of us all—because a knife through the eye and into the brain was perhaps one of the quickest ways to go.

But nothing about this was quick. The lingering images, intrusive thoughts, and the guilt. Those were going to be with us long after the physical wounds became scars.

The intel that confirmed everything we'd been telling Dale's government arrived on the afternoon of the fifth day. Yes, Kassian was dead. And the chemist. And Mordecai. Elysian, Mordecai's sister, had also reportedly gone missing; whether she was dead or had simply evaded arrest, no one could be sure. The king, however, had apparently escaped the explosion and was being held in the dungeons beneath the new palace in Northgate. In part, it was for his safety, because people all across his nation were furious; they were calling him mad, just like his "mad chemist," for his plans to conquer and destroy with the explosive—his lies and secrets about a weapon seemingly brought up from hell. The council chambers in Northgate were emptied, the advisors fleeing before they too were put under lock and key, awaiting a trial that could only go one way. With story after story of needless death emerging, including Fort Ketta and explosive tests that had been going on for years, the king was practically already at the gallows.

That left a nation at war with itself, picking up the pieces, with an empty throne sitting in the middle of the carnage.

As for the trace amounts of Nightfire that Dale had procured off our clothes, they said they'd already destroyed them. "Better to have nothing left," declared the queen, "not a spec of that vile powder left for anyone to ever find and try to make more."

But with Brighton fighting to get back on its feet and an empty throne, Dale decided they wanted to keep all of us within their grasp. Anything we knew, anything we'd seen and heard, would come in handy if Brighton's new leaders tried to go against Dale again. "Until peace is truly established, we are keeping you in the city," was the king's ultimatum. "Under observation, clearly. But your honesty thus far has made a good case for each of you."

On the sixth day, Nickolai's family was granted passage out of Orvalia and across the still heavily guarded channel that separated Dale from the rest of the world. Their wayward child was found, and he would finally get to return home.

We all tried to make it a surprise, but Nickolai could see right through us. As we walked down one of the main hallways toward the great hall, trailed by the set of young guards in charge of keeping an eye on our whereabouts, he said, "You can stop with the bad acting, I know something's up."

"This is just my face," Evander countered as he limped along with us. He was doing better than Harris in that department, finally able to walk without the crutch. But he was still grinning from ear to ear and completely blowing our cover.

Nickolai smiled cautiously. "What is it?"

"Relax, you'll figure it out in a minute," contended Malcolm. His shoulder was still bandaged, and his right arm remained in a sling, but every day was getting a little better now that the stitches were healing.

Nickolai examined our faces, and I concentrated on keeping my gaze forward as I failed to repress a grin. We were nearly to the great hall, so the ruse didn't need to last much longer. Voices carried from the vast room toward us.

Nickolai froze in place. His eyes grew wide as he recognized one. An instant later, he sprinted ahead of us, dashing around the corner into the vast room and shouted, "Mom!" when his eyes confirmed what his ears already knew.

By the time the rest of us were around the corner, Nickolai was already swarmed by his parents, older brothers, and younger sister.

A warm bubble expanded in my chest and I crossed my arms. "They're never letting him out of their sight again, are they."

"Not a chance," agreed Harris.

The surprise idea was Ithaca's to begin with, but she and Tobias were already acclimating back into their work at the infirmary and couldn't be present. Guards trailed them as well, but the lead physician insisted that he and his master apprentice go back to doing the work that was so invaluable for the city. Any impressions of treason directed at them after Ithaca disappeared had virtually turned to dust; traitors wouldn't care about helping a population that had nearly been thrown into war, and anyone with eyes could see that they loved their home, its people, and their work in regard to both.

On day seven, the navy captain commissioned Taz to paint the explosion above the main archway leading into the coliseum, where it would be seen by every soldier who trained there. "Let it be ugly, let it be honest," directed the towering commander in his spotless green uniform. "But most importantly, let it be a reminder of what too much power can do when it's in the wrong hands."

Taz nodded vigorously, and I hadn't seen him look so determined since we first decided to destroy Brighton's stockpile of Nightfire. "I'd be honored to do it. You won't regret it."

And every day he went to work on the mural, without fail, Evander was always with him. No matter how much Taz tried to protest, insisting Evander should be resting and not overworking his injured calf, they both walked across the northern end of the city together.

The generals and advisors who sat in on our initial interrogation had similar plans for Harris, asking that he recreate the rigged timer he made to set off the explosives. Not just to prove his story and ensure it was the truth, but to explain how he came up with it—to see what someone who 'dabbled in engineering' was apparently capable of.

"Simplicity usually yields the best results, and I find this to be a perfect example," noted one of the older, impressively even-tempered advisors. "Have you done anything else like this before?"

"Once, when I was still in an orphanage, I built a slingshot big enough to throw my bunk-mate's laundry out the window and onto the street," Harris admitted sheepishly. He cringed, "But that's obviously not what you meant—"

The advisor laughed, waving off his doubt. "No need to recant; I could use one of those for all the paperwork in my office."

And the rest of the advisors at the table joined the laughter.

"He wasn't kidding, apparently," Harris later told me. "He actually wants me to build a slingshot, but he wants me to work with some of the other navy men and shipbuilders so that we might attach some to warships and see how it works. So, they'll have the battering rams on the front, and slingshots on the sides."

"Well, if anyone could have given them an unstoppable fleet, it's you." I punched his arm lightly. "Don't be afraid to leave some damage on the way."

He shrugged. "How else would they be expected to test ten-foot catapult?"

The eighth day was easy. It was the first day that I didn't feel like there was a weight pressing down on my chest, like maybe there was some hope of normalcy returning—even if we were all still technically being kept under careful observation by Dale's government.

I met Ithaca in the infirmary after her latest shift, the late afternoon sun shining golden across the white floor.

"How are your hands?" she asked. She didn't even need to look up from the papers she was arranging into the vertical filing slots to know it was me.

"They're absolutely perfect."

Her gray eyes flicked in my directions like silver coins. "They're still far from done healing."

"But they're healed enough for this," I cupped her face and kissed her lightly, adding, "and that's all that matters."

Her cheeks were a delightful shade of pink as she smiled up at me. "This might just be the most excited I've ever seen you."

I plucked the last few sheets from her grasp and shrugged. "Just anxious to prove myself as a student." I surveyed the narrow rows of words on the pages, all beyond my reach. For now. Because Ithaca had agreed to teach me how to read. I draped an arm over her shoulders and winked at her out of the corner of my eye, "I promise I'll behave."

She hummed, took the papers back, and was already grinning when she remarked, "I'll believe it when I see it."

And she did. I didn't miss a single word she said as we ran through the letters I already knew and the ones I didn't. I hardly blinked while watching her demonstrate how to write my own name on a blank paper—and hardly breathed while I tried to mimic it. Not a single crumb of information slipped past me.

I kept waiting for the childish urge to stare into the void and plot the best escape route to show up, but it never did. *Wanting* to learn made more difference than I expected. Even though it grew exhausting, listening to her was better than music. When we were done, I already felt like I had a better grasp of the world around me, like the ground was more solid under my feet.

The next morning, nine days since the explosion, Serafina arrived outside the meeting room early with a tense angle to her shoulders. We were both early, being the only ones there except for the guards who continually hovered on the edges of the room. She was twirling the plain band of gold on her finger, the ring from my father, as she said, "I'm not good at this sort of thing, but," she retrieved a twig of greenery from her pocket and extended it to me. After I took the sprig, she elaborated, "A literal olive branch. For the last twenty-one years, for the lies." She lifted her chin, as if deciding on something. "If possible, I'd like to try starting over."

I smiled down at the small, spear-tip leaves. A tiny branch had never carried so much weight, and I suspected I was going to keep it until it turned to dust.

"You helped us blow up a castle and stop a war." I extended my free hand to her. "That was the real olive branch. When it mattered most, you climbed into the mess with me and helped me get back out."

She smiled and fit her hand through mine.

"I won't forget it," I added with a gentle squeeze.

She nodded and turned her gaze to the closed doors of the meeting room before us. "We still have a lot of work to do, the two of us. But I'm glad that now we have a place to start."

On day ten, Malcolm handily kicked my ass at a game of cards. No bets or gambles, just a plain old game for fun.

He fidgeted with his arm sling while I reshuffled.

"It's a shame he's dead," he decided, as he swatted away a spec of lint. "It would have been interesting to ask him questions and hear his reasoning—why he did what he did."

"Is it *reasoning*, or just being a piece of shit? How cruel and unfeeling does a person have to be, to lie and deceive everyone they know so that they might kill an entire family? He hurt everyone he'd ever been close to for that rebel cause." But Xavier was long dead, and even if he wasn't, I couldn't decide if I'd want to hear his explanation at all. "He got what he wanted, I suppose. But at least he also got what he deserved." I began redistributing the cards between us.

"You can't choose your family—as the saying goes." He didn't pick up his hand of cards when I was done dealing them out, but rather stared at them like there was a hidden message printed across their backs. So, I didn't pick mine up either, waiting for whatever he was going to say. A few moments passed before he added, "But you can pick your friends. And you should know that you were my friend before I knew you were my family."

I wasn't expecting to feel like I'd been kicked in the chest or to find my eyes stinging. I sat back in my chair, letting the ache dissipate, and smiled across the table. "You were my friend too. You are, still." Grinning, I added, "I don't allow just anybody to nearly *shatter* my hand, either; only the people I care about get that honor."

He chuckled, finally picking up his hand of cards. "You're never letting me live that down, are you?"

I grinned and wriggled my undamaged fingers at him. "Not in a million years."

He nodded once. "Fair enough."

At last, I picked up my own hand of cards—and winced at the dismal spread. "Someday, I'm going to best you at this damn game."

Surveying his hand, he didn't even bother maintaining a poker face and smiled, his eyes shining with ruthless, game-winning joy. "Just not today."

It had now been eleven days since the explosion in Northgate. Gray and brown loomed in the sky to the east, like a shred of tea-stained parchment across the horizon. If the wind blew right, I could smell the dry ash and smoke, too, and there had been days when it clouded the air in Angel's Landing enough that we could barely see the shape of the coliseum through the haze.

Today, however, the air was clear. We all stood within the first arched entryway into the coliseum, staring up at the mural spanning the curved wall above it.

Ithaca had a hand clutched to the collar of her dress, and did not break her stare from the still-drying paint as she said, "Taz, in the best way possible, it is truly the most haunting thing I've ever laid eyes on."

Taz nodded vaguely, his hands and forearms streaked with black and red paint. He'd smudged some across his brow too. "That means I've done something right. Thank you."

He'd done everything right—because over the smell of paint, I could swear the art radiated a smokey undertone. If I squinted, the black clouds seemed to tumble and roll upward, just like the real thing. The fiery bursts and sparks were done in such a way that they glowed. Real torches, real flames, might look dim when put side by side with it.

I swallowed around the lump in my throat. "It's like being there all over again."

Malcolm and Evander nodded in agreement, and beside them, Harris folded his arms. "And to think, that would have been the fate of everyone here if Brighton's king and his chemist had their way."

"All because they thought Dale was harboring the man responsible for the first royal family's deaths; a man who's long been dead," added Malcolm. "Is it too soon to call that ironic?"

"Not at all," I answered.

"Somebody's got to see the humor in it," Evander agreed.

With his hands in his pockets, Tobias sighed. "As long as the world has learned its lesson."

"As long as it never happens again," amended Serafina.

I crossed my arms. The tattoo flared with warmth, and I took comfort in knowing that the stained-glass dome that inspired it had been destroyed along with the rest of the old palace.

For a long time I had considered finding a way to have it covered with something else, or removed altogether. Now I knew I wanted to keep it as it was. With the palace gone, with Xavier dead—now it truly belonged to me, Malcolm, and my mother. And unless that son of a bitch planned on returning from the dead to claim it, I saw no need to erase the symbol that had ultimately brought us back together.

AN EYE FOR AN EYE

The king's cell was at the bottom of a long cavern beneath the new palace and the existing dungeons. The stairway leading to it was chiseled out of the limestone walls, and oak beams crisscrossed the airy expanse overhead to keep it from collapsing on itself. The highest level of security was really only a gaping hole in the earth.

It made him sick.

He knew a storm was raging above ground over the city of Northgate, because water tricked down the gray walls and dripped from the beams above his cell, dampening his clothes until he began to shiver like some pathetic rat holed up in a sewer.

He'd kill to be above ground again, to begin searching for the cowardly members of his cabinet who had fled as soon as the old palace exploded into ash, and to hunt down those wretched simpletons who'd destroyed his plans, killed his brilliant chemist, and murdered his son. They should all have counted themselves lucky that he was locked away and quickly approaching a date with the gallows.

He was glaring into a murky, soot-stained puddle on the far end of his cell when he noticed movement in its reflection.

In the last few days, his eyes had adjusted to the constant darkness, and he peered upward through the beams and iron bars as someone descended the curved stairway.

He wiped the dirt from his face with his ragged sleeve. "About time someone came to make sure I'm still alive. There's still a trial—I'm still a king. You should all be ashamed of yourselves."

The man who strode onto the flat, stone ground outside the cell door didn't speak. But his silhouette didn't match a guard's. He wasn't in a uniform or carrying a spear. Instead, he wore a long black coat with a hood, and he was taller than any of the guards the king had seen in the dungeons before. His shoulders were wide. Strong.

The king strained his eyes to see through the dark, sitting forward. He couldn't make out the stranger's face. Part of him almost *hoped* an assassin had crept down to this insufferable death just to end it.

"It's been a long time, hasn't it, Hector?"

He knew that voice—that deep, smooth rumble that echoed off the curved walls. His insides instantly turned to cold mush, and a single breath of laughter escaped him. "You truly do heave a death wish—coming here."

"I had to. You know I can't resist a good dance with death. Not to mention your city has been belching black smoke into the sky for days; I'd have to be blind not to notice." The wanted man took a few measured steps forward, blue eyes gleaming as dark as the sea before a storm, and stopped just beyond the cell door. "I wanted to get a good look at the mess you've dug yourself into." His teeth flashed into a wicked smile. His red hair hadn't been cut in a long time, and strands of it curled from beneath his hood, the ends dripping rainwater.

The king found himself wanting to punch that row of infuriatingly straight teeth.

"Word on the street tells me that the ragtag crew who bested you and your chemist fled to Dale. That they've been giving them intel on what happened here." He gripped the iron bars with his massive, calloused hands, and the king resisted the urge to scoot to the back wall of his cell, even if that was where most of the water was pooling. "What say you?"

"All I've heard is that they took a ship," the king crossed his arms, fighting down the shivering that was getting worse. "Chunks of my palace were falling from the damn sky—I was a little preoccupied. What gives you reason to care? Isn't it enough that you've seen this city in ruin, that I'm rotting in this grave of a cell?" A wheeze of laughter bubbled from his lips, cold and empty, as he realized one other thing. "You were never in Dale, were you? Our reports were wrong from the beginning."

The former captain of the guard chuckled, but never broke his stare. That razor-sharp gleam in his eyes seemed to say, *you poor, stupid fool.* Then they darkened, and his smirk vanished. "Where are they?"

The king saw the shift in his eyes, heard the sharpening of his tone. He couldn't help but smile, even as the rain picked up, and the water dripping into his cage took on a swifter drum beat. That was hunger and desperation if he'd ever seen it. "Who?" he asked.

"You know who. Don't play with me, old man." He reached into his black coat, extracting two folded slips of parchment, and tossed them between the iron bars.

Gray water dotted through the pages, but as the king unfolded each, he easily recognized the two faces on the wanted posters; the tall one with the dark hair, and the other one with the red hair. Two of his unwilling spies, each partly responsible for his downfall.

"I won't ask again," declared the former captain.

The king licked his dry, cracked lips. "You're a dead man if anyone catches you, Mr. Karabian. The reward on your head will never expire, not even after they kill me."

On the other side of the bars, Xavier waited, watching the king, like the answers he wanted would appear scrawled across his enemy's forehead. "I like a challenge," he mused, taking a step back from the cell door. He shielded his eyes from the dripping water and gazed up through the tangle of beams, like he had sensed the approaching guard rotation well before the king heard boots scuffing on the limestone stairs far above.

Blind joy swelled in the king's chest as he took in a breath meant to scream at the guards, alerting them of the presence of the most wanted man in the nation, but stopped just short. He looked at the second poster, then back up at the man before him. He stared at the former captain's profile, fitting the pieces together like shards of glass —the broken edges linking together perfectly.

If not for the difference in age, the two men could have been twins. He remembered thinking that his redheaded spy had looked familiar —but thought nothing of it at the time.

And the other one, the one with the tattoo…

The ancient, stained-glass dome of the old palace flashed through his memory. The sun had shone through that red star beautifully on the day he took the throne, the caskets of his cousin and his family still in the room. Their assassination had happened two nights before. The gravesites were mapped, but still untouched by shovels.

The breath he'd taken slowly leaked from his chest, and he just kept staring.

The wanted man glanced at him from the corner of his eye and smirked, like he knew what the king was thinking. "If you'll excuse me, I think it's time I go pay a visit to the giant in the west. I hear Angel's Landing is stunning in winter."

"I could have killed them both…" the king mumbled. He could have ended the blight that was the Karabian bloodline, could have severed it at the root. He could have balanced the scales once and for all—an eye for an eye, a family for a family—if only he'd been able to see those two boys for what they were.

The wanted man winked, turned his back, and ascended the stairs, melting into the tangled shadows that spiraled up above the cell.

The king gathered enough wit to scream then, but somehow, he already knew it was too late. His throat was raw by the time the guards slid to a stop at the bottom of the stairs, faces perplexed, clueless that another man had managed to slip past them.

Xavier Karabian was already long gone.

"Are you out of your mind?" demanded one of the guards.

The other one was shaking his head. "He truly is mad. I think it's getting worse."

Their words barely made sense in his ears as he tried to see through the cavern above, through the rainwater dripping onto his face.

If they truly were in Dale, if they were both that man's sons, they had every reason to be afraid. Wanted men didn't emerge from hiding after twenty-two years on a whim. Not unless it trumped the 8,000-mark price on his head.

ACKNOWLEDGMENTS

Writing this book was harder than I expected and more rewarding than I ever dreamed it would be. None of this would have been possible without the help of many people. First, I want to thank my parents, who have always supported and encouraged me, and who continue to inspire me every day. Thank you so much mom and dad.

Which leads me to thank all of my teachers. Especially those of you who had to deal with the hyperactive, dyslexic little gremlin who refused to sit still. You taught me how to love stories, to see more than just words on a page, and for that I am forever grateful.

A tremendous thank you to Stacy Dymalski, my amazing story editor. There's quite simply no other way to say it; she's an icon, she's a legend, and she is the moment. Your insights into every aspect of this process are invaluable, and you helped me transform that rickety, half-finished draft into a real novel that I am proud to have my name on. This book never would have existed without you. For literally helping me make my dreams come true, thank you x a million!

To Michelle Rayner of Cosmic Design, my immensely talented cover designer. I imagined what the cover of this book might look like for ten years, and you exceeded my grandest hopes and dreams. I never knew a book could be so perfect and beautiful before working with you. Thank you for everything.

I'd also like to thank Callie Miller, my proofreader. Working with you and putting the final polish on my manuscript was one of my favorite parts of the whole process. Your expertise was key to making all of those words truly shine.

And, last but not least, I'm grateful to all of my friends. Thank you for your support and long suffering, thank you for listening to me ramble on and on about this book, and thank you for being the best network of people I could ever hope to have on my team. You're my favorites and I love you!